WETLANDS

WETLANDS

Charlotte Roche

Translated from the German by Tim Mohr

Grove Press
New York

Originally published in Germany under the title *Feuchtgebiete*

Printed in the United States of America

FIRST EDITION

ISBN-13: 978-0-8021-1892-9

Grove Press
an imprint of Grove/Atlantic, Inc.
841 Broadway
New York, NY 10003

Distributed by Publishers Group West

www.groveatlantic.com

09 10 11 12   10 9 8 7 6 5 4 3 2 1

For Martin

I place a lot of importance on the care of the elderly within a family. I'm also a child of divorce, and like all children of divorce I want to see my parents back together. When my parents eventually need to be taken care of, all I have to do is stick their new partners in nursing homes and then I'll look after the two of them myself—at home. I'll put them together in their matrimonial bed until they die.

WETLANDS

As far back as I can remember, I've had hemorrhoids. For many, many years I thought I couldn't tell anyone. After all, only grandfathers get hemorrhoids. I always thought they were very unladylike. I've been to Dr. Fiddel, my proctologist, about them so many times. But he always said to leave them there as long as they didn't hurt. And they didn't. They just itched. And for that he gave me a zinc salve.

For exterior itching, you squeeze a hazelnut-sized dollop from the tube onto your finger with the shortest nail and rub it onto your rosette. The tube's also got a pointed attachment with lots of holes in it that allows you to shove it up your ass and squeeze salve out to quell the itchiness inside.

Before I had the salve I would scratch at my butthole in my sleep so much that I'd wake up in the morning with a brown stain in my underwear the size of the top of a cork. That's how much it itched, and that's how deep I'd stick my finger in. So yes, I'd say it's very unladylike.

My hemorrhoids look strange. Over the years they've worked their way farther and farther out. All around the rosette now there are cloud-shaped lobes of skin that almost look like the arms of a sea anemone. Dr. Fiddel calls it cauliflower.

He says removing it would be strictly an aesthetic move. He'll only take it off if someone is really burdened by it. A good reason for removing it would be if my lover didn't like it, or if the cauliflower gave me anxiety during sex. But I'd never admit that.

If somebody loves me or is even just hot for me, something like the cauliflower shouldn't make a difference. And anyway, I've had very successful anal sex for many years—from the age of fifteen up to now, at eighteen—despite the ever-expanding cauliflower. By very successful I mean that I can come with just a cock up my ass, not being touched anywhere else. Yep, I'm proud of that.

It's also a good way to test whether someone is serious about me. During one of the first few times I have sex with somebody new, I get us into my favorite position: doggy-style, me on all fours with my face down, him behind me with his tongue in my pussy and his nose in my ass. He's got to work his way in there, because the hole is covered with the vegetable. I call this position "stuff your face," and so far nobody has complained.

When you've got something like that on an organ that's so important for sex (is the bum even an organ?), you have to train yourself to relax. This in turn helps enable you to let yourself go and loosen up during, for instance, anal sex.

And since the ass is obviously part of sex for me, it's also subject to the modern shaving regime, along with my pussy, my legs, my underarms, the upper lip, both big toes, and the top of my feet as well. Of course, the upper lip doesn't get shaved but rather plucked, because we all know you'll develop a mustache if you shave it. As a girl you don't want that. I used to be happy enough without all the shaving, but then I started with that crap and now I can't quit.

Back to shaving my ass. Unlike other people, I know exactly what my butthole looks like. I look at it every day in the bathroom. Standing with my bum facing the mirror, legs spread, my hands holding my ass cheeks apart, and my head practically on the floor, I look back between my legs. I shave my ass exactly the same way. Except that I have to let one cheek go in order to hold the razor. The wet blade is put against the cauliflower and then pulled bravely in a straight line outward from the center. Right on out to the middle of the cheek, occasionally leaving behind a stray hair. Since I'm always conflicted about the idea of shaving, I always rush it and end up pressing too hard. Which is exactly how I caused the anal lesion that's the reason I'm lying here in the hospital now. Blame it all on lady-shaving. Feel like Venus. Be a goddess.

Perhaps not everyone knows what an anal lesion is. It's a hairline rip or cut in the skin of your rosette. And if this small open wound gets infected as well—which down there is highly likely—then it hurts like hell. Like with me right now. Turns out your butthole is always in motion. When you talk, laugh, cough, walk, sleep, and, above all else, when you go to the bathroom. But I only realized this once it started to hurt.

The swollen hemorrhoids are also pushing with all their strength against the razor wound, ripping the lesion open even farther and causing the worst pain I've ever experienced. By far. In second place is the pain I felt run down my spine—*ratatatatat*—the time my father accidentally slammed the hatchback door of our car on my back. The third worst pain I've ever felt was when I ripped out my nipple ring taking off a sweater. That's why my right nipple looks like a snake's tongue now.

Back to my bum. In excruciating pain I made my way from school to the hospital and showed my cut to every doctor. Immediately I got a bed in the proctology unit— or do you call it the internal-medicine unit? Internal medicine sounds better than specifying "ass unit." Don't want to make other people envious. Maybe we can just generalize with internal medicine. I'll ask about it later, when the pain is gone. Anyway, now I'm not allowed to move. I just lie here in the fetal position. With my skirt hiked up and my underpants pulled down, ass toward the door. That way anyone who enters the room immediately knows what the story is. It must look really infected. Everyone who comes in says, "Ooh."

And they talk about pus and an engorged blister that's hanging out of the wound on my butthole. I picture the blister like the skin on the neck of one of those tropical birds that puffs its throat out when trying to mate. A shimmering, inflated, red-blue sac. The next proctologist who comes in says curtly, "Hello, the name is Dr. Notz."

Then he jams something up my asshole. The pain bores its way up my spine and into my brain. I nearly pass out. After a few seconds of pain I feel a wet squishiness and cry out, "Ow! Give me some warning. What the hell was that?"

His response: "My thumb. You'll have to excuse me, but with that big blister there I couldn't see anything."

What a way to introduce yourself.

"And now? What do you see?"

"We've got to operate immediately. Have you eaten anything today?"

"How could I with this pain?"

"Good. General anesthesia then. It's better given the situation."

I'm happy, too. I don't want to be conscious for something like this.

"What exactly are you going to do during the operation?"

The conversation is already straining me. It's tough to concentrate on anything but the pain.

"We'll make a wedge-shaped incision to cut out the infected tissue."

"I can't really picture that—wedge-shaped? Can you draw a picture for me?"

Apparently the esteemed Dr. Notz hasn't often been asked by patients to sketch a diagram right before an operation. He wants to leave, glances at the door, stifles a sigh.

Then he pulls a silver pen out of his chest pocket. It looks heavy. Expensive. He looks around for a piece of paper to draw on. I can't help him and hope he doesn't expect me to. Any movement hurts. I close my eyes. There's rustling and I hear him ripping a piece of paper out of something. I have to open my eyes—I'm anxious to see the drawing. He holds the piece of paper in his palm and scribbles with the pen. Then he presents his creation. I read: savoy cabbage in cream sauce. No way. He's ripped the paper out of the hospital menu. I turn the paper around. He's drawn a circle. I figure it's supposed to be my butthole. And out of the circle a triangular wedge has been cut, as if someone has made off with a piece of cake.

Aha, got it. Thanks, Dr. Notz. Ever thought about putting all that talent into a career as an artist? The sketch doesn't help me at all. Though I'm still no better informed, I don't ask any more questions. He isn't interested in helping enlighten me.

"Surely you could cut out the cauliflower with just a little flick of the wrist?"

"It'll be done."

He walks out, leaving me lying in the puddle of water from the blister. I'm alone. And worried about the operation. I think of general anesthesia as something dangerous, as if every second patient never wakes up. I feel courageous for going ahead with it. The anesthesiologist comes in next.

The sandman. He pulls up a low stool and sits down with his face right in front of mine. He speaks softly and has a lot more compassion for my situation than Dr. Notz. He asks how old I am. If I were under eighteen there would have to be a legal guardian here. But I'm not. I tell him I've come of legal age this year. He looks incredulously into my eyes. I know. Nobody ever believes it; I look younger. I know this drill. I put on my serious you-can-trust-me face and lock eyes with him. His gaze changes. He believes me. On with the discussion.

He explains how the anesthesia works. I'll count and then just fall asleep at some point without even noticing. He'll sit by my head throughout the operation, monitor my breathing, and check that the anesthesia is agreeing with me. Aha. So this sitting-too-close-to-my-face thing is an occupational hazard. Most people don't notice anyway—they're knocked out. And he's probably supposed to be as unobtrusive as possible and hunker down close to the patient's head so as not to disturb the real doctors. Poor guy. The standard position while practicing his trade? Squatting.

He's brought a contract that I'm supposed to sign. It says the operation could result in incontinence. I ask how it could affect my pissing. He grins and says this refers to anal incontinence. Never heard of it. But suddenly I realize what this means: "You mean I might lose control of my sphincter muscles and then I could just crap myself anytime and anyplace and would need a diaper and stink all the time?"

The sandman: "Yes, but that rarely happens. Sign here, please."

I sign it. What else am I supposed to do? If that's what it takes to have the surgery. I can't exactly go home and operate on myself.

Oh, man. Please, dear nonexistent God, don't let this happen. I'd be wearing a diaper at age eighteen. You're not supposed to need those until you're eighty. It would also mean I'd only have managed to live fourteen years of my life without diapers. And you certainly don't look cool in them.

"Dear anesthesiologist, would it be possible for me to see what they cut away during the operation? I don't like the idea that a part of me could end up in the trash along with aborted fetuses and appendixes without my being able to picture it. I want to hold it in my hand and examine it."

"If that's what you want, then sure."

"Thanks." He sticks a catheter into my arm and secures everything with surgical tape. This is where they'll pump in the anesthesia later. He says that in a few minutes a nurse will come to take me to surgery. Now the anesthesiologist too leaves me lying in the puddle of moisture from my blister and walks out.

The thought of anal incontinence worries me.

Dear nonexistent God, if I manage to get out of here without anal incontinence, I'll stop doing all the things that give me a bad conscience. Like the game I play with my friend Corinna where we run through the city drunk and grab people's eyeglasses, break them, and then chuck them into the street.

We have to run quickly—some people get so pissed off that they come after us really fast even without their glasses.

The game is stupid anyway because we always sober up from all the excitement and adrenaline. Big waste of money. Afterward we always have to start from scratch again getting drunk.

Actually, I'd like to give that game up anyway—sometimes at night I dream of the faces of the people whose glasses we've just plucked off. It's as if we've ripped off a body part.

I'll give that one up right now, and I'll try to come up with a list of some other things.

Maybe if it's absolutely necessary I'll give up the hookers. That would be a major sacrifice, though. It would be great if giving up the glasses game would suffice.

I've decided to be the best patient this hospital has ever had. I'm going to be extra nice to the overworked nurses and doctors. I'll clean up my own messes. Like the fluid from my blister. There's an open box of rubber gloves on the windowsill. Obviously for examinations. Did Notz have one on when he popped the blister on my ass? Shit, I didn't notice. Next to the carton of rubber gloves is a big translucent-plastic container. Tupperware for a giant. Maybe there's something in there I can use to clean myself up. My bed is up against the window. Slowly, gingerly, I stretch myself out a little without moving my infected bum and manage to grab it. I pull the container onto my bed. Ouch. Lifting it and pulling it tenses my stomach muscles, sending a knife of pain into the infection. I pause. Close my eyes. Breathe deeply. Lie still. Wait for the pain to subside. Eyes open. Okay.

Now I can open the container. What excitement. It's filled to the brim with giant hygienic wipes, adult diapers, disposable underwear, toweling, and bed covers that are plastic on one side and cloth on the other.

I would like to have had one of those under me when Notz came in. Then the bed wouldn't be all wet. Not very comfortable. I need two of them now. One, cloth side down over the puddle. It'll soak it up. But then I'd be laying on plastic. Don't like that. So another one with its plastic side down—plastic on plastic—and the cloth side up. Well done, Helen. Despite the hellish pain, you are your own best nurse.

Anyone who can take care of herself so well will definitely recuperate quickly. I'll have to be a bit more hygienic here in the hospital than I am outside in my normal life.

Hygiene's not a major concern of mine.

At some point I realized that boys and girls are taught differently about how to keep their intimate regions clean. My mother placed great importance on the hygiene of my pussy but none at all on that of my brother's penis. He's allowed to piss without wiping and to let the last few drops dribble into his underwear.

Washing your pussy is considered a deadly serious science in our home. It's made out to be extremely difficult to keep a pussy really clean. Which is nonsense, of course. A little water, a little soap, scrub-scrub. Done.

Just don't wash too much. For one thing because of the all-important flora of the pussy. But also because of the taste and scent of the pussy, which is so important during sex. Don't want to get rid of that. I've experimented with long periods of not washing my pussy. My aim is to get its enticing scent to waft lightly out of my pants, even through thick jeans or ski pants. Men won't consciously notice it but it'll register subliminally since we're all just animals who want to mate—preferably with someone who smells like pussy.

Then, when you're flirting, you can't help smiling the whole time because you know what's filling the air with that deliciously sweet scent. It's what perfume is supposed to accomplish. We're always told that perfume has an erotic effect on those around us. But why not use our own much more powerful perfume? In reality we're all turned on by the scents of pussy, cock, and sweat. Most people have just been alienated from their bodies and trained to think that anything natural stinks and anything artificial smells nice. When a woman wearing perfume passes me on the street, it makes me sick to my stomach. No matter how subtle it is. What is she hiding? Women spray perfume in public toilets after they've taken a shit, too. They think it makes everything smell pleasant again. But I still smell the shit. For me, the smell of plain old shit or piss is better than the disgusting perfumes people buy.

Even worse than women spraying perfume in public toilets is a new invention that seems to be spreading fast.

You go to the bathroom at a restaurant or train station and as you pull the stall door closed behind you, you're misted from above. The first time it happened I was really horrified. I thought someone had flicked water on me from another stall. But then I looked up and saw a dispenser attached above the top of the door. It's actually designed to spray innocent bathroom users with sickeningly sweet disinfectant as soon as they close the door. On your hair, on your clothes, on your face. If that doesn't constitute rape by hygiene fanatics I don't know what does.

I use my smegma the way others use their vials of perfume. I dip my finger into my pussy and dab a little slime behind my earlobes. It works wonders from the moment you greet someone with a kiss on each cheek. Another rule my mother had about pussies was that they get infected much more easily than penises. That they're much more vulnerable to fungus and mold and whatnot. Which is why girls should never sit down on an unfamiliar or public toilet seat. I was taught to piss in an upright crouch, hovering above the rim, never touching the icky pee-pee basin at all. But I've figured out that a lot of the things I was taught aren't true.

I've turned myself into a walking laboratory of pussy hygiene. I enjoy plopping myself down on any dirty toilet seat anywhere. That's not all. I rub the entire seat with my pussy before I sit down, going once around with a graceful gyration of my hips. When I press my pussy onto the seat it makes a smacking noise and then it sucks up all the pubic hairs, droplets, splotches, and puddles of various shades and consistencies. I've been doing this on every sort of toilet for four years now. My favorites are the ones at highway rest stops where there's just one toilet shared by men and women. And I've never had a single infection. My gynecologist, Dr. Broekert, can confirm that.

Once there was a time when I did think my pussy was infected. Whenever I went to the bathroom, sat down, and let my sphincter muscles relax so the piss could come out, I would notice afterward when I looked down—which I like to do—that there was a lovely, big, soft, white clump of slime in the water. With strings of champagne bubbles rising from it.

I have to admit that I'm very wet all day long—I could change my underwear several times a day. But I don't. I like to let it collect. Back to the clump of slime. Was it possible that I'd been sick all along, and that this slimy gunk was the result of a fungal infection of the pussy I'd contracted from all my toilet experiments?

Dr. Broekert was able to allay my fears. It was the result of a healthy, very-active slime-producing mucous membrane. That's not how he put it. But that's what he meant.

I keep close track of my bodily secretions. The whole active mucous-membrane thing used to make me proud when I was younger, hooking up with boys. They might have barely touched my labia with a finger, but inside there was a Slip 'N Slide ready to go.

One boyfriend always sang while we were messing around: "By the rivers of Babylon . . ." These days I could make a business out of it, filling little containers for dry women who have problems producing mucus. It's definitely better to get the real thing than to use some artificial lube.

That way it smells like pussy, too! But maybe women would only be willing to do this with someone they knew—some might be grossed out by a stranger's slime. You could always try it out. Maybe with a dry friend.

I really like to smell and eat my smegma. For as long as I can remember, I've been fascinated with my pussy's creases. All the things you can find in there. I have long hair—on my head—and sometimes I'll find a stray hair lodged between the folds of my pussy. It's exciting to pull the hair out very slowly and to feel it moving in the various places it has twisted its way into. It annoys me when this sensation is over; I wish I had even longer hair so the feel-ing would last longer.

It's a rare pleasure. Like another thing I get a kick out of: when I'm alone in the bathtub and I have to fart, I try to get the air bubbles to glide up between my pussy lips. It doesn't happen very often—even less often than with the long hairs—but when it does, the bubbles feel like hard balls trying to bore their way between my warm, squishy lips. When it happens—let's say once a month—my whole abdomen tingles and my pussy itches so much I have to scratch it with my long fingernails until I come. When my pussy itches I have to scratch it real hard. I scratch up and down between the inner labia—which I call the dewlaps— and the outer labia—which I call the ladyfingers—and at some point I fold back the dewlaps to the right and left so I can scratch right down the middle. I spread my legs wide, until the hip joints crack, so the warm bathwater can flow into my hole. Right as I'm about to come, I pinch my clit—which I call my snail tail. That makes me come so much harder. Yep, that's how it's done.

Back to smegma. I looked up in the dictionary exactly what smegma is. My best friend Corrina told me one time that only men have smegma.

So what's this between my lips and in my underwear?

That's what I thought, but not what I said. I was afraid to say it. But there in the dictionary was a long explanation of what smegma is. That's what it's called in women, too, by the way. So ha! One sentence has stuck with me to this day: "Only through inadequate hygiene can smegma accumulate to a level visible to the naked eye."

Excuse me? That's outrageous. An accumulation of smegma is definitely visible to me with the naked eye at the end of the day no matter how thoroughly I rinse the folds of my pussy with soapy water in the morning.

So what do they mean? Are you supposed to wash yourself multiple times during the day? Anyway, it's good to have a juicy pussy. It's extremely helpful for certain things. The concept of "inadequate hygiene" is flexible—like a pussy. So there.

I take one of the adult diapers out of the translucent-plastic container. Oh man, they're huge. They've got a big, thick square pad in the middle and four thin, plastic tabs to secure at the waist. They'd easily fit around a fat old man—that's how big they are. It's not something I want to need so early in life. Please. There's a knock at the door.

In comes a smiling nurse with his hair sticking up like a cockatoo. "Hello, Miss Memel. My name is Robin. I can see you're already getting familiar with the supplies you'll need during the next few days. You're going to have surgery on your anus, an unhygienic area—the most unhygienic part of the body, in fact. With the items in the container you'll be able to tend to your wound all by yourself after the operation. We recommend that at least once a day you get in the shower and use the showerhead to rinse out the wound. It's best to make sure you spray water up inside. With a little practice, it's easy. It'll be a lot less painful for you to clean the wound that way than to wipe it with towels. After you've rinsed, just pat it dry with a washcloth. I've also got a sedative here. You can take it now. It makes the transition to general anesthesia easier. We're just about ready—it should be some ride."

None of this sounds like a problem. I certainly know my way around a showerhead. And I know just how to get the spray inside. As Robin pushes me through the hallways on my rolling bed and I watch the long fluorescent lightbulbs pass overhead, I discreetly reach down under the sheet and put my hand on my pubic mound to settle myself down before the operation. I divert my attention from the fear by thinking of how I would get myself off with the showerhead when I was younger.

At first I'd just aim the streams of water at my pussy; later I'd hold the ladyfingers aside so the water would hit the dewlaps and snail tail. The harder the better. It should really sting. At some point a few jets of water actually shot up inside my pussy. And I realized this was my thing. To let it fill up and—just as nice—to let it all run out again.

I sit cross-legged in the tub, leaning back with my butt slightly raised. Then I push all the lips to the side, where they belong, and very slowly and carefully slide the thick showerhead in. I don't need any lube—just the thought that I'm about to fill myself up makes my pussy produce plenty of helpful slime. The best lube is Pjur brand because it doesn't clump and it's unscented. I hate scented lubes. It's usually when the showerhead is finally in—which can take a while, because it takes time to stretch out that much—I rotate it so the side the water shoots out of is facing up toward the cervix, toward the spot a guy with a long cock can hit in certain positions. Next the water is turned on, nice and strong. I fold my arms behind my head—both hands are free because my pussy holds the showerhead all by itself—close my eyes, and hum "Amazing Grace."

After what I guess is about four liters, I turn the water off and very carefully pull out the showerhead, letting out as little water as possible. I need the water to get off. I tap the showerhead on my ladyfingers, swollen from being held apart, until I come.

It's usually really fast as long as I'm not interrupted. When I feel totally stuffed—like with the water—it only takes a couple of seconds. Once I've come I press one hand on my lower abdomen and stick the other one deep into my pussy with all the fingers splayed out so the water gushes out with the same force as it went in. I usually come again from the water flowing out. It's an effective way to calm myself. After the big rush of water, spurts of water will still come out for several hours, so I have to line my underwear with sheets of toilet paper—if it soaked through my pants it would look as if I'd wet myself. I don't want that.

Another sanitation device that's perfect for this sort of thing is the bidet. My mother always stressed the importance of quickly freshening up with a bidet after sex. Why should I?

If I fuck someone, I'm proud to have his sperm in every crevice of my body, whether that's on my thighs, on my stomach, or wherever else he may have shot his load. Why the idiotic washing afterward? If you find cocks, cum, or smegma disgusting, you might as well forget about sex. I love it when sperm dries on my skin, when it crusts and flakes off.

When I jerk somebody off, I always make sure that some cum gets on my hand. I run my fingers through it and let it dry under my long nails. That way, later in the day, I can reminisce about my good fuck partner by biting my nails and getting bits of the hardened cum to play with in my mouth; I chew on it and, after tasting it and letting it slowly dissolve, I swallow it. It's an invention I'm very proud of: the memorable-sex bonbon.

The same can be done, of course, with cum that ends up in the pussy. Just don't wash it away with a bidet! Instead, carry it proudly. To school, for instance. Hours after sex it'll ooze nice and warm out of your pussy—a little treat. I may be sitting in a classroom, but my thoughts are back where the cum came from: while the teacher is going on about philosophical attempts to prove the existence of God, I sit there smiling blissfully in my little puddle of sperm. The intermingling of bodily fluids between my legs always makes me happy, and I text the source: "Your warm cum is running out of me—thanks!"

My thoughts return to the bidet. I wanted to spend a few minutes reminiscing about the way I manage to fill myself up with the bidet. But there's no time. We've arrived in the surgery prep room. I can continue that line of thought later. My anesthesiologist is already waiting for us. He attaches a bag of fluid to the IV tube in my arm, hangs it upside down from a rolling stand, and says I should start counting.

Robin, the friendly nurse, wishes me luck and leaves. One, two . . .

I wake up in the recovery room. People are always a bit out of sorts when they wake up from general anesthesia. I think recovery rooms were created to spare relatives from witnessing this.

I'm awoken by my own babbling. What was I saying? Don't know. My whole body is shaking. Slowly the gears in my mind begin to turn. What am I doing here? Did something happen to me? I want to smile to try to hide my sense of helplessness even though there's nobody else in the room. My lips are so dry that the corner of my mouth cracks when I do smile. My asshole! That's why I'm here. It had cracked, too. My hand fumbles for my bum. I feel a huge bandage stretched across both ass cheeks. Through that I feel a thick knob. Oh man, I hope that knob isn't part of my body. Hopefully it's something that will come off with the rest of the bandaging. I'm in one of those embarrassing, apron-like hospital gowns. They love these gowns in hospitals.

It has sleeves and from the front makes you look like a tree-top angel. But it's completely backless except for a little bow tied back there. Why does this piece of clothing even exist? I mean, sure, if you're lying down they can put one on you without having to lift you. But I was lying on my stomach for the operation so they could get at my ass. Does that mean I was essentially naked for the duration of the operation? That's not good. I'm sure they talk about the way you look. And you hear it and remember it subconsciously even though you're knocked out—maybe someday down the road you'll go nuts as a result of the comments and nobody will understand why.

This airy feeling on my backside reminds me of a re-curring nightmare I had as a child. Elementary school. I'm waiting at the bus stop. Just as I often forgot to take my pajamas off before putting on my jeans, today I've forgot-ten to put underwear on beneath my skirt. You don't no-tice that kind of thing at home as a kid. But you'd rather die than have people discover in public that you're bare-assed under your skirt. And this was at exactly the age when the boys think it's funny to lift girls' skirts.

Robin walks in. He speaks very deliberately, saying everything went smoothly. He pushes my gurney into an ele-vator and then along hallways, always slamming his fist on the game-show buttons that open the automatic doors. Oh, Robin. The lingering effects of the anesthesia make for a hypnotic ride. I use the time to find out about my asshole. It's a funny feeling that Robin knows more about it than I do. He's got a clipboard with every detail about me and my ass on it. I'm feeling talkative and all kinds of jokes about bum surgery occur to me. He says I'm so relaxed and funny because the anesthesia's still affecting me. He parks my bed back in my room and says he could talk to me for ages but that he has other patients he needs to check on. Too bad.

"If you need pain medication, just press the call button."

"Where's the skirt and underwear I had on before the operation?"

He walks to the foot of my bed and lifts the sheet. The skirt is carefully folded there with my underpants on top of it.

This is the situation my mother always feared. The underwear is folded with the crotch facing up. Right side in, not inside out. But I can still see a shiny stain where pussy juice has soaked through and dried. My mom thinks the single most important thing for a woman going to the hospital to do is to wear clean underwear. Her primary justification for her ridiculously obsessive approach to clean undies: If you get run over and end up in the hospital, they take your clothes off. Including your underwear. Oh my God. And if they see any evidence of your pussy's totally normal discharge—oh my, can you imagine?

I think mom pictures everyone in the hospital going around talking about her, saying what a dirty whore Mrs. Memel is. Saying her well-put-together exterior is nothing but a lie.

Her dying thought at the scene of an accident would be: How long have I been wearing these panties? Are there any wet spots on them?

The first thing doctors and EMTs do with a bleeding accident victim, before starting to resuscitate? They have a peek at the blood-soaked underwear so they know what kind of woman they've got on their hands.

From the wall behind me Robin pulls out a cable with a call button on the end of it. He lays it on the pillow next to my face. I won't need that.

I look around my room. The walls are painted light green —so light it's barely perceptible. Supposed to be calming. Or optimistic.

To the left of my bed is a built-in wardrobe. I don't have anything to put in it, but someone will bring me things soon, I'm sure. Beyond the wardrobe the room goes on around, probably to the bathroom—or let's call it the shower room.

Between my bed and the wardrobe is a rolling metal nightstand with a drawer. It's extra tall so you can get at it from the high hospital bed.

To the right is a long bank of windows hung with white, see-through curtains that are weighted at the bottom to keep them hanging crisply. They've got to look neat and straight. Like concrete. They mustn't billow in the breeze if the window is open. On the sill is the container of diapers and, next to it, a box with one hundred pairs of rubber gloves in it. It says so on the box. Though there's probably fewer than that in there now.

On the wall opposite me is a framed poster—you can see the little metal tabs that hold the glass. It's a photo of a tree-lined avenue, and written in yellow letters at the top it says, *Walk with Jesus.* What—take him for a stroll?

A small crucifix hangs over the doorway. Someone has decorated it with a bough. Why do they do that? The boughs are always from the same kind of plant. The kind with little arched leaves, dark green, with an artificial shine to them. The boughs always look like they're made out of plastic, but they always turn out to be real. I think they come from some kind of hedge.

Why do they stick pieces of greenery on crosses? The poster and the crucifix have got to go. I'll convince mom to take them down. I'm already looking forward to that discussion. Mom's a practicing Catholic. Wait. I've forgotten something. Up high is a TV. I hadn't looked up there. It's suspended in a metal frame and tipped way down toward me. It looks as if it could fall on me at any moment. I'll ask Robin to shake it later. Just to make sure it's secure. If there's a TV, there must be a remote—or do I have to get somebody to turn it on and off for me? Maybe it's in the drawer. I reach over and pull it open and am suddenly aware of my ass. Careful, Helen. Don't do anything stupid.

The remote is in a plastic compartment in the drawer. Everything's cool. Except the anesthesia is wearing off. Do I need to ring and ask for painkillers already?

Maybe it won't be that bad. Right, I'll wait a bit and see how I feel. I'll try to keep my mind on something else. Like, say, the last unicorn. That won't work. I clench my teeth. My mind is fixated on my wounded ass. I'm tensing up all over. Especially in my shoulders. My good mood has disappeared. Robin was right. I don't want to come across as a whiner, though—especially after yapping so much to Robin. I can hold out a little longer. I close my eyes. I put one hand gently on my bandaged ass and the other on the call button. I lie there and the pain throbs. The anesthesia is getting weaker and weaker. The wound burns. My muscles cramp. The throbbing gets faster.

I push the button and wait. An eternity. I panic. The pain is getting worse, stabbing at my sphincter like a knife. They must have stretched the sphincter wide open. Of course. How else would they get in there. Down my throat? Oh God. The hands of a full-grown man went into my rectum and went to town with scalpels and retractors and suture thread. The pain isn't directly on the wound but all around it. A blown sphincter.

He's finally arrived.

"Robin?"

"Yes?"

"Do they stretch your butthole open wide enough to fit multiple hands into it?"

"Yes, I'm afraid so. That will be the source of most of the pain when the anesthesia wears off in a few minutes."

Hmm. In a few minutes? I need pain medication right now. The thought that it might take a while for painkillers to work scares me so much that I think I'm going throw up. I've held out against the pain too long and now I'll have to wait ages for this shit on my ass to stop hurting. I've got to learn to give in to pain and become a patient who'd rather ring too soon for medication than have to make it through the minutes it takes for the stuff to kick in. There's no medal for holding out against pain, Helen. My asshole has been fatally distended.

It feels as if the hole is as big around as my entire ass. There's no way it will ever close normally again. I think they purposefully inflicted additional pain during the operation.

I was in this same hospital a few years ago. It was the greatest acting job of my life. I was failing French class and was supposed to take an exam the next day. I hadn't studied and had been skipping class. I had faked being sick for the previous exam. I had pretended I had a migraine so mom would give me a note. This time it had to be something more convincing. I just needed some time to study.

An excused absence would mean I could make up the exam some other time. First thing in the morning I told my mom I had palpitations in my lower left abdomen. And that they were getting worse. Mom started to worry because she knew this was a sign of appendicitis. Even though the appendix is on the right side. I know that, too. I started to double over in pain. She drove me straight to the pediatrician. I still go to the same doctor I went to as a child. It's closer to home. He laid me on a stretcher and began to press on my abdomen. He pressed on the left side and I shrieked in pain. He pressed on the right and I didn't make a sound.

"It's unmistakable. Acute appendicitis. You've got to take your daughter to the hospital right away. There's no time to stop off at home for her pajamas. You can drop them off later. This kid's got to get to the hospital. If it ruptures it'll infect the entire body and she'll need a blood transfusion." I thought to myself, What kid?

Off to the hospital. This one. Upon arrival I put on the same show. Left, right, all the right reactions. Like a game. Emergency operation. They cut me open and find an appendix that's not infected or swollen at all. They take it out anyway. You don't need it. And if they left it in and sewed you up, you might just come back at some stage with real appendicitis. Which would be doubly annoying. But they didn't tell me they took it out. My mother did.

When she caught me lying another time, she said: "I can't believe anything you say. You lied to me and all the doctors just to get out of a French exam. They took an uninfected appendix out of you."

"How do you know that?"

"Mothers know everything. The doctors told me outside the operating room. They had never encountered anything like it before. So I know what a liar you are."

At least I knew it was out. Before that conversation with my mom I figured the doctors had opened me up, seen it wasn't infected, and left it in. So I had always worried I might really get appendicitis. And what could you say then, when you'd supposedly already had appendicitis? So that's what had happened. Good to know. A lot of needless hours of worrying. Right after you've had your appendix taken out, it hurts incredibly badly to laugh, to walk, to stand, to do much of anything, because it feels as if the stitches are going to rip open. I tensed and curled up just like now with my ass. Is it possible the doctors recognized my name? Did it cause a sensation in the hospital back then—that a girl would endure an operation just to trick her teacher? Did they go out of their way to make this operation particularly painful—oops, I slipped—as payback? Am I paranoid because of the pain? Because of the painkillers? What is going on? It hurts so bad. Robin. Bring the pills.

Here he comes. He hands me two tablets and says something. I can't concentrate. I'm writhing in pain. I slurp the pills down. Please, let them work fast. Now. To calm myself down, I put my hand on my pubic mound again. I always did this as a kid, too. But back then I didn't know it was called a pubic mound.

As far as I'm concerned, it's the most important part of the whole body. Nice and warm. Perfectly positioned for your hand to reach. My center. I stick my hand into my underwear and run my hand around. This is the best way to put myself to sleep.

I root around like a squirrel down there, and just as I'm falling asleep I have the impression there's a log of crap poking out of my ass. The bandages feel exactly like that. I dream that I'm walking across a wide field. A field of parsnips. I can see a man in the distance. A Nordic walker. One of those guys who hikes with a pair of ski-pole-like walking sticks. I think: Look, Helen, a man with four legs.

He approaches and I can see a giant cock is hanging out of his form-fitting sports leggings. I think: Nope, a man with five legs.

He walks past me and I turn and watch him go. It pleases me to see he's pulled his pants down in the back and a huge log of crap is hanging out of his ass, bigger even than his cock. I think: Wow, six legs. I come to and I'm thirsty and aching. The hand on my pubic mound wanders to the back to feel my wound. I want to see what they did back there. How can I have a look? I can look at my pussy if I bend way forward, but I've never been able to see my own ass. A mirror? No, a camera. Mom needs to bring me the camera.

Will she be here when I wake up? Message.

"It's me. Can you bring the camera when you come? And can you wrap up the bulbs in my room without break-ing the shoots? And bring the empty glasses, too, please. But hide them when you come in, Okay? You're not allowed to have anything but cut flowers here. Thanks. See you soon. Oh yeah, can you also bring about thirty toothpicks? Thanks."

I grow avocado trees. Besides fucking, it's my only hobby. As a kid avocados were my favorite fruit or vegetable—whatever they are. Cut in half with a dollop of mayonnaise in the hole where the pit's been removed. And a bunch of hot paprika powder sprinkled on top. I would play with the pits afterward. My mother would always say kids didn't need toys—a rotten tomato or an avocado pit did just fine.

At first the pit is shiny and slimy from the avocado oil. I like to rub it on the backs of my hands and up and down my arms. Spread the slime all over. Then you have to dry the pit.

If you leave it on the radiator it only takes a few days. Once the moisture has dried, I run the soft, dark-brown pit across my lips. When they're dry they feel so soft. I like to do it for minutes on end, with my eyes closed. It's like when I would run my dry lips across the greasy leather cover of the pommel horse in the school gym—until someone would interrupt me. "Helen, what are you doing? Stop that."

Or until the other kids would laugh at me. Then you spare yourself the embarrassment by doing it only during the few moments you can sneak into the gym alone. It's about as soft as my ladyfingers when they're freshly shaved.

You've got to peel the brown shell off the pit. To do that I stick my thumbnail into the shell and keep cracking it. Just be careful not to let any pieces of the shell jab under your nail.

That hurts and it's hard to get the pieces out even with a needle and tweezers. And trying to finish ripping open the shell with splinters under your nail hurts worse than the initial pain of them getting jammed in there in the first place. It'll leave ugly bloody marks under your nail, too. The blood doesn't stay red, either. It turns brown. It takes a long time for it to grow out. In the meantime your nail looks like a sheet of floating ice with a piece of driftwood frozen into it. Once the shell's completely removed you can see the pleasant color of the pit—either light yellow or sometimes pale pink.

Then I hit it with a hammer. But not so hard that it crushes. After that I put it in the freezer for a few hours to simulate winter. Once you've had enough of winter, you pull it out and insert three toothpicks into the pit. Then you suspend it in water in a glass, using the toothpicks to hold it at the right height.

An avocado pit looks like an egg. It's got a thick, round end and a more pointed end. The narrower end has to stay above the water. About a third in the air and two-thirds submerged. It'll stay this way for a couple of months.

A slimy film grows on the part of the pit in the water. I find it very inviting. Sometimes I take the pit out of the water and put it inside me. I call it my organic dildo. Obviously I only use organic avocados for my starter pits. Otherwise I'd end up with toxic trees.

You definitely want to take the toothpicks out before you put it inside you. Thanks to my well-trained pelvic muscles I can shoot it back out afterward. Then it's back into the water with the toothpicks stuck back in. And then you wait.

After a couple of months you'll see a crack in the round end. It'll get wider, a deep crevice in the pit. It looks as if it's about to split in half; then a thick, white, taproot will start to grow out of the bottom. It curls into the bottom of the glass—there's no other direction for it to grow. Once that gets pretty long, if you look closely at the crack on the top side of the pit, you'll see a tiny green sprout starting to grow. Now's the time to transfer it to a pot full of potting soil. Soon a stem grows with big, green leaves.

I'll never get closer to giving birth than this. I looked after that first pit for months. Had it inside me, pushed it out. And I take perfect care of all the avocado trees I've started that way.

As far back as I can remember, I always wanted to have a child. There's a recurring pattern in my family. My great-grandmother, my grandmother, my mother, and me. All first-born. All girls. All neurotic, deranged, and depressed. But I broke the cycle. This year I turned eighteen and I've been waiting for that moment. One day after my birthday—as soon as I didn't need parental approval—I had myself sterilized. Since then the thing my mother says to me so often doesn't sound so threatening: "How much do you want to bet that when you have your first child it's a girl?" Because I'll only be having avocado trees. Apparently you have to wait twenty-five years for a tree to bear fruit. Which is also about how long you have to wait to become a grandmother. These days.

While I've been lying here thinking happily about my avocado family, the pain has subsided. You always notice when it begins; but you don't notice when it stops. That moment doesn't grab your attention. But I realize the pain is completely gone now. I love painkillers and try to imagine what it would have been like to have been born in another era when there were no good painkillers. My head is free of pain and now there's room for everything else. I take a few deep breaths and, exhausted, fall asleep. When I open my eyes I see mom leaning over me.

"What are you doing?"

"I'm covering you up. You're lying here totally exposed."

"Leave it the way it is. The sheet's too heavy on my wounded ass, mom. It hurts. It doesn't matter how it looks.

Do you think they haven't seen it here a thousand times before?"

"Then stay that way. Good God."

That reminds me.

"Can you please take down the crucifix over the door? It bugs me."

"No, Helen, I won't do that. Stop being so ridiculous."

"Fine. If you won't help me, I guess I'll have to get up and do it myself."

I start to move one leg off the bed, bluffing that I'm going to stand up, groaning with pain.

"Okay, Okay, I'll do it. Please stay in bed."

No problem.

She uses the lone chair in the room to reach the cross. As she's climbing onto it, she speaks to me in an artificially friendly, sympathetic tone. I feel sorry for her. But it's too late.

"How long have you had this condition?"

What is she talking about? Oh, right. The hemorrhoids.

"Always."

"Not back when I used to bathe you."

"So I got them sometime after I was too old for you to be bathing me."

She climbs back down off the chair, holding the cross in her hand. She looks questioningly at me.

"Put it here in the drawer." I point to the metal nightstand.

"You know, mom, hemorrhoids are hereditary. It's just a question of who I got them from."

She closes the drawer firmly.

"From your father. How was the operation?"

We learned in health class that divorced parents often try to manipulate their kids into taking their respective sides. One parent will bad-mouth the other in front of their kids.

What those bad-mouthing parents fail to realize, though, is that they are always insulting one half of the child. If you consider a child half the mother and half the father.

Children whose mothers constantly insult their fathers will eventually take revenge against their mothers. It all comes back like a boomerang.

So for years the mother has tried to get the child on her side only to have the opposite happen. She's just pushed the child closer to the father.

Our teacher was right.

"I don't know. I wasn't there—they used general anesthesia. They say it all went well. It hurts. Did you bring my avocado pits?"

"Yes, they're over there."

She points to the windowsill. Right next to the diaper container is a box with my beloved pits. Perfect. I can even reach them myself.

"Did you bring the camera?"

She pulls it out of her handbag and puts it on the nightstand.

"What do you need it for here in the hospital?"

"I don't think you should record only the happy moments in life—like birthdays—but also the sad ones, like operations, illness, and death."

"I'm sure it will be a joy for your children and grandchildren to look at an album of those pictures."

I grin. If you only knew, mom.

I hope she'll leave soon. So I can take care of my ass. The only situation in which I would want to spend more time with her would be if there was a legitimate hope of getting her together with dad. He's not coming today. But tomorrow for sure. A hospital with your daughter in it is the perfect place for a family reconciliation. Tomorrow. Today: ass photos.

She says her good-bye and tells me she's left pajamas in the wardrobe. Thanks. How am I supposed to get at them? It doesn't matter—I'd rather lie here bare-bottomed anyway, with all those bandages. Air is good for the wound.

As soon as mom's gone I ring for Robin.

Waiting, waiting. There are other patients, Helen, hard as that is for you to imagine. Here he comes.

"How can I help you, Ms. Memel?"

"I have a question for you. And please don't say no right away."

"Shoot."

"Can you help me . . . actually, can you not call me Ms. Memel. It's too formal for what I want to ask."

"Sure. Happily."

"You're Robin and I'm Helen. Okay. Can you help me take a picture of my ass and the wound on it? I want to see what it looks like."

"Um, let me think for a second—I don't know if I'm allowed."

"Please. Otherwise I'll go crazy. There's no other way for me to figure out what they did back there. You know, Dr. Notz can't even explain it. And it's my ass after all. Please. I can't tell from feeling it. I've got to see it."

"I understand. Interesting. Most patients don't want to know. Okay. What do you want me to do?"

I go to the menu on the camera and set it to close-up. First try will be with no flash. It always looks better. I pull off the outer bandages and the plug of gauze. It takes a while. They've stuffed a lot of gauze in there. I carefully turn on to my other side, my face to the window, and hold my cheeks apart with both hands.

"Robin, now take a picture of the wound as close-up as possible. Hold it steady—the flash is off."

I hear it click once and he shows me the test shot. You can't make anything out. Robin doesn't have a steady hand.

Other talents, though, I'm sure. We'll have to use the flash. And repeat the whole thing.

"Take a few pictures from various angles. Up close and from farther away."

Click, click, click, click. He won't stop.

"That'll do it, Robin, thanks."

He carefully hands me the camera and says, "I've worked here in the proctology unit for ages and I've never been able to see the actual surgical work. So I thank you."

"No, thank you. Can I look at these on my own? And would you do this for me again if it's necessary?"

"Sure."

"You're really cool, Robin."

"You, too, Helen."

He walks out grinning. I stuff the gauze stopper back in.

I'm alone with the device in which the pictures of my wound are saved. I have no idea what to expect. My pulse quickens and I start to sweat with anticipation.

I turn the little wheel mechanism next to the display to the "view pictures" option and hold the camera right in front of my face. It shows a photo of a bloody hole. The flash has cast light deep inside. My ass is wide open. There's nothing to suggest the closure of a sphincter.

I can't make out any crinkled, red-brown skin of a rosette. Actually, I can't make out anything familiar at all. So this is what Notz meant by "wedge-shaped incision." Poor description. I'm appalled at my own asshole—or rather, what's left of it. More hole than ass.

So: I'll never be an ass model. It's just for private use now. Or am I holding the camera wrong? No, that can't be possible—Robin would have held the camera the same way to take the picture.

Yikes. You can look right in. I feel much worse now that I've seen it. The pain comes back suddenly, too. Now that I know what I look like down there, I can't believe the pain will ever go away. There's no skin at all around the entire opening, just red, naked flesh.

I have to let the skin grow back. How long will it take? Weeks? Months? What do you have to eat to help the skin of your ass grow? Mackerel?

Do they want me to push a dump past open flesh? No way. How many days and weeks can I hold it in? And if I do manage to hold it in for a long time, the crap will get really big and harden and hurt even worse when it has to pass. I'll ask. They'll have to give me something to cause constipation so the wound can heal. I push my SOS button.

Waiting. While I wait I look through the other shots Robin took. Not one makes the wound look any less gruesome. What is that beside the wound? All sorts of red pimples. What the hell is that? I feel around both ass cheeks with my fingertips. I can feel the bumps. I didn't notice them before. My sense of touch is stunted compared to my sense of sight. I need to improve my sense of touch, this is no good. Where did these pimples come from? Allergies? Am I allergic to butt operations? I look at the photos again. Ah, now I know. It's razor burn. They shave you before an operation. Obviously not too daintily. Chop-chop, run the blade across. The only thing that matters is to get the hair off as quickly as possible. Probably without water or shaving cream. Just run the blade over, dry, to rip the hair out.

They're even more unceremonious about shaving than I am on my own. I used to not shave at all. I thought there were better ways to fritter away the time in the bathroom. And I found better ways. Until I met Kanell. He's from Africa. Ethiopia to be precise. One Saturday he stopped at the fruit-and-vegetable stand where I work to earn a little spending money. I set the stand up at four in the morning and sell produce until afternoon. My boss, the farmer who owns the stand, is a racist. Which is hilarious. Because he thinks he needs to stock exotic fruits and vegetables. A gap in the market. But who besides people from Africa, India, South America, or China knows how to prepare dishes with pomelos, sunchokes, and taro root?

So my boss rants all day long about foreigners, about what an insult it is that they want to shop at his stand, and about their accents. This despite the fact that he's attracting them because of what he's selling. Kanell didn't understand the farmer's question: "That it?"

He had to ask the farmer what he meant. The farmer was so patronizing in his explanation that I slipped away from the stand afterward to apologize.

I ran along the rows of stalls looking for him. Finally, I was standing behind him. I tapped him on the shoulder and he turned around. All out of breath, I said: "Hi. I'm sorry. I just wanted to say I was ashamed of the way my boss acted."

"I could tell."

"Good."

We laughed together.

Then I got nervous and couldn't think of anything better to say than: "I'm going back to the stand."

"Are you shaved?"

"What?"

"I asked whether you were shaved."

"No, why do you ask?"

"Because I'd love to shave you sometime. At my place."

"When?"

"Right after work. Whenever the market closes."

He writes his address down for me, folds the piece of paper up small, and pushes it into my dirty palm like a little present. This definitely qualifies as one of my most impulsive dates ever. I shove the note into the chest pocket of my green apron and walk proudly back to the racist's stand.

I don't want to think too much over the next few hours about what to expect at his apartment. Otherwise I'll get too anxious and might not even go. That would be a shame.

When I'm done for the day I shove my under-the-table wages in my pocket and head for the jotted-down address. I ring the bell labeled *Kanell*. Apparently it's his last name. Or perhaps he's got such a complicated name that, like some soccer players, he's just picked out a pseudonym that stupid

Europeans can pronounce. He buzzes the door open and calls down the staircase: "Second floor."

I step inside the entryway and the door closes hard behind me. It practically hits me and a cold breeze rustles my hair. The mechanical arm that closes the door is set too tight. There's a screw someplace in it that you can loosen so the door closes more elegantly. My father taught me that. If I start coming here often, I'll bring a screwdriver sometime and fix it.

I hike up my skirt and wriggle my hand into my underwear. I stick my middle finger deep into my pussy and leave it in the warmth for a moment before taking it back out. I open my mouth and stick my finger all the way in. I close my lips around my finger and pull it out slowly. I lick and suck as hard as I can in order to get as much of the taste of the slime on my tongue as possible.

There's no way I can spread my legs for some guy—to get thoroughly eaten out, for instance—without knowing myself how everything looks, smells, and tastes down there.

In our bathroom are all kinds of useful mirrors that help me look at my own pussy from below. A woman looking down over her stomach at her pussy from above sees it from a completely different perspective than a man with his head hung between her legs in bed.

A woman sees just a tuft of hair sticking up and two bumps hinting at the outer labia.

A man sees a gaping, hungry mouth with knots of flesh all over it. I want to see everything on me the same way a man sees it; they see more of a woman than she does herself because everything down there is oddly hidden, just out of view. In the same way I want to be the first to know how my slime looks, smells, and tastes. And not just lie there and hope everything comes out alright.

Whenever I go to the bathroom I dip my finger into my pussy before I piss and do the same test. I dig around, scoop out as much slime as possible, and sniff it. For the most part it smells good—as long as I haven't eaten a lot of garlic or Indian food.

The consistency varies a lot. Sometimes it's like cottage cheese, other times like olive oil, depending on how long it's been since I washed. And that depends on who I want to have sex with. Lots of guys prefer cottage cheese. You wouldn't think so. But it's true. I always ask in advance.

Then I suck it all off my finger and slurp it around in my mouth like a gourmand. Most of the time it tastes good. Except once in a while when the slime has a sour aftertaste. I haven't figured out what causes that yet, but I will.

The test has to be conducted every time I go to the bathroom because I often run into the dilemma—or unexpected pleasure—of spontaneous sex. Even in those situations I want to be up-to-date on my pussy's slime production. Helen leaves nothing to chance. Only when I know exactly what's going on with my beloved, precious slime can a man slurp it up with his tongue.

I've done the taste test and am happy. I'm ready to be looked at and tasted. The smegma has a bit of age to it, a truffle flavor, and that makes guys hot. Usually.

I climb the stairs. Not slowly, as if I do this all the time. No games. By walking up quickly, I show him how excited and curious I am. At the door he takes my hands in his and kisses me on the forehead. He leads me into the living room. It's very warm. The radiator is boiling away. Someone could comfortably hang out naked here for a good, long time. It's dark. The blinds are down. There's just a little table lamp with a twenty-five-watt bulb. It illuminates a bowl of steaming water on the floor. Next to that is a folded washcloth and an old-fashioned men's razor and a can of shaving cream. The entire couch is covered with big towels.

He quickly undresses me. The skirt is the only thing that gives him trouble—complicated clasp. Lifting it up isn't good enough for him. It's all got to go, the clothing. I help him. Then he lays me down at an angle on the couch. My head in the back corner, my butt on the front edge. I put a foot up on the arm to brace myself, so I'm lying there as if I'm at the gynecologist—Dr. Broekert position.

He undresses completely in front of me. I hadn't expected that. I thought I'd get undressed and he'd stay clothed. All the better. His nipples are hard and he has a partial erection. He has a very thin cock with an acorn-like tip, and it dangles to the left. That is, to my left.

He has a loaf of bread tattooed on his chest. The shape is more like a round sourdough than a loaf of rye or multi-grain bread. Gradually my breathing calms down. I get used to unusual situations quickly. I fold my arms behind my head and watch him. He's readying everything and seems pleased. Looks like there's nothing for me to do except lie back. We'll see.

He leaves the room and returns with a miner's lamp on his head. I have to laugh and tell him he looks like a Cyclops. We've just been reading about them in school. He laughs, too.

He puts a pillow on the floor and kneels on it, saying he doesn't want to get calluses on his knees. Then he dunks both hands into the hot water and rubs it onto my legs. Aha. He starts all the way down at my ankles, moving upward.

Then he sprays shaving cream into his hand and spreads it on my legs. He dunks the razor in the hot water and tracks it down the entire length of the leg. Where he's run the blade, the foam is gone. He makes one straight line after another. Like a lawnmower. After each razor run, he shakes the blade clean in the water. Hairs and foam are swimming on the surface. Fairly quickly, both legs are naked. He says I should have my armpits done the same way. Crap.

I was already looking forward to having my pussy shaved. If he's even planning to do that.

He wets both pits with water and sprays in the shaving cream. He has a harder time under the arms because the hair is longer. He has to go over some of the same spots several times to get it all off. My armpits are also very deep, so he has to pull the skin tight in various directions in order to be able to shave across flat surfaces. He throws a circle of light on my skin with his miner's light. When he gets close—to get a better view—the circle tightens and the light intensifies. When he pulls back, the lamp throws dim light on a wide area. The circle of light always illuminates the exact spot where he's looking at any moment. And the intensity of the light tells how carefully he's looking at the spot. I see the light fall frequently on my tits. More often on the right one, the one with the snake-tongue nipple. My face seems to hold little interest. Once everything is smooth, he ladles water from the bowl into my armpits to rinse away the shaving cream. Then he dries me off. And I dab myself with a towel, too. We smile at each other.

"And now," I say, patting my hair-covered pussy.

"Hmm."

He wets both hands and dampens the whole area. From my bellybutton down, left and right along my thighs, and then on down between my labia to my butthole and on to the top of my ass crack. He looks closely at the cauliflower. A shaving obstacle course. Then he sprays shaving cream on all the dampened areas. It tingles on the labia. Zhhhh. He massages the foam into the skin a little and reaches for his razor. He starts on the thighs. The pubic hair growing down my legs is shaved away. He puts the blade just below my bellybutton and stops. He leans back to get an overview of the area and a crease appears on his brow.

He says: "I like that the hair grows up that far. There I'm going to leave everything. I'll take a little off the sides so we'll have a long, dark stripe down to the split. Then from there all the way back, everything is coming off." He doesn't look me in the eyes, but talks instead to my pussy.

It answers: "Understood."

On the sides he mows the lawn down to a stripe. He tapers the stripe right to the point where the tops of the lady-fingers rise. Now he's on to the labia. Finally. Finally. He puts his head between my legs. That's the best way he can light up my pussy with his lamp. It must look like a hairy lantern. Glowing red inside. He carefully shaves my lady-fingers. Then he has to spread them because he wants to work on the inside edges, too. Again and again he makes his way through all the crevices. Until there's no foam to be seen anywhere. I want him to fuck me. Which he obviously will after the shaving. Have a little patience, Helen. He says I should spread my legs wider but bring my knees up closer to my body so he can get at my ass. He asks whether the bulges on my butt hurt.

"No, no, that's just hemorrhoids that have worked their way out. If you're gentle, I think you can shave right over them."

There's much less hair in back. He runs the razor up and down my butt crack a few times and once around the anus in a circle. Done. Once again I'm drizzled with what is now no longer hot water from the bowl. The shaving of my crack made my pussy produce a lot of slime. Now it mixes with the water and is dabbed dry by Kanell. But it oozes more immediately.

"Do you want to fuck me now?"

"No, you're too young for me."

Stay cool, Helen. Otherwise that nice feeling down below will disappear.

"Too bad. Do you mind if I fuck myself here then? Or do I have to wait until I get home to come?"

"Please go ahead. You are very welcome to do it here."

"Give me the razor."

I hold the blade end and shove the handle into my wet pussy. The handle's not as cold as I expected. Kanell's hands have warmed it up.

With rhythmic motions I let the handle glide in and out. It feels like the finger of a fourteen-year-old. Like Hansel's finger of bone. I rub the handle hard between my labia, back and forth. Harder. It's the same motion as cutting bread. Hard bread. Forward, back. Forward, back. Sawing. Sawing. Deeper.

Kanell watches me.

"Can you put the lamp on my head? I want to light myself up."

He stretches the elastic headband around my head and adjusts the lamp so it's exactly in the middle of my forehead. I look at my pussy and thereby light it up. Kanell walks out of the room. Ooh la la, shaving's got me hot. I lay the razor on my stomach and stroke my smooth-shaven, naked labia with both hands. Dear nonexistent God are they soft. Soft like kid leather, soft like avocado pits. So soft that I can barely even feel them with my fingers. I rub them faster. And come.

And now? I'm sweaty and out of breath. It's so hot in here. Where is Kanell? I get dressed. It's even warmer. He comes in.

I ask: "Do you want to do this again?"

"Love to."

"When?"

"Every Saturday after work."

"Good. That'll give me a week to grow the hair back for you each time. I'll give it my all. See you then."

That was the first time I shaved. Or rather, that I was shaved. Anyway: my first shave. Since then we see each other almost every week. Once in a while he doesn't buzz me in. Or he's not home. Then I have to run around for two weeks with stubble. I hate it. Either totally shaved or hairy. It always starts to itch worse and worse. So I have to do it if he doesn't. But I never do it anywhere near as well as he does. Not as slowly and not as affectionately.

Shaving myself is stupid—I'm spoiled in that regard now. I'm used to being shaved. I think that if men want shaved women, they should take over the shaving. Don't saddle the women with all the work. In the absence of men, women wouldn't care at all how hairy they were. The best arrangement I can imagine would be for men and women to shave each other in whatever way they find most pleasing. That way each would have the exact hairstyle that got their partner the hottest. Better than just hoping for the best from the other person or trying to explain it. That's nothing but trouble.

For me it's all about just getting it done. I shave myself fast, zigzagging all over the place, and rip myself to shreds. I'm usually bleeding afterward, and the open razor-burn bumps gets infected. Whenever Kanell sees that, he scolds me for treating myself that way. He can't stand it. But even I'm not as careless as the person who shaved me before the operation on my ass.

A nurse walks in. Unfortunately, it's not Robin. Oh well. I can ask her, too.

"What happens if I need to have a bowel movement?"

That's what they call it. I can break out that phrase, too, if I feel like it. Depending on who I'm talking to.

She explains that as far as the doctors are concerned, it's desirable that you take a crap as soon as possible. So no log jam develops. She says it's better for the wound to heal with regular bowel movements so that everything grows back together properly and is able to stretch normally. They must be out of their minds. She says Dr. Notz will be right in to explain everything. She walks out. While I'm waiting for Notz, I think about all the things that can cause constipation. So many things come to mind. Notz comes in. I greet him and look him right in the eyes. I always do that when I'm trying to intimidate someone. It occurs to me what long, full eyelashes he has. I can't believe it—why didn't I notice that before? Maybe I was too distracted by the pain. The longer I look at him, the longer and fuller his lashes become. He's telling me, I think, important things about my bowel

movements, my diet, and my recovery. But I'm not listening. I'm counting his eyelashes. And making noises every
now and again that are supposed to make it seem as if I'm
listening closely. Uh-huh.

Eyelashes like that I call eye-mustaches. I can't stand
it when men have beautiful lashes. Even on women it bugs
me a little. Eyelashes are a constant theme in my life. I always pay attention to them. How long they are, how thick,
what color they are, whether they're dyed, done up with
mascara or with a lash curler, or both, whether they're stuck
together with sleepy seeds. A lot are light at the ends and
darker at the base so they look much shorter than they really
are. If you were to put mascara on them, they'd suddenly
look twice as long. Me, I had no lashes at all for many years
of my childhood. But I know that before that I used to get
lots of compliments on my long lashes.

One day a woman asked my mom if it didn't bother
her that her six-year-old daughter had fuller lashes than she
herself did, even though she used mascara and a lash curler.
Mom always told me there was an old Gypsy saying: if you
get too many compliments about one particular thing, that
thing will eventually disappear. That was always her explanation, too, whenever I asked why I no longer had any
lashes. I have a lingering mental image, though: In the
middle of the night I wake up and mom is sitting on the
side of my bed where she usually sits to read me stories. She's

holding my head still, and I feel cold metal along the edge of my eyelids. Snip. On both eyes. And mom's voice says, "It's only a dream, my child."

With my fingertips I'd always touch the stubs of the lashes. If mom's Gypsy story were true, the lashes would have fallen out completely. But I can't really pin it on mom, either, because I often blur the distinctions between reality, lies, and dreams. These days in particular I can't keep things straight because of all the years I took drugs. The wildest party I ever had happened when my friend Corinna realized Michael, my drug-dealer boyfriend at the time, had forgotten his stash of drugs at her house. There was no occasion for a party. It's just what you say you're doing when you take drugs. Partying.

Michael kept all his blotters and pills and packets of speed and coke in a fake soda can. It looked just like a normal can of cola, but you could screw the top off.

Michael always tried to stuff enough drugs into it so it weighed exactly as much as a real can of cola would.

Corinna said: "Check it out, Helen—Michael's can. He wouldn't mind, would he?"

She grinned at me, wrinkling her nose in the process. That always means she's genuinely excited.

We blew off school, bought some red wine at a kiosk, and left a message for Michael on his answering machine: "If you're looking for cola, we found a whole case in Corinna's room. You won't get pissed if we start drinking without you, will you?"

We were big on using badly coded language over the phone. When you're taking drugs you get paranoid and confuse yourself with Scarface. You think you're being listened to and there's about to be a raid, arrests, and a court proceeding during which the judge will say, "So, Helen Memel, what do the words 'laundry detergent,' 'pizza,' and 'painting' really mean? At no point during this time were you doing laundry, eating pizza, or painting. We didn't just tap your phone; you were also under surveillance."

Then began our race against time. The idea was to take as many drugs as possible before the first one took effect and before Michael showed up. Anything we didn't slurp down we'd have to give back. At nine in the morning we started taking two pills at a time, washing them down with wine. It didn't seem right to snort speed and coke so early in the morning, so we made minigrenades out of toilet paper.

Half a packet for each us—which is half a gram—poured onto a little piece of toilet paper, skillfully wrapped up, and gulped down with lots of wine. Maybe there was less than a gram per packet—Michael was a good businessman and he messed with everyone a little on the amounts. So he could earn more. One time I weighed something that was supposed to be a gram. Not even close. But people can't exactly register a complaint with the police. That's just the way it is on the black market. No consumer protection.

Anyway, these paper grenades are very tough to get down. It takes practice. If it doesn't get washed down your throat right away, the minigrenade opens up and the bitter powder sticks to your mouth and gums. You definitely don't want that.

I guess everything started to kick in. I can only remember the highlights. Corinna and I laughed the whole time and made up stories set in a fantasy land. At some point Michael came by to pick up his can and cursed us out. We giggled. He said if all the stuff we'd ingested didn't kill us, we would have to pay him back. We just laughed.

Later we puked. First Corinna, then me from the sound and smell of hers. In a big, white bucket. The puke looked like blood because of the red wine. But it took us a long time to figure out why it looked like that. And then we realized there were undigested pills floating around. This seemed like a terrible waste to us.

I said: "Half and half?"

Corinna said: "Okay, you first."

And so for the first time in my life I drank someone else's puke. Mixed with my own. In big gulps. Taking turns. Until the bucket was empty.

A lot of brain cells die on days like that. And this, along with other similar parties, definitely took a toll on my

memory. There's another memory that I've never been sure
is even a memory. I come home one day from elementary
school and call out hello. Nobody answers. So I think
nobody's home.

Then I go into the kitchen and lying there on the floor
are my mom and my brother. Hand in hand. They're asleep.
My brother's head is resting on his Winnie the Pooh pillow
and mom's is on a folded-up, light-green dish towel.

The oven door is open. It smells like gas. What to do?
I saw a movie once where somebody struck a match and the
whole house blew up. So, nice and slow, I carefully creep
over to the oven—there are people sleeping here—and turn
off the gas. Then I open the windows and call the fire department. I can't think of the number for the hospital in
order to get an ambulance. Oh, both are on the way . . . yes,
they're still sleeping . . . I can ride with them. Two ambu-
lances. A whole crew. Flashing blue lights. Sirens. They
have their stomachs pumped at the hospital and dad comes
directly from work.

Nobody in the family has ever spoken about it. At
least not with me. That's why I'm not sure whether maybe
I dreamed it or made it up and have just convinced myself
it's true over the years. It's possible.

Mom trained me to be a good liar. To such a degree
that I believe most of my own lies. Sometimes it can be fun.

Other times it can be maddening, as in this case. I guess I could just ask mom.

"Mom, did you used to cut off my eyelashes out of jealousy? And another thing: Did you try to kill yourself along with my brother? And: Why didn't you want to take me with you?"

I never find the right moment.

At some stage my eyelashes grew back and I always curled them and used mascara to make the best out of them —and to piss off my mother in case that memory is a genuine memory. Top and bottom, I want my real lashes to look like plastic false eyelashes from the sixties. I mix cheap and expensive mascara to make the ultimate lashes. The best way is to use the end of the brush, where the mascara accumulates, and just glob it onto the lashes. The goal is for people half a mile away to think: "Wow, she's a walking set of lashes."

Mascara is always advertised as not being sticky, and the brush is always supposed to keep the lashes separate so there are no clumps. But for me those are reasons *not* to buy a mascara. When my relatives and neighbors figured out that I never remove the mascara and just put more on every day, a panic broke out.

"If you don't remove the mascara from your lashes, they never get any light or air—and then they'll fall out."

I thought: It couldn't be any worse than it used to be. And I thought up cool tricks to avoid water ever getting on my lashes. After putting so much money and effort into my lashes, I can't just let them get ruined in the shower. And besides, when months' worth of mascara slowly dissolves in hot water and runs into your eyes, it burns. You definitely don't want that. So I shower in stages. First I wash my hair and wrap it in a towel so the water can't get into my eyes. Then I do the rest of my body from the neck down. For a while I missed my neck and black, greasy smudges would accumulate in the three indentations at the base of it.

When that happens, if you rub your neck, dark, sticky little rolls form that smell like pus. So you either have to wash from the face down or you have to rub these rolls off your neck regularly. But the important thing is that your face never comes in contact with water. I haven't put my head underwater for years—not in the bathtub or in the school swimming pool. I have to climb into the pool by the stairs like a granny, and I can only swim the breaststroke because your face, or parts of it, go under water with any other stroke. If someone tries to dunk me, I turn into a fury and scream and beg and explain that it would ruin my lashes. That's worked so far.

For years I haven't seen water from below the surface. Obviously that means I never wash my face either. I think it's overrated anyway. When you take your makeup off with makeup remover and cotton balls you're kind of washing your face. Just keep your distance from the eyelashes. That's the way I've been doing it for years. Only one or two lashes have gotten stuck in the curler. And they grew back. So I've proved that your lashes don't all fall out if you don't remove your mascara every night.

My ex-boyfriend Matt watched me curl my lashes once and asked me whether a row of eyelashes was the same length as the inner pussy lips.

"Yeah. Approximately."

"And you have two of these curlers?"

"Yep."

A gold one and a silver one.

He laid me down on the bed. Spread my legs. Pushed aside the ladyfingers and gently clamped my dewlaps with the eyelash curlers. That way he could hold the inner labia away from the hole and look deep inside. A bit like when they force Malcolm McDowell's eyes open in A Clockwork Orange. He asked me to hold the curlers and pull them as far apart as felt good. Matt wanted to fuck me immediately and cum on my stretched lips. But first he wanted to take a picture so I could see how pretty my pussy looked all stretched apart. We clapped our hands with joy. Well, he did. My hands were busy.

When you stretch these crinkly flaps of skin all the way out, the total surface is as big as a postcard. At some point Matt drifted out of my life, but his good idea stayed with me.

I like the feeling I get from stretching my lips with the lash curlers until they look from my perspective like bat wings. Actually, I wonder if that's why they're so big and peek out from the ladyfingers? No way. I'm sure they were always so big and long and frayed grayish pink along the edges. All of this goes through my head as I'm ignoring Dr. Notz. Now he wants to leave.

But here comes Helen with the photos of her ass.

He needs to tell me which side is up. I can't make out an asshole anywhere. No matter which way I turn the camera.

I look at him. He looks at the photos and quickly away again. He's disgusted by the results of his own surgical work. No wonder he didn't want to tell me beforehand what he had in mind.

"At least tell me which way I need to hold it to see what it looks like down there."

"I can't tell. In my opinion the photo was taken too close up. I can't tell which way it goes, either."

He sounds angry. Is he crazy? He's the one who did this to me. I didn't mess around with his ass. As far as I'm concerned, I'm the victim and he's the culprit.

He keeps glancing at the photo and then looking immediately away again. Hopefully he's able to keep his eyes on wounds for a bit longer when he's in the operating room. What a sissy. Or does he enter another world in the operating room? Looks at everything closely in there and just can't stand to be confronted with it afterward?

Like somebody who always goes to a brothel and does the wildest, most intimate, filthy things with the same hooker, but who, if he runs into her on the street, looks away and would never say hello.

He didn't greet my asshole very nicely.

He doesn't want to see it again.

I see panic in his eyes: Help! My little operating room asshole can speak, ask questions. It's even taken photos of itself.

There's no point. He just doesn't know how to communicate with the people attached to the asses he operates on.

"Thanks a lot, Mr. Notz." That's supposed to signal that he should leave. I dropped his professional title. That does the trick. He walks out.

After the operation and the explanation by the esteemed Dr. Notz, I should now be crapping merrily. One sentence in his long-winded talk caught my attention: I will be discharged from the hospital only after a successful bowel movement with no bleeding. That is the indicator that the operation's been a success and that everything's healing properly.

From this point on, people who have never been introduced to me before come in every few minutes and ask whether I've had a bowel movement. Noooo, not yet! The fear of the pain is insurmountable. If I were to press a log of crap past that wound, my God, what would happen? It would rip me open.

Since the operation I've had only granola and whole-grain bread. They tell me my granola shouldn't sit in the milk too long before being consumed. It should make it into the stomach and intestines in a fairly dry state. That way it will absorb fluid in the body and swell, pushing against the intestinal walls from the inside and thus signaling that it wants out.

The urge to crap should be greatly heightened that way. They're chucking bombs in the top but down below I'm all cinched up with fear. I'm not going to crap for days. I'll just do as my mother does—wait for everything to disintegrate inside.

Can you eat pizza while you're waiting to take a crap? I don't ask anybody; I decide that it's important for rectal healing to eat things you like. I call my favorite pizza delivery service, Marinara. I know the number by heart. It's easy to remember, like those phone-sex lines. I'm really excited, but I don't let it show. I try to sound as belligerent as possible: "One mushroom pizza. Two beers. Saint Mary's Hospital, room 218. The name is Memel. And make it quick. It better not be cold when it gets here. Just go to the front desk and they'll call me."

I hang up as quick as I can.

There's an urban legend that made the rounds a while ago; I think a lot about it. Two girls order a pizza. They wait and wait but the pizza never comes. They call the delivery service a few times and complain. Eventually the pizza shows up.

It looks a little funny and tastes odd. By coincidence, one of the girls is the daughter of a food inspector, and instead of munching the rest they put it in a bag and take it to dad.

They all think maybe the pizza's gone bad or something. Instead it comes out in the lab analysis that there are

five different people's sperm on the pizza. This is how I picture it getting there: The guys at the delivery service are
annoyed by the phone calls. Since the complaints are being
made by girls, the delivery guys have rape fantasies. The
usual. They talk about it, come up with a plan, and all whip
out their cocks to jerk off on a pizza. The pizza baker sees
all the other guys' cocks. And not just in their normal state.
Fully erect. Being jerked off and coming. That's why I'm
envious of men. I'd like to see the pussies of my friends and
schoolmates. And the cocks of my friends and schoolmates.
Especially when they're all coming. But you hardly ever have
the chance. And I don't dare ask.

I only get to see the cocks of men I'm fucking and the
pussies of women I pay.

I want to see more in life.

That's why I love to break into the public pool and go
drunken skinny-dipping after a night out clubbing.

The whole trespassing thing is a little problematic. But
at least you get to see a few cocks and pussies.

Anyway. I'm always extra mean whenever I order pizza.
And I complain even when it doesn't take long. I'd love to
eat a pizza with sperm from five different guys on it.

It would be like having sex with five strange men at
the same time. Okay, maybe not exactly sex. But it would
be like having five strange men blow their loads in my
mouth at the same time. That would be something for the

memory vault, right? To be able to say you'd done that: well done.

I can't even walk. So there's no way I can pick up the pizza. Shit. Now I'm leaking. No way. I'll have to ask someone to pick it up for me. There's no way the receptionist is going to walk around passing out pizzas. Robin will have to do it. The emergency buzzer. Is that wrong? Oh, well.

A different nurse comes in. His name tag says Peter. It makes me smile. I like the name Peter. I was with one once. I called him Piss Peter. He was really good at going down on me. He would do it for hours. He had quite a unique technique.

He would clamp the dewlaps between his teeth and his tongue and then rub his tongue over them. Back and forth. Or with his tongue flattened out and a lot of spit he'd lick from my asshole up to my snail tail and back down. Pressing hard against all the folds.

Both techniques were very good. I usually came multiple times. Once so hard that I pissed in his face. He was mad because he thought I had done it on purpose. It was a little humiliating—the way he was kneeling there and then that happened.

I patted him dry and apologized. I thought he should be proud. Nobody else had ever accomplished that. To make me come so hard that I lose control of my bladder. And I wasn't drunk or anything.

After a while he realized how impressive it was. I learned that day from Piss Peter that it burns when you get piss in your eye. How else could I have ever found that out?

"Where's Robin?"

"Shift change. I'm the night shift."

Is it already that late? Do the days in a hospital go by that fast? Apparently. I'm losing my mind. Fine. It's not so bad here, Helen. Time flies when you amuse yourself with your own thoughts.

"How can I help you?"

"I wanted to ask Robin a favor. I'm a little uncomfortable asking you. We don't know each other."

"What was the favor?"

"I ordered a pizza. It's going to be delivered downstairs soon and I can't go get it. I need someone who can walk and is willing to bring it up here."

Maybe a nurse like this isn't interested in real nourishment, and this plan will fall flat.

"Aren't you supposed to eat high-fiber foods after the operation? Granola, whole-grain breads?"

Shit.

"Yes. I am. Doesn't pizza have any fiber?"

Super idea. Play dumb.

"No. It's actually counterproductive."

Counterproductive—against production. Everybody here thinks only about bowel movements. It's my choice.

"But it's also important to eat things your stomach is accustomed to. Sudden changes in diet aren't good, either, for encouraging bowel movement. Please."

The phone rings.

I answer.

"Is the pizza here?"

I hold the phone to the side and smile at Peter, eyebrows raised in question marks.

"I'll go get it. We'll see what happens," he says, smiling handsomely as he leaves.

"Nurse Peter will come get it. Don't give it to anyone else. Thanks."

I'm lucking out with these male nurses. They're much nicer than the female ones.

I lie back and wait for Peter.

It's dark outside. I can see myself reflected in the window. The bed is very high so the nurses don't hurt their backs maneuvering the patients. The glass goes the entire length of the wall from right to left and from the ceiling down to the radiator. When it's dark outside and light inside it functions like a giant mirror. I didn't need the camera at all, eh? I turn my ass to the window and crane my head as best I can. It's all blurry. Of course. It's double-pane glass. It reflects two images, slightly staggered. Good to have the camera after all. When it's dark out I can lie with my ass to the door and see who's entering the room without turning around. Cool. But can everybody outside see me now? Oh, who cares. They know it's a hospital. It's impossible not to recognize it. At worst they'll think it's a poor little crazy girl who, out of her head on medication, left her bare ass facing the window—and they'll feel sorry for me. That works for me.

Here in the hospital I'm becoming sort of a nudist. I'm not usually like that. Well, when it comes to things pussy-related I guess I am. But not when it comes to my ass.

I just lie here and, because any motion hurts my ass so bad, I don't even bother to cover myself. Anyone who comes in sees my gaping flesh wound and a bit of my peach. You get used to it quickly. Nothing is embarrassing anymore. I'm an ass patient. Anyone can see that, and I behave accordingly.

The reason I have such a healthy attitude about my pussy while I'm normally so uptight about my ass is that the way my mother raised me made it difficult for me to crap. When I was a little girl she told me all the time that she never went to the bathroom. And never farted. She held everything inside until it disintegrated. No wonder I had trouble.

As a result of being told all of this, I get totally ashamed if someone hears or smells me going to the bathroom. In public toilets, even if I'm just pissing and a fart escapes when I loosen the muscles down there, I'll do anything to avoid the person in the next stall being able to put a face to the noise. I'm the same way with the smell of my crap. When people are coming and going in the stalls around me and I've stunk the place up, I'll wait in my stall until there are no more witnesses around. Only then will I come out.

As if crapping is a crime. My schoolmates always laugh at me for my exaggerated sense of shame.

I also don't like to get dressed in my room at home. There are posters everywhere of my favorite bands. They're always looking right into the camera for the photos, so it feels as if they are following my every move with their eyes. So if I'm changing in my room and they could get a peek at my pussy or tits, I hide behind my couch. Though around real boys and men I don't care.

Someone knocks. Peter walks in. He places the pizza on the metal nightstand and puts the two bottles of beer down—a little too loudly—next to it. It all just barely fits.

He looks me in the eye the whole time. I stare back. I'm good at that. I think he likes taking care of someone roughly the same age as he is. It's nice for him.

"You want one of the beers?"

"That's nice of you, but I'm working. If I walk around here with beer breath there'll be hell to pay."

I hate being told no. I should have been able to figure out that he's not allowed to drink on the job. Embarrassing. This is a hospital, Helen, not a bordello.

His gaze starts to wander. Is he looking out the window? Past me? Wait, no, he must be looking at my peach reflected in the window. His nightshift is starting off well. I like Peter.

"Okay, thanks. I guess I'll eat."

He leaves. I open up the pizza box and look at it. I wonder how I'll be able to eat it without any utensils. The Marinara guys haven't even cut the crust with a pizza roller. Should I rip bites out of it like an animal? Suddenly Peter walks back in. With silverware. And walks back out grinning. And then comes in again. What now? In his hand is a plastic baggie with a piece of tape on it. There's something written on the tape.

"It says here I'm supposed to give this to you. Something to do with the operation. Do you know anything about it? Did they find something on you and need to return it?"

"I wanted to see the wedge of skin after they cut it out of me. I couldn't let something be cut out of me while I was unconscious and then not see it before it was tossed in the garbage."

"Speaking of garbage, it's my job to ensure this baggie and its contents are properly disposed of in the special medical-waste bin."

He takes his duties very seriously. He speaks in such a highbrow manner about them. He could have just said he had to make sure the stuff got thrown out instead of "properly disposed of." It would make him seem more human and less like a robot repeating orders. He hands me the baggie but doesn't leave. But I'm only going to open it when I'm alone. I hold the baggie in my hands and stare at Peter until he finally leaves. My pizza is getting cold. But this is more important—and besides, I've heard real gourmets don't eat things really hot because it masks the flavors. Really hot soup tastes like nothing at all. It must be true of pizza, too. If you make something poorly, just serve it as hot as possible and nobody will notice it tastes bad because they'll all have charred their taste buds. It's true of the other extreme, too: cold. You drink nasty drinks—like tequila—as cold as possible so you can get them down.

The baggie is see-through, zipped shut. A little slide is all it takes to open it. Inside is another bag, smaller and white instead of see-through. I can feel the cut-out piece inside it. No more packaging. If I just pull it out it'll make a mess here in the bed. I rip off the top of the pizza box. It's easy. It's perforated along the edge, probably for just such a situation. When you need something to put a bloody piece of flesh on. I put the cardboard box top in my lap beneath the baggie. Do I need rubber gloves to pull this thing out? No. It's from my own body. So I can't catch anything, no matter how bloody it is. I touch what used to surround this clump of flesh—my gaping wound—all day long without gloves. Okay. So out it comes. It feels like liver or something else from the butcher shop. I lay out all the pieces on the cardboard. I'm disappointed. Lots of little pieces. No wedge. Notz's description made it sound as if it would be a thin, oblong piece of flesh that would look like the venison filets mom makes when we have guests in the fall and winter. Dark red and slick before being roasted, kind of shiny, like liver. But this here is goulash. Little pieces. Some pieces have yellow spots—the infection, no doubt—that look the way freezer burn does in commercials. They didn't cut it out in one motion, not all together in one single piece. Of course, I'm no dead deer, but a living girl. Perhaps it's better that they took care of it in small increments. And paid attention to the sphincter. Rather than carving out a magnificent anal filet just for the sake of a good presentation. Relax, Helen. Things are always different than you anticipate. At least you tried to picture something, imagined the smallest details, asked questions to try to verify things—and now you know more as a result. I learned that from dad. To try to figure things out so thoroughly it makes you puke. Anyway, I'm happy to have seen the pieces before they're cremated along with the other medical waste. I don't repack the pieces into the baggie. I just put the baggie on top of them and push it down so it sticks to them. I put the box top with the pieces of flesh and baggie on it on the metal nightstand. My fingers are covered with blood and goop. Wipe them on the bed? That would make a real mess. Not on my tree-top-angel outfit, either. Same mess. Hmm. Well. It is all stuff from my own body. Even if it's infected. I lick my fingers off one at a time. I'm always proud of myself when I come up with an idea like that. It's better than sitting helplessly in bed and hoping somebody happens by with wet wipes. Why should I be disgusted by my own blood and pus? I'm not squeamish about infections. When I pop pimples and get pus on my finger, I happily eat that. And when I squeeze a blackhead and the translucent little worm with the black head comes out, I wipe that up with a finger and then lick it off. When the sandman leaves puslike crumbs in the corners of my eyes, I eat them in the morning, too. And when I have scabs on a cut, I always pick off the top layer in order to eat it.

I eat my pizza by myself.

I don't like eating alone. It scares me. When you stick something in your mouth, you should be able to tell someone else what it tastes like. My ass begins to twitch. What have you learned, Helen? Don't suffer any more than necessary. Ring the emergency buzzer. Peter comes in and I tell him I need painkillers because the pain is starting up again. He looks confused and says there's nothing about overnight pain medication on the chart he's been given. With a big piece of pizza in my mouth I say, "There must be, Robin said all I had to do was ask and I'd get them."

This can't be happening. I finally ask before it gets bad and now I can't get any for the entire night? Help. Peter leaves to call the doctor at home. He says he doesn't have the authority to do anything that's not specifically listed on the chart. I'm feeling sick with fear. I was operated on today and I can't get any pain medication on the first night? I open both beers with the handle of the fork. I'm one of the few girls I know who can do that. Very practical. Hi ho, hi ho, it's off to work I go. I drink the beers down as fast as I can, one after the other. My ass is getting worse and worse, and my insides are cold from the beer.

Peter, Peter, Peter, hurry up. Bring me medication. I close my eyes. The pain is getting stronger and I'm beginning to cramp up. I know this drill. I cross my hands on my chest and I'm nothing more than my ass.

I hear him come in and, with my eyes still closed, ask whether I'll get something.

"What are you talking about," says a female voice.

I open my eyes and see a woman in a nurse's uniform but one that's a different color from all the others here. The others all wear light blue and she's in light green. Maybe she had a laundry mishap.

"Good evening. Please forgive me for disturbing you so late. The rounds took longer than usual today. I'm a candy striper."

What? She must have broken out of the psychiatric ward. I just look at her. She must be crazy, I think, and I'll leave her to believe what she wants. My ass hurts bad. And it's getting worse. That's the only thing I could possibly say to her. That would be a great conversation: "I'm a candy striper." "Yeah, and my ass hurts."

I watch her with tired, half-open eyes like a grandmother. It seems to me she talks very slowly—each word seems to echo.

"That means I'm a volunteer. I try to make things more comfortable for the people here in the hospital. We candy stripers"—there are others!—"run errands for patients, get them phone cards, pick up their mail, that sort of thing."

Very well.

"Can you get me painkillers?"

"No, we're not authorized to do that. We're not nurses. We just look like them." She snorts. It's supposed to be a laugh.

"Please leave me alone. I'm sorry, but I'm in pain and I'm waiting for a nurse and some medication. Normally I'm nicer. I'll call you if I need anything."

As she leaves, she asks, "Where would you call?"

Get out. I need peace and quiet.

I'm not going to be able to keep it together much longer. I take deep breaths. And blow them back out loudly. My hand wanders down to my pubic mound and I pull my knees up toward my chest. Although this position hurts, I stay in it. Into the pain with you, Helen. The other hand I put over my ass crack. This is bad. The kind of pain that makes you feel extremely lonely and scared. I think to myself, no patient should have to be in pain in a country as rich as this; I think, there's enough medicine for every-one here. I ring the buzzer. Peter comes running in. He apologizes that it's taken so long. He couldn't reach the doctor at first. He found out that the day shift had made a mistake. I was supposed to get an electronic device so I could self-administer pain medication. They were supposed to have the anesthesiologist attach one that would allow me just to click with my thumb to get doses of the medicine through the catheter in my arm. They forgot. Forgot? I'm at their mercy. Forgot. And now?

"You can have strong tablets upon request all night long. Here's the first one."

I pop it into my mouth and wash it down with the dregs of the beer. Peter clears away the pizza box. He's probably forgotten he's responsible for the medical waste. Hospital of the forgetful. My painkillers forgotten, my rectal goulash forgotten. We'll see what else gets forgotten. The half-eaten mushroom pizza sits on top covering everything. My goulash ends up in the normal trash. I like that. I don't say anything. He also throws out the beer bottles, very carefully so they don't bang against each other. Very delicate, Peter.

Because of the pain, my shoulder muscles are pulled all the way up to my ears, stretched taut like rubber bands. Now, after taking the pill, they begin to slowly relax and I can breathe more easily. I need to piss from the beer, but I can't get up. No worries. I fall asleep.

When I wake up it's still dark. I don't have a clock. Wait, my camera has a clock in it. I turn it on and take a picture of the room; when I view a shot, it always says when it was taken, right? 2:46 a.m. Too bad. I'd hoped the pill would allow me to sleep through the night. Did Peter leave more pills here?

I turn on the light. It's terribly bright and white. I'm dizzy. I guess these tablets they're giving me are pretty strong.

I'm having trouble thinking straight. My eyes adjust to the nightmarish light. Why did I bother with the clock in the camera? I have a mobile phone. You're funny sometimes, Helen. It must be the medication. I hope. I see a tablet in a little plastic cup on the nightstand. Down the hatch. I can do it without a drink. It tastes disgustingly chemical. It takes a long time before I have enough spit to swallow it. Gulp. And it's down. I turn off the light and try to go back to sleep. Can't. My bladder's full. Very full. At least it's my bladder bothering me and not my ass. There's a noise bothering me. It's a loud hissing. From outside, I think. Sounds like the exhaust pipe of the hospital's air-conditioning system. They must have moved it right outside my window while I was asleep. I refuse to go to the bathroom. You're going to have to fall asleep with a full bladder, Helen, or not at all. To block out the hiss I put the pillow on top of my head. Top ear blocked by the pillow, bottom ear by the mattress.

The hiss in my head is now as loud as the air conditioner outside. I press my eyelids together and try to force myself to sleep. Think about something else, Helen. But what?

I smell something.

I fear it's gas. I sniff and sniff again. It still smells like gas. A gas leak. I can almost hear it. Sssssssss. Just to be sure not to make a fool of myself, I wait a little while longer. I hold my breath. I count a few seconds and then take another deep breath. It's definitely gas. Turn on the light. I stand up. The motion hurts. But who cares. Better to have your ass hurt than to get blown sky high.

I go out into the hall and call.

"Hello? Is anyone there?"

Mom always forbid us to call out "hello." She thought it sounded as if you were talking down to handicapped people.

I'll make an exception. It's an emergency.

"Hello?"

It's silent in the hallway. Hospitals are creepy at night.

A nurse comes out of the nurses' station. Thankfully it's not a man. Where's Peter?

"Can you come check this out? It smells like gas in my room."

Her face becomes very serious. Good, she believes me.

We go into my room and sniff around. I can't smell it anymore. The strong gas smell. It's gone. No gas, no nothing. It's happened again.

"Oh, no, I guess it doesn't. My mistake." I exaggeratedly raise the corners of my mouth.

I'm hoping to make it look as if I was joking.

I don't pull it off very well. I can't believe I've fooled myself again. For the hundredth time. Approximately.

She looks at me full of disdain and leaves. She's right—it's nothing to joke about. But it wasn't meant to be one.

The worst gas incident so far—except for the real one—happened at home. One night when I was trying to fall asleep I was sure I smelled gas. The smell just kept getting stronger. Because I know gas is lighter than air—even though it's hard to believe—I thought I was well situated lying there in bed. It's not far off the floor.

I also know it takes a long time for all the rooms of a building to fill with gas and for the gas to slowly descend from the ceiling and spread out. I was sure my mom and brother were already dead. Whether the leak was in the basement or the kitchen, their rooms would be full by now.

I lay in bed a long time with my eyes nearly closed—because of lack of oxygen, I thought, though it turned out to be from sleepiness—thinking about what I should do.

I thought if I got out of bed I might cause a spark and it would be my fault if the apartment blew up and I died. The others were already dead—it wouldn't matter to them if the place exploded.

I decided to climb out of bed very slowly and inch my way outside on the floor.

The apartment was silent. If I made it out alive I would still have my father, who, luckily, didn't live in that deadly building. That's the one advantage to having divorced parents.

Lying on the floor I reached up for the handle of the front door and opened it. It took a long time to make it down the hall, snaking my way across the carpet. As soon as I was outside I took a few deep breaths. I'd made it.

I walked away from the building so I wouldn't be hit by any flying bricks if the place blew up.

I stood on the sidewalk in my nightgown, lit up by the only street lamp on our block, and looked at the tomb of my mother and brother.

There was a light on in the living room. I could see mom on the couch with a book in her hand. At first I thought she had suffocated and was frozen in that position. Rather improbable.

Then she turned a page. She was alive, and I realized I had fooled myself again.

I went back in and flopped down in bed. Real hard, to cause sparks.

There's no way for me to know whether I'm imagining it or not when I smell gas. It always smells strong. And it happens pretty often.

It's actually a pleasant smell.

Fear makes you tired. Painkillers, too. I lie down in the hospital bed and fall asleep.

I sleep through the rest of the night. Only two tablets. Not bad. I convince myself that's a small amount of pain medication. To be honest, yesterday evening I had pictured a more difficult night ahead. In a shotglass-sized plastic cup on the nightstand is a pill. Another one. Very generous, Peter. Pain medication, I assume. I slurp it down. Today I'll try to stand up. I also need to go to the bathroom. Bad. It doesn't smell good in here. It's not gas this time. It can only be my ass. What else?

I feel around in back and find it wet. Blood? I look at my fingers. Not red. A hint of light brown. I smell them. Definitely crap. How did that get there, inspector Helen?

From the container on the windowsill I pull out gauze bandages and wipe myself up. It's brown water that smells like crap. In the photo yesterday my butthole was wide open and I think everything must just be running out because the hole is still not tightly closed the way it normally would be. The seal isn't watertight. I christen the stuff coming out "ass piss" and I'm already used to it. I figure out a folding technique for the bandages: I hold my ass cheeks apart and shove my folded masterpiece up as close to the wound as possible so it stems the flow of ass piss. When I touch the wound itself with the bandages or my fingertips, it hurts bad. I gingerly let go of my ass cheeks. They hold the bandages in place. All set. Problem solved.

It really doesn't smell too good in this room. I'm afraid my ass is definitely air-incontinent. A constant flow of warm air is coming without warning out of my intestines. You can't even call them farts. My ass is just wide open. Farts have a beginning and an end. They noisily find their way out, sometimes with a lot of pressure. That's not the case here. It just billows out. And fills the room with all the smells that should stay inside me until I decide to let them out. It smells like warm pus mixed with diarrhea and something acidic that I can't seem to identify. Maybe it's from the medication.

Now when somebody enters the room they know as much about me as if under normal circumstances they had shoved their head up my ass and taken a big whiff.

I'm in a good mood because I slept so well, I think. The next problem: going to the bathroom. I lie on my stomach and drop my legs slowly toward the floor. It's a long way down. These tall beds. Bad. My feet touch the ground. I brace myself with my forearms and lift my upper body upright. I stand up. Ha! Turn around and slowly shuffle with tiny steps—otherwise it hurts my butt too much—what seems like a long way to the bathroom. Three yards. Plenty of time to think of something nice. The smell of this watery ass piss seems familiar to me.

When I know I'm going to have sex with someone who likes anal, I ask: with or without a chocolate dip? Which means: some guys like it when the tip of their cock has a little crap on it when they pull it out after butt fucking—the smell of the crap their cock's pulled out turns them on. Others want the tightness of the asshole without the filth. To each his own. For those who would rather have it clean, I ordered something from an online gay sex shop. It looks like a dildo with holes in the tip. It's made out of surgical steel. I don't know what that is, but it sounds good—and looks good.

First I unscrew my friendly showerhead so I can attach the threaded base of this device. It's handy that everything is standardized. Then it's time to clean the rectum. I smear the tip of the steel thing with Pjur lube. Then I work the thing past my cauliflower and shove it in as far as I can. At least that's the way I used to do it—the cauliflower's gone now. Should make it easier. Pushing it in turns me on—usually when something goes up my ass like that it's a cock. Is that Pavlovian conditioning?

The device is colder and harder than a cock. I turn on the shower full blast, but not too hot because I don't want to boil my innards. This is the best part of my internal cleansing. It feels like you're being pumped up like a balloon. We're more used to the feeling of being filled up from flatulence than from having water in our intestines. So you tend to picture gas, not water. Soon you feel like you're going to burst, like there are liters of water inside you. I get a strong urge to crap.

I turn the water off and crouch down as if I'm going to piss in the shower. I push all the water out of my intestines. It's like pissing out of your ass. Like having severe diarrhea. You need to take out the hair strainer and the tub stopper because a lot of crap comes out, in big and small chunks. I repeat this process three times until there are no more mini-chunks of crap visible. No cock, no matter how big or long, is going to unearth anything in my rectum now. I'm perfectly prepared for clean butt sex, like a blow-up doll.

If somebody does like a chocolate dip, I'll only do it if I've already had good sex with him a few times. It's a real sign of affection. Anal sex without cleaning my ass out in advance. It takes a lot of trust to let someone decorate his cock with my crap. If I haven't emptied my insides right before sex—either with the anal flushing device or on the toilet—there's crap ready to be found just a few centimeters inside the entrance. It doesn't get any more intimate than that as far as I'm concerned. Everything smells like my innards during sex like that, too. I have to smell my own innards the whole time. He only has to have stuck it in for a second and come in contact with the crap. Then when he pulls it back out and we try out another position, his cock functions like a fluttering crap-scented air freshener.

Right now, though, I can't imagine ever doing it again. Either thing. Ass cleansing or ass fucking. Which would be a shame.

I've made it. I've arrived in the bathroom. I don't need to pull my underwear down because I don't have any on. I just gather my tree-top angel outfit together on my stomach and tie it in a knot so it doesn't dangle into the toilet. I carefully try to sit down, but as I start to squat I realize it won't work. I can feel the wound straining. I'll have to stand upright and straddle the toilet bowl. That works. This is how French women piss, right? On the wall to my left is a grandma grab-bar to hold onto. Probably designed more to help lift yourself up if you've sat down and can't get back up. I'm misusing it to keep my balance while pissing standing up. I brace myself on the right against the plastic wall of the shower stall. I get most of the piss in the toilet. Am I supposed to take a crap like this? Can't possibly imagine that. Though I can't imagine taking a crap in any position. I'm not ready to try. Naturally, I don't wash my hands after pissing.

If I were able to sit down on the toilet seat I'd do what I usually do at home: read the labels of the various soaps and shampoos on the rim of the tub. Apparently mom has put a few things around the sink here for me. But I can't reach them right now. At home I know a lot of the label information by heart. My favorite is a bubble bath: "Toning and Invigorating." No idea what that's supposed to mean. Invigorating I understand, I guess. But toning? I've tried to picture mom toned. It's not a pretty picture. And ever since this word entered my vocabulary, I've been calling my brother Toning instead of Tony. He doesn't find it amusing. But I do.

Quickly—but slowly—back to bed.

It's going to take an extremely long time to get there. I never would have thought the butthole was so integral to the process of walking. During this turtle-speed walk I have plenty of time to think about all the things I want to do today. I'm sure my father and mother will visit. I'll get them back together. I also need to set up my avocado pits and fill the glasses with water. I'll have to find a hiding place for them or they'll be taken away. I've made it as far as the Jesus poster. I take it off the wall and carry it with me toward the bed. It'll fit perfectly between the metal nightstand and the wall, where no one can see it. Beautiful. An atheist hospital room. I crawl up onto my bed like a cripple and I've made it. What's this? There are drops of liquid on the floor. A long trail. From the bathroom to the bed, with a detour to the wall. It's drops of pee. I didn't wipe. Never do. But usually it goes into my underwear or whatever I'm wearing. Here I'm not wearing anything down below so it all drips onto the floor. Funny. There's no way I can go back and wipe it up—I can't walk that far again much less squat down to wipe something at floor level. It'll have to stay there. I count the drops I can see, as far as the bathroom door. Twelve. The sun streaming in the window reflects off drops nine and ten so they look like little circles cut out of aluminum foil or something else shiny. My father is a scientist and he taught me that some beams of light are broken and diffuse in a drop of liquid. That's why it looks as if light has been trapped inside a droplet. The rest of the light is reflected by the surface of the liquid. That's why it shines.

There's a knock at the door and someone in white medical clogs walks along the pee path. The socks are gleaming white. Nothing in our house ever stays white. Anything white takes on a different shade after the first washing. A dirty pink or grayish brown. More people walk in. The drops get all trampled. All these people have my pee on the bottoms of their shoes. That's my kind of humor. I imagine how all day long they'll be walking around their various stations and marking my territory for me. What are they doing here other than ruining my pee path?

Aha. It must be doctors and residents, or whatever you call them. They're doing rounds. Why is it called that anyway? They've already introduced themselves. Asked me questions. And I've been thinking about other things. I can continue now. The best spot for the avocados would be the windowsill. Because of the light. I'll just have to screen it off so that nobody standing in the room can see them.

I hear the sentence, "She'll be discharged once she has a successful bowel movement."

Of course. They're talking about me. The bowel movement lady. It's Notz. I hadn't noticed him among all the other doctors. Can I ask someone to fill the avocado glasses with water? I can't possibly go back and forth filling them all. Given the speed I'm walking right now, it could take days. I have glasses for the pits and another one for mineral water. Someone will have to use that one to fill the others, going back and forth between the windowsill and sink. Wait, I've got it. I can use the mineral water for the pits. The nurses always refill my glass. So I don't need to ask anyone to do it for me. I can take care of it myself. Beautiful. Nothing but the finest mineral water for my avocado-pit babies. Rich in calcium and magnesium and iron and who knows what else. They'll grow well in that.

They all walk out again, my pee emissaries. Finally I can start working on my project.

I grab the little box my mom used to transport the pits. First I need to unwrap the newspaper from around the glasses. Packed way too safely. Same way mom drives. Crawling along, coming to a full stop at every speed bump.

To avoid damage to the axles, she says. Maybe in the old days. Modern cars can take such a beating that you could drive over a speed bump at highway speed without anything happening. Says my father.

I put the eight glasses at the farthest end of the sill. Each of the eight pits I stick with three toothpicks and suspend in a glass. I start to pour in mineral water so two-thirds of each pit is submerged. But I need more liguid.

We'll see how they fare after being moved and left out of water for a day and a night. It's the first time I've taken pits on a journey. Now I need something to screen them from the view of all the people who come in and out of the room. Wasn't there a book in the drawer of the nightstand? I open the drawer. A Bible. Of course. These Christians. Always trying to get you. Not going to get me. But as a screen it'll do. I prop it up in front of the pits, open, but upside down so the cross is on its head. That'll piss them off, right? It's a sign of something bad to them. But what? Who cares.

On top of my little greenhouse I put the menu of the week's food choices. That way nobody can see my little secret from above. I'll only be getting whole-grain bread and granola anyway.

My family's all set up. The pit collection makes it feel a bit more like home. As long as I can take care of my avocados I'll have something to do. Filling them up with water or replacing the water. Documenting their progress with the camera. Once in a while scraping off the slime. Pinching off dead or blighted leaves so healthy ones can grow. That kind of thing.

The phone rings. Who had it connected? Is that something the candy stripers do? With what money? Do you have to pay for it? I'll have to look into that. I pick it up.

"Hello?"

"It's me." Mom.

Mom and dad want to visit today. They both want to avoid being there at the same time as the other.

I want so bad for my parents to be in a room together. I want them to visit me here in the hospital at the same time. I have a plan.

Mom asks, "When is your father coming?"

"You mean your ex-husband? The one you used to love so much? At four."

"Then I'll come at five. Will you make sure he's gone by then?"

I say yes but think no. As soon as I've hung up with mom, I call dad and tell him it would be good for me if he came at five.

Dad shows up at five and brings me a book about slugs.

I think maybe it's a reference to my butthole and ask about it. He says he thought I was interested in them because I asked him about them once. I'm sure I did—that's the only sort of topic I can talk about with dad.

Not about real feelings or problems. He's never figured that out. That's why I talk to him a lot about plants, animals, and environmental pollution. He would never ask how my openly gaping wound is doing. I can't think of much to talk about with him. The whole time he's sitting there in the chair at the end of my bed, I keep expecting a knock at the door followed by mom entering the room. I hate awkward pauses. Though as a personal challenge, I try to keep them going. For that, dad is the perfect partner. He doesn't talk. Unless I ask him something. He just doesn't need to talk, I guess. I look at him and he at me. It's horribly quiet. But he doesn't look unfriendly or anything. Actually quite friendly and relaxed. I have no idea why. I guess I could ask. Perhaps I'm afraid of the answer. But that's definitely not a reason to leave someone, just because he sits there, looks at you, and doesn't say anything. There must be a better reason than that. Maybe their love faded. If you really want to promise something worthwhile, try this: I will stand by you even if I no longer love you. Now that's a promise. That really means forever.

In good times and in bad. It's certainly bad times when one person no longer loves the other. To stay only as long as there is love is not good enough if you have children.

Mom comes too late. She's still not there at six. Dad leaves. Failed once again. They repel each other like two negative poles of magnets I'm trying to push together.

My goal is that they see each other and, years after separating, fall head over heels in love again. And get back together. Highly unlikely. But anything's possible. At least that's what I maintain. Though I'm not really so sure.

A lot of time elapses between dad's departure and mom's arrival. I speak even less with mom than I did with dad. She thinks I'm upset because she's late. The perpetually guilty conscience of a working mother. She doesn't know what I know. That she just missed her future husband. I don't let on. She can go ahead and try to convince herself that my bad manners have to do with my pain.

Her visit was a lot shorter than dad's. Your own fault, Helen.

They both plan to come back tomorrow. So I'll try again. The longer I stay in the hospital, the more chances I'll have to bring them together. At home I'm either at my mom's, where dad will never go, or at my dad's, where my mom will never go.

So it would be better not to have a bowel movement. For my own recovery, of course, the opposite is true—better to have a bowel movement soon, if the doctors are to be believed. I can secretly have a bowel movement and not tell anyone. That way I'll be able to stay in the hospital longer without having to worry about my bum.

That's what I'll do. Also, maybe by injuring myself again I can force another operation. Then I'd have many more days to work toward my goal.

Maybe something will occur to me. Definitely. I certainly have enough time here in my boring, atheist room to think up all sorts of possibilities. My parents were each here for only a short time. I'm not talking enough to people. I always realize I'm not when I fall into a state of brooding and start to have bad breath. When I don't talk for a long time—don't open my mouth and give it a chance to air out—the leftover bits of food and the warm saliva in my closed mouth begin to ferment. At night your mouth is the perfect, body-temperature petri dish—bacteria multiplies and the food between your teeth decays. That's what's starting to happen to me now. I need to talk to someone. I push the buzzer. Robin comes in. I have to think of a reason why I pushed the call button. Ah—a question.

"When am I getting the device from the anesthesiologist so I can self-administer pain medicine?"

"He was supposed to have been here a long time ago."

"Good. So anytime, then. Otherwise I would ask for tablets now, as the pain is starting up again."

That's a lie. But it makes my use of the call button more believable. He reaches for the door handle.

"Are you okay, Robin?"

Typical of you, Helen. He's a nurse. Yet I think I have to look after him and make sure he has a nice shift.

"Yes, I'm doing fine. I've been thinking a lot about your wound and about how cool you are about it. I even talked about it with a buddy. Don't worry—nobody from here at the hospital. He thinks you're an exhibitionist or whatever you call it."

"Show-off is what I always say. And it's true. Is that bad?"

"No, I wish more girls were that way. Like the girls I meet at clubs."

To keep the conversation going and maybe also a little to try to turn Robin on and get him into me, I tell him about my nights out.

"Do you know what I always do when I go to the disco?"

I do a cool thing when I'm meeting a boy and want to fuck him. To prove that I'm the one who initiated the fuck that night. To show that what happens later on is no coincidence. A night like that always starts out a little uncertain. You know how it is. Do you both want the same thing? Will you manage to have sex at the end of the night? Or was the date all for nothing? To make totally clear what I wanted from the get-go, I cut a big hole in my underwear so you can see the hair and the lips. Basically, the whole peach should peek out. Obviously I wear a skirt. I start to make out with him and we grab at each other. After he's stroked my breasts for long enough, at some point his finger wanders down to my thigh. He thinks he has to painstakingly work his way into my underwear and is worrying whether I want to go that far. You're not going to discuss that kind of thing when you haven't known each other long. Then, with no warning, his finger comes into direct contact with my dripping wet pussy.

Boys all react the same way to this gift. The finger has a heart attack and pauses for a second. Then there's more feeling around because he can't believe what his finger has found. They always think, She's not wearing underwear. Once they realize—like they're playing a sensory perception game—that there's a hole in the underwear, it becomes clear that I got ready for this and tinkered with them hours prior. This always causes a broad, dirty grin to spread across the face of my prospective partner. That is, my prospective fuck partner.

I break out into a bit of a sweat just telling the story. What would possess me to do this? I think I just got a rush from his compliment. Always have to dial it up a notch, eh, Helen?

Robin stands there with his mouth slightly ajar. My story has achieved its desired effect. I can see his cock bulging in his white scrubs. While I've been telling him the story, the call buzzer's been going nonstop out in the hallway. Other patients who want something from Robin. But not the same thing I want.

"Okay, see you later," he says, and leaves.

I've unsettled him. It's like a sport. In any room I have to be the most uninhibited of all those present. This time I've won. But this was an easy opponent; it wasn't even a real contest. More like a blowout.

I'm already curious what the effect will be, whether he'll still be able to look me in the eyes. I put myself in strange situations. Is it possible that *anyone* who works in a hospital—whether they're old or young, good-looking or ugly—seems sexually attractive just because there's nobody else around?

I exhale through my nose to settle my breathing. Better already. I don't have to muster the strength to get up and go brush my teeth. Just push the call button and tell filthy stories and I'll get plenty of fresh air in my mouth. In the old days children who said bad words would have their mouths washed out with soap. Did people really do that, or only threaten to do it? I'll have to try it out. I'll say a bad word and then wash my mouth out with soap. Something else to add to my mental scrapbook. I've already sprayed myself with pepper spray—also just because I wanted to know what it felt like. The brand I used was called Knockout but I know now there's no truth to the name. I didn't pass out. My eyes just started to tear up really bad and I couldn't get them to stop. You cough a lot, and spit runs out of your mouth like a waterfall. The stuff really agitates your mucous membranes. I'm bored here. I can tell from the thoughts in my head. I'm trying to entertain myself with my own old stories. I'm trying to divert attention from how lonely I feel. It's not working. Being alone scares me. Must be one of the afflictions of being a child of divorce.

I'll go to bed with any idiot just so I don't have to be in bed alone or spend a whole night sleeping alone. Anybody is better than nobody.

My parents didn't anticipate that when they split up. Adults don't think about the wide-ranging consequences of a breakup.

I sink my head deep into my pillow and look up at the ceiling. The TV hangs there. That's it. I'll play my old guess-that-voice game. I pull the remote out of the drawer and turn on the TV. Using the brightness button, I keep pushing "minus" until the picture goes dark. Then I turn up the sound and start changing channels. The idea is to pick out the voice of someone speaking. Obviously it only works with familiar people. I came up with this game because I liked to watch TV to stave off loneliness but I started to get annoyed at the shows. It had to do with one thing above all else. When people on TV have sex with each other and the woman stands up afterward, she always covers her breasts with a sheet. I just can't stand that. They've just stuck parts of themselves inside each another and now she's hiding her tits. Not from him, but from me. How am I supposed to get into what's happening on the screen when they keep reminding me that I'm watching? If the man stands up, they only show him from behind. So aggravating. That's how they lost me as a TV viewer. Only unknown actresses show their tits on TV. When somebody is running around with no top on, you can be sure she's unknown. The stars never show anything. That's the way acting is these days. Now I only listen to the TV—for my guessing game. I used to be better at it. When I was young and watched a lot of TV I recognized voices much better.

I stare at the black screen and try to concentrate on the voices. No idea whose they are. I turn off the TV again. I don't feel like playing. It's more fun to play against some-one. I'll ask Robin when he has time. Which is never.

What else can you play here in this room? Something occurs to me.

I push my head back, getting the pillow under my neck, so I can look above and behind me. I haven't looked there yet. That's where the pale light is coming from. On the wall is a row of long fluorescent tubes. A wooden cover hangs in front of them to keep them from being blinding. I look at the grain of the wood and all I can see are pussies. Whenever I see the grain of boards lined up next to one another, I see pussies of all shapes and sizes. Like on the door to my room at home. It's covered with that thin wood laminate that's made in mirror-image panels. It reminds me of something from art class when I was younger. You put a blotch of watercolor and water in the middle of a piece of paper, fold it in half, press it together, then open it up again, and your pussy portrait's done. I try to conjure something else in the grain of the fluorescent light cover. Doesn't work. Just pussies. I ring the call button. What could I want now? Think of something fast.

A knock and the door opens. A female nurse walks in. Actually she opened the door first and then knocked. I'm so generous to this oafish nurse that I switch the order of the two activities in my head so she comes across as more courteous. Robin must have sent her. I've got him too flustered for now. I'll have to work on that. This nurse is named Margarete. Says so on the badge on her chest. I looked at her breasts first and then her face. I do that often. But I'm fascinated by her face. She's unbelievably well-kept. That's what people say: a well-kept woman.

As if being "well-kept" represents something of great value. At school we call kids who look like that "doctors' daughters" no matter what their fathers do. I don't know how they do it, but they always look better washed than the rest of us. Everything is clean and carefully styled. Every little body part has been treated with some beauty product.

What these women don't know: the more effort they put into these little details, the more uptight they seem. Their bearing is stiff and unsexy because they're worried about messing up all their work.

Well-kept women get their hair, nails, lips, feet, faces, skin, and hands done. Colored, lengthened, painted, peeled, plucked, shaved, and lotioned.

They sit around stiffly—like works of art—because they know how much work has gone into everything and they want it to last as long as possible.

Those type of women would never let themselves get all messy fucking.

Everything that's sexy—mussed hair, straps that fall off the shoulder, a sweaty glow on the face—is a bit askew, yes, but touchable.

Margarete looks at me questioningly. I'm supposed to tell her what the story is.

"I need a trash can for my dirty bandages. If I leave them on the nightstand it won't smell too good in here."

Very convincing, Helen. Well done.

She's sympathetic to my put-on wish for additional hygiene in the hospital room, says "of course," and walks out.

I hear noise outside. Something's happening. Probably nothing exciting. The usual hospital things. I bet it has to do with distributing dinner. Here in the hospital you're subject to a strict schedule that must have been designed by a lunatic. Starting at six in the morning the nurses bounce loudly around the hallways. They come in with coffee, they want to clean the room or clean me. You're trapped in a beehive full of worker bees, all flying around and tending to something. Very loudly most of the time. All sick people really want to do is sleep, and that's the one thing they won't let you do here. If after a bad night—and every night is bad in a hospital—I want to catch up on sleep, there are at least eight people conspiring against my doing this. Nobody who works in the hospital pays attention to whether someone is sleeping when they enter the room. They all just yell "Morning" and loudly do whatever it is they have to do. They could just drop the "Morning" and quietly and considerately take care of their duties in the room. They have something against sleep here. I heard once that you're not supposed to let people with depression sleep too much because it intensifies the depression. But this isn't a nuthouse. I sometimes think they use the constant interruptions to make sure the patients are still alive. As soon as one nods off, he has to be saved from certain death: "Morning!"

People come in and out. Each one expects me to be understanding. But that should go both ways. That's how the world works.

The nurse comes back in with a little chrome trash can and sets it on the nightstand. She pushes down on the plastic pedal with her hand and the top flies open. I put in the used bandages from between my ass cheeks. The way Margarete uses the pedal is typical of a well-kept woman. She pays close attention to her nails. She touches everything only with her fingertips. Odd phenomenon. Sure, if your nails have just been painted, you're careful not to touch things until they dry. But some women act the same way even when their nails are dry. It makes them look squeamish. As if they're disgusted by everything around them.

"Thanks a lot. When it comes to hygiene, I'm quite particular," I say with a broad smile.

She nods knowingly—though she doesn't know a thing. She thinks I want to keep things neat here, that the smell bothers me, or that I'm ashamed of the bandages I magically pull out of my behind. In reality, what I'm quite particular about when it comes to hygiene is that I don't give a shit about it, and I despise germaphobes like Margarete.

What's up with me? Why am I so worked up about her? She's hasn't done anything to me.

I'm putting one over on her with my trash can request, not the other way around. When I instantly despise someone for no comprehensible reason, when I want to punch them or at the very least insult them in the harshest terms, it usually means my period is on the way. Just to top it all off.

Margarete says, "Have fun with your trash can."

Yeah. Thanks a lot. You're a barrel of laughs.

I've already lost plenty of blood down there. And I've already got plenty to do to take care of my wounded ass without having to worry about preventing the flow of blood from my period, too. I'm fine with my actual period once the irritability right before it dissipates. Often I'm horny when I'm bleeding.

One of the first dirty sayings I ever heard, when I was very young, was at a party my parents threw, and I had to ask around a lot before I understood it: It's okay to swim in the red river as long as you don't drink the water.

It used to be considered disgusting for a man to fuck a woman who was bleeding. But those days are long gone. When I fuck a boy who likes it when I'm bleeding, we leave behind a huge, blood-splattered mess in the bed.

When I have any control over the particulars, I try to get fresh, white sheets to use. And I change positions and move around the bed as much as possible so there's blood all over the place.

When we're fucking I like to be sitting or squatting so gravity helps as much blood as possible flow out of my pussy. If I simply lie there, the blood just pools.

I also love it when someone goes down on me while I'm bleeding. It's kind of a test of mettle for the guy. When he's finished licking and looks up with his blood-smeared mouth, I kiss him so we both look like wolves who've just ripped open a deer.

I like to have the taste of blood in my mouth when we finally fuck. I find it extremely exciting, and I'm always sad when after a few wolf-days my period ends.

But I'm lucky. From what I hear from other girls, some of them are in pain for days on end. Doesn't exactly make you want to have sex.

All that happens to me is that shortly before it starts, I get into a really bad mood—like right now—and I'm extremely aggressive toward random people I encounter. Then the blood starts to flow. No pain. No cramps.

Back when periods were still something new to me, I used to think I really was just in a bad mood. And then I'd be caught by surprise by the blood. Usually in school. Clearly visible to everyone as a red stain on the back of my skirt, because I'd be sitting when it started. You're always sitting in school.

Or during a visit with my relatives at my aunt's house. I went to bed because I didn't feel well. I didn't know why.

The next morning I got up and saw that I'd covered the bed with blood. A huge puddle. I was too self-conscious to go to my aunt and say that I'd had a bit of an accident. There was just nothing I could do.

I had slept and hadn't noticed anything. I didn't know how to describe what had happened to me, either. I decided just not to say anything. I left the next morning like nothing had happened, leaving the mess behind without comment.

My aunt must have gone into the room to tidy up and noticed it right away. I hadn't even covered it with the blanket. All those liters of red were right out in the open for my aunt to see. Ever since then I've been uptight around my aunt. Though she's never said anything about it.

Typical of family.

I can't think of anything else when I see her. Until I get so ashamed I can hear the blood pulsing in my ears.

When it comes to my period, I don't care about hygiene, either. It's blown completely out of proportion. Tampons are expensive and unnecessary. When I have my period, I use toilet paper to make my own tampons while I'm sitting on the toilet. I'm proud of that.

I've developed a special balling and packing technique so they stay in for a long time and hold in the blood. But I have to admit that my toilet paper tampons really just stop up my pussy and dam up the blood rather than absorbing it the way commercial tampons do. I asked my gynecologist, though, whether it was harmful to the pussy to keep the blood inside and then let it flow out while sitting on the toilet. And he said it was a common misconception that the bleeding had some kind of purifying effect. So from a medical perspective, my blood-dam system is harmless.

A few times I went to the gynecologist because I'd lost a tampon inside me. I was sure I'd stuffed one in but, when I went to pull it out, I couldn't find it anymore. Of course, that's a small disadvantage of my homemade tampons: there's no turquoise-colored string to pull it out with. And my fingers are kind of short, so I don't get too far when I'm looking for something in my pussy.

A couple of times when I found myself in this situation at my dad's house, I had to fish around in there with his nice barbecue tongs. There's usually charred bits of meat and fat stuck to them. I couldn't be bothered to clean the tongs before they went inside me. So I laid myself down in Dr. Broekert position and tried as best I could to locate the clump of toilet paper in my pussy. With all the stuff from the grill still on them. Often without finding anything. Just as I don't clean the tongs before I shove them inside me, I don't wash them before they land back on dad's grill after my gynecological insertion. I always have a broad grin on my face during barbecues with friends of the family.

I ask everyone "Doesn't it taste great?" and wave to my father who waves back with the tongs, smiling. My third hobby. Spreading bacteria.

If I'm unsuccessful in my search with the barbecue tongs and start to worry that the bloody toilet paper will rot inside me and I'll die a horrible death from infection, I go to the gynecologist.

He calls it my Bermuda Triangle problem. Sometimes he can help me, but often he can't find anything, either. He has really long fingers and all kinds of medical barbecue tongs made out of steel. And still there are times when he doesn't find the clumps.

"Are you sure you inserted a tampon?"

Cute. He always says "inserted." I always say "shoved in."

"Yes, absolutely sure."

I'm a real mystery to him. As my pussy is to me. I have no idea where the clumps go. Hopefully I'll live long enough to figure out this mystery. Dr. Broekert does an ultrasound to make sure there's nothing hiding up there.

Often I'm too lazy to craft new tampons. So I don't throw away the old one—that took me so long to fold up—in the toilet every time I go to the bathroom. I pull it out with my finger after I've sat down. And I put it on the floor. The dirtier the floor, the better.

If I can add a bloodstain to all the other stains on the floor, great. Once I'm finished with whatever I had to do on the toilet, I grab it off the floor and shove it back in. I like the smell of old blood that's gushed out of my pussy.

But then, I like the smell of truffles. I've heard horror stories about what happens if you don't always replace your tampon regularly. You get the worst infection—some women even die from toxic shock. Since I've been getting my period—that is, for six years —this is how I've dealt with my body and my pussy and my bacteria, and my gynecologist hasn't had any moments of anguish over me.

I used to have a close friend, Irene. I always called her Sirene. It suited her better. And we came up with a cool idea: Whenever we had our period at the same time—which didn't happen very often, as you can imagine—we would do the following.

Each of us in a stall. Just a divider between us. The usual eight-inch gap between the base of the divider and the floor. We both take out our tampons—back then they were minis with light-turquoise strings—and then, one, two, three, go, we'd pass each other our tampons beneath the divider. And then, when we were finished peeing and dabbing ourselves dry, we each shoved in the other's tampon. Through our old, stinky blood, we were bound together like Old Shatterhand and Winnetou. Blood sisters.

Sirene's tampon always looked interesting. Before I stuck it in each time, I would examine it closely. Very different from mine. Who knows what another girl's used tampon looks like? Okay, okay. Who even wants to know? Besides me. I know.

Recently during one of my exciting trips to a brothel, I learned something else about bleeding and tampons. I go to brothels a lot now to explore the female body. It's not like I can ask my mother or my friends. Whether they'll spread open their pussies for me so I can satisfy my thirst for knowledge. Couldn't bring myself to do that.

Now that I'm eighteen, I can show my ID and get into a brothel. I look way younger, so they always ask to see it. My life has gotten a lot better since I turned eighteen, but also a lot more expensive. First the sterilization. That was nine-hundred euros including the anesthesia. Here in this same hospital. I paid for it myself. Now all the visits to the brothel. I have to earn it all working for the racist at the market.

Older men always take guys to brothels on their eighteenth birthdays so they can have their first hooker-fuck. In the old days it was probably their first fuck of any kind. These days there's no way that's the case.

I waited patiently until my eighteenth birthday, but nobody offered to take me there. So I did it all by myself. I found the numbers of brothels in our town, called them up, and, with hope in my voice, asked them whether any of the hookers working there dealt with women. Not many did.

One of the brothels, though, immediately said it had a large selection of hookers open to women. It's called the Sauna Oasis. The madam said it would be better if I came early in the evening as the male johns often got annoyed at female johns. Or do you call them johnettes? Whatever.

I was okay with that and now I go there often.

I wanted to pick out the right hooker for me in the waiting room. She looked like a black version of me. By that I mean she was built like me. Thin, small breasts, a wide, flat ass, but overall petite. And long, straight hair. But I think her hair was made out of plastic. Island braid extensions. I went over to her. I already knew she was willing to go with women. That didn't need to be discussed. When I'm picking, the only women in the waiting room are ones there for me, a female client. All those who service only men—maybe on religious grounds?—disappear into a back-room while I'm selecting. I go over to her, as determined as possible. I feel very awkward in this brothel setting. No won-der men always have to get hopelessly drunk before they get up the nerve to go. And then they can't get it up or can't remember their expensive fuck afterward. You really feel as if you're doing something unbelievably taboo, something crazy. I wish I were drunk, too, when I'm there. But I worry I won't remember afterward what the pussies look like. In which case it would all have been for nothing. That's why I'm doing this, after all. Studying pussy. So I go sober. I have too much respect for the women there and for the situation. I look forward to a time when I don't feel so uncomfortable anymore, once I've gotten used to it. At the moment I still get a lump in my throat and my heart races. Only after a few minutes with one of the women do I start to chill out. Back to that first time with the girl who looks like me. I ask her what her name is.

"Milena."

I tell her my name.

She asks me in front of all the other hookers whether I have my period. What made her think that? I think I know. She smelled it through my pants. I had a school friend from Poland whose nose was so sensitive she could tell from her seat who in the class was having their period. She fascinated me. She was like a dog. I got a real kick out of her skill. Almost every day I would ask her who was bleeding. She didn't like knowing and was disgusted by bleeding girls. She didn't want to be near them. Unfortunately, she moved back to Poland. Girls who for stupid reasons of preserving their virginity used pads were easier for her to smell. Because they carried their blood around all day on a platter. With girls who trapped their blood inside with devirginizing tampons, she had to work a little harder. But she'd sniff them out. And now they've sniffed me out here.

I answer her with a yes. She says she doesn't want to fuck me because of AIDS. Great. A few of the hookers giggle.

Milena smiles and says she has an idea. "Come with me. Have you ever heard of sponges?"

"The things you wash up with?"

She nods yes. Things are looking up, I think.

What does she have in mind? I follow her into a room. Number four. Is this her room? Or do they share rooms? I'll ask everything in the half hour I have ahead of me. For fifty euros. I can't decide what would be more enjoyable: to fuck a hooker or to ask her about all the things men have done with her or that she has done with them. Actually, each possibility turns me on as much as the other. But both at the same time—fucking and quizzing her—would be the best of all.

Naked, as she already is, she walks in her high-heeled shoes over to a cabinet and pulls out a big cardboard box. I have a chance to take a long look at her from behind. I love her ass. When she goes down on me, I'm going to bore my finger deep into her ass the whole time. What she's holding in her hands is a family-pack of something. She takes one out—it's something I've never seen before. A round piece of foam packed in clear plastic. Looks like a fortune cookie, only soft.

"This is a sponge. When we have our periods we're not allowed to work because of the risk of infection. And if we use normal tampons, the clients can feel them with their cocks. Tampons are too hard. We shove these sponges as far inside our pussies as we can and it holds the blood out of the way for a while. The sponges are so soft no cock in the world is going to notice it touching its tip. It feels just like

your cunt—even to a finger. You can try it. Lie down. I'll
push it in. Then I'll go down on you, even though you have
your period."

Milena swims in the red river and drinks the water.
And she says "cunt," too. I wouldn't dare.

I've asked in all the drugstores and pharmacies. You
can't get sponges as a normal person. Maybe you need some
kind of proof of prostitution or something. I could definitely
use sponges. Because not every guy I fuck likes to dip into
the red river. In those cases I could hide the blood the good
old hooker way. Otherwise I miss out on a fuck here or there
when I have to confess to blood-averse boys I've got my
period. Sometimes Helen is out of luck.

By the way, another thing that really needs to stop is
the way my period always sneaks up on me by surprise.

I am constantly surprised by it. It was true before I was
on the pill, and it's still true now that I'm on the pill—
obviously no longer to prevent pregnancy but to prevent
pimples. My period never comes regularly or when it's supposed to. Never the way it's described on the package. It's
made a mess of every single pair of my underwear. Particularly the white ones. When I bleed in them and have to walk
around for a while, the blood has a chance to really soak in
at body temperature and then it won't come out even if you
wash them on the hottest setting. Even if you were to wash
the white underwear in boiling water. No chance.

So my entire collection of underwear has a brown stain right in the middle. You get used to it after a few years. Do other people have it, too? What girl or woman could I ask? None. It's always the same. With everything I really want to know.

There are probably other, more hygiene-obsessed, girls who run around their entire lives wearing panty liners to protect their underwear from their own discharges.

But I'm not one of them. I'd rather have everything stained with blood than do that.

Those girls definitely don't have the nice light-yellow crust in their crotch, either, which during the course of the day gets thicker as it continually gets re-moistened.

Sometimes a bit of the crust will hang like a dreadlock from your pubic hair, spun around the hair like pollen on a bee's leg by the rubbing motions of walking.

I like to pull this pollen off and eat it. It's a delicacy.

I just can't keep my fingers off anything on my body. I find a use for everything. If I notice a booger has slowly hardened in my nose, I have to pick it out.

When I was little I would do this in class. Even today I don't see anything wrong about someone eating boogers. There's no way it's unhealthy. I see people all the time on the highway who, when they think they aren't being watched, pop a snack from their nose into their mouth.

In school you get teased for it and quickly stop doing it. At some point I quit doing it except at home, either alone or in front of my boyfriend. I thought it was only reasonable. It's a part of me after all, this habit. But I could see in his eyes that he couldn't deal with it.

Since then I've maintained a second life in the bathroom. Whenever I piss or take a crap, I munch my nose empty of boogers. Creates a liberating sensation in your nose. But that's not the main reason I do it. If I can grab a dry booger and, by picking it out, manage to set something in motion and pull out a long piece of snot attached to it, it turns me on. Similar to pulling out the hairs stuck in my pussy. Or the crust on a pubic hair. It hurts and it turns me on. And all of it makes its way into my mouth and gets slowly chewed with my front teeth so I can really taste it. I don't need any tissues. I'm my own garbage disposal. Bodily secretion recycler. I get the same thrill out of cleaning my ears with cotton swabs. Sticking them in a little too deep.

That's another distinct childhood memory. I'm sitting on the rim of the bathtub and my mother is cleaning my ears with a cotton swab dipped in warm water. A nice, tingling feeling that immediately turns to pain if you go in too far. I'm constantly told that I shouldn't use cotton swabs because you might pack the earwax in and damage the ear. And that it's bad to use cotton swabs too often because your ears will be too clean and the earwax is necessary to protect the inner ear. I don't care. I don't do it to clean my ears but to get myself off. More than once a day. Preferably on the toilet.

Back to the hygiene freaks. They throw out the lovely crust with their panty liners each time they go to the bathroom and have to start collecting it all over again from scratch.

And I'm sure these girls never forget they're about to get their period. Even while in pain in the hospital. The highest imperative in their lives: leave no stains. With me it's the opposite.

It's starting to flow, the blood. I knew it. I take the giant Tupperware container off the windowsill, put it on my lap, and root around in it until I've found some gauze squares. I estimate them to be about four inches by four inches. I decide to experiment and instead of making a tampon out of toilet paper as usual, I make one out of gauze.

It should be easier, and unlike toilet paper it should be absorbant. We'll see. I pull out a square and put the container back on the windowsill. I fold one side a little bit so I have a starting point to roll it up. Now it looks like a sausage. Then I fold it over like a horseshoe or a long apple strudel, so it fits in the oven with the thick, folded side shoved as deep in my pussy as possible.

Whenever I can cheat the tampon industry, it makes me feel good.

I smell the finger I used to stuff in my homemade tampon. I can already detect a musty pussy scent.

At one of my numerous brothel visits a hooker told me that some men get off on coming in with their cocks dirty and making a hooker suck them off. She said it was a power game. Those are their least favorite clients, the dirty ones. The purposefully dirty ones. They don't have anything against inadvertently dirty ones.

I wanted to try that, too. I didn't wash myself for a long time and then had a hooker go down on me. For me there was nothing different about it from having someone go down on me when I'm clean. Power games aren't my thing.

What can I do now to divert my attention from my numbing loneliness?

I guess I could try to think of all the useful things I've learned over the course of my young life. I can entertain myself well that way—at least for a few minutes.

I once had a really old lover. I love to say "lover." It sounds so old-fashioned. Better than "fucker." He was many, many years older than me. I learned a lot from him. He wanted me to experience everything about male sexuality so that in the future no man could ever pull one over on me. Now I supposedly know a lot about male sexuality, but I don't know whether all of what I learned applies to all men or only to him. I still have to see. One of his cardinal rules was that you should always stick your finger up a guy's ass during sex. Makes him come harder. So far I can certainly concur. It's always a hit. They go wild. But you shouldn't discuss it with them beforehand or after. Otherwise they'll worry they're gay and get all uptight. Just do it and afterward pretend nothing was ever in there.

This older boyfriend also showed me lots of porn films. He thought not only could men learn a lot from them, but women, too. It's true.

It was in one of those films that I saw a black woman's pussy for the first time. That's something. Because they have dark skin, the interior colors of the pussy really pop when it's spread open. Much more than with white women, where the contrast isn't as extreme. Something to do with complementary colors, I think. Pussy-pink next to light-pink skin tone looks a lot more boring than pussy-pink next to dark-brown skin tone. Against dark brown the pussy-pink looks dark-lavender-bluish-red. Swollen and throbbing.

I'm telling you. Complementary colors. Brown skin complements pussy-pink.

It impressed me so much that since then I always put makeup on the inside of my pussy when I have a date to fuck. I use standard makeup that you'd normally put on your face. I have yet to find pussy makeup at the drugstore. A gap in the market.

Like when you're putting makeup on your eyes, I make it darker the closer you get to the center. I start with light pink and pink tones, lip gloss and eye shadow, and work my way through the folds until I'm right at the entrance to the tunnel, where I use dark red, lavender, and blue. I like to color the brown-pink of the rosette with a few dabs of lipstick, too, rubbing it on with my finger.

It makes the pussy and rosette more dramatic, deeper, more beguiling.

Since I learned that black women have the reddest pussies, I only go to black hookers. There are no other black women in my world—not in my school, not in my neighborhood. Prostitution is my only chance. I'm sure plenty of men understand my problem.

I had a really bad experience with a white hooker. She had skin as pale as cheese and light-red hair. She was a little chubby and—totally unnecessarily—completely shaved. And I mean everything was bare. Not a single pubic hair anywhere. Her crotch looked like a sculpture of a newborn baby made out of cheese.

I had been looking forward to her tits. From beneath her shirt they made a good impression. Big but still pointing upward. When she undressed and took off her bra, it was a big disappointment. She had big droopy breasts with flat nipples.

Flat nipples are something really bad.

All a nipple is supposed to do is stick out. Flat nipples don't do that. It's as if someone had pushed the nipple back into the breast and it stayed there, cowering in fear. Like a little collapsed soufflé.

I thought, well I'm already here and I'm going to have to pay so I might as well close my eyes and go for it. Some of the hookers had told me that men who weren't happy with their hooker once she got naked just walked back out without paying and picked a different one. I could never do that. I'm too much of a beginner—and too polite.

I would have to tell her to her face that she didn't look good. I'd rather not. I wouldn't have the heart.

I convince myself that it's also an important experience to have sex with someone I find ugly, and immediately I go down on her on the bed.

She puts her hands behind her head and does nothing. I'm doing all the work. I lick her and grind my pussy on her bent knee. I come fast. I'm the queen of grinding. She hasn't moved an inch the entire time. A very lazy hooker. Didn't know there was such a thing.

After I've come, she starts looking around for something to munch on. Finds something. She knocks back a glass of the expensive champagne I paid for and munches on goldfish crackers. She can't believe how fast I came and asks whether I've ever had anal sex.

I don't understand why she's asking. But I answer truthfully and say yes.

"How is it? Doesn't it hurt?"

What? Who's the hooker here? I decide that as a young client it's not my job to explain anal sex to a hooker. I leave. But I pay. I did come, after all, even if the collapsed soufflés were no help at all. It was simple mechanics.

The hookers are always older than me—even the youngest ones. That's why I always assume they've had more experience than me when it comes to sexual experimentation. But that's not the case. They limit what they do professionally. They'll say, for instance, no kissing and no anal. So they never learn anything new. I suppose they have their reasons.

Maybe there are a lot of johns who don't properly prepare the asshole before they fuck it. That can hurt. And guys like that probably pretend not to notice the pain they're causing, and that makes it hurt even worse.

Depending on how long and thick the cock is that's supposed to go up there, I like to take plenty of time to stretch it out, or at least have a lot of alcohol or something else numbing.

Anal sex is great—even though sometimes you don't notice until the next day that you overestimated your ability to stretch.

Overall it was a bad experience with the redhead. Now whenever I see a light-skinned redhead, I chuckle inside and think to myself she's lazy in bed, has no hair—anywhere, like an alien—eats goldfish and has never had anything up her ass. And her nipples don't stick out.

My dad, drunk at a party, once said to a redhead friend of my mother's, "Ginger hair, always moist down there."

Not at all!

And now, Helen? What are you going to do now? Got a plan?

I could look out the window and ponder nature for a while. It's summer. The chestnut trees in the hospital yard are in full bloom. Someone—probably a landscaper—has made planters by cutting off the top halves of what look like big, green-plastic trash barrels. If I'm seeing them correctly from this distance, they're planted with fuschia and bleeding-heart flowers. Those are my favorites. It sounds so romantic. Bleeding-heart. My father taught me the name. I remember everything my father has taught me. Always. The things my mother's taught me, not so much. But my father doesn't try to teach me things as often—maybe that makes the lessons easier to remember. My mother blathers on all day about things I'm supposed to remember. Things she thinks are important for me. Half of it I forget immediately; as for the other half, I purposefully do the opposite. My father teaches me things that are important to him. Everything about plants. He'll say out of the blue: "Did you know you should dig up dahlias in the fall and let them winter over in the basement? And that you plant them again early in the year in the garden?"

Of course I didn't know that. But duly noted, now I do. Dad derives great pleasure from knowing so much about the natural world. Mom's afraid of the natural world and her knowledge of it. She always seems to be fighting against it. She fights against dirt in the household. She fights against various insects. In the garden, too. Fights against bacteria of all kinds. Against sex. Against men and against women. There seems to be nothing my mother isn't bothered by. She once told me that sex with my father caused her pain. That his penis was too big for her insides. This is not information I wanted to know. Wait, I was actually hoping to focus on the natural world outside the hospital. That'll put me in a better mood than pondering sexual intercourse between my parents. Unfortunately, I always picture things in intricate detail. Sometimes the images aren't very pretty.

Helen, kill these thoughts of yours.

Boredom is creeping back.

Mom always says, "Boring people are bored."

Oh well. She also says, "We aren't put on this earth to be happy."

Not your kids, anyway, mom.

Try again, Helen. If you're bored, you can always make a date with yourself to look out the window. Good idea. Busy yourself getting to know your environment. No reason to stay fixated on things down below. Now would be a good time.

I snap my head to the side and stare out the window.

Lawn. Trees. Chestnuts. What else? I see a huge staghorn sumac tree. I guess I don't even have to say it's big. Staghorn sumac trees are always big. They scare me. My father taught me that, too. To be scared of staghorn sumac trees. They're not from here. They're not native. Asian or something. And they grow a lot faster than our trees. When they're still small—which is the case for only a short period—they send up a long, thin, rubberlike trunk that puts all its energy into gaining height.

That way they overtake all the surrounding plants. Once they've exceeded the height of everything around them, they sprout a broad crown over everything else. That kills everything else had been growing beneath it—light no longer gets through, and the roots of the fast-growing staghorn sumac suck up all the water.

But it's not all bad. Since the trunk shoots up so fast, it's unstable compared to our trees. Entire branches break off in the slightest breeze. Serves it right. But the branches often hit people who don't realize they're standing under an Asian tree unable to withstand wind because it busies itself trying to outpace everything else in terms of height and forgets to build a sturdy base for itself.

I always walk in a wide arc around staghorn sumac trees. I wouldn't want one of them to become the epitaph on my gravestone.

When I walk the streets, I see staghorn sumacs all over the place. They seem to grow out of every crack in the earth. They propagate like mad. The city government must be constantly removing them—otherwise they would have completely taken over long ago. Sometimes I notice people who have let one grow in their garden after it appeared. They have no one to blame but themselves. Soon it'll be the only thing in the garden. But I can't ring all of their doorbells and warn them. That would be too much work. Unfortunately, not everyone has a father like mine who can teach them such useful things.

The staghorn sumac fronds are big. In the middle a long stem, at the top end a little leaflet like a head, and then a series of very symmetrical lance-shaped leaflets along each side. Left and right, like ribs. I'll pick out a branch from here and count the leaflets. I've got to do something. Twenty-five leaflets on one frond. Eagle-eyed Helen. Not really— like I said, they're big. Too big. The trunk is smooth and greenish. It looks like uncut brown bread. It feels nice—if you're brave enough to walk under one and touch it.

Enough about nature. My turn again. For a while now I've felt something on my right upper arm. I'm going to look at it. I shift my shoulder forward, grab the fat on my upper arm, and roll it toward me. Now I can see it. Just as I thought —a blackhead. I have no idea why my upper arm is full of them. My own poor explanation for it goes like this: hair tries to grow there but because of the friction from T-shirt sleeve edges, individual hairs stay under the skin and get infected.

And so I come to one of my biggest hobbies. Popping zits. I've noticed a big blackhead in Robin's ear. More precisely in the flat area just outside the ear hole. I've often seen people with exceptionally large, black things like that right in the same area. I think people just don't tell each other and the blackhead then has years to fill itself with dirt and grease. Several times I've forgotten to ask people ahead of time and have just reached for their zit in order to pop it. I practically grabbed Robin's ear. I could barely control myself. But a lot of people aren't cool with that. When you just pop their zit without asking. They think it's overstepping a boundary. I'll ask Robin, though, once we know each other better. I'm sure we'll get to know each other better. Not going to escape. The blackhead in Robin's ear, I mean. That's reserved for me. I clench the blackhead on my upper arm between the thumb and pointer finger of my left hand and, with a squeeze, out comes the worm.

It goes directly from my thumb into my mouth.

With that taken care of, I examine the little wound.

There's a drop of blood in the hole left behind by the blackhead.

I wipe it off. It doesn't disappear. It just smears.

Just like on my legs when I've shaved them instead of Kanell. Fast and careless. Often I get goose bumps from the cold water and from standing around in the tub. When I shave over them, I tear open every bump. Then I think I looked better with hair because now there's a pinpoint of blood where every hair was. At some point I put on a pair of nylons over my bleeding legs and discovered an interesting effect. The almost see-through, skin-color nylons smeared each speck of blood into a stripe as I pulled them up my legs. By the time I had them all the way up, they looked like an expensive pair of patterned nylons. I wear them that way a lot when I go out.

Wearing nylons over my bloody legs has another advantage, too. I like to eat my scabs. At the end of a night out, when I take the nylons off again, they rip off the dried blood, and new scabs form. Then, once they've hardened, I can pick them off and eat them.

Tastes almost as good as sleepy seeds. The snack brought by the sandman and left in the corner of your eye closest to your nose.

When I treat my little wounds so poorly, eventually a pore or two will get sealed and keep a hair from coming out. The hair still grows, but it coils up beneath the skin. Like the roots of the avocado in the base of the glass. At some point it gets infected and then Helen enters the game. I've been very patient. Despite the fact that the whole time the hair was calling to me, "Get me out of here, I want to grow straight like the other hairs, in the fresh air," I've kept my fingers off it. It's difficult. But it's worth the wait.

First I stick a needle into the infected lump and squeeze out the pus. From my fingertip into my mouth with that. Then it's the hair's turn. I poke around in the wound as long as it takes to get at the hair. It always looks a bit stunted since it's never seen the light of day and has had to grow in tight quarters. I grab it with tweezers and pull it slowly out with the infected root. Done. Often another little pleasure will grow in the same spot a few weeks later.

A magpie is hopping across the shortly cropped hospital lawn. In children's books magpies steal shiny objects like bottle stoppers, aluminum foil, and rings. In reality they steal eggs from small songbirds. They peck them open and slurp them out. I always try to picture just how a magpie hacks a hole in the shell of a songbird's egg and then uses its beak as a straw to suck out the egg. Or do they do it completely differently? Jump on the egg until it breaks and slurp the puddle of goop off the ground?

Eggs are a constant theme with me. Years ago kids would chant, "Go climb a pole, you egg hole." For no reason; just because it rhymes. But I always read a lot into it.

I told Kanell once what I thought it meant, and one afternoon we acted it out.

The pussy was the hole, obviously.

Into it an egg. For egg hole.

At first we tried a raw egg. But it broke in Kanell's hand at the entrance to the pussy. The pieces of shell didn't cut me or anything. It's just that everything was covered in goop, and it was cold.

So then we discussed whether it had to be a raw egg. Actually it didn't. So we boiled one. Hard. Eight minutes. Very hard.

And inserted it. So I finally had the egg hole I'd always imagined from this playground rhyme.

Since then it's been our inside secret. In the most literal sense of the phrase.

There's one other thing I'd like to do with Kanell.

I've always loved to play around with the lymph nodes in my groin. I slide them around under my skin. The same way you can move your kneecap around. Recently I've had the desire for Kanell to trace them with a Sharpie. To accentuate them. The same way you accentuate your eyes with makeup. Is that a sexual fantasy? Or just a new form of body art? It would only be a fantasy if thinking of it made me hot. And that it does. What would happen the first time the fantasy were realized? He's good about exploring my fantasies, just as I've supported his with every fiber of my being, right from the start.

Out on the lawn one magpie is fighting with another. Over what?

We humans think of magpies as evil animals because they eat the young of other birds. But we eat the babies of almost every animal that appears on our menus. Lamb, veal, suckling pig.

Outside, Robin is strolling with a female nurse. The magpies fly off. I look at the two of them, appalled. I'm jealous. No way. I feel a claim to him just because he's taken a picture of my wounded ass and I gave him a titillating lecture about modifying my underwear. And because the nurse can walk and I can't. Well, I can, but only very, very slowly. They're both smoking. And laughing. What is there to laugh about?

I want to be able to walk again. I'm going to walk right now—to the cafeteria. There is one here, right Helen? Yes. The candy striper said something about it. I'm going to slowly go to the cafeteria and get a cup of coffee. Good, Helen, do something normal. Don't think anymore about Robin and his fuck-pie or about my parents in bed boning each other. I have plenty of time. Good idea. I should have been capable of thinking of it without the two strolling strangers. Coffee always makes me have to go to the bathroom. I'd like to secretly have a bowel movement, without telling anyone here. Just for me. Just so I know I still can and that I haven't grown together and sealed shut. I won't tell anyone. That way I can still use this venue to try to bring my parents together. That way the things that are supposed to be together will grow together.

I roll onto my stomach and let my legs slowly drop to the floor. I grab a painkiller from my pill supply and slurp it down. I'll get some use out of it along the way. Inside, I'm prepared for the long voyage. But not on the outside. I'm still wearing just this tree-top angel outfit, still gathered and knotted at the front. Nothing on the bottom. You can't walk around like this, even in a hospital, Helen. Even as an ass patient. There are a lot of people running around the halls and in the cafeteria. I go at a snail's pace to the space-saving, built-in wardrobe. Mom said she had left things for me in there. I open the door. Only pajama bottoms and T-shirts. I'll never be able to manage that. To put on a pair of pajama bottoms you have to bend down and put in first one leg and then the other. Oh, man. That'll stretch my ass too much. Mom didn't think of a bathrobe or something simple like that. Now what, Helen? I walk slowly back to the bed and pull off the sheet. I wrap it around myself and tie it at the shoulder so I look like a Roman on the way to the public baths. This is fine for walking around a hospital. The two ass-piss stains could have been caused by something else. They could be the result of my drooling on the sheet while sucking on a Werther's Original. Very believable, Helen. Nobody's going to ask you about it. People aren't like that. They don't want to know.

Off we go. To the door. I haven't left this room in three days. Am I even allowed to wander around? Come on, I'm not going to get in trouble for walking. But am I allowed to walk in the hall as slowly as a dying grandmother? If someone catches me, they can send me right back. Better not to ask in advance. Open the door. There's a lot going on in the hallway. Everyone is busy doing something. They all seem to know each other here, and everyone is laughing and pushing things around. To my eyes it looks as if they're doing things just to look as if they're busy in case the supervisor happens to walk past. They don't want to be caught smoking in the nurses' station. Better to chat on the hallway while shifting something around. They can't fool me. I creep past them. Nobody acknowledges me. I think I'm going so slow they can't see me with their hurried glances.

It's just as bright in the hallway as in my room. The linoleum reflects the light back up from the floor. It looks like gray water. I walk on the water. It must have something to do with the pain medication. I still know the way to the elevator. You retain that even over the course of several days. The escape route. I lie there in bed the whole time in pain and know exactly how to get out—without even being conscious of the fact that I know. Out and around to the left. There are bad religious paintings hung all over the place. The nurses probably put them up to please their parents. They all end up here sooner or later. The parents. Proctology unit. Oncology. Palliative care. Something will bring them here. Unless they care for them at home, which I think is the best way.

I bend over and hold my stomach because I can't reach my ass in this position. It hurts. I've made it to the glass door of the central part of the building. I just have to pound the buzzer like Robin and the giant glass door will open automatically. I stand there and don't go through. I have no money with me. Crap. Have to go back the whole way. No one acknowledges me on the way back, either. I guess I am allowed to wander around. I'm also allowed to take care of my wound myself. It's in an extremely unhygienic spot. Pretty much the most unhygienic spot Robin can imagine. Room 218. Mine. Open the door and in I go. Back to peace and quiet. Thanks to my idiotic forgetfulness I've wasted a lot of energy. I look in the drawer of my metal nightstand. There are a few small bills in it. Mom must have put them in there while I was sleeping. Or did she tell me she had? Or did I dream it? My memory's gone to shit. In any event, I've got money now. I hold it in my hand as I walk. They don't make sheets with pockets yet. My ass is getting used to the motion. I'm a bit quicker now than on the first trip. Probably because the pills are taking effect. I stare at the floor the whole way. We'll see how far I get before someone comments on my attire. I punch the button. The automatic door swings open and this time I go through. Beyond is a whole new world. Here different diseases mingle. Ass patients and ass nurses aren't the only ones out and about. An old woman with tubes in her nose is walking around. The tubes run into a backpack that's attached to a walker.

She obviously has something wrong with her head— not a proctology case. That's a change of pace. She has beautiful white hair that's in a long braid coiled on top of her head. And a nice bathrobe on. Black with three-dimensional pink flowers on it. And nice slippers. Made of black velvet. You can see the shape of a bunion through the slippers. Like a tumor on her big toe. It's growing sideways over the other toes. And by doing that it pushes the joint of the big toe farther and farther to the outside. Until it's quite far away from the rest of the foot. A bunion like that is a destructive force. It bursts out of all your shoes over time. It's about to destroy those velvet slippers. The toes end up like teeth in a jaw, crowding and displacing each other and becoming crooked. But the big toe always wins the battle. I know it. I have a bunion, too. Everyone in our family does. Father's and mother's side. Very bad genes, all things considered. The big toe always wants to go where the other toes belong, so little toes keep having to be surgically removed. My uncle, my grandmother, and my mother hardly have any toes left. Their feet end up looking like devil's hooves.

I want to think about something nicer so I try to find a pleasant end to my granny observations.

Okay, even her spider veins are pretty. I used to call these weblike formations varicose veins. But they're actually called spider veins. Everything about her is pretty. Except for the bunion and the tubes. The tubes will soon be taken out, I'm sure. Hopefully she won't have to die with them in.

I push the button for the elevator, cross my fingers for the handsome old woman, and say hello to her very loudly. In case she's already hard of hearing.

Old people are sometimes startled when someone addresses them. They've already gotten used to being invisible to those around them. Then they get happy that someone has noticed them.

The elevator arrives from above.

I can tell from the red arrow. If I still remember correctly from my sterilization, the cafeteria's in the basement.

The elevator doors pull apart from each other with a loud screech and invite me in. Nobody else in the elevator. Good. I push the button marked B.

Cafeteria is written next to the B. I use the ride down to hoist up my toga with the hand holding my money and pull out my homemade tampon with the other hand. Bloody and slimy as it is, I'll put it near the panel of buttons, the most scrutinized place in this moving crate. Just below the button panel is a bar you can pull down, like a handrail. I yank the horseshoe-shaped bar down and balance the bloody, sticky lump right in the middle of it. Success. Toga down as if nothing's happened. The doors open and two men are standing there. Perfect. Looks like a father and son. None of the important things in life are discussed much in this family, either. I look at both of their faces. The father is ill. His face is yellowish gray and he's wearing a bathrobe. Lung cancer? The son must be here visiting. I greet them, beaming with joy. "Good day, gentlemen."

And walk out with perfect posture. It takes a minute. The men have gotten in. The curtains close. I let myself slump back into my bent-over posture and hear from the elevator a weak, old voice, revolted: "What is that? Oh my God."

There's no way they'll clean it up themselves. They'll never figure out that it's just harmless menstrual blood. It looks like something that fell out of a wound. You can't even recognize that it's gauze. Soaked with blood as it is. It could even be a piece of flesh. Human flesh. These days everybody's afraid to come in contact with blood. They'll tell someone on the floor where they get out. The father will hold the doors open to keep my bloody clump from traveling onward. The son will have to go find a nurse on the hall. The nurse will then have to find a rubber glove and a garbage bag so she can remove the clump. And eventually a wet cloth to wash off the dirty grab-bar.

She'll thank the father and son. Showing such civil courage in the cause of hygiene. Then my masterpiece will end up with the medical waste.

I've arrived at the cafeteria. The bills have in the meantime been passed between both hands and smeared with blood. The finger that was inside me also clearly has blood under the fingernail. Blood turns brown when it's exposed to the air. So it looks more like crap or dirt. So my period-hands now look more like the dirty hands of a kid on a playground. I'll nibble it all out from under my nails later. Cleaning your nails with your teeth in public looks as if you're chewing your nails—and I hate that. Chewing your nails is considered by almost everyone to be a sign of psychological weakness. Insecurity. Nervousness. It's something that belongs behind closed doors. Kill or be killed. Coffee, please. As a reward for the long trip here, I'll treat myself to caramel flavor.

I pay with a bloody bill. Pleased that this bill will sooner or later make the rounds. First it'll be clamped under the spring-loaded plastic clip in the drawer of the cash register. Until it's handed out as change. Then it'll wander into a sick person's wallet and, later, when that person is released, will be carried out into the world. Whenever I get a bill with blood on it, my first thought is always of a nose bloodied from snorting too much coke. A bit of blood often gets on the part of the rolled-up bill that was stuck into the nose. Bit of snot, bit of blood. Maybe I should rethink that. There's more than one way to get blood on a bill. I take my coffee and my change to an empty table in the cafeteria. I've done it. I'm sitting here like a normal hospital patient drinking a cup of coffee. I have a long journey behind me, and I've disturbed at least three people through hygienic transgressions. A good day.

While I'm drinking my coffee, I need to figure out how I can manage to stay in the hospital for a while longer. Somehow I need to inflict another injury on myself or else reopen the one I already have. But how, without it looking purposeful? So my parents don't get suspicious. Not to mention the doctors. The cafeteria is slowly beginning to fill up. It's teatime. Most of the people here want to get out of the hospital as fast as they can. I want to stay as long as possible. I think the only other people who want to stay in the hospital as long as possible are the homeless. In our town there's Blind Willy. I don't know why everybody calls him that, because he's not blind. At least not when I talk to him. I always want to give him something. Mom says if you give them money they just drink themselves to death that much faster. Or they buy drugs. She has no clue. Whenever I was downtown without her I would talk to him and get close to his face so I could smell his breath. Not a whiff of alcohol. She was wrong on that count. And I asked him about the drugs. He just laughed and shook his head. I believe him. So I stole some money out of mom's purse and put it aside. Then the next time I went into town without mom, I gave it to him and told him it was from my mother. She sends her best. I told him he shouldn't ever thank her, though, because she wouldn't want it to seem as if she were seeking a public show of gratitude. He took her for a generous, humble lady rather than a hypocritical Christian. I also stole a sleeping bag, food, and clothing for Willy from home. As far as he knows, it all came from her. Whenever I walked past him with mom, he and I would look at each other briefly and then lower our gazes with knowing smiles.

Willy is probably happy when there's something wrong with his leg or something so he can spend a night in the hospital.

If I'm to have any chance at all of bringing my parents together, I need a lot more time here. I would pay to have any of these people's diseases. But there's no point in even thinking about that. It won't work. Just like trading breasts with my friend Corinna. She has big breasts with soft, light-pink nipples. I have small breasts with hard, maroon nipples. Whenever I see the way her tits bulge out of a T-shirt, I want to trade. I picture the two of us going to the plastic surgeon and each having our breasts removed and then reattached on the other. I always have to convince myself to stop think-ing about it because no matter how badly I want it, it'll never work. It breaks my heart that something like that isn't yet possible. And besides, I'd still have to ask Corinna whether she was cool with it. I couldn't do it without her consent. Or maybe I could. But then I'd definitely lose her as a friend. But I can't do it anyway because it's simply impossible. Get it through your head, Helen! Quit torturing yourself by let-ting your mind wander down these hopeless cul-de-sacs. It's just as much of a waste of mental energy to think about how much you would pay the people here for their various dis-eases. It won't work.

This is no place to figure out a plan to extend my stay here. I'm just too distracted by the other inmates.

I also notice that the coffee is having its usual effect on me. My innards are starting to gurgle and rumble. I react to a cup of coffee the same way a native in the rain forest

would to the first cup of his life. With symptoms of poison-
ing. Half a cup of coffee in the top, diarrhea immediately
out the bottom. I did a coffee piss-test once. My dad taught
me how. When you get up in the morning, you usually have
to pee because your bladder has stored it up all night. So
when you've pissed yourself empty in the morning, you can
pretty much assume there's basically no more pee left in your
body. Now, if you drink a cup of coffee with breakfast, your
body feels so poisoned that it leeches water from itself in
order to wash out the poisonous drink as quickly as possible.
You have to go to the bathroom as soon as you finish drinking it and piss out more fluid than you just drank in the form
of coffee. I've confirmed this by using the coffee mug as a
measuring cup. The pee always sloshes over the edge. So to
the delight of my father I proved the dehydrating effect
of coffee. My mother wasn't pleased, though, because she
doesn't think urine belongs in a coffee mug.

I've got to get back to my room. It's go time. My body
is starting to fend off the coffee. There's no way I can use a
public toilet down here in case I have to crap. I'm scared of
that and need peace and quiet. It might also hurt so badly
that I have to scream. This isn't the place for that. That's
something I'd want to do on my own. Quick, back to my
room. Though it's not like me, I don't take my cup to the
cart at the exit for dirty dishes—despite the fact that I want
to be a model patient. In an emergency you can leave your

cup. Just stand up and make your way slowly to the elevator. And cinch closed what's left of your sphincter muscle
so nothing ends up in the sheet.

Just in the nick of time I remember that I got rid of
my do-it-yourself tampon for the sake of a prank. I'm squeez-
ing everything down there together as best as I can. In the
front, too. A Roman with a bloody toga walking around the
cafeteria. That would create quite a sensation. Don't want
that. Thanks to my pussy's good musculature, I can hold blood
in for quite a while. Then, when I sit on the toilet and relax
my muscles, it all sloshes out of me at once. At the elevator
I tell myself I've already made it halfway. Once I get on the
elevator I'll just have to stand still and then when I get out
on my floor I'll only have to make it the same distance I did
from the chair in the cafeteria to the elevator.

Ding. It's here. I immediately look for what I left behind. Nothing. As I thought. Tampon gone. Not even a hint
of a drop of blood. Drops of blood have a very short half-
life in a hospital. When the doors have closed, I stick the
tip of my pointer finger into my blood-holder and dab an
oval of blood—like a potato print in school—in the exact
spot where my goods were. They won't catch me. The doors
open. I walk to my room so fast it hurts. The pressure is
building. I'm worried about what's going to come out and
how. I stand over the toilet bowl with my legs spread apart,
pull the gauze plug out of my ass and let nature take its

course. I don't need to paint a picture, but it takes a while, hurts a lot, bleeds heavily, and now I've done it. The thing everyone here is waiting for me to do. But they're never going to know. I make a new plug out of toilet paper. Air this place out. The telltale scent has got to go. First I turn on the shower full blast. Somebody once told me the water pulls bad smells down the drain. I leave the door to the bathroom open and walk even more buckled over than before to the window next to my bed and open it as wide as it goes. I walk gingerly because of the postfecal pain. But I'm in a hurry. Back to the bathroom door. I open and close the door, fanning the air in the direction of the window. I don't smell anything anymore. But that will need to be confirmed. I go back out into the hall and close the door to my room. I take a few deep breaths in and out until I have only fresh, stench-free air in my nose and lungs. Then I go back in, just as any nurse would, and sniff. The smell is gone. Everything's clean. No evidence. Mission accomplished. I turn off the water and make a new homemade tampon to handle my menstrual blood. Done. Calm. What should I do now? I'll lie down and close my eyes. Let's simmer down—or at least get worked up over something else.

I'm thinking of Robin. I undress him. Lay him totally naked on my hospital bed and lick him from his tailbone all the way up his backbone to his neck. He has a lot of dark moles. Maybe he should visit the skin doctor. It would be a shame if he died of skin cancer. He's a nurse, after all. A nurse shouldn't die of something overlooked. A nurse should get run over by a car or kill himself because he's fallen hopelessly in love with someone. Like me, for instance. I lick each vertebrae all the way back down. To his butt crack. I spread his cheeks apart and lick his asshole. At first just in a circle. Then I make my tongue pointed and stiff and bore into his tightly closed sphincter. My left hand makes its way underneath to his cock. It's so hard it's like a stone column wrapped in warm skin. I shove my tongue deeper into his ass and hold my closed hand against his bell-end. I want him to come so hard into my pressed-together fingers that it streams out the other side. Which is exactly what he does. There's nothing else he can do. I don't let go of the tip of his cock. Hold it tight. I open my eyes again. He's a pig, this

Robin. I have to laugh. I love my emergency sex fantasy. I don't need TV to entertain myself.

A knock at the door. With my luck it'll be Robin and he'll instantly figure out what I was just picturing. Nope. A female nurse. She asks whether I've had a bowel movement.

"No, have you?"

The nurse gives a pained smile and leaves.

Helen, you wanted to be a good patient. Yes, but with the constant questions and the phrase "bowel movement" it's tough to be nice. And now. I'll combine two things in one trip. I'll pee and go out into the hall to get mineral water for my hidden avocado pits. I slide out of bed backward, as always, dropping my feet to the ground until they are both solidly planted. Twinges of pain are beginning. The anesthesiologist warned me about this. It's on the way. I waddle to the washroom, lift my hospital gown and piss standing up, just the way an ass patient is supposed to. No need to flush. Nobody else is going to use it but me. Drives hygiene-freaks nuts. From the sink I grab the glass you're supposed to use to rinse your mouth out after you brush your teeth and fill it to overflowing with water. Dad taught me that water can stay in a glass even if you fill it above the rim— because of the surface tension or something like that. I can't remember exactly anymore. I'll ask him again when he shows up. Now I've already got a conversation topic prepared. You need to do that with him. And this is just the sort of thing he loves to talk about for long periods of time. There won't be any embarrassing pauses in the conversation.

I drink the entire glass in one go. Nice change. Still water instead of sparkling.

I leave my gown gathered and tied in front. I'd be ashamed to have any of my schoolmates visit me, but I don't care if everyone here sees me undressed all day long. They've seen it all here, that's for sure. From the bathroom I don't go back to bed but out into the hall. I stand there for a minute and look around. On the way to the cafeteria I saw a little seating area for visitors. Where you can make tea or get coffee out of a big urn. And right there was a tower of stacked water-bottle crates. Surely they're self-serve. I'll try it out. Because to fill the pit glasses I need more than one bottle. And the nurses only bring a new bottle once the last one is empty. It's too indulgent for me to make a nurse take several trips back and forth. I head for the seating area. There's a family sitting there speaking to each other very quietly. The nurses should follow their lead. One of the men in the group is wearing pajamas and a bathrobe. That signals to me that he's the ass patient of the bunch. I don't feel like saying hello. I take three bottles out of the top crate and head back. I can hear that my rearview has created a stir among the family. Have a ball. I walk as quickly as I can back to my protected cave.

I squeeze into the far corner between the windowsill
and the bed without letting my ass brush up against anything. Back to where I've hidden my avocado greenhouse
with the Bible. Shielded from the view of the doctors and
nurses and from Robin. Although Robin's allowed to see
them. I'll show him at some point. He's already seen a lot.
Come to think of it, he could take some pictures of the
current condition of my ass.

I lift up the Bible carefully and refill the glasses. In the
sun here on the windowsill the water evaporates pretty fast.
Don't think you have nothing to do, Helen. There are living
things depending on you. You can do a better job keeping
them watered. Some of the pits are already out of the water,
and here you are saying you're bored. Tsk, tsk. They all look
to be doing okay, though. Sometimes one here or there will
start to mold and I have to part with it despite all the effort
I've put in. The roots aren't yet sticking out of most of them.
But one has started to split, and another has a root growing
out of the bottom. Things are going well with my pits. All
healthy. I put the Bible back and shield them from view again.

I think I'd like to stand here for a minute. The room
looks completely different from here.

Up to now I've mostly looked out from the bed. From
here the room looks bigger. Of course. I'm in the farthest corner. With all my power I push the bed a few inches into the
room and then let myself slide down into the corner until my

ass touches the floor and my legs are bent so much that my knees touch my breastbone. I feel the cold linoleum on my peach and ass cheeks. I don't even know if it is linoleum, but that's what people always say is in a hospital. This position is straining my ass too much. I need to straighten out my legs under the bed. I can hide here. If I can't see the door, nobody who comes through the door can see my face either. My legs yes. But they'd have to purposefully look under the bed first. Nobody who comes in will have any reason to look under the bed. Everyone will just look at the bed and, if it's empty, think that I'm wandering around somewhere or that I'm on the toilet. I feel between my legs with my hand. I stick two fingers in and use them like tweezers to pull out my home-made tampon. I put it on top of the shoulder-high radiator. The tampon wobbles back and forth unsteadily so I press it down between two ribs of the radiator. I don't want it to fall on me. I don't want to have any bloodstains in strange places on my back or wherever that nobody can explain—and that I can't either because I can't even see them. As soon as I've positioned the tampon securely—it's a bit sticky now, too, which helps—I take my middle finger and put the tip of the nail directly on my snail tail. I press on it with the edge of the nail. That must make an indentation. Nobody sees it though. It's the fastest way to get wet. My pussy immediately begins to drip with slime. One hand is busy with the snail tail—I alternately press on it and rub it; I need two fingers of

the other hand to shove into my pussy. I spread the two fingers apart inside my pussy and make a twisting motion. Normally, as I get more and more into it I stick my pussy fingers
in my ass. That's not going to happen, though. The ass is fresh
from surgery and already occupied by a plug. I could try to
feel that, though. I move the pussy fingers inside me toward
the back. It feels like a very thin dividing wall between pussy
and ass. I can feel the plug. Even though I'm in the pussy. I
know this feeling. But not from a plug, of course. From shit.
It's often lined up at the exit before it's allowed to leave. And
if you're in the pussy you can feel the log of crap through the
thin dividing wall. I wonder if men have ever felt one in me
when we were hooking up?

They would never say anything about it anyway. It
wouldn't seem like the most appropriate thing to say right
before you stuck your cock in someone.

"Hey, wow, you know what I just felt inside you?" Not
likely.

I also like to feel the sphincter work from my pussy. I
tighten it, cinch my ass closed, and feel it from inside.

There's a cow on the grass, hallelujah. Opens and closes
its ass, hallelujah.

Now I want to feel the front wall of my pussy. The back
wall has been sufficiently investigated.

By turning my fingers all the way around—a feeling
that really turns me on, I love quick twisting motions in-

side me—I'm touching the front wall of my pussy, directly
behind the pubic bone. Here the pussy feels like a washboard. You say a muscular man has a washboard stomach,
too. But that's not a very good comparison. The front wall
of the pussy feels like an actual washboard, in miniature.
Like a cheese grater. That's it! A cheese grater. It's a hard
landscape of bumps like that—like the top of your mouth
but with bigger bumps. The way the roof of a lion's mouth
looks when it yawns and you can see inside it. That's exactly how the front wall of the pussy feels. When I press hard
against it, it feels as if I'm going to piss all over my hand
and I usually come immediately. When I come that way, a
fluid often shoots out, too, like sperm. I don't think there's
much difference between men and women. But that's not
how I want to come today.

I have to stop exploring the inside of my body.

I need both hands now. I rub my dewlaps really hard
with both pointer fingers. Almost there, almost there. One
hand works its way up. I want to brace myself on the windowsill. When I come I like to hold onto something sturdy.

I come fast. Usually.

Suddenly there's water all over me. It's ice cold. No way
I can come now. I've knocked over one of the avocado glasses
and the water's spilled onto my head and run down my chest.

I look down at my body. My hospital gown is see-through
now from the water. My maroon nipples show and they're

sticking out because they're cold. If there's a wet T-shirt con-test at the hospital today I'll win.

But first I'll finish my mission. I press my middle fin-ger against my little snail tail again and make tiny circular motions with it. This gets me back in the mood again and starts to warm me up from below. But that feeling that spreads across your pelvis just won't come back because of the chill of the water. It's just not going to work. I can't even quietly give myself a handjob hidden under the bed in my own hospital room. Usually the easiest task.

Sorry, Helen.

I want to get back up. Just as I've lifted my ass a few inches above the puddle, there's a knock at the door. As always, the door opens simultaneously. Nobody here waits for a "come in."

They must already have their right hand on the door handle as they knock with the left. As they are knocking they open the door.

They keep catching me with my hand on my pussy. I've given up trying to quickly pull my hand away. It's even more obvious than just leaving your hand there.

There are no secrets in the hospital. I've given up on secrets. Otherwise I'd have to hate all these intruders too much.

I can see feet and a handle with a big mop attached to the bottom of it. The cleaning woman is making her rounds.

I don't want her to see me. The mop snakes softly around the floor. An animal that's coming in my direction. I hold my breath. People always think their breathing will give them away. But that's stupid. I normally breathe very quietly. She starts at the door and works her way past the front of the wardrobe, toward the bed. Snaking lines. Back and forth. I see her corral some crumbs and push them around. I notice some hair, long and dark, probably mine—who else's?—just before the wet mop gets them. The mop also pushes dust bunnies. Those things that form when hair or splinters or lint tangle themselves up into little bird's nests. She slowly mops until she reaches the metal nightstand. She'll probably slide the mop under the bed; I grimace as I pull my legs up. She does. Good prediction. I see the handle lean on the bed now. She's stopped mopping. There's a metallic banging. She's opened the chrome trash can on the nightstand.

"Bah."

What does that mean? Bah. She must have seen the towels in the trash can. She shouldn't look so closely. There's nothing else I could have done with them.

I hear the drawer of my nightstand open.

No way. What is she doing in there? Get out! There's nothing to clean in there—only something to steal. Money.

The drawer closes again. I'll look to see what's missing. That was a favorite game for us at home. In a wardrobe or on a table, my father would make us look away and then remove something. Then we'd have to figure out what was gone.

I'm good at it. Just you wait . . .

I look at the newly washed, still wet, glistening floor. She leaves footprints on the freshly mopped surface. Right. Of course. She did it wrong. No way. She started at the door and then tracked dirt right back over everything. When she leaves, everything will look dirtier than before. Maybe she's new. I could tell her how to do it, just a little tip. I see her leaving footprints as she walks toward the door. But she pulls the mop behind her, snaking it back and forth. Footprints gone. All upset for no reason, Helen. Interesting technique.

She pulls the door closed behind her. I've already started to hoist myself up onto the bed.

As fast as the plug in my ass allows me, I circle the foot of the bed and go around to the metal nightstand.

I open the drawer and look and look. I realize nothing's missing. It's a great relief. It would be horrible if the cleaning woman were stealing from hospital patients. I would have to have registered a complaint and she would have probably lost her job.

So why did she open the drawer?

Maybe she just wants to see what people have. Maybe it's a tick or a fetish of hers. You could also call it a hobby, I guess.

I'll never know. Even if I asked her, I know she wouldn't answer honestly. That's just the way people are.

I would divulge my fetishes. But nobody asks me. Nobody thinks to.

I scrutinize the drawer once more. Think. But it's true. Not even the smallest thing is missing.

I get back into bed and ring the emergency call button. A nurse comes in surprisingly quickly. I tell her the cleaning woman has just been here but that she didn't notice a big puddle of water in the corner. I lie and say I spilled a glass of water. Very believable, Helen. Sometimes you're strange. How is that supposed to have happened? Unless you purposefully dumped a full glass over there. The nurse doesn't ask any questions or show any signs of suspicion— at least I don't notice it if she does. And she calls the cleaning woman back into the room.

She comes in and opens her eyes wide with surprise because I'm suddenly there in bed. I hold the sheet in front of my wet, see-through shirt.

The nurse points behind the bed and explains in a nasty tone of voice—like a command, in exaggeratedly simple words—what the cleaning woman needs to do.

The nurse disappears through the magic door. Without asking, the cleaning woman shoves me and my sickbed away from the windowsill. It's a nice feeling, like being on a flying carpet. Or rather, what you imagine it might be like on a flying carpet—they don't exist, right? But I don't let myself show the pleasure of the sensation. You're supposed to be upset when someone just shoves you around in your bed as if you were an object or you were in a coma.

Unlike when I'm in a car, I'm very sensitive to turns and stops here. When she suddenly stops the bed after the two-yard drive, I nearly fall out. I let out a high-pitched cry. I always do that when something happens to me, good or bad. I scream loud. If I stumble over something I let out a major scream. Let it all out, that's my motto—otherwise you'll get cancer. I'm very loud in bed, too. I'm in bed now, of course. But this is different.

As I scream I can see the corner of the cleaning woman's mouth twitch—upward, not downward. Ha. She's taking pleasure in my misfortune. That pisses me off. I promise myself that if she's ever in the hospital, lying there helpless, I'll push her around like Aladdin and when she screams I'll let the corner of my mouth turn up like that so she can see how it feels. I swear I will. Helen. Very impressive.

While I'm dreaming up my *One Thousand and One Nights* revenge fantasy, she's already set about cleaning up the puddle. She's quick with the mop. She keeps moving it over the same area in the form of the sign for infinity we learned in school, soaking up the water. A figure eight. Again and again.

Something suddenly occurs to me. My lungs, or my heart, or something else in there, makes a sickening jump. My gaze wanders up the radiator and there is my bloody wad. Oh no. Forgot about that. She hasn't noticed it up to this point. The slots of the built-in radiator are probably not a main area of focus for her duties. I might get lucky and she'll just swish around in the corner and never raise her eyes above the level of the mop. I try to calm my fears with this possibility. I really hope she doesn't see the bloody wad. Funny how things can sometimes be excruciatingly embarrassing and other times perfectly okay. If she said "Bah" to the contents of my trash can, how will she react if she spots that? Please, don't let that happen.

I say thanks and ask her to push me back toward the windowsill even though she still hasn't stopped mopping up. She can just push me back like a patient in a wheelchair and then leave.

She leans the mop against the wall at the foot end of the bed. She grabs the rail that runs around my bed with her strong hands and rams me and the bed far too hard toward the window. Bam. It smacks into the wall and I scream again.

Yep, all her resentment over cleaning up after filthy patients packed into one motion.

She grabs the mop and heads out. Just before she closes the door behind her she says, "Funny—if the glass fell over, why is it sitting there full?"

My heart skips a beat again.

I look over at the metal nightstand and see the full glass of water. I'm terrible at making up fake explanations.

The time between when I hit upon the idea to masturbate in the corner and this moment feels like hours. Very stressful and not at all relaxing as I had imagined it would be.

I toss the bloody clump into the chrome trash can.

Don't be disappointed. Your next self-fuck will be better, Helen.

I look around the room. Have you forgotten anything else you don't want to reveal to others?

Nope, everything's back in place, where it all belongs.

I just need to get out of this wet gown. Undress first and then ring the buzzer, or ring first and then undress? Helen? You wouldn't be Helen if you were to ring first.

I take off my top and cover my breasts with the sheet. It feels nice. The crisp sheet against the skin of my chest. I wonder if the sheets are put through a heated roller press? Is that what it's called? I always read the signs of laundromats as I go past. I know this cool feeling on my chest from home. Mom places a lot of importance on perfect linens. Only for me to sully them.

Now I ring the buzzer.

Please. Let it be Robin instead of somebody else.

Sometimes I get lucky. Robin comes in.

"What's up, Helen?"

"Can I have a fresh gown?"

I hand him the wet one in a bundle and make sure the sheet slips down enough so he can catch a glimpse of both nipples.

"Of course. What happened? There wasn't bleeding, was there?"

He's worried about me. Amazing. After all he's had to listen to from me. And to look at. I can't believe it.

"No, no. No bleeding. I would tell you immediately if that happened. I tried to masturbate under the bed and I accidentally knocked over a glass of water and it spilled on me. Everything got wet."

He laughs and shakes his head.

"Very funny, Helen. I get it. You don't want to tell me what happened. I'll get you a new one anyway. Be right back."

In the short time it takes Robin to go to some cabinet somewhere and find a new tree-top angel outfit, I get bored and lonely. What to do? With one hand I push down the pedal that opens the chrome trash can on my nightstand and with the other I reach in. The homemade tampon's no longer red from fresh blood but brown from old blood. I open the Tupperware container on the other side of the bed and put the lump of bloody toilet paper in with the unused hygiene articles. I hope my bacteria multiplies and spreads in there and—invisible, as bacteria is—gets all over the gauze bandages and pads. The box is steamed up from sitting in the sun. For my purposes it has perfect petri-dish conditions. I'll have to remember to get rid of it at some point. When I'm released, the next patient will be able to further my experiment by proving to me and the world that nothing bad happens when you use bandages with other people's bacteria on them to stop the bleeding in your open wound. I'll keep track of the experiment as a candy striper, knocking on the door, daily, and opening it at the same time, catching ass patients masturbating on the floor. You get to know people fast that way.

Robin comes back in.

He hands me the gown, smiling. I drop the sheet into my lap. I act as if it's nothing to me for him to see me completely topless. I strike up a conversation, more to keep myself from losing my cool. I pull the gown over my arms and ask him to tie it in the back. He ties a little bow in back and says he has to get back to work. But he also says "unfortunately."

He's gone for a while and then there's a knock at the door again. He must have forgotten something. Or he wants to tell me something. Please.

Nope. It's my father. Surprise visit. I'll never get the two of them in the room together at this rate. My parents, that is. If they come and go as they please without listening to the visit coordinator. My father has something strange in his hand.

"Hello, my daughter. How are you doing?"

"Hi, dad. Have you had a bowel movement?"

"You're outrageous," he says, laughing. I'm sure he can figure out why I'm asking him this question.

I put out my hand the way I always do when dad's supposed to have something for me. He puts whatever it is he's brought in my hand. Some strange thing made out of clear plastic.

"Is it a balloon? A gray balloon? Thanks, dad. I'm sure it'll help me get well soon."

"Open it. You've jumped the gun, my daughter."

It looks like an uninflated neck pillow, but instead of being horseshoe-shaped it's round, like a life preserver for really small people.

"Stumped? It's a hemorrhoid pillow. So you can sit without it hurting. The sore part goes in the middle of the ring so it floats in the air. If it's not touching anything, it can't cause you pain."

"Oh, thanks, dad." He's obviously spent a lot of time thinking about me in pain and wondering what he could do to help. My father has feelings. And feelings for me. Nice.

"Where can you buy such a thing, dad?"

"One of those stores that sells surgical equipment and health-care products and whatnot."

"Aren't they called medical-supply stores?"

"Yes, that sounds right. A medical-supply store."

This is already a long conversation for us, given the circumstances.

I rip open the plastic wrap. And start to blow up the pillow ring. I guess lying around and imagining having sex with the nurse doesn't make your lungs any stronger. After a few puffs I'm seeing stars in front of my eyes. I hand the pillow over to dad so he can finish the job.

I left an extra gob of spit on the inflation valve on my last puff. Dad puts it in his mouth without wiping it off. That's the precursor to a French kiss. Wouldn't it be considered that? I can definitely imagine having sex with my father. Years ago, when I was young and my parents still lived together, they would always walk naked to the bathroom in the morning. A thick club grew from my father's groin. Even as a kid I was fascinated by it. They thought I didn't notice. But I did. And how.

I didn't know about morning wood back then. I only learned about that much later. Even after I was fucking boys I still thought for a long time that morning erection was because of me. It was a big disappointment to learn men have them to keep their piss from running out. Major disappointment.

I watch my father blowing up the pillow and have to laugh. The way he's concentrating so seriously and putting his all into it reminds me of earlier times. We were on vacation at the beach and he blew up a bunch of huge inflatable animals and air mattresses for me and my brother—he was completely exhausted. That's fatherly love. He was also supposed to put sunscreen on my back to protect me from getting burned. I rubbed it onto all the places I could reach by myself. I never got burned in those places. But my back, which my father was responsible for, was always burned. Sometimes really badly. When I would look at my sunburned back in the mirror in the evening, I could tell dad had done a lazy job. There was a big white question mark on my back, and everything else was fiery red. He had obviously squirted a blob of sunscreen into his hand and just made a quick arc across my back and called it a day. I always thought it took him far too little time. So much for fatherly love. Maybe he was just too depleted from blowing up all those inflatable toys to be able to properly cover me with sunscreen. Maybe it was just too much to ask for. Probably. I do that all the time. Ask for too much.

He notices me smiling.

"What?" He doesn't even take his mouth off the valve.

He's thoroughly mixed his spit with mine. Does he find that as interesting as I do? Does he think about such things, too? If you don't ask, you never find out the answer. And I'll never ask.

"Nothing. Thanks for the hemorrhoid pillow and for blowing it up, dad."

The door opens. Now they've stopped knocking altogether.

It's a new nurse. How many are there here?

I already know what she wants.

"No, I haven't had a bowel movement."

"That's not what I wanted. I just wanted to change the plastic bag in your trash can. You produce such a steady stream of used gauze pads."

"Well my ass is producing a steady stream of blood and ass piss."

The nurse—Valerie according to her nametag—and my father just stare at me in shock. Go ahead, stare. So what? All the belittling by the nursing staff is slowly starting to get on my nerves.

The nurse quickly pulls the plastic bag out of the chrome trash can, puts a knot in the top of it, snaps open a new one like a windsock, and puts it into the trash can. She watches my father continue inflating the pillow.

She lets the top of the trash can close loudly and says, as she's walking out, "If that pillow is supposed to be for the patient, I'd advise against it. It'll tear everything open again if she sits in it. It's not for people who have had surgery."

My father gets up and puts the pillow in my wardrobe. He seems sad that he's given me something harmful.

Now what? He says he has to get going soon. Needs to get to work. What does he even do?

With certain things, if you don't ask about them soon enough you can never ask about them.

Because I've been hanging around boys for so long, I never paid any attention to what my father did. I can only guess from what others used to say at family meals that it has something to do with research and science.

I promise myself that when I get out of the hospital, which shouldn't be too long from now, I'll look through the things in my father's secret cabinet and figure out what he does.

"Okay, dad. Say hi to all your coworkers from a stranger."

"What coworkers?" he says softly as he walks out the door.

My dad has a whole lot of gray and silver hair now. He'll die soon. That means I'll have to part with him soon. It's best if I get used to the idea now so it hurts less when it happens. I'll make a mental note of it in my forgetful, sievelike brain: make peace with the fact that you have to say good-bye to dad. When it actually comes to pass, everyone will wonder how I manage to come to grips with it so well. Winning the battle of mourning by advanced preparation.

One thing my father's short visit accomplished is that I now know how I can remain in the hospital longer. All I have to do is sit on the ring pillow with a lot of pressure and my wound will rip open again. That's what the huffy Valerie promised would happen. I just can't get caught. I take a pain-killer. A little numbness is something I'm definitely going to want.

Using my proven method I turn onto my stomach, shimmy down off the bed, and, hunched over with pain, walk over to the wardrobe. I open the doors my father closed. Down on the bottom is the would-be culprit. The normal squatting down by bending my legs won't work. Hurts too much. I'll have to figure out another way to reach down and pick it up. I keep my legs straight and bend at the waist. Keep my back straight, too. I look like an upside-down L now. I can just barely reach the ring with my hand. Success. Raise my back upright again. And retrace my steps. Back beside the bed, I put the ring down near the edge of the mattress so I can sit directly on it from a standing position. I turn my ass to the bed and sit myself down like a bird on a nest. I wiggle around on my ass. A little this way, a little that way, it's not difficult. With the movement, the skin of the wound really strains. I stand up and feel around back there with my hand. I look at my hand. No blood! You promised too much, Valerie.

What now? It was a good plan to reopen the wound. Won't work with the pillow. I'll have to find something else to rip open my ass. Concentrate, Helen. You don't have a lot of time. You know how often the door opens and witnesses come in. I look at all the available objects in the room. Metal nightstand: useless. Bottle of water on the nightstand: you could stick it in, but I don't think you'd be able to hurt yourself with it the way I need to. Television: too high. The spoons on the table: too harmless. Granola bowl: you can't do anything with that. My gaze falls on the bed. There. That's it. The brakes on the bed's rollers. The wheels are big and metal with a rubber coating. They're equipped with some sort of foot brakes, operated by a metal pedal that sticks out. You've got the job, pedal. I go as fast as I can to the end of the bed. I line my back up with it and slide awkwardly down, letting my ass land on the pedal. Now I sit on it. I wiggle back and forth. I have to scream with pain and put both of my hands over my mouth. If this doesn't work I don't know what I'm going to do. I can feel the pedal penetrating the wound. Pressing down hard I make it bore in deeper. This is going to have to do. Valiant Helen. Well done. I'm crying and shaking with pain. It must have worked. My test hand makes its way down and wipes around. I look. My entire palm is covered with fresh, red blood. I need to lie down fast or I'm going to faint right here. That would ruin the whole exercise. I need to be found lying in bed so I can pretend it just happened to me as I was lying there. I lie down.

It hurts like hell. I'm still holding my mouth shut. Tears stream down my face. Should I call somebody now or wait so the wound makes more of an impression? I'll wait. I can manage. Be sure to wipe off the brake pedal, Helen, and get rid of the evidence. The hemorrhoid pillow I hide under the covers. I can take care of that later. More and more blood is gushing out. I reach back with my hand again and this time it's even more covered with blood than the first time. The feeling in my crotch and down my legs is just like when you wet yourself as a kid. When body-temperature liquid is running down you, the first innocent thought is of piss—since that's what it's usually been in past experience. I lie in a pool of my own blood and cry. I open my eyes and see an upside-down bottle cap from the mineral water on my nightstand. I take it in my hand and try to catch my tears. I can distract myself from the horrible pain with this challenge, and maybe I'll find a use for the tears later. I almost never cry. But now its just spewing out of me. Tears up top, blood down below.

I hold the bottle cap up near my tear ducts and after a few seconds look to see what I've managed to collect. At least the bottom of the cap is wet. Helen, you've fooled around long enough. I push the emergency buzzer. As I'm waiting for someone to come, I hide the bottle cap at the back of my nightstand behind everything else. So none of these idiots knock it over. There's a lot of pain in that little vessel.

I think it's high time somebody showed up. I am, after all, losing a lot of blood. Regardless of whether I did it to myself or it just happened. They have to help me stop the bleeding now. So much has gushed out of me that it's dripping onto the floor. How is that possible? Shouldn't the bed soak it up? I know. Because of the plastic lining. The blood is pooling beneath me and not soaking in to the mattress. It's trickling past me onto the floor. I lie in bed and look at my blood on the floor. There's more and more.

Interesting view. It's beginning to look like a butcher's shop
in here. Only the butcher's floor slopes into a runoff channel so the blood can drain. They should think about doing
that here in the proctology unit. Though not many patients
do to themselves what I've just done to my ass. Forget putting a drainage channel in the floor. Bad idea. I push the
buzzer again. Three times, one after the other. I can hear
out on the hall that it doesn't help. Pushing three times still
only creates a single tone in the nurses' station. They don't
want to be driven crazy by the patients. Though they could
use a more clever system for communications between the
patients and staff. One buzz: I need a little more butter for
my whole-grain bread. Two buzzes: please bring a flower vase
with water. Three buzzes: help, blood is gushing out of my
ass so fast that I hardly have enough left in my brain to think
straight and I'm stuck here thinking up stupid ways to improve the hospital.

I can see the blood-smeared brake pedal. I've got to
wipe that clean or I'm going to get it. I stand up quickly and
nearly slip over in my own blood. I brace myself on the bed
and go slowly toward the foot of it. The blood splashes up
between my toes and onto my foot. I have to be careful not
to hydroplane on the blood. I squat down and wipe the pedal
with a corner of my gown. Evidence gone. Well. At least
the evidence on the brake pedal. Squatting hurts. Walking
hurts. I'm about to collapse. Come on, Helen, you can make

it into bed. Lie down, little one. Made it. I press both hands to my face.

I wait an eternity. You always have to wait. I could also go to them and cause a big commotion by leaving a trail of blood down the hallway. I'll restrain myself from doing that.

I'm getting dizzy. It smells like blood in here. A lot of blood. Shall I use the time to clean up a little? After all, I want to be the best patient they've ever had. But maybe that's asking too much of myself. I don't need to tidy up right now.

Knock. The door opens. Robin. Good. He can do it. Do what exactly, Helen? Whatever. I'm going downhill fast.

I explain right away: "I don't know what happened. I think I must have moved in an odd way and all of a sudden the blood started to gush. What should we do now?"

Robin's eyes open wide. He says he's going to call the doctor right away.

He comes up to me. Didn't he say he was going to call the doctor?

He says I look pale. He's stepped in the pooled blood and as he goes out he tracks bloody footprints all over the room.

I think to myself afterward: be careful you don't hydro-plane on the blood. I hold both hands on the bleeding, try-ing to slow it. My hands fill with blood. What a waste. Don't some people have too little blood? Or is it that they have diseased blood? How should I know?

Anemic. That's what it is. There are people they describe as anemic. You will be, too, soon, Helen, if you keep this up.

The anesthesiologist comes in. He asks if I've eaten anything. I have. I had a lot of granola for breakfast. He finds this a shame. Why?

"Because then you can't have general anesthesia. There's too much risk you'll vomit in your sleep and suffocate. An epidural is the only possibility."

He runs out and returns with a form and needles and some other stuff.

That's what pregnant women get, pregnant women who can't manage a normal birth. Cowardly mothers. Ones who want a natural birth but with no pain, thanks. I've heard about it from my mother.

I have to sign something. I'm not sure what it is because I wasn't listening. I trust him. It definitely makes me nervous that this otherwise calm man is running around. I begin to worry about myself. He seems to be in a major hurry.

They think I've lost too much blood too fast. Once I realize they think the same thing I do, I'm sick with fear—afraid I may die as a result of my plan to get my parents back together. That wasn't part of the plan.

He says I need to sit up, bend forward, and arch my

back like a cat so he can disinfect my back, insert a thick catheter between my lower vertebrae, and then administer the injection. It doesn't sound good.

I hate anything that gets near my spinal cord. I worry they'll screw up and I'll be permanently paralyzed and never feel anything again during sex. Might as well forget sex then. Everything he says he also simultaneously does. I can feel it as he searches around back there, wipes, inserts, and injects. Sitting in this position increases the pain. It feels as if my ass is ripping open even more.

He says it takes exactly fifteen minutes for everything from the tube to my toes to go numb. It seems like a long time to both him and me. Calculated in liters of blood per minute. He goes out saying he'll be right back. Good. I look at my mobile phone to check the time. Ten past. At twenty-five past I'll be ready for surgery.

Robin comes in and tells me the doctor is getting ready for an emergency operation. That's why he can't come see me. Robin described to him how much blood I had lost. The doctor immediately ordered the emergency surgery.

Emergency operation. Man oh man, that sounds bad. But also important and exciting. As if I'm important. This is a good time to lure my parents here.

I write down my parents' numbers for Robin and ask him to call them during the operation and tell them to come down here.

The anesthesiologist comes in and wants Robin to
wheel me to the operating room. I touch my thigh and can
feel my hand make contact. Wait. I can still feel everything.
They can't operate on me. Not yet. I look at my mobile.
Quarter past. Only five minutes have gone by.

They can't be serious. They're not going to wait for the
anesthesia to kick in? They're in more of a hurry than I
thought. Very unnerving.

Robin pushes me out into the hall. They won't let me
take my mobile. Because of all the equipment. What equipment? Are we flying there or something? Whatever.

If I remember correctly, clocks are hanging in all the
halls and waiting rooms. Those giant black-and-white train
station clocks. Why do they have train station clocks in a
hospital? Are they trying to tell us something? I'm not going
to let them stick their tools up my ass until fifteen minutes
have elapsed. Whether I bleed to death or not. Very defi-
ant, Helen, but stupid. You don't want to die.

It would be the perfect reason for my parents to reunite,
though. In their mourning they would drift back toward each
other. They wouldn't be able to take comfort in their respective new partners because they know the partners never
accepted their stepchildren. If the stepchild dies, the new
partner is exposed. Then it'll be clear who won the power
struggle and who lost. Great plan, Helen, except you wouldn't

be able to experience their reunion. If you die, you won't be watching down from above.

You know that there's no heaven. That we're just highly developed animals. Who, after death, simply rot in the earth and are eaten by worms. There's no possibility of looking down after death at your beloved parental animals. Everything is just devoured. The reputed soul, the memory, every little recollection and bit of love will be turned into worm shit along with the brain. And the eyes. And the pussy. Worms can't tell the difference. They eat synapses as happily as they eat clitorises. For them there's no big picture of what or whom they're eating. Their only concern is that it's tasty.

Back to the time. We pass several clocks but hardly any time is passing. Robin is in a hurry. He bumps into the walls a lot. I can feel the puddle of blood I'm lying in getting deeper.

The depression my ass creates in the mattress has long since overflowed. That I can still feel these things is a bad sign. If I've understood the anesthesiologist correctly, I should feel like a quadriplegic before they start. If I have this much feeling left in my legs, then I must also still have it in my ass.

We've arrived in the prep room. There's a train station clock in here, too. I knew it. Clock-memory contest won. It's eighteen minutes past. I stare at the long hand. Robin explains that we'll be ready to go as soon as the operating room's cleared out. Without looking away from the long hand, I tell him: "I'm not a stickler when it comes to tidiness. They don't need to clear the place on my account. I'm happy to have a look at what was going on in there before."

Robin and the anesthesiologist laugh. Typical, Helen. Even in the worst situation you've still got a zinger on the tip of your tongue. It's just so none of them notice how scared I am of them and of having their hands up my ass. I'm very proud of the flexibility of my sphincter muscle during sex, but several adult-male hands is too much for me. Sorry. I just can't see anything good about it.

Now, unfortunately, I know what a blown-out sphincter muscle feels like. And this time they're going to do it without general anesthesia.

These sick pigs. I'm scared. I grab Robin's hand. It was near me, and I hold it tight. He seems used to it. It doesn't surprise him at all.

Every granny probably does the same thing. Most people get really nervous before an operation. Like before a big journey. It really is like a journey. You never know whether you'll return.

A journey of pain. I squeeze Robin's hand so tight that his skin goes white from the pressure. I bore my long nails

in so I'll leave a different pattern in his skin than the grannies do. The big motorized doors of the operating room open
and a nurse with a surgical mask says, muffled, "Here we go."

Bitch. Panicking, I look at the clock. The long hand
jerks down to the four. Tick. Twenty past. The clock hand
is still jiggling.

They have to wait five more minutes. No. Don't. I can
still feel everything. Please don't start, I think. But don't
say. Your own fault, Helen. You wanted to bleed and this is
what you got yourself into. I think I might throw up. I don't
say that either. If it happens, they'll see it anyway. Nothing
matters at this point.

"I'm scared, Robin."

"Me too, for you."

Understood. He loves me. I didn't know. Sometimes
it happens that quickly. I put my other hand on his, holding his hand tightly between both of mine. I look him in
the eyes and try to smile. Then I let go.

They wheel me in. Lift me onto another bed. The nurses each take one of my legs and loop them in straps hanging from the ceiling. They are fastened at the ankle and then pulled tightly upward. Some kind of pulley. My legs are sticking straight up. Like an extreme version of a gynecological position. So everyone can crawl up my ass. I see long lashes above a surgical mask. Dr. Notz. Robin's gone. Probably too nervous to watch. The anesthesiologist sets up next to my head. He says they have to start now because I'm losing so much blood. He says it only seems as if I can feel everything because there's a miniscule amount of feeling left. In reality, he says, I'll only feel a tiny fraction of what's being done. They've hung a light-green drape between my head and my ass. Obviously so my ass can't see my horror-stricken face.

I ask the anesthesiologist very quietly what exactly they are doing.

He explains to me, as if I am six, that they have to use stitches now, which they normally try to avoid. During my first operation they cut away quite a lot but they were able to leave it open to heal. It's much more pleasant for the patient. Now all of us—and first and foremost me—have had a bit of bad luck. They have to stitch up each and every bloody spot and afterward I'll feel very uncomfortable from the tension. It's really going to pinch. For a long time. And here I was thinking it couldn't get any less comfortable. Oh, Helen, all the things you do for the sake of your parents. Heartwarming. Ha. As the anesthesiologist has been sketching out my painful future for me, I haven't even been paying attention to my ass. Meaning I must be fully numb. I ask the anesthesiologist for the time. Twenty-five minutes past. Feeling gone, to the minute. Very precise with his work. He smiles happily. I do, too.

Suddenly I'm very relaxed, as if nothing is happening.

We can segue into small talk. I ask him inconsequential things that cross my mind. Whether he has to have lunch in the basement cafeteria, too. Whether he has a family. Or a garden. Whether the anesthesia has ever failed to work. Whether it's true that it's more difficult to anesthetize people who take drugs. During the pauses in conversation I picture my parents already waiting together in my empty room, sick with worry over me. Talking about me. About my pain. Nice.

And soon they're done with the stitches. I have feeling in my feet again. I ask the anesthesiologist whether that's possible. He explains that his goal is to numb me just enough. He knows through experience how long these operations last, and numbed me only enough for this amount of time. It looks as if this makes him very proud. Soon I'll feel everything again, including, unfortunately, the pain. For that he gives me a pill. He says it's going to be tough to combat the pain of the tension in my anus with pills. I should prepare myself for serious pain. No comparison to the pain I've experienced up to now. What have I done? My legs are lowered from the ceiling. Feeling begins to trickle up my legs. I'm plugged up again down there, lifted onto another bed, tucked in, and wheeled back to my room. By some random nurse I don't know and who can't wheel beds very well. Worse than Robin earlier in his agitated state.

She parks me in my big, lonely room and walks back out. If I need anything, I should buzz. I already know that. I've been here long enough to get that.

And now? After nearly bleeding to death, lying around in bed is boring. There's something I need to take care of. Get rid of the hemorrhoid pillow. I lift the covers and it's no longer there. Where is it? Who has it? Oh man, Helen, are you out of it. Must be the medication. Of course they made up the bed with fresh linens after the explosion of blood. So where has the pillow gotten to now? I can't ask, and don't want to. Maybe some stupid nurse just threw it out without even thinking. That would be the best. If somebody else had already taken care of the pillow.

I probably won't feel any pain for a while. So I might as well do something now. But what? I'm sure I'm not allowed to walk around. I'd rather not anyway—don't want everything to get ripped open again.

A knock.

Robin?

No, it's the candy striper. Something to keep me busy. This time I won't be as snippy as last time.

"Good day," she says.

I greet her back. Good start. I would love to keep her here for as long as possible, to stave off the boredom.

She can solve the telephone riddle.

"Do you guys pay to have the phone switched on for newly arrived patients?"

"Yes, we did that for you. You were so out of sorts from the pain that we figured we'd take care of that. We pay out of our funds. The patients repay us."

Too bad. I thought Robin had done it.

"Earlier this year I was here to be sterilized. Nobody did that for me then."

Come on, Helen, this information is of no concern to her.

"It's a new service we're providing."

I ask her for a favor. I would like a coffee from the cafeteria. And as long as she's down there, she could bring me some fresh grapes and a packet of trail mix. She can take the money for it out of the drawer in the metal nightstand. Along with whatever was advanced for the phone.

She agrees and leaves with the money.

While she's gone, I fill my glass with mineral water from a bottle I took from the hospital supply. Bottoms up into my mouth and then I spit it back into the bottle. I hold my thumb over the top and shake it around. I repeat this process three times.

I wait for her to return. I notice how tired I am. Close my eyes. Despite the pills and the fact that the anesthesia is probably still working a bit, I can feel the pain. It feels as if they are still sewing up skin in my colon with metal needles. They pull the thread tight and cut the end with their teeth. Just the way mom always does it when she's sewing. She does a lot of things with her mouth. Dangerous things, too. I remember as a kid watching her hang pictures with tacks. She would always put all the tacks in her mouth and balance herself on a chair, taking one tack after the other out of her mouth as she needed them. I close my eyes with pain. Hold them closed for a long time.

I'm awoken by a knock as the candy striper returns. That was fast. Of course she was faster than I was—she's not an ass patient. It seemed like a long way to me.

I thank her for bringing me the things. And then I ask her whether she would mind my asking her a few questions. It's tough for me to maintain a normal conversation. Something's really brewing down inside me. The more painful it gets the more normal I try to come across. She says go ahead. I offer her some mineral water and she gratefully accepts. She goes to the nurses' station to get a clean glass. Stripers are allowed in there. And yet they can't give you a shot.

She comes back with a glass. She fills it to the brim and gulps it down. It makes me happy. It's as if we've already kissed. Without her even knowing, of course. Against her will even. As if she had been unconscious and I kissed her. That's how I'd describe our relationship. Kissing to dull the pain. It doesn't do much.

I feel close to her and smile at her. Suddenly I notice how nicely she's made-up. She's drawn a thin, light-blue line along the very edge of her bottom eyelids. It takes years of practice to be able to do that so well. She must have been making herself up for years. Probably started doing it back in school. Very good.

I ask her everything I can think of about her duties as a candy striper. How do you become one? Where do you apply? Are there many applicants? Are you allowed to pick which department you'll work in?

I think I must be talking funny. I wrench the questions out of myself. I'm almost too weak to talk. But with this feeling down there, I don't want to be alone. Now I know the most important aspects of the field of duty I'll join as soon as I am released.

I thank her sincerely. She understands and leaves.

"Thanks for your generous offer of water." She tit-ters. She thinks it's funny because she has emphasized the word "generous" for comedic value, since it's just the hospi-tal's own mineral water. I find it funny, too. But for other reasons.

As soon as she's gone, I'm filled with nasty thoughts. Where are my parents? For fucks sake! This is not happen-ing. They've abandoned me here. I figured after Robin's call they'd be worried and come straight here. Nothing. Nobody here. A gaping abyss. I think much more about them than they do about me. Maybe I should stop thinking about them so much. They don't want me to take care of them. And I should finally give up on expecting anything from them. It doesn't get any clearer than this. I'm lying here having gone through an emergency operation and nobody turns up. That's the way it goes in our family. I know that if one of them had something like what I have, I wouldn't leave their side. That's the big difference. I'm more their parents than they are mine. I've got to stop that. Give it up, Helen. You're an adult now. You have to make your own way. Wake up to the fact that you're not going to change them. I can only change myself. Exactly. I want to live without them. Change of plan. It's just, in what way am I going to change my plan? What next? I need something to do. So I can think more clearly. When your hands are working, you brain works better, too.

Not to mention that I get sad when I have nothing to do.

I take the grapes and lay them in my lap on top of the sheet. Then I lean over to the metal nightstand and grab the bag of trail mix. I rip it open with my teeth. With my long thumbnail I slit open a grape along one side. Just the way you would a bread roll with a knife. I root around in the bag for a cashew nut, pull it out, and separate its two halves. It's easier than I thought it would be. As if they were already partially separated. I find a raisin in the bag and put it between the cashew halves. This stuffed cashew I push into the cut-open grape until it's in the middle. Now I just have to squeeze the grape back together so you can hardly see the cut. As if nothing's been done to it. Stuffed without a trace. My little masterpiece is finished. The truffle of poor students. The idea came to me the second I saw the candy striper. I knew I had to give her something to do for me—that's why they're here. These candy non-nurses in their odd-colored uniforms. And I wanted whatever she did for me to give me something to do later. It worked perfectly. I'm proud.

I'm going to transform all the grapes and trail mix into student truffles to give to my favorites. Lovely task you've found for yourself, Helen. The finished creations I place on the metal nightstand.

I love to stuff things into other things. What made me think of stuffing things when I looked at the candy striper I don't know. Sometimes I only realize after the fact, when someone has turned me on. Maybe that's what's going to happen in this case.

Back when we were still a cohesive family, mom would make stuffed birds on Christmas. She'd stuff a quail into a small chicken, the chicken into a duck, the duck into a small goose, and the goose into a turkey. The anus of each fowl would have to be widened with a few snips for the next one to fit through it. And then she'd roast the whole thing in the extra-large oven we had just so she could do this. A professional stove. A lot of gas comes out of those if you want it to. Between each set of birds mom would put strips of bacon because otherwise it would all dry out since it had to roast for so long for the heat to penetrate all the layers.

When it was done, we kids loved to watch it be sliced open.

The pain is practically knocking me out. I can't take it anymore. Helen, keep thinking about Christmas dinner. Keep your thoughts away from your butt. Back to your family. Think of something nice. Don't give in to the pain.

With the help of some big, sharp kitchen shears, the whole thing would be cut right down the middle so you'd get a perfect cross section of all the birds. It looked as if each one were pregnant with the next smaller one. The turkey was pregnant with the goose, the goose had a duck in its belly, the duck was pregnant with a chicken, and the chicken with a quail. It was hilarious. A parade of pregnant fetuses. And parsnips from the field next to our house roasted along with them. Delicious.

Once, a long time ago, I overheard my father late at night in the living room telling a friend of his that it was pretty awful for him to have to watch my birth. They had to give mom an episiotomy or else she would have torn from her pussy to her asshole. He said it had sounded as if they were cutting a stringy chicken down the middle with kitchen shears, through cartilage and other gristly parts. He imitated the sound several times that night. *Sniiip.* He was good at it. Each time the friend laughed loudly. You always laugh loudest at the things that scare you the most.

Just before I've used up all my student-truffle supplies, I go to put another finished work on the nightstand. With this motion, the stem with the last of the grapes attached to it falls to the floor.

I can't get out of bed now to pick it up. With the stitches in my ass, I don't want to move at all. With nothing more to do and my thoughts brought to a halt, I notice the pain getting worse and worse. I need a distraction and some stronger painkillers. I hit the buzzer. A nurse should be able to take care of it for me. While I'm waiting for help, I do nothing, for a change. I sit there and stare at the wall. Light light light green. What a subtle shade. I hate it when I can't take care of myself. It bugs me that I can't just hop down there and pick everything up. I don't like to depend on others. Doing things yourself is the best way. I trust myself the most. When it comes to applying sunscreen, for instance. But in all other matters in life, too.

She floats in. Pretty quick. Must not be too much buzzer action in the unit at the moment.

"Can you do me a favor and hand me those grapes?"

She crawls under the bed and collects them.

Instead of giving them back to me she takes them over to the sink. What does she think she's doing?

"I'll just rinse them off. They were on the floor, after all."

These hygiene fanatics would never think to ask: Do you want me to wash your grapes for you since they were on the disgustingly filthy hospital floor that's mopped twice a day? They just do it because they think everyone is as afraid of bacteria as they are. But that's not the case. In fact, in my case, it's just the opposite.

She rinses the grapes for quite some time in running water.

As she's rinsing them she says that she has the feeling they haven't been washed anyway, that they might still have toxic pesticides on them. They're still covered with that fuzzy, white film. A sure sign of having not been washed. Oh, please!

I don't say anything. I'm screaming inside, though. This idiotic notion of washing pesticides off fruit and vegetables is the biggest joke there is. My dad taught me. These days you learn it in school, too. In chemistry. The chemicals that are sprayed on produce to keep away vermin and fungus are so strong that they penetrate the skin of tomatoes and grapes. You can wash them until your fingers shrivel. Nothing comes off. If you don't want to eat pesticides with your fruit and vegetables, you shouldn't buy them at all. You're not going to cheat the poison industry with a few seconds of running water. I never wash fruit and vegetables. I don't think it removes any of the poisons.

The other reason the nurse feels the urgent need to wash my property is that people like her always think the floor is extremely filthy because people walk on it. In the imagination of these people, there must be a tiny particle of dog shit every few inches. That's the worst contaminant a hygiene fanatic can imagine. If kids pick things up from the ground and put them in their mouths they're always told: Be careful, there could be dog crap on that. Even though it's highly unlikely there's dog crap anywhere on it. And what if there is? What would be so bad about that? Dogs eat canned meat. The canned meat is turned into canned-meat-crap in their intestines and then lands on the street. Even if I ate spoonfuls from a pile of dog crap, I'm sure nothing would happen to me. So if a whiff of a trace of an unlikely particle of dog crap that somehow made its way into my hospital room sticks to a grape there beneath my bed and winds up in my mouth, nothing's going to happen.

She's finally finished with her nonsense.

I have my work materials back, washed against my will. I don't thank her.

"Could you please ask whether I can have some stronger pills or can take two at a time? What I've got isn't stopping the pain."

She nods and leaves.

I'm pissed off as I finish up my work. These stupid hygiene freaks drive me crazy. They are so unscientifically superstitious about bacteria. This pain is also driving me crazy. But I've hit upon my next good idea.

I know what I'm going to do now. I'm going to have a bowel movement. I can't stand up. I'll force myself. I need to make sure I can take care of myself. Which I normally don't have to worry about. Better to try to take my first bowel movement after emergency surgery here in a controlled environment near doctors than wherever I'll end up doing it if I'm discharged. I'm all out of sorts. I'm dizzy.

I'll make myself do it. It can't be that difficult. Maybe I'm still numb from the operation. It's possible that the pain will just keep getting worse from now on. In which case I'd rather try now. Now or never. Bite the bullet, Helen, and do it. And given what I've eaten in the last few days— granola as hard as wood chips—I should be ready to drop one. Off to the bathroom. First I need to get rid of the plug. What they manage to stuff up there is very long. I position myself in the reliable spread-legged stance above the bowl and think of the pain I felt when I ripped myself open. This is nothing by comparison. It works. I manage it. I do it well. In a death-defying feat, I push everything past the stitches and I'm home free. I don't need to tell anyone I was able to do this. But it's good for me to know. I'm one step closer to recovery. If I do end up abandoning my plan for my parents, this will have been a big waste of strength and suffering. We'll see. I rinse myself off and pat myself dry. Robin was right. It's a lot better than wiping with toilet paper. All the things he knows. We're a good match.

I go back over to the bed and stand next to it.

I have to do something. Have to. Doesn't matter what. The main thing is not to think about my parents or the pain in my asshole. My hands are shaking. I'm all tense. I wipe cold sweat from my brow. Cold sweat is creepy. The only other time you experience it is right before you faint. Little death. Aren't men's orgasms called that, too? Or is it something you say about animals? Which ones? I can't think straight. Not an enjoyable experience. This. Everything. I climb back into bed. I put all the trail-mix sculptures in my lap. I twist around so I can reach the back edge of the metal nightstand. I carefully lift up the bottle cap of tears and move it gingerly across the surface of the nightstand. I put it down on the edge closest to me, so I can easily reach it, and dunk the tip of my pointer finger in the salty water. I let a drop fall from my finger into the cut in each stuffed grape. I work carefully, as if my finger were an eyedropper. I have to conserve my tears so there's enough to go around. I already know to whom I'll offer them. I manage not to notice my pain for several minutes thanks to this tedious task. Once each grape has a drop in it, I put them all back in the trail mix bag.

As soon as I don't have anything to do, I panic. Think of something, Helen, anything. None of my friends, or I guess I should call them classmates, know I'm here. Only my parents know. And my brother. So the only visits I can hope for would be from my family.

And I might end up waiting a long time for that.

I didn't want to tell any of my classmates why I had to go to the hospital. I don't like the idea of them visiting me in the proctology unit. They all think I'm home with the flu. When I took off—how many days ago now?—because my ass hurt so bad, I told them I felt a flu coming on. That I was feeling achy. Nice word. Achy. And that I had to go home. I didn't have to worry about having my cover blown because none of them would stop by my house anyway. Nobody wants to hang out with a sick person. They like to go out, party, hang out in the park. They drink a lot and smoke pot, and you can't do that while visiting a sick person at home with their parents around. We only go around to people's places when their parents are on vacation. Otherwise, being outdoors is the best place for our hobbies. My parents are always pleased I get so much fresh air. But obviously, for me and my friends, hanging out isn't about getting fresh air in our lungs.

Robin comes into the room.

In his hand he's holding a plastic shot glass with two pills in it. These pills are shaped differently from any of the others. I guess the nurse said something about my pain. I don't even ask what they are. I hold out my hand, he plunks the two fat pills onto my palm, and I smack my hand to my mouth. Just like in the movies. The pills hit the back of my throat and I almost hurl. Quick, chase them with some hospital water. I cough. The uvula is a sensitive spot.

And unfortunately it's very closely tied to the gag reflex. Which can be very disruptive during sex. God didn't think that one out very well when he designed human beings. If I suck a cock during sex and want him to come in my mouth, I have to pay a hell of a lot of attention to make sure he doesn't shoot his sperm on my uvula. Because then I would puke immediately. Been through it all, our Helen. Obviously I want to take the cock as deep into my throat as I can—it really makes a striking visual impact. I look like a sword swallower. But I really have to watch out for my uvula. It's a pain. Everything has to tiptoe around it.

"Robin, did you call my parents before the emergency operation?"

"Oh, you know what, I forgot to tell you with all the commotion. I was only able to leave messages. Didn't reach them directly. Sorry. I'm sure they'll come at some point. Once they've listened to their messages."

"Sure."

He tidies the room. The table at the foot of the bed, something in the bathroom. He neatly organizes everything on the metal nightstand.

I stare straight ahead and say under my breath, "Any other parents whose daughter was in a situation like this would either stay with her in the hospital the whole time or sit by the phone at home so as not to miss any emergency calls. The trade-off, I guess, is that I have more freedom. Thanks."

I ask him if he wants to taste my new specialty. I've invented a new dish. It's that boring for me here, Robin.

I hold out the trail mix bag with the tear-grapes in it. If someone eats a woman's tears, the two of them are forever bound to each other.

I explain what he has in his hand. I leave out the part about the tears. He bravely sticks the modified grape in his mouth. First I hear the skin of the grape burst, then the crack of the nut. With his mouth full he says he likes it and asks if he can have some more. Of course. He eats one after the other. He continues to clean up and keeps coming back to the metal nightstand to pop another grape in his mouth.

The pills aren't working yet. I'm tense and tired. Pain is exhausting. It's very hard to create attachments with people in a hospital room. I have the feeling everybody wants to get out of my room quickly. Maybe it doesn't smell good in here. Or I don't look good. Or maybe people just want to distance themselves from sickness and pain. The nurses' station has a magical pull on all the nurses and caregivers, including Robin. I can hear them laughing out there in ways they never do in here. As a patient I'll soon be gone; as employees they'll still be here. That creates a barrier. But I'll break it down soon. Even with no medical training I'll join them as soon as I'm released. As a candy striper I'll be allowed in their break room and drink sparkling water with them. For the first time, I have the feeling that Robin is trying to stay near me. He doesn't leave. He keeps tidying. In places he's already just cleaned up. It makes me happy. I've managed to create an attachment.

I pick up the phone. I dial mom's number. Nobody answers. Answering machine.

"Hi, it's me. When is somebody going to come visit me? I'm in pain and I have to stay here longer than I thought. At least send my brother by. He hasn't been here yet. I would visit him if he had an operation down under."

I hang up. Slam it down. Of course, on an answering machine you can't tell the difference between a friendly hang up and an angry one.

I pick up the phone again and ask the dial tone: "And why did you try to kill yourself and Tony, mom? Are you sick? What's wrong?"

You coward, Helen.

I'm spent.

I'm talking to myself, and a little bit to Robin.

"I can't take it anymore. Not by myself. I have to constantly beg for painkillers. I lie to everyone about my bowel movements so I can stay here as long as possible in order to bring my parents together in this room. But they never come. And they'll never show up at the same time. How is my plan supposed to work? What a load of shit. A massive load of shit. I'm an idiot and want things nobody else wants."

I can feel the muscles in my shoulders tightening up. That always happens when I realize that everything's pointless and that I can't control things. My shoulders start to rise toward my ears because of the tension and I cross my arms and try to push them back down with my hands. I close my eyes and try to calm myself with exaggerated deep breathing. Doesn't work. Never works. My butt is burning, it's killing me, and my shoulders are attaching themselves to my ears.

My grandmother has been so tense for her whole life that she doesn't have any shoulders at all anymore. Her arms come right out of her ears. Right next to her head. Once, when I was still young and nice, I went to massage her and she immediately let out a bloodcurdling scream. Then she told me that the muscles there had been so tense for so many years that the lightest touch felt to her as if someone were poking around in an open wound. But that's not reason enough for her to try to do something about it. She just has all her blouses altered at the tailor so the arms are sewn right onto the collar—otherwise the extra flower-print fabric of the shoulders would hang there in big pouches. If I don't want to end up like that, I'm going to have to come up with a way to avoid it. But how? Gymnastics? Massages? Ditch my family?

As a result of getting my back slammed in the car door, my doctor used to have me get regular massages. The first thing I'd ask each new masseuse was whether they'd ever had a male client get a hard-on during a massage.

Every one of them said yes. I'd act as if I was sympathetic, that I was as disgusted as they were about the boners.

Ah, men. In reality I was hoping to hear a story that would turn me on. I mean, what do these people think?

How can a man avoid getting a hard-on when a woman is massaging all around his cock and balls, like on his upper thigh? I get wet from that, too. It's just that with women you can't see the excitement.

I'll start with that. I need to take the bull by the horns so I don't end up like grandma. When I get out of here, I'm scheduling some more massages.

Where is Robin? I can hear him puttering around in the bathroom. Is it possible he's worried about me? Though I have downed some strong medicine—maybe he's just obligated to keep an eye on me. That could be it.

When was the last time I ate something?

Who cares. I only want to eat painkillers. Nothing else. The pain in my ass keeps getting worse. My head is spinning.

Grandma can probably lie on her side very easily. The breadth of normal shoulders can get in the way when lying on your side. When she lies on her side, it's a straight line from her ear right down along her arm. Much more comfortable. Maybe I won't make any appointments for massages after all. I should have a closer look at grandma. Then I'll decide.

Robin comes over to the bedside.

"Is it bad?"

"Yes."

"In my experience, it'll start to get better by tonight at the latest. Tomorrow you'll probably be able to handle it without any medicine, and if you have a bowel movement with no bleeding, you'll probably be allowed to go home."

That's not possible. They'd send me home in this condition? That's it for my plan. Definitely. But I had already screwed it up. Pointless. This whole thing.

"Home? Nice."

Shit.

Robin, I don't want to go home. And I already had a bowel movement. I've fooled you all. Sorry. All because of my messed-up family. I have nowhere to go. I have to stay here. Forever.

I don't want Robin to leave.

Maybe I can distract myself from the pain with a bit of conversation until the medicine starts working.

"Robin, can I tell you a secret?"

"Oh, man. What is it, Helen?"

"It's not what you think." Of course. I need to dispel the reputation I have with him. "It's got nothing to do with my ass or nakedness or anything. I just wanted to show you my little family."

He looks annoyed, but nods.

I turn to the windowsill and lift up the Bible.

"What is all that?" he asks.

I put the Bible down next to me in bed.

I give him a long lecture about my hobby, growing avocado trees.

He listens closely. I manage to keep him in my room for a long time. For the moment I don't have to share him with other ass patients.

As I bring my presentation to a close, he takes off his white hospital clogs and climbs onto my bed. He looks at the avocado pits up close. This makes me very happy. Nobody's ever shown so much interest in this hobby of mine.

He says he wants to try it out himself at home. Says they look pretty.

"If you want, you can pick one out and take it home with you."

"No, I couldn't do that. You've already put so much work into them."

"Yes, and for exactly that reason, you should take one."

He hesitates. He must be trying to figure out whether or not it's allowed. Strong sense of duty it seems to me. Always following the rules, this Robin.

"Well, okay. If you're absolutely sure you want to give one away. I'll take this one here."

He points to the nicest one of all. A light-yellow pit with touches of light pink. And a healthy, dark green sprout. Good choice.

"It's yours."

He picks up the glass and carefully lifts it across the bed, keeping it balanced so the water doesn't spill. He slips back into his shoes and stands in front of my bed with the avocado pit. He seems really happy. We smile at each other.

He walks out.

I wrap my arms around my rib cage. It occurs to me that I'll be released soon. My body and I shrug inwardly, and with that comes a gush of something down below. Warm. It could be anything. Out of any opening. I can't distinguish anything down there at the moment.

I feel around with a finger. My first thought is that it's a fluid leaking out pussywise. I make my finger magically reappear from under the sheet and see that the fluid is red. Got it.

I forgot to put in a tampon. With all the unusual bleeding I completely forgot about the routine bleeding. The bed is covered. I'm covered. Smeared with blood.

Okay. This is my own problem. I'm not going to ring for Robin and ask him to run and bring me something again. I don't want him to think I've fallen in love with him and I'm just sitting here thinking up reasons to ring. I am in pain and really did need the pills. It's fine to ring for that. But this would be too much. I don't want to get on his nerves.

Though it's also all right if he thinks I've fallen in love with him. Because I have. So there's no reason he can't be the first to know. But I can handle menstrual blood by myself. I've always managed to in the past—except that one time at my aunt's.

I grab the plastic container from the windowsill and pull out two squares of gauze and a piece of paper towel. I also take the opportunity to pull out my old tampon. Time for it to go. I'm sure it's already spread enough bacteria. Into the trash it goes before anyone has noticed it.

I can see condensation in the plastic container. It's warm on the windowsill. On the inside of the box, droplets of moisture have formed. When they get too big and can't hold on to the sides of the container anymore, they drip down, pulling other droplets with them. The droplets running down the sides seek the easiest path and leave a tiny, zigzagging trail of destruction behind, the same way a river does on a bigger scale. Then the droplets can join to form a fetid, fermenting puddle and bubble up into new steam droplets to cling to the sides of the container. Whoever stays up longest . . .

I need to examine my gown. If there's blood on it, I'll flip out. There's no way I'm asking for another one.

Lucky. All clean. I hadn't pushed it under myself properly. Good. I shift to the side to have a look at the mess. Not as much has come out as I thought. Good.

I lay one piece of the padding down with the plastic side up and the other on top of it with the plastic side down.

I can do it with my eyes closed now. Nice to have something to do again.

I rip the paper towel in half and with one half wipe all around the folds of my pussy, soaking up as much blood as possible.

The other half I fold lengthwise so I have a long, thin, flat piece of toweling. I roll this up into a short, thick sausage and shove it as far into my pussy as I can. Take that, American tampon industry!

Then I sit on the soft gauze pads.

Ta-dah!

Done.

How well you take care of yourself, Helen.

I'm proud of myself. That doesn't happen very often, and it makes me smile warmly inside.

If I'm in such a good mood and thinking such nice thoughts, that must mean the pain medication has kicked in.

I concentrate on trying to feel my wounded ass and realize nothing hurts. I just veer back and forth from pain to no pain in here.

I want to get up and walk around.

I've perfected my method of slowly getting out of bed so well that it would be a shame if I were pronounced healed and released.

I lie on my stomach and scoot my body, feet first, sideways toward the edge of the bed until I'm in the shape of a right angle with just my upper body on the bed and my feet on the ground. I call this gymnastics position "Helen kicks herself out of bed."

The best view of it is from the doorway. Open tree-top angel gown, naked, wounded ass spread open to the door. I snap my upper body up and stand.

I stretch my right arm high in the air the way we were taught to after a tumbling routine. Smile wide and stretch your body so far out in the direction of your hand that your heels briefly leave the mat. I snap my right hand down to the side of my thigh. Nod my head, curtsy, and wait for applause. Silence. Wipe the smile off my face. What can you do, Helen, you always give your best performances when nobody's watching. It's just the way you are.

I'm not in any pain and want to move my body. Where should I go? Not outside. Don't feel like running into other people. And besides, I'd either have to put on an ass parade in the hallway or put on underwear.

Do I even have any underwear here? I can't remember what mom brought me.

There's the first thing I can do on my tour of the room. Have a look. I go to the wardrobe. Open the door. It's true. Pajama pants and T-shirts. Untouched. I've used hospital gowns right from the start. Haven't put on any of my own things.

Robin said I might be released as soon as tomorrow.

Time to pack my bag if it's going to go according to that plan.

I'm not going to be able to make it work with my parents. It was a good plan. But they haven't even shown up despite the emergency operation. I would love to continue trying to make my plan work. But it's not going to happen here. They don't visit often enough, and I'd have to have something much worse to be able to stay any longer. They won't let me stay here long enough to pull it off. It's nice here. Nicer than at home, at least.

Maybe I can go somewhere else beside home if I'm going to get kicked out of here so soon?

I pick up the empty bag on the bottom of the wardrobe and ball it up as small as I can. I stick it into the chrome trash can on the metal nightstand. Now my things will just have to stay in the wardrobe—they don't have a bag to travel in.

Come on, Helen, that's absolutely ridiculous. You can think of somewhere to go.

I have an idea. I take the bag back out of the trash can.

Move around some more. As long as I can't feel my ass, it's almost as if I'm here on vacation. On drugs.

From the nightstand I move along the edge of the bed to the corner that sticks out into the room. Then around the short side of the bed to the windowsill.

And back. Once. Faster. Twice. With ever-faster steps I go back and forth five times until I'm winded.

All this walking strains my legs. My muscles have already atrophied in the few days I've been lying around.

Still standing, I hike up the gown so I can look at my legs. I stretch one leg out onto the bed, then I take it back down and stretch out the other one to have a look. They're thinner. They look funny. A bit like granny legs—hardly any muscle, white skin, and long hair. Ugh.

I hadn't thought about that at all during the entire time here in the hospital. When you're in pain, you don't necessarily feel like shaving.

Now, though.

I throw myself onto the bed. Too hard. Despite the pills I feel pain rise from my ass up through my back. Take it easy, Helen, don't flip out.

It's nice not to have any pain and you want to keep it that way for a while. So watch it with the jerky movements.

I grab the phone and dial mom's number. Answering machine again. Have they all gone on vacation in my absence? When was the last time I saw one of them?

It's been days.

It's difficult to figure out exactly how long it's been. Or how long I've been here. Probably has something to do with the painkillers and the pain and with my general drug consumption. These gaps in my memory.

"It's me again. Did you get my other message? If either of you is still even thinking of visiting me, do it fast. Tony, you haven't come to see me at all. If you do come, can you bring one of mom's dresses and a pair of her shoes? Thanks. See you soon. It's already evening."

Oh, man. It sucks when you have to depend on blood relatives. Now I have to wait until somebody brings me those things.

I get out of bed in slow motion and walk to the door. I open it a crack and peek out. There was some kind of noise coming from out there. Something's going on.

Dinner service. They're pushing around multilevel towers stacked with trays and stopping in front of each door. Maybe I'll get some normal food tonight. Not the usual granola and whole-grain bread. If I were to tell them I've long since had a bowel movement, I'd get something better to eat. But I'm not saying anything.

I slowly go back to bed and get in to wait for feeding time.

There's a knock at the door.

I offer a very friendly "Good evening." It's some female nurse. I can't tell them apart. All of them unfuckable.

"Good evening. In a good mood, are we, Miss Memel? How are you—had a bowel movement yet?"

"Not yet, but thanks for asking. What's on the menu tonight?"

"Unfortunately just whole-grain bread for you. You know that's the situation until your first bowel movement."

"I'd rather have granola."

I already have everything I need for that right here.

"What are the other patients having tonight?"

"The meat dish is a roast with peas, potatoes, and gravy. The vegetable dish is a cabbage stew."

That sounds like paradise to me. For one thing because it's warm. I only get cold food, and after awhile it leaves you cold inside, too. I'm on the verge of telling this nanny that I shat ages ago.

But then, although I'd get one warm meal, I'd just be sent home. That's too high a price to pay.

I need some more time to figure out where I'm going when I leave.

"Thanks. I can mix it up myself."

With slouched shoulders, I shovel three spoonfuls of granola into the bowl then pull the trail mix bag out of the drawer and put three grape creations on top. Tonight Helen's having granola with tears.

When I can't feel the pain, life is fun. I pop the aluminum cherry of the little milk container by sticking a hole in it with the plastic tube stuck to the side of the box. I turn the box upside down and squeeze the milk into the bowl until the box is empty. Dad used to lecture us about not using the word "straw" because the things weren't made of straw anymore. But I can't believe they were ever made out of straw. How could you pop the cherry on a drink box with a piece of straw? It would buckle immediately. Surely they were always made out of plastic and are called straws just because somebody thought they looked like stalks of straw.

I eat my cold dinner fast.

There's a soft knock on the door as I'm downing the last bite.

That's not a nurse. They always knock louder and more confidently. And nobody walks in. Definitely not a nurse. I'm betting it's my father. He also has a weak handshake. Everyone complains about it. Guess he doesn't have muscular hands. Not strong enough to knock solidly on doors, either.

"Come in."

The door opens slowly. Man, oh, man, so gingerly compared to the nurses.

It's my brother's head. Must be genetic. Inherited weak hand muscles from our father.

"Tony."

"Helen?"

"Come on in. You just missed dinner. Thanks for visiting me."

He has a bag in his hand.

"Did you bring the things I wanted?"

"Of course. But what are they for?"

"It's a secret."

He looks at me. I look at him. Is that all the conversation we're going to manage?

Okay, damn the torpedoes.

"Tony, you don't like hospitals, do you? That's why you haven't visited me up to now."

"Yeah, but you know that. I'm sorry, Helen."

"Do you want me to tell you why you don't like it here?"

He chuckles. "As long as it's not bad."

"It is."

His smile disappears. He looks at me anxiously.

Go ahead, Helen, out with it.

"When you were really small, mom tried to kill herself. She wanted to take you with her. She put sleeping pills down your throat and took a bunch herself. When nice little Helen came home, you two were lying unconscious on the kitchen floor and gas was streaming out of the oven. Against mom's will, I saved you guys before the house blew up or you suffocated to death. At the hospital they pumped your stomachs and you guys had to stay here a long time."

He looks at me sadly. I think he already suspected it. His eyelids take on a light-blue hue. Handsome boy. But the muscles around his eyes are weak, too.

He's silent for a long time. Doesn't move an inch.

Then he stands up and slowly makes his way to the door. He opens it and, as he's walking out, he says, "That's why I always have those fucked-up dreams. She's going to get hers."

My family is even farther up shit's creek than it already was.

Is that my fault?

Just because I told Tony the truth?

You can't be silent forever. Lies. For the sake of keeping the peace in the family? Peace through lies. We'll see what happens. With a lot of things I do, I only think about the consequences after I've already done them.

The plan to get my parents back together is now completely out the window.

This is driving me slowly crazy. I'm confined here and everyone else just comes and goes as they please. And I'm sure they're all doing things out there I don't know about. I'd love to be doing things with them, I think for a second. But that's bullshit. Out there our family's even more torn apart, each of us only out for ourselves. At least with my ass bound to this bed my relatives' paths cross mine every once in a while.

There's a knock and someone rushes in. I think for a second my brother has come back to talk more about his near-death at the hands of my mother.

But the person standing there is wearing big, white hospital clogs and white linen pants.

A doctor.

I look up. Dr. Notz.

He better not release me. I'll chain myself to the bed.

"Good evening, Miss Memel. How are you feeling?"

"If you want to know whether I've had a bowel movement, just ask, please. There's no point in beating around the bush."

"Before I discuss your bowel movements, I want to know how you're doing with the pain."

"Fine. The nurse gave me some pills a few hours ago. Supposedly the last ones, if I understood correctly."

"Exactly. You'll have to get used to dealing with it without pills. And all this pressure to have a bowel movement doesn't seem to be working, either. With some patients we have to abandon our usual requirement of their having a bowel movement with no bleeding here at the hospital. The pressure is too much for them and they get too tense."

What? He's just going to release me right now and have me crap at home?

"For that reason I'd like to suggest you go home and see how it goes in peace and quiet. And if it starts to bleed again, just come back. Our opinion is there's no point to keeping you here."

Our opinion? I only see one person. Whatever. Crap. What now? What am I going to do? My wonderful plan irrevocably ruined by Notz.

"Yeah, sounds sensible. Thanks."

"You don't seem to be as pleased as most patients are when they're released. I like to deliver the happy news personally."

I'm sorry to spoil your fun, Notz. But I don't want to go home.

"I'm happy, I'm just not showing it."

And now get out of here, you. I need to think.

"I won't say 'see you later' because I would only see you later if something went wrong at home with the healing process. So, hopefully, see you never."

Yeah, I get it. Ha ha. I'm not a moron. See you never.

"I'll say 'see you later.' Once I'm better I'm going to become a candy striper. They already know. Do something meaningful with my life. I've already applied. I'm sure we'll run into each other in the hall at some point."

"Lovely. Good. See you later."

Out. Door closed.

Think!

My last chance. To leave my family. I'll call my father and tell him I've been released. He should pick me up tonight. I dial his number. He answers. He doesn't apologize for not being there after the emergency operation. As expected. I tell him everything, tell him I've been released, tell him he should come get me.

Come on, Helen, what's the point. Just ask.

"Dad, what do you do?"

"Are you serious? You don't know?"

"Not exactly."

Actually not at all.

"I'm an engineer."

"Aha. And would you like it if I became an engineer?"

"Yes, but you're no good at math."

Dad often hurts my feelings. He never notices, though.

Engineer. I write it out in my head and read it back to myself.

I do the same with my mom. No asking her what she does. I already know that: she's a hypocrite. I leave another message, telling her I'm being released tonight and that she needs to pick me up, preferably with Tony. It's possible she never wants to see me again after what I told Tony. We'll see.

Now, Helen, you have to do what you planned.

I get out of bed. Finally. I won't be getting back in it. I pick up the bag that I'd previously hidden in the trash can.

I stuff all the clothes from the wardrobe into it. I throw in all the stuff from the bathroom. The bag smells a bit like old menstrual blood. But I'm the only one who would notice that.

I put the bag aside and lean over the bed. I snatch the Bible and rip out a few pages.

I go back and forth to the sink to empty the avocado glasses. I dump out all the water.

I stack the glasses inside each other, put them in the bag and wrap the leg of my pajama pants around them.

I leave the toothpicks in my babies and wrap each one in a page of the Bible. Wrapped up, I put them all in the bag.

Now to clean out the nightstand drawer. I'll leave the crucifix here. I look around the room. I sit on the edge of the bed and let my legs dangle like I did as a child.

There's no sign of me left in the room. It's as if I was never here. All that remains are some invisible bacterial clues here and there. Nothing visible.

I ring the buzzer. Hopefully he's still around.

It occurs to me that they may have actually been worried about me. That they may have thought I was holding it in out of fear of the pain. I'm sure that happens all the time in this unit. But for such an extended period of time?

I'd like to have seen whether they would try more aggressive measures at some point. Like an enema. It wouldn't have been a problem for me. Let them come at me with their tubes and liquids. They couldn't wear me down with that.

It takes a while for someone to come. Though I'm hoping it's Robin who comes, not just someone.

I hoist my legs up onto the bed and turn myself around. I want to look out the window. Can't see anything. There's nothing out there. Just me and my room reflected in the glass. I stare at myself for a long time and notice how tired I look. Amazing how pain and painkillers break you down. They could go ahead and add some happy-happy uppers to the mix.

I don't look good. Not that I ever do. But I really look bad now. My hair's greasy and sticking up all over the place. It's the way I imagine I'll look when I have my first nervous breakdown. All the women in my family have nervous breakdowns. Not that they have so much to do. Maybe that's the problem. I'm sure it'll strike me like a bolt of lightning one day. Just sitting there doing nothing one minute, crazy the next.

Maybe before all hell breaks loose here I can wash my hair.

There's a knock at the door. Please, please, nonexistent God, let it be Robin.

The door opens. Some woman is standing there. At least she's dressed the same way as Robin.

"Has Robin already left?"

"His shift is over, yes, but he hasn't left."

"Could you do me a huge favor and ask him to stop by for a second before he takes off?"

"Sure."

"Great, thanks."

Thank you, thank you, thank you. Run. Fast. Little nurse.

There's something brewing with the Memels.

If Robin's gone, that's it for my plan.

What's this about washing your hair, Helen? Normally you don't care how you look in a situation like this, right? Robin thought you were cute when you had a blister hanging out of a lesion in your ass. And that's gone. Clearly an aesthetic improvement.

The greasy hair can function like my stuff-your-face position, to test whether he really likes me.

The hair stays dirty. I comb it down a little with my fingers.

The door opens. Robin.

"What's up? I'm just about to head home. You're lucky —you barely caught me."

You, too. Because if you want to, you can take me home with you.

"You've packed up your things? Have you been released?"

He looks sad. He thinks he has to say good-bye now. I nod.

He's covered his white uniform with a light-and-dark-blue checkered raincoat. Looks good. A timeless classic.

No time to lose.

"Robin, I've lied to all of you. I've already had a bowel movement. By that measure I'm healthy. You know—no bleeding. Well, in the front. But not in the back. You understand what I mean. I just wanted to stay in the hospital as long as possible because I thought I could bring my family together here. We're not even a family anymore, actually, but I was hoping to get my parents together again in this room. But that's crazy. They don't want that. They have new partners whom I ignore so much I don't even know their names. I don't want to go home to my mom. Dad's left. My mom's so unhappy she tried to kill my little brother. I'm eighteen. I can decide for myself where I want to go. Can I come live with you?"

He laughs.

Out of embarrassment? At me? I look at him appalled.

He comes up to me. He stands in front of me and wraps his arms around me. I start to cry. I cry more and more. I sob. He strokes my greasy hair. He's passed the test.

I smile briefly midsob.

"I guess you have to figure out whether it's allowed."

His jacket is tear-repellent.

"Yes."

"Yes you have to find out whether it's allowed, or yes I can come home with you?"

"Come with me."

He picks up my bag and helps me out of bed.

"Can you take my bag to the car and pick me up? I have to clear something up with my family."

"I'd love to. But I don't have a car. Just a bike."

Me on the back with my fucked-up ass. That's the last thing I need. But that's what we'll do.

"Is your place far? I could make it a little ways on a rear rack."

"It's not far. Really. I'll take your bag to the nurses' station and wait for you to ring the buzzer. Then I'll pick you up. I have your bag so there's no turning back."

"You won't have to wait long. Can I get one thing out of the bag?"

I root around inside and find my pen. I need that. And a T-shirt and a pair of socks.

He caresses my face, kisses me, and nods at me a few times. I guess it's supposed to give me courage to deal with my family.

"No turning back," I say to him as he leaves.

The door closes.

I pull my mom's dress and shoes out of the bag Tony brought me.

I stuff the bag into the wardrobe. Don't need it anymore. It would only ruin the picture.

I lay the dress out on the floor with the neck opening facing the wall. I place the shoes below the bottom of the dress at roughly the proper distance.

The T-shirt I fold up so it looks like a piece of children's clothing. I roll the socks a little so they look like kids' socks. I lay these things next to the adult female "body." From the Tupperware container I pull out two square gauze pads and fold them up. I lay them where the figures' heads would be. Their pillows.

The larger figure gets long hair. I pull out one strand after the other from my head and lay them one at a time on the pillow. You can't see them. I keep stepping back to see whether they're noticeable if you're just standing in the room and don't know what you're looking at. At some point I stop pulling them out one at a time. Taking too long. I yank hair out of my scalp in bunches and lay it on the pillow until I think you can make it out well enough. It doesn't hurt as much as I thought it would. Probably because of the painkillers. And now the child's hair. It needs to be short. I can rip every strand I pluck out into three pieces of hair for the child. I lay enough short hair on the child's pillow so it's clearly visible.

Now it's obvious that a woman and a boy are lying there.

With the pen I draw an oven and burners on the wall at the heads of the bodies. With a bit of perspective, as if the stove's receding into the wall.

At the top of the oven door I cut into the wallpaper with the pen. I use my fingernails to claw along the oven door and then pull at the wallpaper, ripping it down from the top to the floor. Now it looks like a real, open oven door.

I step back and take a good look at what my relatives are about to discover.

My good-bye letter. The reason I'm leaving. Silence.

There they are. My mother and my brother. Just the way I found them. They all hoped I'd forget. You can't forget something like that. And through their silence it loomed ever larger for me. Never faded.

I ring the buzzer one last time and wait for my Robin.

The entire time I'm waiting I stare at mom and Tony. I can smell gas.

Robin comes in.

"Get me out of here."

We leave.

I close the door behind me. I press a big puff of air out of my lungs, exhaling loudly.

We walk slowly down the hall.

We don't hold hands.

Suddenly he stops and puts the bag down. He's changed his mind.

No. He steps behind me and ties the gown closed over my bum. He wants to cover me up in public. Good sign. He picks up the bag again and we walk on.

"If I'm living with you, I guess you'll want to sleep with me?"

"Yeah, but I won't do you up the ass for now."

He laughs. I laugh.

"I'll only sleep with you if you can suck a pony's insides out through its asshole."

"Is that even possible—or do you not want to sleep with me?"

"I just always wanted to say that to a guy. Now I have. And I do want to. But not today. I'm too tired."

We walk to the glass door.

I smack the button, the door swings open, I throw back my head and scream.

About the Author:

Charlotte Roche was born in England in 1978 and raised in Germany, where she still resides with her husband and daughter. A longtime presenter on *Viva*, the German equivalent of MTV, she is a well-known and award-winning television personality. *Wetlands* is her first novel.

About the Translator:

Tim Mohr is a staff editor at *Playboy* magazine. His writing has also appeared in other publications, including *The New York Times*. Prior to joining *Playboy*, he spent six years as a club DJ in Berlin. His translation of *Guantanamo*, by Dorothea Dieckmann, won the Three Percent prize for best translation of 2007.

The translator wishes to thank Andrej Huesener for his advice and his careful read of the draft manuscript.

AMERICAN
SOCIAL
MOVEMENTS

THE SEXUAL
REVOLUTION

Mary E. Williams, *Book Editor*

Daniel Leone, *President*
Bonnie Szumski, *Publisher*
Scott Barbour, *Managing Editor*
Stuart B. Miller, *Series Editor*

GREENHAVEN PRESS
SAN DIEGO, CALIFORNIA

THOMSON

GALE

*Detroit • New York • San Diego • San Francisco
Boston • New Haven, Conn. • Waterville, Maine
London • Munich*

495297846

Every effort has been made to trace the owners of copyrighted material. The articles in this volume may have been edited for content, length, and/or reading level. The titles have been changed to enhance the editorial purpose.

Library of Congress Cataloging-in-Publication Data

Williams, Mary E., 1960–
    The sexual revolution / by Mary E. Williams.
        p. cm. — (American social movements series)
    Includes bibliographical references and index.
    ISBN 0-7377-1051-9 (pbk. : alk. paper) —
ISBN 0-7377-1052-7 (hardback : alk. paper)
    1. Sex customs—Juvenile literature. 2. Sexual ethics—Juvenile literature. [1. Sex customs. 2. Sexual ethics.] I. Title. II. Series.

HQ12 .W538 2002

                                                        2001008358

Cover photo: © Hulton/Archive

CONTENTS

Chapter 3 • THE SEXUAL REVOLUTION OF THE LATTER TWENTIETH CENTURY

work contributed to both the feminist and the gay
and lesbian liberation movements.

Chapter 4 • THE LEGACY OF AMERICA'S SEXUAL REVOLUTION

FOREWORD

Historians Gary T. Marx and Douglas McAdam define a social movement as "organized efforts to promote or resist change in society that rely, at least in part, on noninstitutionalized forms of political action." Examining American social movements broadens and vitalizes the study of history by allowing students to observe the efforts of ordinary individuals and groups to oppose the established values of their era, often in unconventional ways. The civil rights movement of the twentieth century, for example, began as an effort to challenge legalized racial segregation and garner social and political rights for African Americans. Several grassroots organizations— groups of ordinary citizens committed to social activism— came together to organize boycotts, sit-ins, voter registration drives, and demonstrations to counteract racial discrimination. Initially, the movement faced massive opposition from white citizens, who had long been accustomed to the social standards that required the separation of the races in almost all areas of life. But the movement's consistent use of an innovative form of protest—nonviolent direct action—eventually aroused the public conscience, which in turn paved the way for major legislative victories such as the Civil Rights Act of 1964 and the Voting Rights Act of 1965. Examining the civil rights movement reveals how ordinary people can use nonstandard political strategies to change society.

Investigating the style, tactics, personalities, and ideologies of American social movements also encourages students to learn about aspects of history and culture that may receive scant attention in textbooks. As scholar Eric Foner notes, American history "has been constructed not only in congressional debates and political treatises, but also on plantations and picket lines, in parlors and bedrooms. Frederick Douglass, Eugene V. Debs, and Margaret Sanger . . . are its architects as well as Thomas Jefferson and Abraham Lincoln." While not all

American social movements garner popular support or lead to epoch-changing legislation, they each offer their own unique insight into a young democracy's political dialogue.

Each book in Greenhaven's American Social Movements series allows readers to follow the general progression of a particular social movement—examining its historical roots and beginnings in earlier chapters and relatively recent and contemporary information (or even the movement's demise) in later chapters. With the incorporation of both primary and secondary sources, as well as writings by both supporters and critics of the movement, each anthology provides an engaging panoramic view of its subject. Selections include a variety of readings, such as book excerpts, newspaper articles, speeches, manifestos, literary essays, interviews, and personal narratives. The editors of each volume aim to include the voices of movement leaders and participants as well as the opinions of historians, social analysts, and individuals who have been affected by the movement. This comprehensive approach gives students the opportunity to view these movements both as participants have experienced them and as historians and critics have interpreted them.

Every volume in the American Social Movements series includes an introductory essay that presents a broad historical overview of the movement in question. The annotated table of contents and comprehensive index help readers quickly locate material of interest. Each selection is preceded by an introductory paragraph that summarizes the article's content and provides historical context when necessary. Several other research aids are also present, including brief excerpts of supplementary material, a chronology of major events pertaining to the movement, and an accessible bibliography.

The Greenhaven Press American Social Movements series offers readers an informative introduction to some of the most fascinating groups and ideas in American history. The contents of each anthology provide a valuable resource for general readers as well as for enthusiasts of American political science, history, and culture.

The Sexual Revolution: An Overview

Many enthusiasts of American culture associate the sexual revolution with the liberalization of sexual values that occurred after the introduction of the birth control pill in 1960. As its defenders point out, the birth control pill increased female access to reliable contraception and thus afforded women greater control over their sexual and reproductive lives. This expansion of women's options regarding sex coincided with a youthful countercultural movement that questioned traditional social standards and explored political protest, alternative lifestyles, and freer sexual behavior. Sexuality and gender, moreover, became focal points around which new social movements—including the women's liberation movement and the gay and lesbian liberation movement—were organized. By the 1970s, an increased acceptance of nonmarital sex, cohabitation, sexual experimentation, and abortion was often cited as the legacy of the 1960s sexual revolution.

The trend toward more liberal sexual values, however, actually began early in the twentieth century and has precursors in nineteenth-century reform movements and communities that challenged prevailing sexual standards.

HARBINGERS OF THE SEXUAL REVOLUTION

During the nineteenth century, what would later be known as a "nuclear family" structure emerged in American cities, with husbands working in factories and businesses to earn income and women remaining at home to raise children and attend to household duties. Most middle-class families attempted to adhere to the so-called Victorian sexual ideals of the day. Named after Queen Victoria, who ruled England from 1837 to 1901, Victorian values emphasized the importance of male strength, female purity, and the restraint of sexual desires. Women and men were seen as serving distinctly different roles: Men were expected to be aggressive, competitive, and suited for work in the public world, while women were expected to be gentle, chaste homemakers who provided stable moral guidance for their families. Sexual passion was seen as a potentially destabilizing force that needed to be controlled. As historian Mary E. Odem explains,

> A new ideology of sexual restraint [became] prevalent among middle-class Americans. . . . Disseminated by physicians, ministers, and health reformers in medical texts and advice literature, this ideology promoted male continence and female purity. Physicians and reformers urged men to avoid all sexual stimulation before marriage and to practice sexual control within marriage. They warned that excessive sexual indulgence destroyed a man's physical and mental powers and undermined his ability to rule his family and compete successfully in the business world. Some advice manuals recommended that married couples limit coitus to once a month and then only for the purposes of procreation.

Although so-called sexual impropriety—nonprocreative sex and nonmarital sex—was publicly condemned, it was quietly tolerated among men, who were assumed to have relatively strong sex drives. Women, however, were considered to be pure, virtuous, and sexually passionless, and thus were held to a different moral standard than men. Because of this presumption, most middle-class Americans saw women as the moral guardians of the home, charged with curbing the lustful natures of male family members. Any woman who had sex outside of marriage was deemed "fallen" or permanently "ruined."

This sexual double standard was reflected in nineteenth-century attitudes toward prostitution. While prostitutes were criticized for their lack of respectability and for their immorality, their customers rarely received such censure. In fact, prostitution was sometimes seen as a "necessary evil"—a marital safety valve that allowed men to satisfy their supposedly stronger desires while sparing their wives from unwanted sex. After the Civil War, police and medical authorities supported attempts to legalize and regulate prostitution as a means to control the spread of venereal disease. In the 1870s, a coalition of women's rights activists, temperance reformers, former abolitionists, and Protestant clergy—a "social purity" movement—arose to oppose this effort to license prostitutes. They contended that prostitution was a vice for both the prostitute and the customer, and that women *and* men should be held to a single standard of sexual morality. By the late 1880s, these reformers succeeded in defeating all nineteenth-century attempts to establish state-regulated prostitution.

Many purity reformers, particularly the suffragists, also advocated the notion of "voluntary motherhood"—the right of wives to abstain from sexual intercourse to avoid unwanted pregnancies and assert some control over family size. These reformers' support of voluntary motherhood and their opposition to the double standard were among the first of the broad-based endeavors to place women on equal footing with men.

UTOPIANISTS AND FREE LOVERS

A few smaller and more radical nineteenth-century groups also challenged Victorian sexual norms. Several communitarians, freethinkers (those opposing religious authority), and anarchists founded collectives and utopian colonies that rejected the traditional concept of marriage. In 1848, John Humphrey Noyes founded the Oneida Community in New York, a utopian society in which all members were considered to be married to each other. Oneidans were encouraged to limit pregnancies by practicing nonprocreative sex. Eschewing contraceptives, Noyes's followers learned the method of *coitus reservatus*, in which men had intercourse without ejaculation. In Noyes's view, this practice allowed a couple "the most essential freedom of love, [while] at the same time [avoiding] undesired procreation and all the other evils incident to male incontinence." Unlike those who upheld Victorian values, Oneidans believed that female sexual pleasure was natural and healthy.

In the 1850s, two short-lived "free love" communities emerged in Long Island, New York, and Cleveland, Ohio. During the nineteenth and early twentieth centuries, the term free love referred not to promiscuous or multiple-partner sex but to the notion that a man and a woman are entitled to have an intimate love relationship without being married. After the Civil War, the free love movement reached a wider audience as feminist reformer Victoria Woodhull gave public lectures condemning marriage as a barbaric institution that forced women to submit to men and stifled the possibility of genuine love between the sexes. Only love that was freely chosen and rooted in mutual "passional attraction," and not in a license from church or state, would lead to sexual equality and social harmony, Woodhull argued. Other free love advocates, such as Ezra Heywood and Moses Harmon, extolled the benefits of sexual passion and sex education; some proponents also endorsed contraception and occasional abortion.

Although the concept of free love gained some acceptance among cultured New England elites, the majority of the American public shunned it as a dangerous idea that threatened the traditional family and basic moral values. Moreover, because some free love advocates were anarchists, social analysts and commentators associated free love with violent political revolt. In the early 1870s, moral crusader Anthony Comstock founded the New York Society for the Suppression of Vice with the aim of suppressing "obscene and subversive" art and reading material. With financial support from wealthy businessmen, Comstock lobbied state and federal legislatures to strengthen anti-obscenity laws. In 1873, Congress passed the Comstock Law, which banned the mailing of "indecent and lascivious" materials, including books and pamphlets containing information about contraception and abortion. This federal law enabled Comstock to arrest and imprison many free love advocates, who often published speeches, journals, and tracts containing ideas about sexuality that were considered obscene at the time.

The utopianists' and free lovers' promotion of sexual pleasure, sex education, birth control, and nonmarital sexual partnership was considered radical in the nineteenth century. In
the twentieth century, however, much of the middle class
would eventually embrace these ideas—particularly the notion of separating sexual activity from reproduction through
contraception.

TWENTIETH-CENTURY CHALLENGES TO VICTORIAN SEXUAL STANDARDS

At the turn of the twentieth century, the pace of American
industrialization and technological innovation accelerated
rapidly. The growth of the manufacturing and retail sectors of
the economy created a great demand for labor in the cities.
Rural Americans moved to urban areas to take advantage of
the new opportunities, as did millions of immigrants arriving
from Europe. A plethora of mass-produced goods flooded the
market, fostering a shift in middle-class values. As Odem explains, "The production of a wide array of . . . goods and the
increased standard of living of many Americans led to a major reorientation of values within middle-class culture. A new
ethic of consumption and self-gratification replaced the Victorian emphasis on thrift, sobriety, and self-denial."

A change in values was also reflected in the lives of young
people, especially young women. Many middle-class daughters left home to attend college or pursue professional careers,
postponing or abandoning marriage and domestic life, and a
growing number of working-class women sought jobs in factories, stores, and offices. This movement into the urban workforce afforded women some economic stability and a new
sense of independence. In the meantime, the growth of commercialized recreation and leisure activities in the cities gave
young people more freedom from the community constraints
that had previously encouraged sexual modesty. Instead of the
family- or church-based diversions of the past, unescorted
youths frequented amusement parks, movie theaters, and dance
halls. In these new social spaces, away from parental supervi-

sion, young men and women could explore romantic and sexual possibilities. Statistics reveal an increasing incidence of youthful sexual experimentation: Premarital pregnancies rose from a 10 percent rate of occurrence in the mid–nineteenth century to 23 percent in the years between 1880 and 1910.

By the second decade of the twentieth century, more Americans were beginning to evaluate the meaning of sexuality beyond its procreative function. In 1909, psychoanalyst Sigmund Freud lectured at Clark University in Worcester, Massachusetts, introducing an American audience to the notion that sexuality is a central part of human identity and development. Although critics argued that Freud's emphasis on the harmful effects of sexual repression would encourage immoral behavior, others believed that a reexamination of sexual attitudes would benefit marriage. Buttressed by the writings of Freud, English physician Havelock Ellis, and other experts, a growing number of Americans rejected the Victorian ideal of sexual restraint, believing that it undermined marriage by causing frustration and adulterous affairs. They instead promoted the modern "companionate marriage" that recognized the importance of sexual pleasure for husbands and wives. Some also advocated contraception for married couples to enhance sexual activity while avoiding unwanted pregnancy.

In the early 1910s, espousing artificial means of birth control remained controversial. Although contraceptive information was available in the United States, it was generally restricted to obscure medical texts, and the Comstock Law still forbade distributing such information through the mail. In 1914, socialist and public-health nurse Margaret Sanger was arrested for publishing *The Woman Rebel*, a newsletter that contained articles on sexuality and birth control. During her years working as a nurse in poor New York neighborhoods, Sanger had been horrified by the misery of impoverished women who gave birth to numerous children, sometimes at great risk to their own health. These women often asked her for the secret to preventing pregnancy, but at the time Sanger knew of no consistently reliable methods. Determined to find a safe and effective contraceptive—and fleeing her criminal trial—Sanger traveled to Europe, where she learned about diaphragms and spermicides. After the charges against her were dropped in 1916, Sanger opened America's first birth control clinic in Brooklyn, New York.

Over the next few years, Sanger and other activists gained national support as they wrote and lectured widely on the issue of birth control. Her sympathizers included women's rights advocates and radical anarchists such as Emma Goldman, who gave provocative speeches praising contraception and criticizing marriage and sexual chastity. By the 1920s, however, Sanger and her followers distanced themselves somewhat from feminism and political radicalism and sought backing from the relatively conservative medical profession. With the support of physicians, birth control came to be seen as an important component of public health, family planning, and population control. In 1921, Sanger founded what would later be known as the Planned Parenthood Foundation of America. Within a decade after its founding, more than three hundred clinics throughout the United States were providing contraceptive information and devices to women.

THE ROARING TWENTIES

The decade of the 1920s is sometimes referred to as America's first sexual revolution. Young men, many of whom had experienced the more relaxed sexual attitudes of Europe during military service in World War I, encountered bolder, more independent-minded American women who wore shorter skirts, sharper hairstyles, and brighter makeup. Economic affluence gave the middle class more leisure time and more money to spend on consumer goods, luxury items, and entertainment. With the advent of the automobile, youths could experience even more freedom in their romantic encounters as they went out on "dates" to movies, parties, and cabarets. Unsupervised dating allowed an increase in "necking" and "petting"—the terms used to describe a range of erotic activity short of intercourse, from kissing to physical fondling. A growing number of people also engaged in premarital sex.

Many social analysts maintain that the popular culture of the 1920s reflected and influenced American tastes and behavior. Literature, advertisements, songs, and movies were saturated with sexual imagery. Vamped-up sex idols starred in popular films, sexual advice columns appeared in newspapers, and advertisers used sex to sell myriad goods and services. Although the sale of alcohol was outlawed in 1919, many cities were peppered with speakeasies and nightclubs selling bootleg liquor, where one might encounter stylish "flapper girls" dancing wildly to jazz music. "By comparison with the past," write cultural historians John D'Emilio and Estelle Freedman in their book *Intimate Matters*, "American society in the 1920s seemed to embrace the sexual. Sex was something to be discussed and displayed, whether through popularizations of Freud, the true-confession magazines, or the romantic imagery of Hollywood films. As one popular magazine described it, . . . 'sex o'clock' had struck in America."

Despite the sexual liberalism of the era, mainstream society still adhered to a version of the old double standard. Husbands and wives were expected to conform to conventional gender roles: Men had to be vigorous, strong breadwinners, and women were to be nurturing and passive. Women were also reminded to "keep the thrill in their marriage" by carefully maintaining an attractive feminine appearance. Although women were expected to be sexually alluring, female promiscuity was still largely frowned upon; male sexual licentiousness, however, was covertly allowed.

The sexual exuberance of the 1920s faded after the stock market crash of 1929, largely because the consumerism and commercialized entertainment that invited sexual adventure temporarily dwindled. Birth control information and devices, however, became even more widely available in 1936 after a federal appeals court overturned the anticontraception stipulations of the Comstock Law. Condoms were obtainable in grocery stores, gas stations, and restaurants, and sexual activity was no longer presumed to be purely reproductive.

The 1940s and 1950s

By the 1940s, many middle-class Americans had embraced fairly liberal attitudes toward heterosexual activity. Sexual satisfaction was considered an important component of successful marriage and individual happiness. There was also a greater tolerance for youthful sexual experimentation, which was frequently seen as a phase that preceded maturity and married life.

As had happened during World War I, the Second World War contributed to the liberalization of sexual values. American servicemen engaged in nonmarital sex overseas. Pictures of scantily clad "pinup" girls, which were thought to boost military morale, proliferated in army barracks and navy ships. Concerns about the spread of venereal disease in the armed forces resulted in heightened educational and preventative efforts and more straightforward discussions about sex. Although promiscuity was discouraged, sexual expression was perceived as an innate need, as one medical official's statement reveals: "We cannot stifle the instincts of man, we cannot legislate his appetite. We can only educate him to caution, watchfulness, and the perpetual hazards of promiscuous intercourse and furnish him with adequate preventative measures."

Toward the end of World War II, pharmaceutical companies were able to produce large quantities of medicinal penicillin, which proved to be effective against syphilis and gonorrhea. While many saw this "VD magic bullet" as a cause for celebration, others feared that it would encourage promiscuity, and postwar arguments for a more conservative sexual morality regained strength.

Penicillin was not the only reason that the latter part of the 1940s and much of the 1950s were characterized by a stricter condemnation of sex outside of marriage. Many analysts connect the renewed conservatism to the fear of communism during the cold war era. As historian Margo Horn points out, "a range of high-level officials and influential thinkers linked communism with sexual depravity. . . . According to this logic, sexual excess or degeneracy made individuals easy prey for

Communist tactics. It was feared that Communist agents would use evidence of homosexuality or extramarital affairs to blackmail government officials into handing over top-secret information." Gays and lesbians, who had encountered a degree of tolerance in the early 1940s, faced severe harassment and discrimination during the early years of the cold war. Heterosexuality, premarital abstinence, and marital fidelity came to be seen as crucial to national security.

The sexual behavior of Americans, however, apparently conflicted with mainstream society's professed sexual values. Such was the conclusion drawn by behavioral researcher Alfred Kinsey in his landmark 1948 study, *Sexual Behavior in the Human Male,* a book that stayed on the *New York Times* bestseller list for twenty-seven weeks. In 1953, Kinsey published *Sexual Behavior in the Human Female*, and the two books became known as the Kinsey Report. According to Kinsey, 90 percent of the men and 50 percent of the women surveyed had engaged in premarital sex, and half of the men and a quarter of the women had had extramarital relations. Moreover, 50 percent of the men acknowledged feelings of sexual desire for other men, and a third admitted to engaging in homosexual activity as adults. Kinsey's data and research techniques were challenged by some critics later in the twentieth century. But many among Kinsey's 1950s audience appreciated the seemingly objective, scientific approach to the study of sexuality. As an editor of *Look* magazine wrote, "For the first time, data on human sex behavior is entirely separated from questions of philosophy, moral values, and social customs."

THE SEXUAL REVOLUTION OF THE 1960S

Despite Kinsey's revelations about sexual behavior in the United States, most Americans in the 1950s did not openly question the established sexual norms that held that sexual activity should be heterosexual and largely reserved for marriage. It was not until the 1960s that several social trends converged in a way that encouraged a significant segment of the population to boldly challenge—and change—mainstream sexual values.

In 1960, after a decade of investigations and experimental efforts by a group of Planned Parenthood–supported scientists, a contraceptive pill was approved for use in the United States. Inexpensive, convenient, and highly reliable, "the pill" offered American women a previously unseen measure of control over their own fertility. Women could now enjoy sexual intercourse with more spontaneity and without risk of pregnancy. Because of its role in separating the pleasurable aspects of sex from reproduction, the birth control pill is often seen as the catalyst of the sexual revolution.

This view of the contraceptive pill as inciting the sexual revolution is somewhat oversimplified, however. In and of itself, access to reliable birth control was not an inevitable affront to marriage-oriented sexuality or traditional gender roles. Other social factors played an even greater role in the confrontation against prevailing sexual norms. According to historians D'Emilio and Freedman, one contributing factor was the economic prosperity and consumerism that predominated in the postwar years of the 1950s. They maintain that "the first major challenge to [mainstream sexual values] came . . . from entrepreneurs who extended the logic of consumer capitalism to the realm of sex." In 1953, entrepreneur Hugh Hefner published the first issue of *Playboy*, a popular upscale magazine featuring glossy photos of nude women, male sexual fantasies, and articles on culture and current events. Hefner strongly condemned marriage and rejected societal constraints on sexual gratification, encouraging *Playboy* readers to "enjoy the pleasures the female has to offer without becoming emotionally involved." The naked women in his magazine were, in his words, "a symbol of disobedience, a triumph of sexuality, an end of Puritanism." The pursuit of unlimited sexual pleasure was depicted as the entitlement of successful, prosperous men.

Similarly, Helen Gurley Brown's 1962 best-seller, *Sex and the Single Girl*, rejected marriage and encouraged women to sexually use men, who she claimed were "cheaper emotionally and a lot more fun by the dozen." She advised single women to pursue liaisons with married men, arguing that "an affair between a single woman and her lover can be unadulterated, cliff-hanging sex." Hefner, Brown, and other such promoters of sexual carousing tapped in to the desires of a certain segment of rebellious young Americans who were simultaneously influenced by a consumerist ethic. An urban "singles culture" soon emerged, characterized by weekend parties, singles bars, dating services, and youth-oriented apartment complexes.

While some middle-class youths adhered to a consumerist ethic in their rebellion against traditional sexual standards, others challenged sexual norms as they rejected the materialism and political complacency of the "establishment," or mainstream culture. Inspired by the black civil rights struggle of the early 1960s, some middle-class college students began engaging in protests to demand free speech on campuses and to oppose the war in Vietnam. With each passing year, more and more young people joined a burgeoning cultural and political critique of American society. This countercultural protest was multifaceted, denouncing the hypocrisy of a value system that seemingly accepted racial inequality in a democracy, poverty in a land of prosperity, consumerism among dwindling resources, and sophisticated warfare against peasant nations. For many disaffected youth, engaging in nonmarital sexual activity was also part of the generalized rejection of establishment values. "Make love, not war" became the countercultural rallying cry.

The most noticeable participants in the countercultural movement were the hippies, who openly mocked their own middle-class roots by denouncing materialism, growing their hair long, taking hallucinogenic drugs, and abandoning sexual restraint. Although in the nineteenth century the term free love had referred to a committed sexual partnership rooted in love rather than marriage, hippies tended to define free love as open sexual unions or as sex with multiple partners. In February 1967, *Newsweek* reported that

> For the hippies, sex is not a matter of great debate, because as far as they are concerned the sexual revolution is accomplished. There are no hippies who believe in chastity, or

look askance at marital infidelity, or even see marriage itself as a virtue. Physical love is a delight—to be chewed upon as often and as freely as a handful of sesame seeds.

Some hippies expressed their rejection of the traditional nuclear family by forming communes and loose extended families that raised children in common—a development that brought them strong condemnation from mainstream America. Hippies were denounced as moral degenerates, political subversives, and sexual anarchists.

In spite of this open criticism of aspects of the counterculture, American attitudes toward sexuality were undergoing a noticeable change by the end of the 1960s. On the one hand, upholders of the consumerist ethic were adopting a "sex sells" strategy—as had occurred in the 1920s—and fashion, movies, magazines, advertising, and other facets of popular culture became infused with sexual innuendo and imagery. On the other hand, the sexual rebelliousness of the counterculture began to reach beyond the confines of campus protest groups and hippie enclaves, as more middle-class Americans abandoned the post–World War II ideal of stable, marriage-centered sexual relationships. As a November 1967 *Newsweek* editorial noted, "The old taboos are dead or dying. A new, more permissive society is taking shape."

Other Challenges to the Sexual Status Quo

The consumerists and counterculturalists of the 1960s were not the only groups challenging traditional sexual norms. In 1963, writer and journalist Betty Friedan published *The Feminine Mystique*, a book that questioned the widespread assumption that women find fulfillment mainly through becoming housewives and mothers. Friedan wrote of "a problem that has no name"—the painful malaise experienced by middle-class women who were suppressing their intelligence and creative potential in order to conform to traditional gender roles. Friedan's thoughts struck a nerve among many American

women who were frustrated by their lack of life choices, professional opportunities, and political power. In 1966, Friedan
and others founded the National Organization for Women
(NOW), a group whose purpose was to confront "the conditions that now prevent women from enjoying the equality of
opportunity and freedom of choice which is their right as individual Americans, and as human beings." NOW was instrumental in initiating a feminist movement that would take up
many of the challenges that had not been addressed by the
women's rights movement of the early twentieth century.

While NOW's appeal was mainly to middle-class, suburban
housewives, many younger women who were involved with
the civil rights struggle, the countercultural movement, and
other left-wing causes took up a more outspoken feminist activism with zeal. They questioned the "gender caste system"
of male-led political movements that often exploited female
labor or devalued women's contributions. They also confronted the presumptions of male activists who expected revolutionary women to be sexually available. Although the
counterculture was rejecting traditional sexual values and the
pill had made it easier for women to have sex whenever they
pleased, feminists decried the fact that men often saw them as
sex objects and that sex was yet another means by which men
exploited women. Radical feminists criticized the sexual objectification of women during one of their first political actions, the 1968 Miss America protest, by crowning a sheep as
pageant queen and throwing bras, girdles, high heels, and false
eyelashes into a "freedom trashcan." Women's liberationists, as
these younger feminists called themselves, argued that "the
personal is political," protesting the gender inequities that existed in heterosexual relationships, marriages, and family life.

One battle taken up by both NOW activists and women's
liberationists was the fight for reproductive freedom. Although
the pill had given women greater control over their sexual and
reproductive lives, access to legal abortion remained limited in
the late 1960s. Arguing that abortion was a woman's right,
feminists sponsored teach-ins, petition drives, and acts of civil

disobedience as they worked to repeal state restrictions on abortion. The 1973 Supreme Court decision in *Roe v. Wade*, which legalized abortion in all states, was celebrated as a major legislative victory.

Another social movement that evolved as part of the sexual revolution was the gay and lesbian liberation movement. During the cold war, when homosexuality was seen as a threat to national security and to the traditional family, gays and lesbians faced severe repression, including criminal prosecution, if their sexual orientation became public knowledge. Although this pervasive discrimination ruined many lives, it also fostered a kind of community consciousness among homosexuals. In the 1950s, two small organizations—the Mattachine Society and the Daughters of Bilitis—initiated a "homophile movement" that quietly worked for the integration of homosexuals into mainstream society.

The style and the pacing of gay politics changed radically after the Stonewall riot of 1969, an incident in which homosexuals battled against a police raid of a gay bar in Greenwich Village. The event became known as the "shot heard around the homosexual world" because it was the first time that gays and lesbians were seen openly resisting harassment by police. An energetic gay liberation movement, influenced by the ideas and strategies of the feminist and black power movements, emerged in the wake of the riot. Denouncing the notion of homosexuality as depravity or illness, gay activists proclaimed that same-sex desire was a normal variation of human sexuality that had been suppressed by mainstream heterosexual values. Throughout the 1970s, gay liberationists encouraged millions of American homosexuals to "come out"—to publicly reveal and take pride in their gay identity. In 1974, the American Psychological Association removed homosexuality from its list of mental disorders. By the end of the 1970s, several major cities had passed ordinances forbidding discrimination on the basis of sexual orientation. Despite the onslaught of AIDS, a new disease that killed large numbers of gay men, and defying resistance from powerful political opponents, gay and lesbian organizations proliferated in urban areas during the 1980s and 1990s.

THE LEGACY OF THE SEXUAL REVOLUTION

Contemporary social observers who applaud the sexual revolution are grateful for the increase in opportunities and rights for women, the broader recognition of a diversity of family forms, greater tolerance of sexual minorities, improved sex education, and widespread acceptance of nonprocreative sexual activity. Others, however, maintain that the sexual revolution resulted in higher rates of teen pregnancy, sexually transmitted disease, abortion, marital infidelity, and divorce. Conservatives lament the apparent decrease in traditional romantic courtships and lifelong marriages, contending that a decline in stable families and committed love relationships has led to pervasive loneliness and unhappiness. Some advocate a return to traditional values that allow sexual activity only within the confines of marriage. Moreover, progressive critics of the sexual revolution often denounce the exploitation of sexuality seen in the advertising and entertainment industries. As Sarah van Gelder, executive director of the Positive Futures Network, writes, "The mysteries of sexual ecstasy are trivialized—all is laid out in magazines and videos. There is little discussion of the effects of inundating the culture with superficial images of sexuality and associating those images with consumerism, violence, and exploitation rather than love and creativity."

Today, the forces of both sexual liberation and restraint continue to mold sexual ideals, and the results of the so-called sexual revolution still elicit controversy and debate. Sexuality and gender will likely be the site of various struggles and conflicts in the future. Perhaps the best way for Americans to prepare themselves for these skirmishes is to become better educated about sexuality so that they can put its importance into reasonable perspective.

CHAPTER 1

PRECURSORS TO A REVOLUTION

AMERICAN
SOCIAL
MOVEMENTS

Sex Wars of the Nineteenth Century

JOHN D'EMILIO AND ESTELLE B. FREEDMAN

In the following selection, John D'Emilio and Estelle B. Freedman discuss the sexual politics of nineteenth-century America. Physicians of that era, who generally believed that middle-class women should maintain their traditional roles as homemakers and mothers, clashed with women's rights activists—particularly after the medical profession recommended the legalization of prostitution as a means to protect public health. A "social purity" movement then arose and effectively fought off legalized prostitution. By the end of the nineteenth century, purity activists—many of them women who were entering the paid workforce—were demanding that women be given more control over marital sexuality and reproduction. Advocates of "free love" also promoted sexual equality in relationships, but they actually opposed marriage itself, claiming that men and women should have the right to choose sexual partners based on mutual love and without the need for licensing from church or state. Although many free-love activists were arrested and imprisoned on obscenity charges, their initially radical-seeming ideas on romance, sex education, and birth control became acceptable in the twentieth century. D'Emilio is a professor of gender and women's studies and of history at the University of Illinois in Chicago. Freedman is a history professor at Stanford University.

I n the process of expanding their authority, some nineteenth-century doctors seemed to be waging a covert battle against women. New theories of reproductive science reinforced the concept of the separate sexual spheres by exaggerating the centrality of the womb to women's health. Particularly in the new

Excerpted from *Intimate Matters: A History of Sexuality in America*, 2nd ed., by John D'Emilio and Estelle B. Freedman (Chicago, IL: University of Chicago Press, 1997). Copyright © 1997 by The University of Chicago Press. Reprinted with permission.

specialization of gynecology, women were seen as merely reproductive beings, ideally confined to the home and to lives of repeated childbearing. As Dr. Horatio Storer wrote in 1871, woman was "what she is in health, in character, in her charms, alike of body, mind and soul because of her womb alone." Harvard physician E.H. Clarke argued in his 1873 book *Sex in Education* that women should not participate in higher education. Alarmed at the declining birth rates among educated, white middle-class women, Clarke reasoned that the energy women expended in studying depleted their reproductive capacities. Some nineteenth-century physicians, such as J. Marion Sims and Robert Battey, employed radical gynecological surgery, including female castration, to "correct" masturbation or other expressions of sexual passion. Similarly, women diagnosed as neurasthenic or insane sometimes had their ovaries removed on the grounds that the reproductive organs determined a woman's overall physical and mental health.

In addition to their efforts through medical advice and private practice, doctors joined political movements to maintain the traditional reproductive framework of marital sexuality. Regular physicians opposed the irregulars who profited from the trade in contraception and abortion. One doctor wrote in outrage in 1867, claiming that married women received circulars "offering information and instrumentalities, and all needed facilities by which the laws of heaven with regard to the increase of the human family may be thwarted." Obstetricians such as Horatio Storer and Augustus Gardner joined Anthony Comstock's campaign to limit access to contraception, which culminated in the passage of the Comstock Act in 1873. [This act banned the sending of "indecent" material by mail, including information on contraception and abortion.]

OPPOSITION TO ABORTION

The medical response to abortion further suggests that doctors viewed women primarily as mothers. In the early nineteenth century, neither doctors, women, nor judges had necessarily condemned abortion as long as it was performed before "quickening," when the mother felt the fetus move within her at about three months. Antebellum laws retained the quickening doctrine and attempted to protect women from unwanted abortion, rather than to prosecute them. After 1860, in response to increasing alarm about the commercialization of abortion and its growing use by married women, doctors began to organize to outlaw abortion and place it under the strict regulation of the medical profession. Horatio Storer led a crusade to punish not only those who performed the operation but also the women who sought them. Unwilling mothers, Storer claimed, who selfishly sought "the pleasures of a summer's trips and amusements," used abortion to evade their maternal duties. Storer mobilized the fledgling American Medical Association, while newspapers such as the New York *Times* popularized his cause and began to ban ads for abortionists and abortifacients. As a result of these efforts, between 1860 and 1890, forty states and territories enacted anti-abortion statutes, many of which rejected the quickening doctrine, placed limitations on advertisements, and helped transfer legal authority for abortion from women to doctors.

Members of the medical profession did not necessarily conspire to limit women to motherhood. Doctors acted independently, but upon widely shared values, when they upheld the legitimacy of the separate spheres. Further, not all doctors supported these efforts, while some women did, including those who opposed abortion and higher education. Some women sought radical gynecological surgery for themselves, whether because they believed the medical opinions or because the removal of womb or ovaries relieved them of the risk of pregnancy. Nonetheless, taken together, these medical constraints suggests that doctors may have gained authority at the expense of women. Just when middle-class women had begun to leave the home, whether as reformers or college students, doctors seemed eager to displace women from the public sphere and reaffirm female domestic and maternal roles.

That many doctors supported not only the separate spheres but also the double standard further indicates a conflict between the interests of women and doctors. Despite their efforts to contain middle-class women within the home and maintain the primacy of reproductive sexuality, the medical profession largely accepted prostitution as a necessary evil. Unlike female reformers of the antebellum decades, doctors at midcentury viewed prostitution not as a moral issue but as a public health problem. In the name of preventing venereal disease, they recommended a system of legalized, or regulated, prostitution that would be overseen by medical authorities. . . .

When doctors recommended that Americans adopt regulated prostitution, they sparked a counteroffensive much larger than their own initial efforts toward regulation. The suggestion that the state should officially recognize prostitution as a necessary evil struck a sensitive chord among clergymen, former abolitionists, and women's rights activists. Together they organized formidable resistance to legalized prostitution. In Missouri, clergy and women succeeded in overturning the St. Louis experiment [in regulated prostitution] in 1874. Susan B. Anthony convened women's meetings to explain the implications for women's rights of the proposed New York legislation to regulate prostitution. Opponents of regulation helped defeat each of the New York state bills. Similarly, Chicago women and clergymen formed a social purity society in 1870 to defeat regulated prostitution. The following year women's club members in Washington, D.C., called mass meetings and formed a committee for preventing the legalization of prostitution. In the West, women petitioned city councils and state legislatures to close down brothels and enforce vagrancy laws against prostitutes. The San Francisco Women's Suffrage Club opposed laws to legalize prostitution on the grounds that the laws provided an ineffective means of controlling venereal disease. Only a single standard of purity, they argued, could insure public health. By 1886, local social purity coalitions had effectively staved off state-regulated prostitution in America.

The battle over regulated prostitution inaugurated a sexual reform movement akin to antebellum moral reform but with more ambitious goals and wider impact. The social purity movement of the late nineteenth century incorporated many of the ideas of moral reform, especially the demand for a single sexual standard. From its local grass-roots origins within the anti-regulation efforts of the 1870s, social purity grew into a national, institutional, and more conservative mold by the 1890s. In the process, it helped transform American attitudes toward sexuality by making women's belief in a single sexual standard the dominant middle-class view. Like earlier moral reformers, and like conservative vice crusaders, social purity advocates resisted the movement of sexuality outside of the private sphere. At the same time, they launched a critique of marital sexuality and attempted to break through the conspiracy of silence regarding the public discussion of sex. Thus social purity unintentionally contributed to the movement of sexuality beyond the family. . . .

Earlier in the century, the ideal of the pure woman in her domestic sphere had helped stabilize the rapidly changing society. By the late nineteenth century, however, more and more women left the domestic sphere, entering the paid work force or attending college before marriage. Once married, the declining birth rates revealed, maternity was less central to women's lives. Some doctors tried to return women to the domestic sphere, but middle-class women organized to expand their maternal authority beyond the home, through movements for social purity and temperance. In order to protect the home and enforce their own vision of moral order, they became active in politics. Their attack on legalized prostitution eventually raised criticisms of marital sexuality, as well. Like free lovers [those advocating the right to have sexual relationships outside of marriage] and utopians, social purity activists grappled with the new meanings of marital sexuality, especially the relationship of sexuality and reproduction. . . .

Although the debate over prostitution inspired the social purity movement, women went on to attack all forms of male sexual privilege. The most radical theorists, such as suffrage leaders Susan B. Anthony and Elizabeth Cady Stanton, drew parallels between prostitution and marriage. In both institutions, women engaged in sexual relations in return for economic support. Marriage and divorce laws trapped women in unhappy relationships, they wrote, and made it impossible for them to escape from drunken or sexually abusive husbands. As remedies, Stanton called for more liberal divorce laws, while Anthony repeated her analysis that women had to become self-supporting in order to prevent unhappy marriages. In the meantime she recommended that women decline offers of marriage from "impure" men and refuse "to continue in the marital relation" if their husbands visited prostitutes or took mistresses. . . .

VOLUNTARY MOTHERHOOD

Short of criticizing marriage as an institution, suffragists and social purity workers insisted that women should have more control over marital sexuality. Their key demand was "voluntary motherhood," or the right to say no to sex unless a woman wanted to become pregnant. Despite the increased use of contraception to limit family size, suffragists preferred voluntary motherhood to either contraception or abortion. They associated contraception with men's privilege to have sex outside of marriage, while abortion, they believed, unjustly burdened women with the costs of unwanted pregnancy. Influenced by Darwinian ideas about the improvement of the species, many believed that children who were conceived during voluntary intercourse would be healthier and more intelligent, while those conceived during unwanted intercourse might become criminals, idiots, or paupers. As suffragist Harriet Stanton Blatch explained in 1891, the "welcome" child— one whose mother chose to perform the labor necessary to proper upbringing—advanced the evolution of the race.

Despite their rejection of "artificial" contraception and their belief that force, not choice, led women into prostitution, social purity workers did not necessarily deny female sexual pleasure. In their marital advice books, social purity leaders Elizabeth Blackwell, Eliza Duffey, and Alice Stockham each recognized women's desires, but they stressed that women could only enjoy intercourse if they truly wanted it. Blackwell termed unwanted marital intercourse a "grave social crime," but she challenged what she termed the "prevalent fallacy" that men had stronger sexual passions than women. In healthy women, uninjured by too-frequent childbirth, "increasing physical satisfaction attaches to the ultimate physical expression of love." Similarly, social purity advocate Ida Craddock encouraged married women not to submit to unwanted or unfulfilling intercourse, yet insisted that they could enjoy sexual relations. In "Right Marital Living" Craddock echoed the spiritualization of sexual relations so prevalent in the middle class:

> the nude embrace comes to be respected more and more, and finally reverenced, as a pure and beautiful approach to the sacred moment when husband and wife shall melt into one another's genital embrace, so that the twain shall be one flesh, and then, as of old, God will walk with the twain in the garden of bliss "in the cool of the day," when the heat of ill-regulated passion is no more.

In short, social purity sought not to oppose all sexuality but rather to control male sexuality and to spiritualize marital relationships. In their approach to prostitution as well as to marital sexuality, women's rights activists concentrated on the problem of gender inequality, not necessarily on the dangers of sexuality itself.

PRESERVING TRADITIONAL MATERNAL AUTHORITY

The social purity view of sexuality must be interpreted in light of women's historical experience. The declining importance of reproduction as a part of sexual life had different meanings for men and women, creating for a time a gap between the extended privileges of men and the traditional responsibilities of women. Despite their shared experience of the heightened importance of sexual intimacy within courtship and marriage, women maintained a closer connection to reproduction, and men had greater access to sexuality beyond the family, without reproductive responsibilities. Not only did women continue to experience the physical consequences of pregnancy and childbirth, at a time when contraception did not always insure their avoidance, but women also continued to perform the social role of mothering. As Linda Gordon has argued, the insistence of women reformers that sexuality and reproduction remain linked served women's interests by preserving their traditional maternal authority when women still had little access to political or economic power outside the home.

Even as the social purity arguments resisted both the separation of sexuality and reproduction and the movement of sex outside the home, its program in fact provided a bridge from the past to the future. Gordon argues, for example, that voluntary motherhood was the first step in an ideological progression toward the acceptance of family limitation and, ultimately, of contraception. In addition, social purity embraced the notion, growing among the middle class, that a romantic, even spiritual, bond should exist between husbands and wives. Fearing the economic and physical costs that women might pay as sexuality became less closely associated with reproduction, social purity theorists, like free lovers, accepted the positive value of the erotic only if love bound partners together.

Finally, women's rights and social purity advocates looked toward the future by rejecting middle-class reticence about discussing sex. Through a "moral education" movement, for example, nineteenth-century reformers issued the first call for sex education in America. Women, they argued, must teach children about sex, lest they learn incorrectly from other sources. As one writer exhorted mothers, "Show your sons and daughters the sanctities and the terrors of this awful power of sex, its capacities to bless or curse its owner." Both women and children needed moral education, Lucinda Chandler argued. For children, special education "to fit them for parenthood" would advance social purity, while women needed to be educated to know that they had the right to control their own person. From their exposés of the evils of prostitution to the "No Secrets" approach of the Moral Education Societies, social purity workers called for a public sexual discourse that, in contrast with the portrayal of sexuality in the male and working-class world of sexual commerce, emphasized love and reproductive responsibility rather than lust. Sex, they wanted children to learn, could be holy; in the absence of love and marriage, however, it defiled woman or man.

By the 1890s, social purity had become a broad-based national movement that included suffragists, temperance workers, and clergy from every denomination. It had succeeded in its goals to the extent that doctors who had originally recommended legalized prostitution now accepted the view that the social evil should be abolished. By the time of the first National Purity Congress in 1893, the single standard had become the common ideal, although not necessarily the common practice, among middle-class Americans. Moreover, key political victories had been won. Cities and states had rejected regulated prostitution and raised the age of consent.

Yet the success of the social purity movement was in many ways illusory. Despite the defeat of regulation, prostitution continued to flourish in red-light districts, away from the view of the middle classes. The sanctity of the home was constantly belied by sweatshop conditions and tenement housing, as well as by a noticeable rise in the frequency of divorce. And even as the revivalistic fervor for social purity swelled, a renewed free-love movement took purity ideals to their uncomfortable yet logical extreme. Indeed, the last quarter of the nineteenth century witnessed an intense battle between those who sought to control sexuality by returning it to the private sphere of the family and those who sought to release it from social constraints.

THE BATTLE OVER OBSCENITY

To some extent, all of the responses to prostitution, from moral reform to social purity, combined a vision of individual control over sexuality with a program of external regulation, whether by family, community, or the state. In the battle over obscenity, however, sharply opposing camps, one embracing individual and the other social control of sexuality, squared off against each other. The attack on obscenity, commandeered by Anthony Comstock, called for direct government involvement in the suppression of sexual expression in the public sphere and the confinement of sexuality to its reproductive function. In contrast, a small but vocal anarchist and free-love movement demanded that neither church nor state should limit the expression of sexual ideas and feelings; whether in private or in public, the regulation of sexual life should be solely a matter of individual choice.

The frequent skirmishes between these two armies of true believers—free lovers committed to exposing all sexual matters to the light of day, and vice crusaders determined to keep all such "obscenity" (that is, open discussion of sexuality and contraception) behind closed doors—portrayed dramatically a central problem of late–nineteenth-century sexual thought. Was sex best regulated by expanding or restricting its public discussion? In the late nineteenth century, the restrictive policy advocated by Comstock triumphed in most of the battles. By the early twentieth century, however, the expansive mode, supported by free lovers, suffragists, and sex educators, would win the war. . . .

The expansion of sexually explicit popular literature [after the 1860s] was met by a new sexual reform movement, one more willing to turn to the state to support its goals. One reform agency, the New York City Young Men's Christian Association, instigated a postwar anti-obscenity crusade. In 1866, a YMCA report bemoaned the decline of paternalistic supervision over the morals of young workers. Employers no longer took notice of the "social and moral interests of young men." In urban boardinghouses, the "virtuous and the vicious" were thrown together; after work, young men frequented saloons and theaters, where they were likely to meet prostitutes or buy the cheap "vile newspapers" that the YMCA believed were "feeders for brothels." The Association tried to redirect young men along the path to pure Christian living by providing alternative housing, reading, and recreation.

One YMCA member, Connecticut dry-goods salesman Anthony Comstock, adopted as his life's work the task of combating sex in print, art, or private correspondence. Story papers and pulp novels, he explained in *Traps for the Young* (1883), bred "vulgarity, profanity, loose ideas of life, impurity of thought and deed." Moreover, Comstock claimed, when impressionable youth read dime novels, they proceeded to act out their plots of seduction, theft, and murder. He implored parents to monitor their children's reading and boycott newsdealers who sold "these death-traps." Comstock's greatest concern, however, was the availability of "obscene literature" and articles through the mails. Only state action could defeat this threat to national morality.

In 1872, Anthony Comstock began a crusade to strengthen anti-obscenity laws. With financial backing from the upperclass businessmen on the board of the YMCA, Comstock tirelessly lobbied state and federal legislatures. He also founded the New York Society for the Suppression of Vice to support his work. Through the Society, Comstock enforced existing obscenity laws; he seized and handed over to the police "bad books" and "articles made of rubber for immoral purposes, and used by both sexes." Comstock's major political victory came in 1873, when the U.S. Congress passed, without debate, "An Act for the Suppression of Trade in, and Circulation of Obscene Literature and Articles of Immoral Use." This revision of the federal postal law forbade the mailing of obscene, lewd, lascivious, and indecent writing or advertisements, including articles that aided contraception or abortion.

Throughout the 1880s and 1890s, Congress strengthened the so-called Comstock law, and the courts upheld its constitutionality. Comstock himself supervised enforcement. As an unpaid U.S. postal inspector, he almost single-handedly prosecuted those who wrote, published, and sold literature or art that he considered obscene. In 1875 alone, his vigilance led to forty-seven arrests, twenty-eight convictions (aggregating thirty years in prison), and ninety-one hundred fines. That year the New York Society for the Suppression of Vice seized twelve hundred pounds of books and destroyed over twenty-nine thousand sexually explicit photos, songs, leaflets, rubber goods, and circulars. The objects of Comstock's attack ranged from penny postcards sold on the Bowery to fine arts exhibited in Fifth Avenue galleries depicting the nude body, from dime novels of seduction to Leo Tolstoy's *Kreutzer Sonata,* an 1889 novel that spoke openly of prostitution. The conviction rate under the Comstock Act—as high as ninety percent of those accused—attested to Comstock's boundless (some claimed prurient) interest in suppressing vice. . . .

Two underlying themes characterized the anti-vice efforts to use the state to regulate sexual expression. First, sexuality had to be restored to the private sphere; therefore, any public expression of sexuality was considered, by definition, obscene. Second, lust was in itself dangerous; therefore Comstock and his allies attacked not only sexual literature sold for profit but also any dissenting medical or philosophical opinion that supported the belief that sexuality had other than reproductive purposes. Thus, even doctors paid heavy fines for publishing discussions of contraception or sex education. In 1874 Comstock arrested Dr. Edward Bliss Foote for including information about condoms and womb veils in his marital advice books. As a result of his conviction and fine, Foote deleted these methods from his text, even as he waged an attack on the Comstock laws. But the severest penalties awaited those radicals who, during the 1880s and 1890s, elaborated the anarchist and free-love theory of sexuality. Comstock hounded free lovers such as Victoria Woodhull, Ezra Heywood, Moses Harmon, and social purity writer Ida Craddock, imprisoning each for a time. Craddock, a spiritualist who had published a guide to marital sex for women, was one of several suicides that resulted from Comstock's ruthless pursuit (others included Madame Restell, the notorious New York city abortionist, and pornographer William Haynes). In a letter to the public, written before she took her life, Craddock accused Comstock of being a "sex pervert" and called for an exposé of his activities:

Perhaps it may be that in my death more than in my life, the American people may be shocked into investigating the dreadful state of affairs which permits that unctuous sexual hypocrite, Anthony Comstock, to wax fat and arrogant, and to trample upon the liberties of the people, invading, in my own case, both my right to freedom of religion and to freedom of the press.

THE FREE LOVE MOVEMENT

Just why these radicals elicited so much of Comstock's rage requires a closer look at the late–nineteenth-century free-love movement, the antithesis of vice suppression. In many ways, the anarchist free-love philosophy formulated in the 1870s resembled social purity. Free lovers opposed prostitution, criticized male sexual dominance in marriage, and envisioned a society in which women would have greater equality with men. Some free-love advocates incorporated other social purity ideals, such as voluntary motherhood and the importance of male continence. Despite these similarities, free love differed fundamentally from social purity in that free lovers wanted to abolish the institution of marriage rather than reform it. In addition, some free lovers believed that erotic pleasure, with or without reproduction, was a valuable goal of sexual relations, but not apart from love.

As its proponents were quick to point out, free love did not mean sexual licentiousness. Rather, free love referred to the right of all men and women to choose sexual partners freely on the basis of mutual love and unconstrained by church, state, or public opinion. Despite their opposition to marriage, many free lovers had long monogamous unions; others practiced what has come to be called "serial monogamy," leaving one long-term partner only when another true love exerted its call. These practices had roots within both anarchist and spiritualist traditions. Many anarchists opposed marriage on the grounds that it represented an unjust intrusion of the state into personal life or because marriage laws made women the property of men. Spiritualists believed that the soul could transcend the boundaries of the material world and were therefore sympathetic to the anarchist critique of societal controls over the individual. Both groups opposed organized religion, which, they believed, supported the enslavement of women to men within the institution of marriage.

Although free love originated in the antebellum period, when Frances Wright and others created short-lived utopian communities, it reached a wider audience in the last quarter of the nineteenth century, when public lectures by Victoria Woodhull attracted national attention. As in the past, free love evoked fears that uncontrolled promiscuity would undermine the moral base of the society—the family. Now, in addition, Americans associated free love with anarchist politics. Especially after the Haymarket Riot of 1886, when seven anarchists were convicted of murder after a bomb exploded at a protest rally in Chicago, anarchism raised the specter of the violent overthrow of the government. As a result, newspaper editors, clergymen, and Comstock crusaded to suppress what they perceived to be a dangerous tendency. They ridiculed, ostracized, and imprisoned free lovers, who nonetheless continued to express their alternative sexual theory. Free lovers remained committed to breaking middle-class taboos on the public discussion of sexuality, the very taboos that Comstock was committed to enforcing. The stage was set for the sex wars of the late nineteenth century.

Victoria Claflin Woodhull

During the 1870s, Victoria Claflin Woodhull issued the clearest battle cry of the free-love-free-speech offensive. Woodhull's personal background prepared her for her later, infamous career. Raised in a spiritualist family, at age fifteen she married a doctor who turned out to be a drunkard. Woodhull abandoned her husband and supported herself as an itinerant spiritualist. In the 1860s, with the help of Cornelius Vanderbilt, she and her sister Tennessee Claflin became the first women stockbrokers on Wall Street. Woodhull remarried Colonel James Blood, whom she eventually left to marry a wealthy

Englishman. First, however, she joined and was expelled from the Marxist International Workingmen's Association, ran for the presidency of the United States, and scandalized American society by publicizing her free-love doctrines.

Woodhull derived her sexual theories from her own personal experience and from the philosophy of Stephen Pearl Andrews, whom she had met in New York. The central theme in her public lectures and articles of the early 1870s was that sexual consummation should only occur when a man and a woman loved each other; marriage restricted this ideal by allowing sex without love between husbands and wives and by preventing loving sex between those not married to each other. In addition to elevating individual sexual choice over the laws of marriage, Woodhull emphasized the positive value of sexuality and condemned marriage for stifling the liberating potential of sexual passion. Anticipating modern notions of the centrality of sex to personal identity, she declared that "[s]exuality is the physiological basis of character and must be preserved as its balance and perfection." To develop human sexuality, a young man or woman "should be taught all there is known about its uses and abuses, so that he or she shall not ignorantly drift upon the shoals whereon so many lives are wrecked." To charges that sexual desire was "vulgar," she responded as a romantic and a libertarian:

> What! Vulgar! The instinct that creates immortal souls vulgar! Who dare stand up amid Nature, all prolific and beautiful, whose pulses are ever bounding with the creative desire, and utter such sacrilege! Vulgar, indeed! Vulgar, rather, must be the mind that can conceive such blasphemy.

Victoria Woodhull's public advocacy of free love might have been tolerated in the 1870s, when many Americans engaged in nonprocreative sex and sophisticated New Yorkers were well aware of the extent of adultery among them. But Woodhull went a step further and broke the conspiracy of silence that protected the middle classes from the contradictions in their sexual ideology. To highlight the hypocrisy of opposition to free love, she announced in public that the prominent Brooklyn minister Henry Ward Beecher was having an affair with a married parishioner, Elizabeth Tilton. Not only did the Beecher family and all of respectable society condemn her for the revelation, but an infuriated Anthony Comstock sent Woodhull to jail for publishing the details in *Woodhull and Claflin's Weekly*. She was ultimately acquitted, but after her marriage and emigration to England, Woodhull no longer spoke out on free love.

THE HEYWOODS AND THE HARMONS

The controversy set off by Victoria Woodhull helped inspire a budding new generation of free lovers, including Ezra Heywood, who founded the New England Free Love League to provide a forum for Woodhull to address. An abolitionist, pacifist, and anarchist, Heywood published a free-love tract, *Cupid's Yokes* (1876), for which Anthony Comstock had him and his publisher jailed. Like earlier free lovers, Heywood considered marriage a form of prostitution. Although he accepted male continence, along with other methods of contraception, Heywood endorsed the ideas of the healthfulness of sexual passion, as did his wife, women's rights and free-love advocate Angela Tilton Heywood. Both Ezra and Angela Heywood believed that frank discussion of all sexual matters was critical to alleviating the sexual ills that seemed to pervade American society. Thus they named their journal *The Word,* and in it they employed direct language. As Angela explained,

> Such graceful terms as hearing, seeing, smelling, tasting, fucking, throbbing, kissing, and kin words, are telephone expressions, lighthouses of intercourse; . . . their aptness, euphony and serviceable persistence make it as impossible and undesirable to put them out of pure use as it would be to take oxygen out of air.

For such plain speaking, the Heywoods, too, incurred the wrath of Anthony Comstock, who twice convicted Ezra Heywood for printing obscenity. Ezra served three years at hard labor, while Angela supported their four children alone. Within a year of his release from prison, Ezra Heywood died, one of many martyrs of Comstock's crusades.

The task of naming the sexual was carried on by Moses Harmon, a Virginia-born minister who converted to "free thought" in Kansas during the 1880s. Between 1883 and 1907, Harmon published *Lucifer, The Light Bearer,* a radical journal opposed to lynching, the Spanish-American War, and women's sexual slavery. *Lucifer* published biblical descriptions of sex, letters from women who complained about their husbands' sexual excesses, and even accounts of oral sex, which, like homosexuality, free lovers condemned as unnatural. Although Harmon shared the social purity–suffragist belief that women should have the right to say no to unwanted sex and motherhood, *Lucifer* was too sexually explicit for Anthony Comstock. In 1886, Comstock prosecuted Harmon for publishing a letter exposing the horrors of marital rape. Harmon served a prison term for his plain speaking; during his absence, Lois Waisbrooker, a women's rights supporter and spiritualist, edited the journal. Harmon's seventeen-year-old daughter, Lillian, also clashed with the law when she "married" Edwin Walker without the blessings of church or state. Publicized in *Lucifer,* their free-love ceremony led to the couple's arrest and imprisonment. Lillian Harmon later opposed the age-of-consent laws because they forced chastity upon young women.

Although sexual radicals and some liberal supporters tried to stop Comstock, they were unsuccessful. Two organizations—the National Liberal League and the National Defense Association—publicly opposed Comstock, and Heywood's publisher gathered seventy thousand signatures on a petition to repeal the Comstock Act. The popular press frequently ridiculed Comstock, but they never undermined his political power. Comstock succeeded until his death in 1915 at least in part because his tactics of intimidation immobilized many critics. On a deeper level, Comstock could remain powerful because his crusade tapped both the fears and the longings of mainstream America. Even as middle-class men and women began to limit family size and value romantic union in marriage, they worried about the specter of sexuality unleashed from traditional controls. At a time when the middle class sought to establish social order in the face of rapid industrialization and immigration, the control of sexuality outside of the family seemed all the more pressing. Whatever new sexual meaning they may have embraced within the private realm of marriage, middle-class Americans increasingly insisted on limiting the public expression of sexual desire. Sex divorced from reproduction was simply too disturbing to unleash in public. Thus public reticence accompanied the private transformation of sexuality.

SEXUAL CHOICE AND SEXUAL CONSTRAINT

In addition to their battles against the suppression of sexuality, late–nineteenth-century free lovers engaged in an internal dialogue about the meaning of sexuality and its relationship to reproduction that mirrored broader, often unspoken social concerns. In the pages of *The Word* and *Lucifer,* and in their novels and political tracts, free lovers struggled with the problem of how to balance the increasing importance of erotic sexuality against the fear that it would lead to sexual chaos. The free-love response pointed in the direction of modern sexual ideas when it affirmed the positive value of the erotic, but its ties to the nineteenth-century theory of sexual control remained strong. Like John Humphrey Noyes's system of *coitus reservatus,* each of the major sexual alternatives endorsed by free lovers combined sexual pleasure with sexual restraint. In *Karezza* (1896), for example, Alice Stockham explained how both men and women could build stronger characters by engaging in sexual relations that stopped short of climax. Karezza, and other theories such as Alphaism, Dianism, and Zugassent's Discovery, differed in their recommended frequency of sexual intercourse, but they all claimed to enhance sexual pleasure by avoiding orgasm. Thus, each method allowed erotic sex to flourish while preventing procreation, and each combined individual sexual choice with individual sexual control. Although some free lovers accepted contraception, and in some cases abortion, they perceived homosexuality as an unnatural vice. As libertarians, they opposed the imprisonment of British writer Oscar Wilde, but their sexual radicalism pressed only to the boundaries of heterosexuality, and not beyond.

Free love remained within the mainstream of nineteenth-century sexual thought in other ways as well. Despite its opposition to marriage, the free-love doctrine was rooted in a perfectionist notion of the family in which the "true love" of a man and woman would produce not only morally stronger characters but also biologically superior children. Free lovers, social purity advocates, suffragists, and some utopians combined this romantic vision with late–nineteenth-century Darwinian theories of natural selection to create what historian Hal Sears has termed "anarchist eugenics," the forerunner of the Progressive-era eugenics movement. Edward Bliss Foote, Stephen Pearl Andrews, the Nicholses, Elmina Drake Slenker, as well as women's rights leader Elizabeth Cady Stanton and social scientist Lester Ward, all supported women's right to control reproduction on the grounds that women would select mates wisely and produce healthier, physically stronger, and morally superior offspring. By justifying free love in the name of race progress, they countered the charges of "race suicide" leveled against Anglo-Saxon women who chose to bear few children, but they did so by accepting the argument that racial purity was a major goal of sexual intercourse.

Anarchist eugenics reflected how closely the free-love vision resembled the sexual thought of the dominant society. Despite the persecution of free-love anarchists, their values were not entirely incompatible with those of most Americans. Indeed, by 1907, when *Lucifer* became the *American Journal of Eugenics,* free love had ceased to occupy the radical fringe. Its once-threatening message of sex education, birth control, and the romantic union of love and sexuality was about to become the dominant middle-class sexual ideology. Along the way, however, the central anarchist theme of individual freedom would be discarded, as church, state, and public opinion gradually joined in enforcing many of the sexual ideas for which nineteenth-century free lovers had been sent to prison.

Free Love:
A Campaign
Against Marriage

VICTORIA C. WOODHULL

Victoria C. Woodhull was a spiritualist, feminist, and social reformer who provoked controversy in the late nineteenth century for advocating "free love"—the idea that a man and a woman who loved each other could have a fruitful sexual relationship without being married. In 1872 Woodhull was arrested and briefly jailed for transmitting obscene literature through the mail; the case was later dismissed. In the following excerpt from her 1874 speech "Tried as by Fire," Woodhull declares war against marriage, claiming that it is a brutal manmade invention that destroys the potential for genuine love between the sexes. In her opinion, marriage forces women to submit to men and makes hypocrites out of couples who remain married for the sake of social convention even when their relationship is loveless. Woodhull maintains that sexual instincts should not be regulated by any community, belief system, or governing body. Instead, couples should be free to establish relationships based purely on mutual love, desire, and benefit. Once free love usurps marriage, Woodhull argues, true brotherhood, justice, and equality will transform society.

I am conducting a campaign against marriage, with the view of revolutionizing the present theory and practice. I have strong convictions that, as a bond or promise to love another until death, it is a fraud upon human happiness; and that it has outlived its day of usefulness. These convictions make me earnest, and I enter the fight, meaning to do the institution all possible harm in the shortest space of time; meaning to use

Excerpted from *Tried as by Fire; or, The True and the False Socially*, by Victoria C. Woodhull (New York: Woodhull & Clafin, 1874).

whatever weapons may fall in my way with which to stab it to the heart, so that its decaying carcass may be buried, and clear the way for a higher and a better institution.

I speak only what I know, when I say that the most intelligent and really virtuous people of all classes have outgrown this institution; that they are constantly and systematically unfaithful to it; despise and revolt against it as a slavery; and only submit to a semblance of fidelity to it, from the dread of a falsely educated public opinion and a sham morality, which are based on the ideas of the past, but which no longer really represent the convictions of anybody.

Nor is this hypocritical allegiance the only or the greatest or gravest consideration that is capturing the opinions of the really intelligent. It is rapidly entering into the public thought, that there should be, at least, as much attention given to breeding and rearing children, as is given to horses, cattle, pigs, fowls and fruit. A little reflection shows that the scientific propagation of children is a thing of paramount importance; as much above and beyond that of personal property as children are above dogs and cats. And this conviction, practically considered, also shows that the union of the sexes, for propagation, should be consummated under the highest and best knowledge, and in such manner and by such methods as will produce the best results. These considerations are so palpable that they cannot be ignored; and they look to the early supercedure of the institution of marriage by some better system for the maintenance of women as mothers, and children as progeny. This is as much a foregone conclusion with all the best thinkers of today as was the approaching dissolution of slavery, no more than ten years before its final fall.

But in the meantime men and women tremble on the verge of the revolution, and hesitate to avow their convictions; but aware of their rights, and urged by the impulses of their natures, they act upon the new theories while professing allegiance to the old. In this way an organized hypocrisy has become a main feature of modern society, and poltroonery, cowardice and deception rule supreme in its domain. The continuation of such falsity for a generation, touching one of the most sacred interests of humanity, will eradicate the source of honesty from the human soul. Every consideration of expediency, therefore, demands that some one lead the van in a relentless warfare against marriage, so that its days may be made short. . . .

MARRIAGE IS A CURSE

But why do I war upon marriage? I reply frankly: First, because it stands directly in the way of any improvement in the race, insisting upon conditions under which improvement is impossible; and second, because it is, as I verily believe, the most terrible curse from which humanity now suffers, entailing more misery, sickness and premature death than all other causes combined. It is at once the bane of happiness to the present, and the demon of prophetic miseries to the future—miseries now concealed beneath its deceptive exterior, gilded over by priestcraft and law, to be inwrought in the constitutions of coming generations to mildew and poison their lives.

Of what in reality does this thing consist, which, while hanging like a pall over the world, is pretendedly the basis of its civilization? The union of the opposites in sex is an instinct inherent in the constitutions of mankind; but legal marriage is an invention of man, and so far as it performs anything, it defeats and perverts this natural instinct. Marriage is a license for sexual commerce to be carried on without regard to the consent or dissent of this instinct. Everything else that men and women may desire to do, except to have sexual commerce, may be and is done without marriage.

Marriage, then, is a license merely—a permission to do something that it is inferred or understood ought not to be done without it. In other words, marriage is an assumption by the community that it can regulate the sexual instincts of individuals better than they can themselves; and they have been so well regulated that there is scarcely such a thing known as a natural sexual instinct in the race; indeed, the regulations have been so at war with nature that this instinct has become a morbid disease, running rampant or riotous in one sex, and feeding its insatiable maw upon the vitality of the other, finally resulting in disgust or impotency in both.

Isn't this a pretty commentary on regulation? Talk of Social Evil bills! The marriage law is the most damnable Social Evil bill—the most consummate outrage on woman—that was ever conceived. Those who are called prostitutes, whom these bills assume to regulate, are free women, sexually, when compared to the slavery of the poor wife. They are at liberty, at least to refuse; but she knows no such escape. "Wives, submit your-selves to your husbands," is the spirit and the universal practice of marriage.

THE SANCTIONING OF BRUTALITY

Of all the horrid brutalities of this age, I know of none so horrid as those that are sanctioned and defended by marriage. Night after night there are thousands of rapes committed, un-der cover of this accursed license; and millions—yes, I say it boldly, knowing whereof I speak—millions of poor, heart-broken, suffering wives are compelled to minister to the lech-ery of insatiable husbands, when every instinct of body and sentiment of soul revolts in loathing and disgust. All married persons know this is truth, although they may feign to shut their eyes and ears to the horrid thing, and pretend to believe it is not. The world has got to be startled from this pretense into realizing that there is nothing else now existing among pretendedly enlightened nations, except marriage, that invests men with the right to debauch women, sexually, against their wills. Yet marriage is held to be synonymous with morality! I say, eternal damnation sink such morality!

When I think of the indignities which women suffer in marriage, I cannot conceive how they are restrained from open rebellion. Compelled to submit their bodies to disgusting pol-lution! Oh, Shame! where hast thou fled, that the fair face of womanhood is not suffused with thy protesting blushes, sting-ing her, at least into self-respect, if not into freedom itself! Am I too severe? No, I am only just!

Prate of the abolition of slavery! There was never servitude in the world like this one of marriage. It not only holds the body to whatever polluting use—abstracting its vitality, prostituting its most sacred functions, and leaving them degraded, debauched and diseased—but utterly damning the soul for all aspiration, and sinking it in moral and spiritual torpor. Marriage not slavery! Who shall dare affirm it? let woman practically assert her sexual freedom and see to what it will lead! It is useless to mince terms. We want the truth; and that which I have about this abomination I will continue to give until it is abolished.

It is useless to cry, "Peace! Peace!" when there is no peace. It is worse than useless to cry, "Freedom! Freedom!" when there is nothing but slavery. Let those who will, however, in spite of the truth, go home and attempt to maintain it there, and they will wake up to find themselves sold, delivered and bound, legally, to serve their masters sexually, but, refusing to do which, there will be a penalty, if not the lash. . . .

If there are any who are in doubt as to what is right and true, I offer a test that will decide it. Let the married who live together, who would separate were the law repealed, rise! Not any here of that stripe; or, if there are, they are ashamed to make a public confession of it. I should be so, too, were I sailing the voyage of life in such a ship. Ask any audience, or any individual, this question, and the result would be the same. What is the inference? Clearly that, if people really do live together who do not love, they are ashamed of it, and, consequently, of the law that holds them; and that they want the world to think that they love each other, and choose to live together on that account, regardless of the law.

Who is there in the community who would like to have it understood that there is no love at home? Isn't it the fact, on the contrary, that those whose homes are loveless, and who fight and wrangle and fuss continually take special pains to conceal these things from the world? Everybody knows it is. What more sweeping condemnation could there be than this, both of the law which compels it and the practice itself? None! It is the hot-bed of hypocrisy, deceit and lust, and is doing more to demoralize the world than all other practices combined.

I am justified, therefore, in concluding that all people who are not practical free lovers, living together for love, are theoretically so, and are ashamed to confess that their practices do not accord with their theories; or, in other words, are ashamed that their practice is enforced lust instead of free love. These are the alternatives, and the only ones, and I don't intend that the people shall escape them. Every one of you—every one of the people generally—either practices Free Love or enforced lust, and the world shall understand when people denounce me as a Free Lover they announce themselves as enforced lusters; and I'll placard their backs and they shall walk up and down the world with this mark of depravity, as they have intended that I should do for having the moral courage, which they lack, to make my theories and practices agree. . . .

INCOME FOR PRIESTS AND LAWYERS

After careful observation I have deliberately concluded that there are two classes only who have anything more than an imaginary interest in maintaining the marriage system: The hypocritical priests who get their fees for forging the chains and the blackguard lawyers who get bigger ones for breaking the fetters. The former have an average of ten dollars a job, and some of them a hundred jobs a year; while the latter, not quite up to the former in number, to keep even with them, raise their average price per job to two hundred and fifty dollars. A thousand dollars a year for the priests! How should people know whether they ought to marry or not without asking their consent? Of course marriage is divine! A thousand dollars a year for the lawyers! How could people be supposed to know whether they ought to separate or not until the lawyer has got his fee? Of course virtue must have a legal standard. How could morality and modesty be preserved unless the priest got his ten dollars; or how could husbands and wives be prevented from killing each other unless the lawyer got his two hundred and fifty? Will the priest ever cease his cant about the former, or the lawyer change the law about the latter so long as the people are fools enough to pay them fees? They who suppose they may, don't yet understand how much divinity there is in this marriage business.

The real question at issue then is one entirely apart from

The Rights of Conscience in Love

A free love advocate denounces church and state authority over sexuality.

I f government cannot justly determine what ticket we shall vote, what church we shall attend, or what books we shall read, by what authority does it watch at key-holes and burst open bed-chamber doors to drag lovers from sacred seclusion? Why should priests and magistrates supervise the sexual organs of citizens any more than the brain and stomach? If we are incapable of sexual self-government, is the matter helped by appointing to "protect" us "ministers of the Gospel," whose incontinent lives fill the world with "scandals"? If unwedded lovers who cohabit are lewd, will paying a marriage fee to a minister make them "virtuous"? Sexual organs are not less sacredly the property of individual citizens than other bodily organs; this being undeniable, who but the individual owners can rightly determine when, where, and how they shall be used? The belief that our sexual relations can be better governed by statute, than by individual reason, is a rude species of conventional impertinence, as barbarous and shocking, as it is senseless. Personal Liberty and the Rights of Conscience in love, now savagely invaded by Church, State, and "wise" free-thinkers, should be unflinchingly asserted.

Ezra Hervey Heywood, *Cupid's Yokes: Or, the Binding Forces of Conjugal Life,* 1877.

law, relating wholly to the conditions that make up the unity, whether they are such as judged by the results, warrant the unity that is sought. What are proper and what improper sexual relations is the problem to be solved, and it is that one which of all others is most fraught with the interests, the happiness and the real well-being of humanity. Upon these relations, as I shall show, depend not only the health, happiness and prosperity of the present generation, but the very existence of future generations.

Purifying the Fountains of Life

That existence is involved in these relations. If they be pure and good and withal natural, which they must be to be pure and good, then the existence which they make possible will be of the same character; but if they be impure, bad, and withal unnatural, which if they are they must be impure and bad, then the existence which they make possible will be of like character. A pure fountain sends forth pure waters, but the stream flowing from an impure source will assuredly be unclean. To make the fountains of life—the sexual relations—pure, is the work of the reformer, so that the streams they send forth may flow through coming ages uncontaminated by any inherited contagion.

There are a few propositions necessary to be laid down that will become self-evident as the subject develops: 1. A man or woman who has perfect physical health, has natural and healthful sexual relations. 2. A man or woman, married or single, old or young, professional prostitute or *roue,* or a professed nun or celibate, who has bad general health—and suffers from any chronic disease—has unnatural and unhealthy sensual conditions. 3. A man and woman, living together, who have perfect physical health, have natural and healthful sexual relations, and will have healthy offspring. Such a union is God-ordained, if it do not have the approval of the law or the sanction of the priest; and no man can put it asunder. 4. If either or both of the parties to a union have generally poor physical health—suffer from any chronic disease—such parties have unnatural and unhealthful sexual relations, and their progeny will be puling, weakly, miserable, damned. Such a union is God-condemned if it have the approval of all the laws, and the blessing of all the priests in the world; and as corollary to all these, this: All diseases not to be attributed to so-called accidental causes are the result of improper, or the want of proper, sexual conditions; and this applies to all ages and to both sexes.

It may now be asked: What are proper sexual conditions? I reply: Sexual commerce that is based upon reciprocal love and mutual desire, and that ultimates in equal and mutual benefit, is proper and healthful; while improper sexual commerce is that which is not based upon reciprocal love and mutual desire, and that cannot, therefore, ultimate in equal or mutual benefit. Children begotten by the former commerce will never be bad children physically, mentally or morally; but such as are begotten by the latter commerce will inevitably be bad children, either physically, mentally or morally, or, which is more likely to be the case, partially bad throughout.

Proper Versus Improper Sexual Commerce

I desire to be fully understood upon this part of the subject. I have been generally denounced by the press as an advocate of promiscuousness in the sexual relations. I want you to fully comprehend the measure of truth there is in this charge. Hence I repeat that there is but one class of cases where commerce of the sexes is in strict accordance with nature, and that, in this class, there are always present, First, love of each by each of the parties; second, a desire for the commerce on the part of each, arising from the previous love; and third, mutual and reciprocal benefit.

Of improper sexual commerce there are several classes: First, that class where it is claimed by legal right, as in marriage; second, where the female, to please the male, accords it without any desire on her own part; third, where, for money, for a home, for any present, as a payment for any claim, whether pecuniary or of gratitude, or for any motive whatever other than love, the female yields it to the male; fourth, where there is mutual love and desire, but where, for any reason, there is such want of adaptation as to make mutual consummation impossible.

This is the promiscuousness that I advocate now, and that I have, from the first, advocated.

Will the representatives of the press, who have covered me with their abuse until I am regarded with horror all over the land as a person whose presence is contamination and whose touch contagion, correct their foul lies by stating these propositions, and, so far as they can at this late day, do me justice? We shall see!

"But," said a prominent woman of this country, with whom I was recently discussing these maxims in sexuality, "how are you going to prevent all this intercourse of the sexes, which you condemn?"

"Ah!" said I, "that's the question. I have no right nor has anybody else any right to prevent it in any such sense as you infer."

This is a matter that must be remanded back from law, back from public interference, to individuals, who alone have the sovereignty over it. No person or set of persons, however learned and wise, have any right, power or capacity, to determine legally for another when commerce is proper or when it shall occur. It is not a matter of law to be administered by the public, but a question of education to be gained by individuals—a scientific problem to expound and elucidate which, should be one of the chief duties of all teachers and reformers. Every person in the world, before arriving at the age in which the sexual instinct is developed, should be taught all there is known about its uses and abuses, so that he or she shall not ignorantly drift upon the shoals whereon so many lives are wrecked.

I advocate complete freedom for sexuality the same as for religion. The charge of promiscuousness is laid in this fact, and some intelligent minds have thought it was a sound charge, until its inconsistency and utter absurdity have been pointed out to them. This is the proposition: I advocate sexual freedom for all people—freedom for the monogamist to practice monogamy, for the varietist to be a varietist still, for the promiscuous to remain promiscuous. Am I, therefore, an advocate of promiscuousness, variety or monogamy? Not necessarily either. I might do all this and be myself a celibate and an advocate of celibacy. To advocate freedom in sexual things and also the right of individuals to choose each for himself to which class to belong, is by no means synonymous with the advocacy of the class which he chooses. Advocating the right to do a thing and advocating the doing of that thing are two entirely separate and different matters. . . .

THE MISUSE OF THE SEXUAL INSTINCT

When a limit is placed upon anything that by nature is free, its action becomes perverted. All the various attractions in the world are but so many methods by which love manifests itself. The attraction which draws the opposites in sex together is sexual love. The perverted action of sexual love, when limited by law or otherwise, is lust. All sexual manifestations that are not free are the perverted action of love—are lust. So, logically, the methods enforced by man to ensure purity convert love into lust. Legal sexuality is enforced lust. All the D.D.'s and LL.D.'s in the world, though they have all the mental gifts and the tongues of angels, cannot controvert the proposition.

This brings us to a still more serious part of my subject. Remember I am to withhold nothing—no fact, no advice. We are now face to face with the most startling and the most common fact connected with the miseries of marriages. But I know of no author, no speaker who has dared to call attention to, or to suggest a remedy for it, or even to hint at it as needing a remedy, or to recognize its existence in any manner.

It will be remembered that early in the evening I showed that marriage when analyzed, is a license to cohabit sexually. Now I am going to show that the enforcement of this method eventually defeats the original object. I state it without fear of contradiction by fact or of refutation by argument that it is the common experience among the married who have lived together strictly according to the marriage covenant, for from five to ten years, that they are sexually estranged. There may be, I know there are, exceptions to this rule, but they are the exceptions and not the rule. It is a lamentable fact that all over this country there is a prolonged wail going up on account of this condition. Sexual estrangement in from five to ten years! Think of it, men and women whom Nature has blessed with such possibilities for happiness as are conferred on no other order of creation—your God-ordained capacity blasted, prostituted to death, by enforced sexual relations where there is neither attraction or sexual adaptation; and by ignorance of sexual science!

Some may assert, as many do, that failure in sexual strength is intellectual and spiritual gain. Don't harbor the unnatural lie. Sexuality is the physiological basis of character and must be preserved as its balance and perfection. To kill out the sexual instinct by any unnatural practice or repression, is to emasculate character; is to take away that which makes what remains impotent for good—fruitless, not less intellectually and spiritually than sexually.

It is to do even more than this. From the moment that the sexual instinct is dead in any person, male or female, from that moment such person begins actually to die. It is the fountain from which life proceeds. Dry up the fountain and the stream will disappear. It is only a question of time, and of how much is obtained from other fountains, when the stream will discharge its last waters into the great ocean of life.

Others again seem to glory over the fact that they never had any sexual desire, and to think that this desire is vulgar. What! Vulgar! The instinct that creates immortal souls vulgar! Who dare stand up amid Nature, all prolific and beautiful, whose pulses are ever bounding with the creative desire, and utter such sacrilege! Vulgar, indeed! Vulgar, rather, must be the mind that can conceive such blasphemy. No sexual passion, say you? Say, rather, a sexual idiot, and confess that your life is a failure, your body an abortion, and no longer bind your shame upon your brow or herald it as purity. Call such stuff purity. Bah! Be honest, rather, and say it is depravity.

It is not the possession of strong sexual powers that is to be deprecated. They are that necessary part of human character which is never lacking in those who leave their names standing high in the historic roll. The intellect, largely developed, without a strong animal basis is never prolific of good in any direction. Evenly balanced natures, in which there are equal development and activity of all departments are those which move the world palpably forward for good; but if superiority of any kind is desirable at all, let it be in the animal, since with this right, the others may be cultivated to its standard. If this be wanting, however, all possible cultivation, intellectually, will only carry the individual further away from balance, and make the character still more "out of tune" with nature. These are physiological facts inherent in the constitution of mankind, and they cannot be ignored with impunity. No reliable theory of progressive civilization can ever be established that does not make them its chief corner stone, because they are the foundation upon which civilization rests.

It is the misuse, the abuse, the prostitution of the sexual instinct that is to be deprecated. Like all other capacities, it needs to be educated, cultivated, exercised rightly, and to do this is to live in accordance with nature and as commanded by the higher law, that law which every one finds deep-seated in his soul, and whose voice is the truest guide. When the world shall rise from its degradation into the sphere of this law, when the sexual act shall be the religion of the world, as it is now my religion, then, and then only, may we reasonably hope that its redemption is nigh. . . .

SEXUAL AND SOCIAL FREEDOM

Sexual freedom, then, means the abolition of prostitution both in and out of marriage; means the emancipation of woman from sexual slavery and her coming into ownership and control of her own body; means the end of her pecuniary dependence upon man, so that she may never even seemingly, have to procure whatever she may desire or need by sexual favors; means the abrogation of forced pregnancy, of ante-natal murder, of undesired children; means the birth of love-children only, endowed by every inherited virtue that the highest exaltation can confer at conception, by every influence for good to be obtained during gestation, and by the wisest guidance and instruction on to manhood, industrially, intellectually and sexually.

It means no more sickness, no more poverty, no more crime: it means peace, plenty and security, health, purity and virtue; it means the replacement of money-getting as the aim of life by the desire to do good; the closing of hospitals and asylums, and the transformation of prisons, jails and penitentiaries into workshops and scientific schools; and of lawyers, doctors and ministers into industrial artizans; it means equality, fraternity and justice raised from the existence which they now have in name only, into practical life; it means individual happiness, national prosperity and universal good.

Ultimately, it means more than this even. It means the establishment of co-operative homes, in which thousands who now suffer in every sense shall enjoy all the comforts and luxuries of life, in the place of the isolated households which have no care for the misery and destitution of their neighbors. It means for our cities, the conversion of innumerable huts into immense hotels, as residences; and the combination of all industrial enterprises upon the same plan; and for the country, the co-operative conduct of agriculture by the maximum of improvements for labor-saving, and the consequent reduction of muscular toil to the minimum. And it means the inter-co-operation of all these in a grand industrial organization to take the places of the present governments of the world, whose social basis shall be all people united in the great human family as brothers and sisters.

So after all I am a very promiscuous Free Lover. I want the love of you all, promiscuously. It makes no difference who or what you are, old or young, black or white, Pagan, Jew, or Christian, I want to love you all and be loved by you all; and I mean to have your love. If you will not give it to me now, these young, for whom I plead, will in after years bless Victoria Woodhull for daring to speak for their salvation.

Trapping the Devil's Trapper

Anthony Comstock rose to prominence in the 1870s as a crusader against sexual obscenity and its corrupting influence on children. With the help of New York congressman Clinton L. Merriam, he drafted a bill that banned the mailing of allegedly "indecent and lascivious" materials, including books and pamphlets containing information about contraception and abortion. In 1873, Congress passed this bill, which became known as the Comstock Law. Comstock was also appointed a special agent of the post office and was charged with enforcing the anti–obscenity statutes. Comstock arrested thousands of individuals over the course of his career, and particularly harsh punishments were reserved for many of the free love advocates of the late nineteenth century. In the following excerpt from *Traps for the Young*, Comstock recounts his arrest of Ezra Heywood, founder of the New England Free Love League.

When a boy I used to construct in the woods what was called a stone-trap. This was formed by taking a large flat stone and setting it up on one edge at an angle of about forty-five degrees, and fastening it there by means of three notched sticks. The end of one directly under the centre of the stone was baited with a sweet apple. The rabbit or squirrel nibbling the apple would spring the trap and be crushed to death.

The thing I mention now crushes self–respect, moral purity, and holy living. Sure ruin and death are the end to the victims caught by this doctrine, which is now becoming so prevalent. It is a bid to the lowest and most debased forms of living, and is dangerous to youth and adults alike. It takes the word "love,"

Excerpted from *Traps for the Young*, by Anthony Comstock (New York: Funk & Wagnalls, 1883).

60 • THE SEXUAL REVOLUTION

that sweetens so much of earth, and shines so brightly in heaven, and making that its watchword, distorts and prostitutes its meaning, until it is the mantle for all kinds of license and uncleanness. It should be spelled l-u-s-t, to be rightly understood, as it is interpreted by so-called liberals.

I can liken it to nothing more striking than the rude stone trap, so far as its results go.

As advocated by a few indecent creatures calling themselves reformers—men and women foul of speech, shameless in their lives, and corrupting in their influences—we must go to a sewer that has been closed, where the accumulations of filth have for years collected, to find a striking resemblance to its true character. I know of nothing more offensive to decency, or more revolting to good morals, than the class of publication issuing from this source. Science is dragged down by these advocates, and made a pretended foundation for their argument, while their foul utterances are sought to be palmed off upon the public as scientific efforts to elevate mankind. With them, marriage is bondage; love is lust; celibacy is suicide; while fidelity to marriage vows is a relic of barbarism. All restraints which keep boys and girls, young men and maidens pure and chaste, which prevent our homes from being turned into voluntary brothels, are not to be tolerated by them.

Nothing short of turning the whole human family loose to run wild like the beasts of the forest, will satisfy the demands of the leaders and publishers of this literature. The chief creature of this vile creed was sentenced to two years in Dedham Jail, Massachusetts, for sending his obscene books advocating his doctrine through the mails. . . .

LUST IN EVERY FACE

My first experience with this crew was in Boston. Their leader had printed a most obscene and loathsome book. This book is too foul for description.

This foul book was advertised at a low price, and a special effort was made for "boy, girl, and women agents" to sell the same. This leader and his wife made it their business to hold

Obscene Publications

In his 1880 book Frauds Exposed, *Anthony Comstock maintains that sexually explicit publications are a danger to family and community. He denounces anticensorship liberals who defend venders of "obscene publications."*

The effect of this cursed business on our youth and society, no pen can describe. It breeds lust. Lust defiles the body, debauches the imagination, corrupts the mind, deadens the will, destroys the memory, sears the conscience, hardens the heart, and damns the soul. It unnerves the arm, and steals away the elastic step. It robs the soul of manly virtues, and imprints upon the mind of the youth, visions that throughout life curse the man or woman. Like a panorama, the imagination seems to keep this hated thing before the mind, until it wears its way deeper and deeper, plunging the victim into practices that he loathes.

This traffic has made rakes and libertines in society—skeletons in many a household. The family is polluted, home desecrated, and each generation born into the world is more and more cursed by the inherited weaknesses, the harvest of this seed-sowing of the Evil one.

And these monsters—these devil-men, or men-devils—

free-love conventions, for the purpose of educating the youth in this line. He appropriated the mails of the United States, and made them his efficient agents in disseminating the book. Every volume had an advertisement for "boy and girl agents."

I secured the evidence, and procured a warrant in the United States Court at Boston for his arrest. I was especially deputed to execute this warrant. I went to his residence, and there learned that he was in Boston, holding a free-love convention. I returned there, reaching the hall where this con-

caught in this cursed traffic, and prosecuted legally, and legally placed where they cannot longer strike their deadly fangs into the vitals of the youth, are made martyrs of, and the so-called "liberals" of this land rally to their defence! and, at the beck and call of this band of ex-convicts and co-conspirators, a combined effort is made to repeal these laws!

There is a mawkish sympathy for criminals, among even good men, that is all for the prisoner, and nothing for the victim. The burglar who enters the house at night and terrifies helpless women and children, or cripples for life the master of the household, if arrested, is an object of special sympathy. Poor fellow! to be shut up behind the bars and deprived of his liberty! The vender of obscene publications, or the keeper of the gambling hell and the rum shop—these fellows *who make criminals,* who bring disgrace on the family and suffering on helpless women and children—are especial objects of sympathy; while not a thought is bestowed upon the youth cursed for life, the wife widowed, the child orphaned, the family disgraced, pauperized, and destroyed. My sympathy is for the family of the prisoner, but not to that extent that I am blinded to the lasting curse the prisoner is daily inflicting on other families in the community.

Anthony Comstock, *Frauds Exposed*, 1880.

vention was being held about 8:30 P.M. I was alone. I went up to the convention, bought a ticket, and as I entered the hall heard the speaker railing at "that Comstock." I took a seat without being recognized. The address was made up of abuse of myself and disgusting arguments for their cause.

I looked over the audience of about 250 men and boys. I could see lust in every face. After a little while the wife of the president (the person I was after) took the stand, and delivered the foulest address I ever heard. She seemed lost to all shame.

The audience cheered and applauded. It was too vile; I had to go out. I wanted to arrest the leader and end the base performance. There my man sat on the platform, puffed up with egotism. I looked at him and at the 250 eager faces, anxious to catch every word that fell from his wife's lips.

Discretion said, It is not wise to make yourself known. Duty said, There's your man, take him. But I was alone. In not one face in all that throng of his sympathizers was there enough manliness to encourage a hope of help, in case I required it.

I left the room with this one sentiment uppermost in my mind: "It is infamous that such a thing as this is possible in any part of our land, much more in Boston. It must be stopped. But how?" I went down the two flights of stairs to the street. The fresh air never was more refreshing. I resolved to stop that exhibition of nastiness, if possible. I looked for a policeman. As usual, none was to be found when wanted. Then I sought light and help from above. I prayed for strength to do my duty, and that I might have success. I knew God was able to help me. Every manly instinct cried out against my cowardly turning my back on this horde of lusters. I determined to try. I resolved that one man in America at least should enter a protest.

MAKING THE ARREST

I had been brought over from the depot in a carriage. I had the driver place his carriage at the door leading up to the hall. I returned to the hall. This chieftain's wife continued her offensive tirade against common decency. Occasionally she referred to "that Comstock." Her husband presided with great self-complacency. You would have thought he was the champion of some majestic cause instead of a mob of free-lusters. I sat down again in the audience. The stream of filth continued until it seemed to me I could not sit a moment longer. Just then the leader passed from the stage into the anteroom. The audience were carried away with the vile talk. The baser the expressions, the louder they applauded.

I followed him out, and said to him quietly, "Is your name [Ezra Heywood]?"

With much self-conceit, he responded in the affirmative.

I simply said, "I have a warrant for your arrest for sending obscene matter through the mail. You are my prisoner."

He gasped out, "Who are you?"

I replied, "I am a deputy United States marshal."

"Well," he said, "if you'll excuse me I'll just go in and address the convention a moment."

I had been expecting this, and said at once, "You are now in custody, and you cannot harangue that crowd any more to-night."

Then he tried other devices to get into the hall; he wanted his overcoat and hat.

I said, "No, you cannot go in there again to-night." I then turned to one of his doorkeepers, a man about six feet two inches high, who was selling these obscene books as the people passed in and out, and said, "Are you a friend of this man?"

"Waal, you bet I am," he replied.

"Then," said I, "you had better get his hat and coat, or he'll go without them."

Then the prisoner wanted to go in and see his wife. I said, "No; call her out." As the six-footer brought the hat and coat, his wife-orator came out, having excused herself for a moment, and, much to my surprise, the audience kept their seats.

It began to be a little warm. Any moment an alarm might be given and this mob break loose. I kept cool, but it required an effort.

She wanted to know what was going to be done with her husband. I quietly replied, "Taken to Charles Street Jail."

"Well," she said, "I'll just go in and adjourn the convention, and then will come out and go with you, if you will wait a few moments."

I felt obliged, out of respect to my wife, sisters, and lady friends, to decline the kind offer of her (select) company. It was about all I wanted to do to have one of that slimy crowd in charge.

I knew that as soon as she returned and announced the arrest there would be a scene. I was in no mood for a bigger show than I had already witnessed. I had my money's worth and more, and was fully satisfied.

The prisoner desired to tarry. He did not readily respond to my gentle hint to come. Time was safety with me then. I said, "Come"; and then took him by the shoulder (or neck, or thereabouts), and he moved toward the foot of the stairs. We got part way down the top flight, and I heard a tremendous yell. Then came, in less time than it takes to write it, a rush of many feet, pell-mell over benches and seats, in their scramble to see who would get out and down first. I took my man by the nape of the neck and we went down the next flight rather lively, and into the carriage. Before the first one of the audience touched the sidewalk, we were half a block away, for before I could get the carriage door closed, my Jehu, thinking discretion the better part of valor, whipped his steeds into a gentle run, away ho! for Charles Street Jail, where we arrived in safety.

Thus, reader, the devil's trapper was trapped.

CHAPTER 2

THE SEXUAL REVOLUTION OF THE EARLY TWENTIETH CENTURY

AMERICAN
SOCIAL
MOVEMENTS

The End of
American Innocence

HENRY F. MAY

In the following excerpt from *The End of American Innocence*, historian
Henry F. May discusses some of the social and intellectual forces that
challenged the conservative sexual morality at the beginning of the
twentieth century. Traditionalists were confronted by feminists who
demanded that women be given access to birth control; conservatives
were also disturbed by the growing divorce rate. Avant-garde and sexually frank publications became more available, spurring increasing calls
for their suppression and censorship. May concludes that despite these
challenges to mainstream morality, the majority of the public held to
their traditional value systems in the years before World War I.

Young Intellectuals constantly attacked Puritanism; actually, nineteenth-century Anglo-Americans were stricter
about sexual morality than their Puritan ancestors. Liberal religion, giving less emphasis than its predecessors to the theo-
logical virtues, gave more to some kinds of conduct. In 1912
religious liberals, respectable freethinkers of the Robert In-
gersoll kind, and staunch evangelical Christians still saw eye to
eye about sexual morality.

   Chastity was, whether by divine precept or common consent, as absolute a good as honesty, and (this was tacitly admitted) far more difficult. Not all Americans agreed with Billy
Sunday about the reality of a personal devil, but most had reason to believe in temptation. Paradox lay at the root of the matter: sexual intercourse in marriage was a sacred duty, romantic
love the most beautiful thing in life, and sexual lust evil. Since
women, except the depraved few, were naturally pure, it was

Excerpted from *The End of American Innocence*, by Henry F. May (New York: Knopf, 1959).
Copyright © 1959 by Henry F. May. Reprinted with permission.

best that they have jurisdiction over the whole field of sexual relations. The duty of men was to make every effort to grow up pure, and especially to avoid the debilitating dangers that arose from evil thoughts. The crown of the whole civilization was the American family, with the father supreme in the economic sphere but the mother, freer and more respected than the women of other countries, in special charge of morals.

The millions of people who believed in this code and tried to live by it knew of course that it was continually broken. Lapses could be forgiven; outright defiance was far more serious. From Shelley to Sarah Bernhardt distinguished foreigners had flouted the code; now there were Americans who openly repudiated the customs of their own country. . . . Every now and then a member of the conservative middle class discovered that some people actually advocated and practiced what sounded to him like sheer deliberate wickedness. He was not surprised when such people turned out to be avant-garde artists or writers.

Women's rights were sometimes a corollary of nineteenth century moral progress, yet some kinds of militant feminism could be disturbing. To some American males it was disquieting in itself to find the weaker sex taking on the roles of athlete, professional, or political agitator. Sexual defensiveness was not far below the surface of some of the ridicule directed against allegedly mannish feminists and their effeminate male defenders.

BIRTH CONTROL

One of the most logical ends of female equality, and one of the most disturbing, was the demand that women take control of their own most important function: childbirth. In 1913 Margaret Sanger, according to her own account, coined the term birth control for a movement that had a long subterranean history. Mrs. Sanger was not hard to connect with the rebellious intellectuals. She had been brought up a socialist and influenced by Emma Goldman . . . and she had summered at Provincetown. Yet she was inescapably respectable, the wife of an architect and the mother of two children. Her interest in the problem had begun in a way the period approved. As a nurse in the New York slums, she had been horrified by abortion, the death of mothers, and the neglect of children, just as other reformers of the period had been horrified by tenement sanitation.

On her lecture tours, in her editorial and clinical work, and during her trial and imprisonment in 1916 Mrs. Sanger obviously ran into a complex whirlpool of public emotions. Expressions of horror and outrage were many; to some her purpose seemed an almost unbelievable apology for lust. Yet there was clearly another side. Many respectable feminists shared her view that motherhood must not be brought about by uncontrolled male passion, and some sociologists believed that the poorer classes at least must be helped to restrict their offspring. Mrs. Sanger's admirers extended far beyond the desperate and frantic women from the slums who saw her as a personal deliverer from slavery and death. The press noticed that limousines drew up outside her Western lectures. The government, goaded by Anthony Comstock and others into persecution, handled Mrs. Sanger with obvious gingerliness and timidity.

Changes in the Family

Dangerous thoughts about birth and marriage were not the whole trouble; the statistics too were alarming. Since 1867 the national birthrate and the average size of families had been declining. As an endless succession of books and pamphlets was pointing out, the decline was sharpest among the well educated, especially those of native New England stock. Divorce was going up. In 1914 the number of divorces first reached a round hundred thousand. This meant about one per thousand in the population; in 1867 the rate had been .35; in 1920 it was to reach 1.6. President Roosevelt, who had frequently denounced divorce in the press, considered the national sin of "wilful sterility" and the menace of "race suicide" serious enough as early as 1905 to give them considerable space in a message to Congress.

Here too public emotions were divided. It was, after all, a progressive era, and a large and respectable minority thought the family should change with the times. Many sociologists, a sprinkling of liberal ministers, and several of the muckraking magazines agreed that marriage itself needed overhauling. This was the message of William E. Carson's *The Marriage Revolt,* a popular summary of liberal doctrine published in 1915. To Carson the divorce rate and the wide uneasiness about marriage did not mean a spread of evil ideas. It meant that people were finally learning to see marriage not as an unchanging ordinance, but as a custom that could be altered for human happiness. To real moral conservatives, no suggestion could have been more shocking.

THE WHITE-SLAVE PANIC

The sharpest indication of sexual malaise was the white-slave panic, which reached its unaccountably hysterical peak in the peaceful prewar year 1913. It apparently started with the muckrakers, who had turned to the enticing subject of prostitution as early as 1907. Their attitude was a familiar one: the "Daughters of the Poor" were innocent victims; the real criminals were members of a secret, mysterious white-slave trust. In 1910 Congress attacked this trust with the Mann Act, designed to end the interstate white-slave trade. In the same year the New York Grand Jury, with John D. Rockefeller as foreman, started an investigation, and in 1911 the Chicago Vice Commission issued its famous report. Within three or four years most of the nation's states and cities conducted some sort of inquiry.

Inevitably, the cause was taken up by sensationalists on the borderline between evangelism, muckraking, and pornography in a number of lurid books about "The Girl Who Disappears." Novelists seized on the subject; the movies devoted a number of full length features to "The Traffic in Souls." Any girl, it seemed, who said hello to a stranger in a large city was likely to be pricked with a poisoned needle and spirited away. She would wake up, helpless, in the brothels of Rio or Constantinople. A correspondent of the *New York World* said that his wife believed fifty thousand women disappeared from Chicago and New York every year, and that more than half the men in the country were working night and day in an organization more formidable than the Steel Trust. Frederick C. Howe, Wilson's liberal Commissioner of Immigration, found himself on Ellis Island the custodian of hundreds of alien men and women, seized on flimsy evidence as prostitutes or procurers. Howe, describing the excitement later, compared it in intensity to the Pro-German hysteria of 1918 and the Red Scare of 1919–20.

By 1913 and 1914, when the panic reached its height, a counteroffensive got under way. H.L. Mencken, among others, jumped with delight on this new, superb example of Puritan gullibility. Sober newspapers assured their readers that the poisoned needle was a myth. In a strange backwash of emotions, the censors started to object to white-slave films and novels. In 1913 *Current Opinion,* seizing a phrase of William Marion Reedy's, lamented that it seemed to have struck "Sex O'Clock" in America. Our reticence about sex was yielding, it said, to a frankness that would have startled Paris, and the center of the trouble was the constant discussion of prostitution.

CONSERVATIVE REACTION

All these and other fears lay behind the reaction of conservative America to the essentially innocent ideas of the Rebellion, and to its favorite literature. No literate American could manage by the mid-teens to ignore Ibsen, Wells, and Dreiser entirely. To many, the solution seemed simple, to tighten the existing censorship. The *Dial,* in 1912, four years before it deserted to the rebels, stated exactly the point of view that the Freudians and others found most abhorrent:

> Now reticence may possibly go too far, but no sane person can deny that there are ugly things in life that had better be kept in the dark corners of consciousness.

Ever since the 1870s Anthony Comstock, for one, had been trying to keep them there, and his activities seemed to be reaching a wild crescendo just before his death in 1915. Armed with the federal and state laws which his efforts had secured, commissioned as a special agent by the Post Office Department, backed by his own New York Society for the Suppression of Vice and a network of similar societies in other states, Comstock was a formidable figure. Since he believed deeply in the pervasive, infectious power of evil thoughts, Comstock drew no lines between deliberate pornography, European classic art, and factual reports of vice commissions. In 1912 he attacked and made famous a painfully decorous picture which had won the medal of honor at the Paris Spring Salon; it was called "September Morning." In 1914 he went after the February issue of the *Chautauquan,* which had on its cover a photograph of a Greek faun recently dug up by a University of Pennsylvania expedition.

To publishers, and especially to new, daring, and vulnerable publishers, Comstock was not by any means a laughing matter, and neither was his slightly less spectacular successor as Secretary of the New York Society, John S. Sumner. Those who defied him might find their books denied the mails and boycotted by booksellers, themselves in court facing an inflamed and hostile jury. In 1913 Comstock led a dramatic raid on Mitchell Kennerley's office and brought the publisher to trial over the novel *Hagar Revelly.* In December 1915 Knopf, barely started, was threatened with attack over Przybyszewski's *Homo Sapiens.* In 1917 Sumner attacked Appleton for publishing *Susan Lenox,* the famous, impeccably uplifting, white-slave novel of the muckraking novelist David Graham Phillips.

CENSORS VERSUS INTELLECTUALS

The climax of prewar censorship battles, and the prelude to many celebrated engagements of the twenties, raged round the battered head of Theodore Dreiser. In July 1916 the Western Society for the Prevention of Vice, aroused by a Cincinnati minister, attacked *The Genius,* got it removed from the bookstores, secured a temporary cessation-of-circulation order from the Post Office Department and filed a complaint with its New York counterpart, Sumner's famous Society. Sumner, following the usual procedure, persuaded Lane to withdraw the book pending a court contest and managed to get it banned throughout the country.

This time, however, Sumner ran into a fight. Despite Mencken's correct warnings that anti-German sentiment would be brought into the contest, Dreiser refused to compromise, and Mencken roused a public protest. He failed to get help from Howells, Brander Matthews, and most of the other custodians of culture. Yet he was able to line up a formidable list of libertarians: in England Arnold Bennett, Hugh Walpole, and Wells; in this country Amy Lowell, Robert Frost, Edwin Arlington Robinson, Willa Cather, William Allen White, Knopf, Huebsch, and many others. The book remained substantially suppressed until 1923, but the defenders of intellectual freedom were aroused to battle as never before.

In this battle, and in the whole war that was opening, both sides were serious. To the intellectuals, censors were nasty and cruel old men, inflicting on others their own frustrations, denying to America the possibility of free and joyous self-expression. To some of the conservatives in the prewar years, a strange flood of filth was welling up from mysterious sources. Erotic plays and books, divorce, free love, lascivious dances, birth control were menacing not only American culture but the possibility of moral restraint, the sheet-anchor of any and all civilization.

The *Nation,* balanced and serious as usual, presented a picture of the situation in 1913 which was fairly accurate, given the *Nation's* assumptions. All was not lost, despite:

> Tango, eugenics, the slit skirt, sex hygiene, Brieux, white slaves, Richard Strauss, John Masefield, the double standard of morality . . . a conglomerate of things important and unimportant, of age-old problems and momentary fads, which nevertheless have this one thing in common, that they do involve an abandonment of the old proprieties and the old reticences. . . .

One must distinguish, said the *Nation,* between the fluttering tastes of the half-baked intellectuals, attracted by all these things, and the surviving soundness of the great majority. It was still only revolt, not revolution.

The Love-Rights of Women

Havelock Ellis

The English doctor and author Havelock Ellis wrote essays on sex and marriage that influenced European and American attitudes toward sexuality early in the twentieth century. In the following selection from his 1922 text *On Life and Sex*, Ellis maintains that women are often deprived of sexual pleasure in marriage because the male-dominated social order deems erotic feelings improper for married women. A double standard which assumes that men—but not married women—desire erotic pleasure has led to an unnatural sexual repression in women and coldness in marriages, explains Ellis. He believes a fundamental change in attitude is needed—one in which men perceive women as equals and a wife's right to sexual joy is seen as natural and healthy.

What is the part of woman, one is sometimes asked, in the sex act? Must it be the wife's concern in the marital embrace to sacrifice her own wishes from a sense of love and duty towards her husband? Or is the wife entitled to an equal mutual interest and joy in this act with her husband? It seems a simple problem. In so fundamental a relationship, which goes back to the beginning of sex in the dawn of life, it might appear that we could leave Nature to decide. Yet it is not so. Throughout the history of civilisation, wherever we can trace the feelings and ideas which have prevailed on this matter and the resultant conduct, the problem has existed, often to produce discord, conflict, and misery. The problem still exists to-day and with as important results as in the past.

Excerpted from *On Life and Sex*, by Havelock Ellis (New York: George H. Doran, 1922).

In Nature, before the arrival of Man, it can scarcely be said indeed that any difficulty existed. It was taken for granted at that time that the female had both the right to her own body, and the right to a certain amount of enjoyment in the use of it. It often cost the male a serious amount of trouble—though he never failed to find it worth while—to explain to her the point where he may be allowed to come in, and to persuade her that he can contribute to her enjoyment. So it generally is throughout Nature, before we reach Man, and, though it is not invariably obvious, we often find it even among the unlikeliest animals. As is well known, it is most pronounced among the birds, who have in some species carried the erotic art,— and the faithful devotion which properly accompanied the erotic art as being an essential part of it,—to the highest point. We have here the great natural fact of courtship. Throughout Nature, wherever we meet with animals of a high type, often indeed when they are of a lowly type—provided they have not been rendered unnatural by domestication—every act of sexual union is preceded by a process of courtship. There is a sound physiological reason for this courtship, for in the act of wooing and being wooed the psychic excitement gradually generated in the brains of the two partners acts as a stimulant to arouse into full activity the mechanism which ensures sexual union and aids ultimate impregnation. Such courtship is thus a fundamental natural fact.

AMONG PRIMITIVE PEOPLES

It is as a natural fact that we still find it in full development among a large number of peoples of the lower races whom we are accustomed to regard as more primitive than ourselves. New conditions, it is true, soon enter to complicate the picture presented by savage courtship. The economic element of bargaining, destined to prove so important, comes in at an early stage. And among peoples leading a violent life, and constantly fighting, it has sometimes happened, though not always, that courtship also has been violent. This is not so frequent as was once supposed. With better knowledge it was found that the seeming brutality once thought to take the place of courtship among various peoples in a low state of culture was really itself courtship, a rough kind of play agreeable to both parties and not depriving the feminine partner of her own freedom of choice. This was notably the case as regards so-called "marriage by capture." While this is sometimes a real capture, it is more often a mock capture; the lover perhaps pursues the beloved on horseback, but she is as fleet and as skilful as he is, cannot be captured unless she wishes to be captured, and in addition, as among the Kirghiz, she may be armed with a formidable whip; so that "marriage by capture," far from being a hardship imposed on women is largely a concession to their modesty and a gratification of their erotic impulses. Even when the chief part of the decision rests with masculine force courtship is still not necessarily or usually excluded, for the exhibition of force by a lover,—and this is true for civilised as well as for savage women,—is itself a source of pleasurable stimulation, and when that is so the essence of courtship may be attained even more successfully by the forceful than by the humble lover.

The evolution of society, however, tended to overlay and sometimes even to suppress those fundamental natural tendencies. The position of the man as the sole and uncontested head of the family, the insistence on paternity and male descent, the accompanying economic developments, and the tendency to view a woman less as a self-disposing individual than as an object of barter belonging to her father, the consequent rigidity of the marriage bond and the stern insistence on wifely fidelity—all these conditions of developing civilisation, while still leaving courtship possible, diminished its significance and even abolished its necessity. Moreover, on the basis of the social, economic, and legal developments thus established, new moral, spiritual, and religious forces were slowly generated, which worked on these rules of merely exterior order, and interiorised them, thus giving them power over the souls as well as over the bodies of women.

The result was that, directly and indirectly, the legal, economic, and erotic rights of women were all diminished. It is with the erotic rights only that we are here concerned.

THE ESTABLISHED SOCIAL ORDER

No doubt in its erotic aspects, as well as in its legal and economic aspects, the social order thus established was described, and in good faith, as beneficial to women, and even as maintained in their interests. Monogamy and the home, it was claimed, alike existed for the benefit and protection of women. It was not so often explained that they greatly benefited and protected men, with, moreover, this additional advantage that while women were absolutely confined to the home, men were free to exercise their activities outside the home, even, with tacit general consent, on the erotic side.

Whatever the real benefits, and there is no occasion for questioning them, of the sexual order thus established, it becomes clear that in certain important respects it had an unnatural and repressive influence on the erotic aspect of woman's sexual life. It fostered the reproductive side of woman's sexual life, but it rendered difficult for her the satisfaction of the instinct for that courtship which is the natural preliminary of reproductive activity, an instinct even more highly developed in the female than in the male, and the more insistent because in the order of Nature the burden of maternity is preceded by the reward of pleasure. But the marriage order which had become established led to the indirect result of banning pleasure in women, or at all events in wives. It was regarded as too dangerous, and even as degrading. The women who wanted pleasure were not considered fit for the home, but more suited to be devoted to an exclusive "life of pleasure," which soon turned out to be not their own pleasure but men's. A "life of pleasure," in that sense or in any other sense, was not what more than a small minority of women ever desired. The desire of women for courtship is not a thing by itself, and was not implanted for gratification by itself. It is naturally intertwined—and to a much greater degree than the corresponding desire in men—with her deepest personal, family, and social instincts, so that if these are desecrated and lost its charm soon fades.

The practices and the ideals of this established morality were both due to men, and both were so thoroughly fashioned that they subjugated alike the actions and the feelings of women. There is no sphere which we regard as so peculiarly women's sphere as that of love. Yet there is no sphere which in civilisation women have so far had so small a part in regulating. Their deepest impulses—their modesty, their maternity, their devotion, their emotional receptivity—were used, with no conscious and deliberate Machiavellism, against themselves, to mould a moral world for their habitation which they would not themselves have moulded. It is not of modern creation, nor by any means due, as some have supposed, to the asceticism of Christianity, however much Christianity may have reinforced it. Indeed one may say that in course of time Christianity had an influence in weakening it, for Christianity discovered a new reservoir of tender emotion, and such emotion may be transferred, and, as a matter of fact, was transferred, from its first religious channel into erotic channels which were thereby deepened and extended, and without reference to any design of Christianity. For the ends we achieve are often by no means those which we set out to accomplish. In ancient classic days this moral order was even more severely established than in the Middle Ages. Montaigne, in the sixteenth century, declared that "marriage is a devout and religious relationship, the pleasures derived from it should be restrained and serious, mixed with some severity." But in this matter he was not merely expressing the Christian standpoint but even more that of paganism, and he thoroughly agreed with the old Greek moralist that a man should approach his wife "prudently and severely" for fear of inciting her to lasciviousness; he thought that marriage was best arranged by a third party, and was inclined to think, with the ancients, that women are not fitted to make friends of. Montaigne has elsewhere spoken with insight of women's instinctive knowledge of the art and discipline of love and has pointed out how men have imposed their own ideals and rules of action on women from whom they have demanded opposite and contradictory virtues; yet, we see, he approves of this state of things and never suggests that women have any right to opinions of their own or feelings of their own when the sacred institution of marriage is in question.

Montaigne represents the more exalted aspects of the Pagan-Christian conception of morality in marriage which still largely prevails. But that conception lent itself to deductions, frankly accepted even by Montaigne himself, which were by no means exalted. "I find," said Montaigne, "that Venus, after all, is nothing more than the pleasure of discharging our vessels, just as nature renders pleasurable the discharges from other parts." Sir Thomas More among Catholics, and Luther among Protestants, said exactly the same thing in other and even clearer words, while untold millions of husbands in Christendom down to to-day, whether or not they have had the wit to put their theory into a phrase, have regularly put it into practice, at all events within the consecrated pale of marriage, and treated their wives, "severely and prudently," as convenient utensils for the reception of a natural excretion.

MASCULINE IDEALS OF SEXUAL MORALITY

Obviously, in this view of marriage, sexual activity was regarded as an exclusively masculine function, in the exercise of which women had merely a passive part to play. Any active participation on her side thus seemed unnecessary, and even unbefitting, finally, though only in comparatively modern times, disgusting and actually degrading. Thus Acton, who was regarded [in the late nineteenth century] as the chief English authority on sexual matters, declared that, "happily for society," the supposition that women possess sexual feelings could be put aside as "a vile aspersion," while another medical authority of the same period stated in regard to the most simple physical sign of healthy sexual emotion that it "only happens in lascivious women." This final triumph of the masculine ideals and rule of life was, however, only achieved slowly. It was the culmination of an elaborate process of training. At the outset men had found it impossible to speak too strongly of the "wantonness" of women. This attitude was pronounced among the ancient Greeks and prominent in their dramatists. Christianity again, which ended by making women into the chief pillars of the Church, began by regarding them as the "Gate of Hell." Again, later, when in the Middle Ages this masculine moral order approached the task of subjugating the barbarians of Northern Europe, men were horrified at the licentiousness of those northern women at whose coldness they are now shocked.

That, indeed, was, as Montaigne had seen, the central core of conflict in the rule of life imposed by men on woman. Men were perpetually striving, by ways the most methodical, the most subtle, the most far-reaching, to achieve a result in women, which, when achieved, men themselves viewed with dismay. They may be said to be moved in this sphere by two passions, the passion for virtue and the passion for vice. But it so happens that both these streams of passion have to be directed at the same fascinating object: Woman. No doubt nothing is more admirable than the skill with which women have acquired the duplicity necessary to play the two contradictory parts thus imposed upon them. But in that requirement the play of their natural reactions tended to become paralysed, and the delicate mechanism of their instincts often disturbed. They were forbidden, except in a few carefully etiquetted forms, the free play of courtship, without which they could not perform their part in the erotic life with full satisfaction either to themselves or their partners. They were reduced to an artificial simulation of coldness or of warmth, according to the particular stage of the dominating masculine ideal of woman which their partner chanced to have reached. But that is an attitude equally unsatisfactory to themselves and to their lovers, even when the latter have not sufficient insight to see through its unreality. It is an attitude so unnatural and artificial that it inevitably tends to produce a real coldness which nothing can disguise. It is true that women whose instincts are not perverted at the roots do not desire to be cold. Far from it. But to dispel that coldness the right atmosphere is needed, and the insight and skill of the right man. In the erotic sphere a woman asks nothing better of a man than to be lifted above her coldness, to the higher plane where there is reciprocal interest and mutual joy in the act of love. Therein her silent demand is one with Nature's. For the biological order of the world involves those claims which, in the human range, are the erotic rights of women.

THE EROTIC CLAIMS OF WOMEN

The social claims of women, their economic claims, their political claims, have long been before the world. Women themselves have actively asserted them, and they are all in process of realisation. The erotic claims of women, which are at least as fundamental, are not publicly voiced, and women themselves would be the last to assert them. It is easy to understand why that should be so. The natural and acquired qualities of women, even the qualities developed in the art of courtship, have all been utilised in building up the masculine ideal of sexual morality; it is on feminine characteristics that this masculine ideal has been based, so that women have been helpless to protest against it. Moreover, even if that were not so, to formulate such rights is to raise the question whether there so much as exists anything that can be called "erotic rights." The right to joy cannot be claimed in the same way as one claims the right to put a voting paper in a ballot box. A human being's erotic aptitudes can only be developed where the right atmosphere for them exists, and where the attitudes of both persons concerned are in harmonious sympathy. That is why the erotic rights of women have been the last of all to be attained.

Yet to-day we see a change here. The change required is, it has been said, a change of attitude and a resultant change in the atmosphere in which the sexual impulses are manifested. It involves no necessary change in the external order of our marriage system, for, as has already been pointed out, it was a coincident and not designed part of that order. Various recent lines of tendency have converged to produce this change of attitude and of atmosphere. In part the men of to-day are far more ready than the men of former days to look upon women as their comrades in the every day work of the world, instead of as beings who were ideally on a level above themselves and practically on a level considerably below themselves. In part there is the growing recognition that women have conquered many elementary human rights of which before they were deprived, and are more and more taking the position of citizens, with the same kinds of duties, privileges, and responsibilities as men. In part, also, it may be added, there is a growing diffusion among educated people of a knowledge of the primary facts of life in the two sexes, slowly dissipating and dissolving many foolish and often mischievous superstitions. The result is that, as many competent observers have noted, the young men of to-day show a new attitude towards women and towards marriage, an attitude of simplicity and frankness, a desire for mutual confidence, a readiness to discuss difficulties, an appeal to understand and to be understood. Such an attitude, which had hitherto been hard to attain, at once creates the atmosphere in which alone the free spontaneous erotic activities of women can breathe and live.

This consummation, we have seen, may be regarded as the attainment of certain rights, the corollary of other rights in the social field which women are slowly achieving as human beings on the same human level as men. It opens to women, on whom is always laid the chief burden of sex, the right to the joy and exaltation of sex, to the uplifting of the soul which, when the right conditions are fulfilled, is the outcome of the intimate approach and union of two human beings. Yet while we may find convenient so to formulate it, we need to remember that that is only a fashion of speech, for there are no rights in Nature. If we take a broader sweep, what we may choose to call an erotic right is simply the perfect poise of the conflicting forces of life, the rhythmic harmony in which generation is achieved with the highest degree of perfection compatible with the make of the world. It is our part to transform Nature's large conception into our own smaller organic mould, not otherwise than the plants, to whom we are far back akin, who dig their flexible roots deep into the moist and fruitful earth, and so are able to lift up glorious heads toward the sky.

The Beginning of My Fight for Birth Control

MARGARET SANGER

Margaret Sanger was instrumental in the formation of the first widespread American birth control movement. In 1921 she established the American Birth Control League, a lobbying group of medical professionals, which became known as Planned Parenthood in 1942. In the following excerpt from her 1931 book, *My Fight for Birth Control*, Sanger discusses her experiences working as a nurse in New York City slums. Witnessing the miserable living conditions and the desperation of poor women who gave birth to numerous children—and women who died from pregnancy complications or crudely performed abortions—fostered Sanger's desire to provide the public with information about reliable contraception.

E arly in the year 1912 I came to a sudden realization that my work as a nurse and my activities in social service were entirely palliative and consequently futile and useless to relieve the misery I saw all about me.

For several years I had had the good fortune to have the children's paternal grandmother living with us and sharing in their care, thereby releasing more of my time and renewed energy for the many activities and professional work of the nursing field. I had longed for this opportunity, and it now enabled me to share in the financial responsibility of the home, which, owing to the heavy expenditures caused by my illness, I felt was the only self-respecting thing to do. I eventually took special obstetrical and surgical cases assigned to me from time to

Excerpted from *My Fight for Birth Control*, by Margaret Sanger (New York: Farrar & Rinehart, Inc., 1931). Copyright © 1931 by Dr. Grant Sanger.

time, and had glimpses into the lives of rich and poor alike.

When I look back upon that period it seems only a short time ago; yet in the brief interval conditions have changed enormously. At that time it was not the usual thing for a poor woman to go to a hospital to give birth to her baby. She preferred to stay at home. She was afraid of hospitals when any serious ailment was involved. That is not the case today. Women of all classes are more likely to have their babies in lying-in hospitals or in private sanatoriums than at home; but in those days a woman's own bedroom, no matter how inconveniently arranged, was the usual place for confinement. That was the day of home nursing, and it gave a trained nurse splendid opportunities to learn social conditions through actual contact with them.

REVOLTING LIVING CONDITIONS

Were it possible for me to depict the revolting conditions existing in the homes of some of the women I attended in that one year, one would find it hard to believe. There was at that time, and doubtless is still today, a sub-stratum of men and women whose lives are absolutely untouched by social agencies.

The way they live is almost beyond belief. They hate and fear any prying into their homes or into their lives. They resent being talked to. The women slink in and out of their homes on their way to market like rats from their holes. The men beat their wives sometimes black and blue, but no one interferes. The children are cuffed, kicked and chased about, but woe to the child who dares to tell tales out of the home! Crime or drink is often the source of this secret aloofness; usually there is something to hide, a skeleton in the closet somewhere. The men are sullen, unskilled workers, picking up odd jobs now and then, unemployed usually, sauntering in and out of the house at all hours of the day and night.

The women keep apart from other women in the neighborhood. Often they are suspected of picking a pocket or "lifting" an article when occasion arises. Pregnancy is an almost chronic condition amongst them. I knew one woman who had given birth to eight children with no professional care whatever. The last one was born in the kitchen, witnessed by a son of ten years who, under his mother's direction, cleaned the bed, wrapped the placenta and soiled articles in paper, and threw them out of the window into the court below.

They reject help of any kind and want you to "mind your own business." Birth and death they consider their own affairs. They survive as best they can, suspicious of everyone, deathly afraid of police and officials of every kind.

They are the submerged, untouched classes which no labor union, no church nor organization of a highly expensive, organized city ever reaches and rarely tries to reach. They are beyond the scope of organized charity or religion; not even the Salvation Army touches them. It was a sad consolation to hear other women in the stratum just slightly above breathe contented sighs and thank God that they had not sunk so low as that.

THE DIFFICULTIES OF POOR MOTHERS

It is among the mothers here that the most difficult problems arise—the outcasts of society with theft, filth, perjury, cruelty, brutality oozing from beneath.

Ignorance and neglect go on day by day; children born to breathe but a few hours and pass out of life; pregnant women toiling early and late to give food to four or five children, always hungry; boarders taken into homes where there is not sufficient room for the family; little girls eight and ten years of age sleeping in the same room with dirty, foul smelling, loathsome men; women whose weary, pregnant, shapeless bodies refuse to accommodate themselves to the husbands' desires find husbands looking with lustful eyes upon other women, sometimes upon their own little daughters, six and seven years of age.

In this atmosphere abortions and birth become the main theme of conversation. On Saturday nights I have seen groups of fifty to one hundred women going into questionable offices well known in the community for cheap abortions. I asked several women what took place there, and they all gave the same reply: a quick examination, a probe inserted into the uterus and turned a few times to disturb the fertilized ovum, and then the woman was sent home. Usually the flow began the next day and often continued four or five weeks. Sometimes an ambulance carried the victim to the hospital for a curetage, and if she returned home at all she was looked upon as a lucky woman.

This state of things became a nightmare with me. There seemed no sense to it all, no reason for such waste of mother life, no right to exhaust women's vitality and to throw them on the scrap-heap before the age of thirty-five.

FEAR AND DESPERATION

Everywhere I looked, misery and fear stalked—men fearful of losing their jobs, women fearful that even worse conditions might come upon them. The menace of another pregnancy hung like a sword over the head of every poor woman I came in contact with that year. The question which met me was always the same: What can I do to keep from it? or, What can I do to get out of this? Sometimes they talked among themselves bitterly.

"It's the rich that know the tricks," they'd say, "while we have all the kids." Then, if the women were Roman Catholics, they talked about "Yankee tricks," and asked me if I knew what the Protestants did to keep their families down. When I said that I didn't believe that the rich knew much more than they did I was laughed at and suspected of holding back information for money. They would nudge each other and say something about paying me before I left the case if I would reveal the "secret."

It all sickened me. It was heartbreaking to witness the rapt, anxious, eager expression on their pale, worried faces as I told them necessary details concerning cleanliness and hygiene of their sex organs. It was appalling how little they knew of the terms I was using, yet how familiar they were with those organs and their functions and how unafraid to try anything, no matter what the results.

I heard over and over again of their desperate efforts at

bringing themselves "around"—drinking various herb-teas, taking drops of turpentine on sugar, steaming over a chamber of boiling coffee or of turpentine water, rolling down stairs, and finally inserting slippery-elm sticks, or knitting needles, or shoe hooks into the uterus. I used to shudder with horror as I heard the details and, worse yet, learned of the conditions *behind the reason* for such desperate actions. Day after day these stories were poured into my ears. I knew hundreds of these women personally, and knew much of their hopeless, barren, dreary lives.

A RETURN TO MISERY

What relief I had came when I shifted my work for a few weeks to the then fashionable Riverside Drive or to the upper western section of New York City, but inevitably I was called back into the lower East or West Side as if magnetically attracted by its misery.

The contrast in conditions seemed only to intensify the horrors of those poverty-stricken homes, and each time I returned it was to hear that Mrs. Cohen had been carried to a hospital but had never come back, that Mrs. Kelly had sent the children to a neighbor's and had put her head into the gas oven to end her misery. Many of the women had consulted midwives, social workers and doctors at the dispensary and asked a way to limit their families, but they were denied this help, sometimes indignantly or gruffly, sometimes jokingly; but always knowledge was denied them. Life for them had but one choice: either to abandon themselves to incessant childbearing, or to terminate their pregnancies through abortions. Is it any wonder they resigned themselves hopelessly, as the Jewish and Italian mothers, or fell into drunkenness, as the Irish and Scotch? The latter were often beaten by husbands, as well as by their sons and daughters. They were driven and cowed, and only as beasts of burden were allowed to exist. Life for them was full of fear.

Words fail to express the impressions these lives made on my sensitive nature. My own happy love life became a reproach. These other lives began to clutch at all I held dear. The intimate knowledge of these misshapen, hapless, desperate women seemed to separate me from the right of happiness.

They claimed my thoughts night and day. One by one these women, with their worried, sad, pensive and ageing faces would marshal themselves before me in my dreams, sometimes appealingly, sometimes accusingly. I could not escape from the facts of their misery, neither was I able to see the way out of their problems and their troubles. Like one walking in a sleep, I kept on.

MRS. SACKS

Finally the thing began to shape itself, to become accumulative during the three weeks I spent in the home of a desperately sick woman living on Grand Street, a lower section of New York's East Side.

Mrs. Sacks was only twenty-eight years old; her husband, an unskilled worker, thirty-two. Three children, aged five, three and one, were none too strong nor sturdy, and it took all the earnings of the father and the ingenuity of the mother to keep them clean, provide them with air and proper food, and give them a chance to grow into decent manhood and womanhood.

Both parents were devoted to these children and to each other. The woman had become pregnant and had taken various drugs and purgatives, as advised by her neighbors. Then, in desperation, she had used some instrument lent to her by a friend. She was found prostrate on the floor amidst the crying children when her husband returned from work. Neighbors advised against the ambulance, and a friendly doctor was called. The husband would not hear of her going to a hospital, and as a little money had been saved in the bank a nurse was called and the battle for that precious life began.

It was in the middle of July. The three-room apartment was turned into a hospital for the dying patient. Never had I worked so fast, never so concentratedly as I did to keep alive that little mother. Neighbor women came and went during the day doing the odds and ends necessary for our comfort.

The children were sent to friends and relatives and the doctor and I settled ourselves to outdo the force and power of an outraged nature.

Never had I known such conditions could exist. July's sultry days and nights were melted into a torpid inferno. Day after day, night after night, I slept only in brief snatches, ever too anxious about the condition of that feeble heart bravely carrying on, to stay long from the bedside of the patient. With but one toilet for the building and that on the floor below, everything had to be carried down for disposal, while ice, food and other necessities had to be carried three flights up. It was one of those old airshaft buildings of which there were several thousands then standing in New York City.

At the end of two weeks recovery was in sight, and at the end of three weeks I was preparing to leave the fragile patient to take up the ordinary duties of her life, including those of wifehood and motherhood. Everyone was congratulating her on her recovery. All the kindness of sympathetic and understanding neighbors poured in upon her in the shape of convalescent dishes, soups, custards, and drinks. Still she appeared to be despondent and worried. She seemed to sit apart in her thoughts as if she had no part in these congratulatory messages and endearing welcomes. I thought at first that she still retained some of her unconscious memories and dwelt upon them in her silences.

But as the hour for my departure came nearer, her anxiety increased, and finally with trembling voice she said: "Another baby will finish me, I suppose."

"It's too early to talk about that," I said, and resolved that I would turn the question over to the doctor for his advice. When he came I said: "Mrs. Sacks is worried about having another baby."

"She well might be," replied the doctor, and then he stood before her and said: "Any more such capers, young woman, and there will be no need to call me."

"Yes, yes—I know, Doctor," said the patient with trembling voice, "but," and she hesitated as if it took all of her courage to say it, "*what* can I do to prevent getting that way again?"

"Oh ho!" laughed the doctor good naturedly, "You want your cake while you eat it too, do you? Well, it can't be done." Then, familiarly slapping her on the back and picking up his hat and bag to depart, he said: "I'll tell you the only sure thing to do. Tell Jake to sleep on the roof!"

With those words he closed the door and went down the stairs, leaving us both petrified and stunned.

Tears sprang to my eyes, and a lump came in my throat as I looked at that face before me. It was stamped with sheer horror.

The Trap of Maternity

In her book Motherhood in Bondage, *Sanger presents case histories of poor mothers "who are pathetically begging for release from the long slavery they have suffered and are still enduring."*

I have tried so hard not to become pregnant but now I am pregnant again after having given birth to fourteen children. It seems to me it was more than one woman should be asked to. It sure makes my heart and hands full. Husband has cancer of the stomach and I have wanted to be all the comfort to him possible but now my heart is broken and makes me feel like giving up. The oldest child is twenty-four and my last baby was three and now I am along three months again. What should a woman do? It sure seems like a woman should have a limited number of children. I love babies but how can one do justice to a little bunch like this. I some times do not see how I ever have stood it all. I don't see why the law should not be in favor of contraceptives; unless it is that it is in man's hands and he does not have to suffer the consequences.

Margaret Sanger, *Motherhood in Bondage*, 1928.

I thought for a moment she might have gone insane, but she conquered her feelings, whatever they may have been, and turning to me in desperation said: "He can't understand, can he?—he's a man after all—but you do, don't you? You're a woman and you'll tell me the secret and I'll never tell it to a soul."

She clasped her hands as if in prayer, she leaned over and looked straight into my eyes and beseechingly implored me to tell her something—something *I really did not know.* It was like being on a rack and tortured for a crime one had not committed. To plead guilty would stop the agony; otherwise the rack kept turning.

I had to turn away from that imploring face. I could not answer her then. I quieted her as best I could. She saw that I was moved by the tears in my eyes. I promised that I would come back in a few days and tell her what she wanted to know. The few simple means of limiting the family like *coitus interruptus* or the condom were laughed at by the neighboring women when told these were the means used by men in the well-to-do families. That was not believed, and I knew such an answer would be swept aside as useless were I to tell her this at such a time.

A little later when she slept I left the house, and made up my mind that I'd keep away from those cases in the future. I felt helpless to do anything at all. I seemed chained hand and foot, and longed for an earthquake or a volcano to shake the world out of its lethargy into facing these monstrous atrocities.

The intelligent reasoning of the young mother—how to *prevent* getting that way again—how sensible, how just she had been—yes, I promised myself I'd go back and have a long talk with her and tell her more, and perhaps she would not laugh but would believe that those methods were all that were really known.

But time flew past, and weeks rolled into months. That wistful, appealing face haunted me day and night. I could not banish from my mind memories of that trembling voice begging so humbly for knowledge she had a right to have. I was about to retire one night three months later when the telephone rang and an agitated man's voice begged me to come at once to help his wife who was sick again. It was the husband of Mrs. Sacks, and I intuitively knew before I left the telephone that it was almost useless to go.

I dreaded to face that woman. I was tempted to send someone else in my place. I longed for an accident on the subway, or on the street—anything to prevent my going into that home. But on I went just the same. I arrived a few minutes after the doctor, the same one who had given her such noble advice. The woman was dying. She was unconscious. She died within ten minutes after my arrival. It was the same result, the same story told a thousand times before—death from abortion. She had become pregnant, had used drugs, had then consulted a five-dollar professional abortionist, and death followed.

The doctor shook his head as he rose from listening for the heart beat. I knew she had already passed on; without a groan, a sigh or recognition of our belated presence she had gone into the Great Beyond as thousands of mothers go every year. I looked at that drawn face now stilled in death. I placed her thin hands across her breast and recalled how hard they had pleaded with me on that last memorable occasion of parting. The gentle woman, the devoted mother, the loving wife had passed on leaving behind her a frantic husband, helpless in his loneliness, bewildered in his helplessness as he paced up and down the room, hands clenching his head, moaning "My God! My God! My God!"

THE REVOLUTION

The Revolution came—but not as it has been pictured nor as history relates that revolutions have come. It came in my own life. It began in my very being as I walked home that night after I had closed the eyes and covered with a sheet the body of that little helpless mother whose life had been sacrificed to ignorance. . . .

I asked doctors what one could do and was told I'd better keep off that subject or Anthony Comstock would get me. I was told that there were laws against that sort of thing. This was the reply from every medical man and woman I approached.

Then I consulted the "up and doing" progressive women who then called themselves Feminists. Most of them were shocked at the mention of abortion, while others were scarcely able to keep from laughing at the idea of my making a public campaign around the idea of too many children. "It can't be done," they said. "You are too sympathetic. You can't do a thing about it until we get the vote. Go home to your children and let things alone.". . .

I had previously cast my lot with the women of the Socialist movement. I listened intently to all debates, arguments and theories of this great school of liberal thought. Their ardent and passionate faith in legislation, however, I could never share. Their answer to the misery of women and the ignorance of contraceptive knowledge was like that of the Feminists: "Wait until we get the vote to put *us* in power!"

Wherever I turned, from every one I approached I met the same answer: "Wait!" "Wait until women get the vote." "Wait until the Socialists are in power." "Wait for the Social Revolution." "Wait for the Industrial Revolution." Thus I lost my faith in the social schemes and organizations of that day.

Only the boys of the International Workers of the World seemed to grasp the economic significance of this great social question. At once they visualized its importance, and instead of saying "Wait" they gave me names of organizers in the silk, woolen and copper industries, and offered their assistance to get any facts on family limitation I secured direct to the workingmen and their wives.

My friend "Big Bill" Haywood came to my aid with that cheering encouragement of which I was so sorely in need. He never wasted words in advising me to "wait." I owe him a debt of gratitude which I am proud to acknowledge. It was he who suggested that I go to France and see for myself the conditions resulting from generations of family limitation. This idea . . . convinced me that I was to find new ways to solve old problems in Europe. I decided to go and see.

The Sudden Popularity of Sex

JOHN MCPARTLAND

World War I had a profound impact on American sexual mores, contends John McPartland in the following selection. Many women began working in factories and offices, earning an income that afforded them a new sense of freedom and independence; meanwhile, men in the armed services became sexually adventurous during their time in Europe. Many young people dealt with the anxieties of war by having sex outside of marriage and engaging in other forms of rebellion against traditional moral standards. These emotional and sexual binges, along with the money that became more readily available during and after the war, set the stage for the "carnival of the Twenties," writes McPartland. Taboos were broken as popular culture, art, and entertainment became more sexually charged, reflecting and influencing American tastes and behavior. This selection is excerpted from the 1947 book *Sex in Our Changing World*, in which McPartland laments the sexual selfishness and national cynicism that he feels resulted from the excesses of the 1920s.

It didn't last long, only from April of 1917 to November of 1918; by the spring of 1919 almost all of the new soldiers had unwound their puttees for the last time, put away the choke-collared uniforms, and had settled down to get rich. In comparison to [World War II] it was a matinee performance, and of our four million soldiers only about two million got further than the training camp. But that little war had more effect on our people and their morals than—at this stage—the incomparably greater World War II. Those nineteen months

Excerpted from *Sex in Our Changing World*, by John McPartland (New York: Rinehart & Co., 1947). Copyright © 1947 by John McPartland.

THE EARLY TWENTIETH CENTURY · 95

seemed to be the gestation period for the changeling American people of the Twenties. . . .

That first World War brought women into factories and offices in great numbers. The real emancipation of our women occurred then with their near equality to men in the matter of making money. They worked in shell plants loading explosives, they operated drill presses and punching machines, and Saturday night they had money of their own in their purses. That made a difference in their attitudes toward men, a difference that remained to alter our whole sex mores. . . .

The soldiers found the army an education; just as our women used the war period to make the most out of their feminine qualities, the boys in the army and navy began to emphasize their maleness. Under the excuse of patriotism a lot of getting together was done with eager girls, free from the inhibitions of peacetime. . . .

THE SUDDEN POPULARITY OF SEX

It was a confusing time. The children who became the young men and women of those war years were the product of schools, homes, and churches which regarded sex as a secret, and rather a disgusting secret. Ellen Keye had not had much effect on the attitude of the nation, guilt was much a partner of sex, and ignorance muddled most of the new freedom. It may be that the mysterious insistence of these young people that they had been forced adrift by what was after all a short and comparatively easy war—"The Lost Generation" idea which was popular through the Twenties—was the result of bewilderment and feelings of guilt in this sudden popularization of sex, a popularization for which most of them were totally unprepared.

The soldiers had a few months of barracks life, and barracks life is an aphrodisiac: the constant maleness, the constant talk of women, and the sharp demands of ego produced by being one in many, all conspire to make men want women as a hungry man wants food—fast, and without regard for quality. The army instructed its men in prophylaxis, and, while the condom had been an article of contraband and illegal commerce for many years, this was the first time that many of these boys from sex-fearing families had ever seen them. Its usefulness as a birth control device was evident, and these returning soldiers produced the sharpest decline in our birth rate in our entire history two years later. . . .

For a large number of our four million men in the services the war represented their first chance to escape the routine of their environments, they were free of wives, fiancées, family, church, and employer. They were concerned only with time, money, and the military police. Fifty thousand, more or less, went AWOL in Paris after the Armistice, a situation regarded by our amateur army as amusing rather than bad. When the two million returned from France they brought with them some degree of rebellion, they never fully returned to the controls that had been so strong in 1915. The other two million seemed to envy them their experiences, and proceeded to emulate them. Twenty years later it was difficult to discover a World War I veteran that had not enjoyed himself in Paris.

Our ladies at home were impressed, and not altogether favorably, by these fine tales of adventure. Some of the sexual looseness which inundated our morals a few years later may have been a form of retaliation. The phrase "sauce for the goose is sauce for the gander" became popular, even though the genders were reversed. . . .

The stage was being set for the carnival of the Twenties. Money is a major ingredient in sophistication, and money we had. We were braggarts, we had learned to leer, and we had broken through more than a century of moral restraints in less than two years. Our women were restless for more excitements after the sensual hysteria they had enjoyed, and they were becoming impressed by the simple truths dramatically demonstrated in the movies: women are desired by men, women can make fools out of men, sex and beauty are all that matter until love comes and makes everything wonderful. The sexes began to experiment in new techniques of fooling each other, techniques that used motorcars, popular songs, movies, flats in the city, birth control, and money. . . .

Changing Sexual Mores

Our sexual mores had been built around an ideal situation, and a common one: the boy and girl grew up together, in a quiet city neighborhood, in the American prototype—the small town, or on neighboring farms. The girl was virtuous, the boy was sincere. They fell in love, married, and produced their children. They worked hard, the girl was a good mother, their children grew and married within their neighborhood. Love, not sex, was important.

Now, coincidental with this war, the framework of the sexual mores was changing. The boy and girl were restless, they were apt to break away from their families and homes, eager for money and success. The boy wanted to be gay and experienced, the girl wanted to be beautiful and admired by many men. Clothes, a city apartment, a car, and smart gaiety were more important than children. Love was the sugar frosting on sex, and it was sex that was beginning to matter.

This change had been going on for some time before the war, but slowly, and not many people were aware of this changing basis of our mores. During the war the change must have been very rapid, because by the beginning of the Twenties this new attitude was causing concern in the churches and among the older people. . . .

The Roaring Twenties

The fun began on the day of the false Armistice in November, 1918, and lasted until October, 1929. The period was something like a magician's box: we entered it as one kind of people, left it eleven years later a wholly different sort of people. We are changelings now, illegitimate sprites left in the places of the real children of our fathers. The America that had existed before the first World War was a country of small-town people, enjoying the small pleasures, looking for happiness at home. The nation that stumbled into the depression of the Thirties was a country of city-minded people, used to superlatives, involved with money, entertainment and excitement. They didn't look for happiness, and they didn't go home.

These were the ingredients of the change: four million boys had gone off to the war, some of them got to France, some of them became combat troops, a good many did not get beyond the training camps, but almost all of them felt that things were "going to be different now;" the war period had been a time of big wages, good earnings, especially for women; the motorcars were really pouring from the factories, and just ordinary folks were buying them; the movies became the most important mass entertainment; prohibition became a national law.

What happened in a matter of five years is best indicated by our women. A girl of seventeen, daughter of a quiet middle-class family, was too young for dates with boys before this change; she used a little powder, sometimes, but believed that rouge and lipstick were unladylike; she might, in moments of excitement, say "darn," but she would feel quite daring; she believed that kisses were reserved for engaged couples, and talked of sex only to girls her own age, with a background of misinformation, and with nervous giggles; she wore knickers, petticoats, shifts, camisoles, corsets, and various other yardages of cloth swaddling her body; her hair was her pride, worn long, with rats to increase its apparent volume; she was proud of her figure—surreptitiously padded to enhance its swelling fore-and-aft. Her social events were confined to church and school, with an occasional family excursion to the ten cent movie house.

In the middle Twenties a girl of seventeen, daughter of a middle-class family, was evaluated socially by her dates—how many, with what sheiks, how expensive, how exciting; she used paint on her face, not as an artifice but in exactly the same ritual fashion as primitive body decoration; she enjoyed saying "God damn it!" and "Hell!"; she had about an even chance of remaining virgin until she met her husband-to-be; she talked about sex incessantly, preferably to boys a little older than herself; she wore high-heeled pumps, silk stockings rolled below her knees, her skirt reached just to her knees, underneath were rayon panties, a pink rayon chemise, and a flat band of cloth that pressed her breasts back against her chest; her dress was a waistless affair designed to show her boyish figure—breastless and hipless; her hair was cropped in a boyish bob. She smoked, drank gin straight from a flask, and prided herself on her familiarity with every expensive roadhouse for miles around the town. She thought her parents were very funny indeed.

Our women responded to this period of change much more dramatically and drastically than did our men. The business of cutting their hair short and flattening their breasts and hips is significant of their escape from womanhood. During this time of social change—the fastest in all history—men took nearly two decades to get rid of their ties and suit coats in hot weather, women practically stripped inside of five years.

"THE LOST GENERATION"

The ingredients of this change worked in this manner: we became convinced that we had survived a terrible catastrophe in World War I (twenty-odd years later we were to go through a much bigger and longer war with considerably less fuss) and the younger people began referring to themselves as "The Lost Generation." The assumption was made that this "Lost Generation" could not be expected to fit in with the ordinary rules. That established the style of the period.

Money had got out of the moral obligation class during the high wage period and had become an instrument of fun. The phrase of the time, "Keeping Up With the Joneses," indicates our national attitude toward money in those years. Among our prewar repressions there must have been a good deal of passive inferiority; money was the tonic for that inferiority—spend it conspicuously on luxuries. If you didn't have it, pretend that you did. Money became the answer to just about everything, especially for the great body of our people that had never before had any spare money. Women found an expanding field of jobs—typists, secretaries, telephone girls, factory girls, beauty shop operators (at one time it seemed that every young girl in the whole country planned to become a beauty shop operator), soda fountain clerks, waitresses, and all such. Women began to plan on working a few years before marriage, or even after marriage. There were getting to be such a lot of things to spend money for, and you simply had to keep up with the Joneses. The birth rate took the sharpest drop in history.

In 1920 the motor industry had a tremendous year, nearly two million cars rolled out of the factories. By 1925 there were nearly four million cars coming off the assembly lines. Everybody wanted an automobile, especially the young folks. The men were leaving the farms and the little towns to go to Detroit and work for Mr. Ford. Big money in the pay envelope every Saturday night, and a shiny car in front of the flat. What more could a fellow want out of life?

POPULAR CULTURE

The impresarios of the nickel show were doing very well also; they had taken the kitchen chairs and the converted stores that made up the movie houses of the pre-war period and run them into the kind of business that could borrow big money from the bank. They built the cathedrals of the silent screen, and the ordinary folks became used to walking across hundred thousand dollar carpets in million dollar marble foyers, while a thousand dollar a week organist titillated their nerve ends with his *vox humana*. They took the rococo cathedrals in fine stride—the best is none too good for us—and sank into soft seats in the perfumed darkness of the theaters. There were lights in changing colors, a hundred piece orchestra playing "Poet and Peasant," dancing girls, and the hypnosis of the myth-world on the screen. Here was love and passion, here were handsome men and beautiful women living in a world of luxury, excitements, and happy endings. For the wives it was a revelation: there was more to sex than an occasional tussle under the covers, the usual old business, a thing of habit with little stimulation or pleasure; these movie people made sex into a wonderful dream. For the men it was disquieting: "If I hadn't got married I bet I could have got me a doll like that. Gee, imagine walking down the street with a number like that on your arm!" For the young folks it was reality, and pretty soon they would actually be living in that world.

The movie magazines began to spread across the country; they were a sort of extension of the hypnosis of the screen. Women and girls would pore through them, lips partially open, eyes faraway in the dream-world. The standards of housekeeping and cooking slumped badly. . . .

PROHIBITION

Prohibition was an ingredient of change probably as important as the motorcar or the movies. Prior to the first War drinking was a masculine affair. There had been a time, half a century and more ago, when everybody in the country drank straight whiskey; for decades church and school had carried on a campaign against drinking with considerable success, by the time of the National Prohibition Act more than half the country was dry, and liquor was under a moral ban. Prohibition produced an unsuspected reversal of this trend—liquor ceased to be morally bad in the eyes of the upper middle class and became fashionable instead. People started to drink as evidence that (a) they could afford expensive things, such as bootleg liquor, (b) they were on the "in," (c) they were as modern as anybody, and (d) they were having fun. These were potent reasons, powerful enough to encourage many a good housewife through a brawling evening of synthetic gin mixed *ad nauseam*. Flask drinking fitted in well with automobiles, the wild new enthusiasm for spectator sports, especially football, and with the general purposes of seduction.

We have never recovered from that period of Prohibition. Sex and social drinking were wedded in those days, and there is no divorce in prospect. The cocktail lounge of today was born in the speakeasy of the Twenties; the intimate night club of Prohibition was a little too vicious to survive except in a few odd places. As a people we learned new tricks rapidly, in those days. We brought our women into the speakeasies, developed a whole tradition of the night club, borrowing much from the old cabarets, of course. We learned to drink expensively, if not well. . . .

THE INGREDIENTS OF A MORAL REVOLUTION

Advertising [previously] had been a slow-footed, clumsy sort of affair. There was little regard for truth, but also little imaginative lying. That changed in the Twenties. The breasts and thighs of lovely women became associated with soft drinks, motorcars, mouthwashes, and cigarettes. The endless theme was a concealed sexuality—be loved, be rich so that you will be loved, appear to be rich. The appeals were made to snobbery; the haunting insinuation about unpopularity sneered from the pages of the magazines; the tom-tom repetition of command—"Get this!" "Buy this!" began, nor has it ceased since. The urge was for showy things, material things that would arouse the envy of others. And always was the secret whisper of sex; for women it was, "Be lovely, be loved, don't grow old, be exciting, be dangerous, be loved!" for men it was, "Be successful, make everybody know that you're successful—how can you get women if you don't look successful?"

This was incessant; it was done in color, by the best artists that money could buy; it was worded by poets and by shrewd cynics; it was a parade of breast and leg, of the smiles of women and the eyes of men. It was sleek, shining, new, expensive, rare, mellow, lovely, priceless, exciting, exclusive—and it could all be yours.

Our factories turned out gadgets—automobiles, toasters, washing machines, furniture, lamps, watches—endless streams of shiny gadgets; perfumes, unguents, creams, oils, powders, rouges, lipsticks, eye-shadow—the tokens of sex; clothes, shoes, hats, shirts, girdles, ties, foundations—the stuff of youth. And something new had been invented—you didn't need money anymore, you could buy youth, envy, love, all on the installment plan.

Those were the ingredients of the moral revolution that began with the ironic false Armistice and ended with the stock market crash. We became excited about sex, money, and liquor in those years. Our women changed, our concept of family changed. It happened quickly, less than ten years produced a completely new set of social patterns. It was tremendous, little towns that hadn't changed since the railroad had come in fifty years before joined the giddy dance with the same excitement as New York and Chicago. It was intense, our whole belief in a sexual moral code was altered, our sexual manners were drastically affected. . . .

The movies, the motorcars, and the advertisements all helped change us into city-minded people. We began to base our culture on the individual, rather than the family. Sex became important as a gratification of the ego, a form of selfishness. Yet, while we were changing our sexual manners we didn't change our announced sexual code. We still pretended to be chaste and monogamous. Our divorce rate went up sharply, and the birth rate dropped, but our mores were ostensibly the same as they had been. Our young people went in for a fashionable promiscuity, but it didn't alter the attitudes or actions of our churches and schools. In our books, and on our stage, there was a new realism to be sure, but the movies and the popular periodicals remained in a dream world. . . .

SEXUAL REALISM

The people were becoming accustomed to sexual realism, in sterilized packages like books or plays. The housewives and theater-goers were beginning to expect their money's worth in sexual realism from certain novelists and certain dramatists.

The New York stage was the high point of this new sexual realism. In the season of 1924, for example, this realism varied from the bitter, ugly, ribald, honest *What Price Glory* through the pedestrian sex of *Desire Under the Elms* and *They Knew What They Wanted* to the high fun and high sex of Lunt and Fontanne in *The Guardsman*. A little number called *White Cargo* was doing very well with some tropical miscegenation. The pulpits and the editorial pages were unpleasant about the four-letter words used on the stage, and predicted a decline of the drama because it was prostituting the theater to realism. The four-letter words were usually just "son of a bitch," "bastard," and "God damn," only one of which has four letters.

The realism consisted mostly of discreet indications that sex was going on, usually suggested by a fast drop of the curtain on the heroine and some man, as they advanced towards each other in the manner of two wrestlers.

Mae West tapped the lode of the out-of-town visitor with a series of ghastly dramas, *Diamond Lil, The Pleasure Man,* and some others now well-forgotten. There were a lot of expensive revues that consisted of handsome naked girls, dancing girls, lavish stages, dirty jokes, and popular songs. The dirty jokes would drift back to the towns across the country as the out-of-towners returned, breathless with stories of the "dirtiest show you can imagine! They all but did you know what right there on the stage! You simply have to see it when you go to New York," and the intimate little night clubs, the speakeasies, the gorgeous naked showgirls, and all of the other entertainment appealing to our sedate upper-middle class. . . .

EVERYTHING CHANGED

Sex was the answer to so many of the questions of the Twenties. Sex made you feel popular, successful, envied. It was selfish sex, not for the physical pleasure nor for procreation—just sex for sin's sake. The maidenheads of the period took a beating; these postwar children had the new freedoms of money, automobiles, and gin. . . .

The whole country did not go in for an orgy of sex and drunkenness in those years, but it seemed like it to observers. There were many families that continued through these times in the same quiet fashion they had lived before the war. The churches continued to attract the faithful; and more than half the girls who went to the marriage bed were still virgin. A great number of families worked in the same old ways, and saw no easy money as a result of their labors. There were a surprising number of people, old and young, who had never seen a movie, ridden in a motorcar, or tasted gin.

But the style of our country was the style of speed, of quick-spent money, of bootleg liquor and jazz, of careless sex. These were the gaudy Twenties, and everything was changed.

These were the collegiate Twenties, the years of the Harding boom, Coolidge prosperity, two dollar a bushel grain, installment buying, shiny new cars, kitchenette flats, racoon coats, silver flasks of gin, dirty jokes, short skirts, rolled stockings, quick and easy birth control, and the devil take the hindmost.

All of this made a profound change in our sexual manners, and a less obvious change in our sexual code, as understood. It was the simultaneous impact of the extraordinary emotional excitement caused by World War I, combined with an excess of money, the new mobility of the motorcar, the quick spread of birth control based on the use of the condom or a douche, the ego desirings and envy inspired by the new techniques of advertising, and the powerful semi-hypnosis of the motion picture, that caused this moral revolution in our people. The tangle of Prohibition which made drinking a fashionable affair was a magnifying factor. These things occurred to a population which had made a major shift from rural to urban, which had a considerable percentage of foreign-born and first generation immigrants, and which had not had a single tradition, or unified code in its sexual mores.

A social typhoon such as the one which struck our country at the close of the first World War has long lasting effects. We are still muddling through the warpings and dislocations that were caused by that social typhoon. While it was widely billed at the time as a process of freeing our people from old hypocrisies and worn-out rules, those hypocrisies and worn-out rules tended to persist. There were taboos that were pretty well smashed, of course—taboos about the body, for example. The Twenties took the human body, especially the female body, out of its musty wrappings and put it out to the sun. A lot of prudishness did disappear in the popular prurience of those times. Divorces and birth control were removed from the sinful category, but mention of venereal disease was generally frowned upon. Literature and the theater broke through most of the old taboos, but the mass entertainment of the motion picture and the newly popular radio remained ridden with a crazy pattern of censorship. This pattern, as far as the movies were concerned, permitted them to be salacious, lecherous, and sexually irritating, but seldom honest.

The children of the Twenties established a sort of Youth tradition which has continued since their day. Before their time adolescents were not much of a social factor, but that has not been true since that era. The adolescent has been given certain sexual privileges, often in an unspoken fashion, and is even encouraged to use these sexual privileges in a moderate manner. This is probably more of that vicarious enjoyment that parents find as one of their possible pleasures.

BURNING DOWN THE HOUSE

On the whole, the Twenties were more on the order of burning down the house rather than remodeling it. We did a much better job of honesty in the succeeding years of the great depression, and our freedoms became less illusory and more the product of understanding. Possibly the Twenties could be termed our national adolescence, our time of rebellion, of gay excitement. The Thirties took the cynicism of the preceding decade and turned it into bitterness, but we have outlived that bitterness as well.

One of the outstanding phenomena of that decade was the failure of our social institutions to meet the new demands of our people. Church, school, settlement house, national, state and local government, all these were left in the ruck. Not until the Thirties did they begin to catch up, and they haven't succeeded in doing their job well to this day.

[World War II] emphasized our heritage from the Twenties. The adulthood of our children, the frequent selfishness of our sex habits, the looseness of our family organization, the hard, biting humor of our national cynicism, the paramount importance of money, and our hard-drinking gaiety were all products of that gaudy decade that now seems so long ago.

The First Modern Woman

ANN WHITE

The following selection, written in 1999 by Washington, D.C., high school teacher Ann White, is intended to refute the notion that sexual fulfillment should be the highest aim in life. White recounts the life of a woman of the 1930s who yearned to be "modern" and emancipated, yet who also longed for the security of a stable relationship. Believing that she was entitled to sexual pleasure and that marriage would allow her to satisfy her deepest needs, this woman tricked a reluctant groom into marrying her. The relationship began unraveling within a few years, but the woman stayed married out of concern for her children and because she was afraid of being alone. Emotionally dead and preoccupied with her own disappointment, she failed to develop a healthy relationship with her children. White concludes that "sex has saved no woman from her discontents or her fears."

Contrary to popular opinion, current American sexual practice began not in the "sexual revolution" of the 1960s but decades earlier, in the youth of our first modern girls, women now in their eighties. The first modern American women grew up in the 1920s and early 1930s, when Americans discovered that women were sexual beings.

Theirs was the first generation to believe that women could do anything. A woman could fly an airplane, like Amelia Earhart. She could drive a taxi, or she could choose a profession—and have a husband and children as well. After women got the vote in 1920, many insisted on the same freedom as men to choose their personal habits, including smoking, drink-

Excerpted from "The First Modern Woman," by Ann White, *First Things*, June/July 1999. Copyright © 1999 by Ann White. Reprinted by permission of *First Things*.

ing, dancing, and wearing provocative bathing suits. The heroine of a 1925 *McCall's* magazine story announced that a flapper's goal was "to live life in one's own way." A woman now could go anywhere alone—into stores, churches, depots, saloons. And a modern American woman could go anywhere she chose with a man, including to bed.

Historians tell us that emancipated young women of the '20s and '30s had sex only with men they loved; you could go to bed with a man if you loved him enough to want to marry him. Most women longed for such love—"I would rather be loved than respected," said one—and on the surface they looked "traditional," linking sex and marriage, keeping a good bit of the old female sexual reserve. But all the while a new idea simmered in their minds: that they were capable of sexual pleasure, entitled to sexual satisfaction, and that the marital sexual relationship would satisfy their deepest needs. Meanwhile, the idea of marriage as a sacred, religious bond seemed outdated.

ONE AMERICAN WOMAN

Let's take a look at how one real woman of the 1930s worked out the new sexual idea. Though our heroine, the "first modern woman," is anonymous here, she is neither imaginary nor a composite of many women. She is one individual American woman, who was born in 1911 and died in 1992.

This first modern American woman wanted to be more modern than her mother, a quiet woman who wore modestly printed cotton dresses and followed a weekly routine of household chores: laundering clothes on Mondays, shopping on Wednesdays, baking on Fridays. Her daughter was more sociable. In college, she sang small solo parts in operettas and began to picture herself as a little bit glamorous and to think the staidness of her mother's life a little old-fashioned. "Modern" to her meant glamorous, with a hint of the sexually suggestive. She loved the new Clark Gable movie, *It Happened One Night*, especially the last scene, when the blanket "wall" separating Claudette Colbert's bed from Gable's came down.

After graduation she found a teaching job in another city.

She thought about getting her own apartment—many young women did this—but settled instead for a rented room in a widow's house. She told herself that her first-year teacher's salary would not cover an apartment, but in the back of her mind she feared being alone. The young women who did live alone craved the excitement of an independent life, though they did not necessarily want to go through life by themselves. It was one thing to imagine pawning valuables to buy an airplane, as Amelia Earhart had done, quite another to carry through such lonely, demanding career plans. Most of these would-be moderns wanted to feel free, but they wanted to feel secure at the same time. They yearned for excitement, but they wanted a reliable companion with them on the way.

The companion, they thought, would be male. Not for them, however, the sedate kind of courtship they imagined their mothers having conducted in their grandparents' front parlors. They would engage in sexual behavior unknown to their mothers before the wedding night, usually but not always stopping short of sexual intercourse. Sex was in the air—had been in the air since they were children. Sex was in movies and novels and public lectures, in intellectuals' arguments that sexual abstinence harmed women's physical and mental health. These modern young women, self-conscious about their own sexual sophistication, said that they cut their hair and wore short skirts for comfort and convenience. But they knew that hair sculpted close to the head was alluring and that short skirts and sheer silk stockings drew attention to their legs in a far from innocent way. They made up their faces to suggest sensuality: pale powdered skin, colored lips, unnaturally arching eyebrows.

SEEKING AN ELIGIBLE MAN

Our heroine found herself attracted to her landlady's handsome and eligible nephew. When he came for dinner one Sunday, she laughed at his jokes and asked him questions about his office supply business. They had frequent weekend dates, which included long, lingering kisses. Would he, she found herself wondering, ask her to marry him? When he stopped calling her, she told herself that he was a businessman like her father and that she really wanted to marry an intellectual.

She moved back home, where she taught junior high school English and, in her spare time, helped with children's and teenage activities at her Lutheran church. Glamorous the church was not. Once upon a time, the Christian Church pulsed with the kind of excitement our heroine sought. In days of apostles and martyrs, Christians were gallant. In Reformation days, Christians were passionate. On nineteenth-century mission fields, Christians were heroic.

But by 1937, few American Christians understood the content of their faith, let alone defended it passionately. To our heroine and to many of her peers, the church seemed stodgy. In her church work, the first modern American girl saw mostly women and children, since the male leaders ran the church but did not study or teach in it. When she did see men at the formal Sunday service, they were middle-aged and older. Her most glamorous dream, of intellectual conversation with an attractive *young* man, looked unlikely to be fulfilled.

Until that surprising Sunday afternoon, when a man whom she had never seen before showed up to help chaperone a group of teenagers. Her handsome co-chaperone, younger than she by four years, was working as a wholesale tobacco salesman because his family could not afford to send him to college. He wished, however, that he were in college. Very intelligent, he mourned his unused intellectual powers. In his spare time he read Schopenhauer, the pessimistic philosopher who wrote about pain's predominance in human experience. But even while contemplating his psychic pain, he did not ignore our attractive heroine, who, for her part, thought she had found the intellectual of her dreams.

They began seeing each other regularly. Our heroine, who had been in a bar only once with her father, felt a tingle of excitement when the young man took her to a nightclub. They drank whiskey and listened to a local singer's rendition of "Night and Day." Many Saturday evenings they returned to the club, sometimes meeting his friends from the tobacco company. He smoked Chesterfield cigarettes; soon, so did she, feeling quite sophisticated as she tapped her cigarette on the table before lifting it to her lips for him to light.

She found him more pliable than her former boyfriend, who had always kept her guessing. This new man basked in her attention. He told her that the Depression made marriage impossible, speaking of no particular marriage, certainly not his. She ignored the impersonal tone and imagined that he was thinking about marrying her. She wanted to get married. She would soon be twenty-five and feared that marriage might elude her. A teaching career did not excite her despite her talent—she had a sense of humor that kept students interested through the dullest grammar drills. A teaching career did not seem modern to her, though, and it did not make her feel important. In modern life women were equal to men, and therefore important. Marriage, she believed, would make her both equal and important.

SEX AS PERSONAL FULFILLMENT

Her mother and her long-skirted nineteenth-century grandmothers had also considered marriage important, but our heroine did so for a different, "modern" reason: she believed that marital sex would bring her personal fulfillment. Intellectuals preached to her generation that women's equality with men required husbands to fulfill their wives sexually. A new era had dawned, wrote sexologist Havelock Ellis, in which sex took on "therapeutic" importance: women should no longer—*would* no longer—be sexually repressed. Sexual fulfillment was their right, the sign of their equality with men.

Our heroine believed she loved the tobacco salesman. He said that he loved her, though usually when he was slightly drunk. Should they sleep together now? He pressed for it; she relented. That is, she told herself she was "relenting" because she loved him so much. Her deepest thoughts were more complex. She now proudly regarded herself as a daring, modern young woman; she also, without quite admitting it to herself, was trying to maneuver the young man into marriage. She didn't worry about his drinking because he never lost control of himself; he just kept talking like an intellectual, gradually becoming sardonic and sad.

Weekend after weekend went by, with nightclubs and sex on Saturday nights, church services on Sunday mornings, and sometimes church activities on Sunday afternoons. On Saturday evenings, our heroine's lover bewailed his lot in life and toasted his self-pity with beer and whiskey. Sunday mornings he seemed cheerful and refreshed, a state that our heroine attributed to sex with her, not to church—salvation came through sex, or so she thought.

One Saturday evening, pretending some nervousness, she told him that she was pregnant. On the inside she was pleased, believing marriage would quickly follow. It did; very quickly. They eloped—glamorously, she thought—as did Claudette Colbert in *It Happened One Night*, when she fled a big church wedding to marry her down-and-out boyfriend. Our heroine told her parents she wanted to spare them the expense of a wedding.

The tobacco salesman had been right when he said that the Depression made marriage impossible. Where could they afford to live on the pittances they were earning? Her parents offered to carve a few rooms of their house into an apartment for the fledgling couple. There, in the bosom of her childhood home, our heroine undertook to enjoy all the sexual pleasures of modern married life—not, however, before telling her new husband in appropriately surprised tones that she was *not* pregnant after all.

REGRETTING MARRIAGE

Our heroine did not grasp the magnitude of her mistake until a few years later, when her husband, self-pitying as ever, had a brief affair with another woman. Then she decided that her marriage had misfired. The first modern American girl, now a modern American woman with two small children, thought of divorce but stayed married, in part for the children but also because she was still afraid to live alone. Another thirty years and she was still married and still thinking of divorce, regretting her marriage every day. Her husband's drinking no longer seemed sophisticated, especially when, drunken and sardonic, he mocked *her*. The joys of sex and then the sex itself gradually left the marriage. So deeply preoccupied was she with her own disappointment that she spent no emotional energy on her children; she fed and clothed them but never tried to understand them. Rather than fulfilling her, marriage deadened her spirit.

Though she began her sexual career optimistically, our modern American girl ended it in quiet tragedy. Feminists claim that such tragedies occurred because women were not truly equal to men—a broader set of career choices would have kept our heroine from wanting so much to get married. But can we not also admit that exaggerated hopes for sex betrayed her? Early–twentieth-century intellectuals exalted sex as a woman's salvation; their promises have echoed down the twentieth century, with hardly a whisper heard about the falseness of such claims. For all its power, sex has saved no woman from her discontents or her fears. It certainly did not save that first modern American woman, our anonymous but real heroine, who died quietly a few years ago. The false promises that marred her life remain virtually uncontested in America's sex-drenched culture.

CHAPTER 3

THE SEXUAL REVOLUTION OF THE LATTER TWENTIETH CENTURY

AMERICAN
SOCIAL
MOVEMENTS

Alfred Kinsey and the Kinsey Report

VERN L. BULLOUGH

Alfred Kinsey was an important pioneer in behavioral research whose work challenged widely held beliefs about sexuality in America, writes Vern L. Bullough in the following selection. Prior to Kinsey, no sex researcher had scientifically classified the various kinds of sexual expression. Kinsey's controversial techniques, which included extensive interviews on sexual behavior with thousands of subjects, resulted in published studies that proclaimed that nonmarital sex was not uncommon, that women experienced sexual pleasure, and that homosexuality was unusual but normal. Kinsey, whose work contributed to the feminist and gay and lesbian rights movements, was "a major factor in changing attitudes about sex in the twentieth century," the author concludes. Bullough is senior editor of *Free Inquiry*, a quarterly journal promoting humanist principles.

The more I study the development of modern sexuality, the more I believe in the importance and significance of Alfred Kinsey. Although his research was on Americans, it came to be a worldwide source of information about human sexuality and set standards for sex research everywhere. In America and much of the world, his work was a decisive factor in changing attitudes toward sex. Within the field of sexuality, he reoriented the field, moving it away from the medical model and medical dominance, to one encompassing a variety of disciplines and approaches. In short, his work has proved revolutionary.

To understand what Kinsey wrought, one must look at the field of sexuality when Kinsey began his studies. One must also look briefly at Kinsey as an individual to understand his accomplishments.

SEX RESEARCH, 1890–1940

The modern study of sexuality began in the nineteenth century, and these early studies were dominated by physicians. It was assumed that since physicians were the experts on body functions, they should be the experts regarding sexual activities. In a sense, this was a divergence from the past, when sexuality had been regarded almost entirely as a moral issue. And although there were still moral issues involved, physicians were also judged as qualified to speak on these issues as well. Although few physicians had any specialized knowledge on most sexual topics, except perhaps for sexually transmitted diseases, this did not prevent them from speaking with authority on most aspects of human sexuality.

Havelock Ellis, one of the dominant figures in promoting sexual knowledge in the first third of the twentieth century, said that he sought a medical degree primarily because it was the only profession in which he could safely study sex. Inevitably, most of the so-called experts were physicians. Equal in influence to Ellis was Magnus Hirschfeld, another physician. Both Ellis and Hirschfeld compiled what could be called sexual histories, as Kinsey later compiled. Ellis, however, acquired almost all of his histories from correspondence of volunteers and, as far as I know, never interviewed anyone. Hirschfeld, later in his career, compiled many case histories based on interviews, but early on he depended mainly on historical data and personal knowledge. Unfortunately, Hirschfeld used only a small portion of his data in his published books, and before he could complete a comprehensive study of sexuality, his files were destroyed by the Nazis.

Although some of the data physicians reported about sex was gathered from their own practices, these were usually interpreted in terms of traditional views and were supplemented by historical materials or reports of anthropologists to increase their authenticity. Simply put, most physicians writing about sex were influenced more by the zeitgeist of the time rather than by any specialized base of knowledge. A few early physician investigators, such as the American obstetrician Robert Latou Dickinson, had over 1,000 case studies, but most had only a handful. As the twentieth century progressed, the ordinary physician probably was regarded as the easiest available authority on sex, but most of the medical writings on sexual topics came from psychiatrists, particularly those who were psychoanalytically trained. Unfortunately, even the most comprehensive sex studies undertaken by psychiatrists, such as that of George Henry, were flawed by the assumptions of the investigators interpreting data. For example, they assumed that homosexuals were ill. Moreover, whether the answers to their questions were valid for determining differences with heterosexuals is uncertain, as there was a lack of any comparative study of heterosexuals.

Still, assumptions about medical expertise remained. When the Committee for Research in the Problems in Sex (CRPS), the Rockefeller-funded grant-giving body operating under the umbrella of the National Research Council, began to explore the possibilities of carrying out surveys of sexual behavior, they first sought out physicians. . . .

Funding for research projects when Kinsey began his work operated much more according to an old-boy network than it does today. There was little advertisement of fund availability and individuals were invited to apply, had to be nominated to apply, or had to have a connection. Certain universities and individuals dominated the disbursement of the money available. To an observer in the 1990s examining most of the research grants given for sex research, the relationships look almost incestuous.

Unfortunately for the committee, sex activity could not be studied exclusively in the laboratory or even in the field by observing animals or gathering historical data. There had been nongrant-supported popular studies of sex, but their samples were not representative and the questionnaires were poorly designed. Moreover, in keeping with its reliance on academia, the committee seemed reluctant to give its imprimatur to individuals conducting such studies. What was needed was a person willing to blaze new trails, dispassionately examining sex without the preconceived notions of most of the physicians then involved in writing about sex. The qualified individual or individuals needed an academic connection, preferably one with an established reputation for scientific studies.

KINSEY ENTERS THE SCENE

It was in this setting that Kinsey entered the scene. He was the right person at the right time; that is, a significant amount of money was available for sex research and there was an interest within the CRPS for some general kind of survey of American sex behavior. Who was Kinsey?

In terms of overall qualification, Kinsey's best asset was that he was a bench scientist, a biologist with a Ph.D. from Harvard, and an internationally known expert on gall wasps. But he was also a broad-based scientist. Unlike most research scientists today, who often are part of a team, researchers in the 1930s in the United States were self-dedicated and carried a major teaching load. Kinsey, for example, simultaneously taught general biology, published two editions of a popular introductory general biology text, two editions of a workbook, and a general text on methods in biology, and carried out major research. His entry into sex seems to have been serendipitous, taking place after he had completed his studies on gall wasps. Professors at the University of Indiana had discussed the possibility of an introductory cross-discipline course on marriage, then a topic beginning to receive some attention in academic circles. Kinsey was not only involved in such discussions but took the lead. In 1938, he was invited to coordinate and direct the new course on marriage and family. As a sign of the time, the course was taught by an all-male faculty from a variety of disciplines, including law, economics, sociology, philosophy, medicine, and biology.

Before the appearance of courses on marriage and family, the academic discussion of human sexuality had been con-

Kinsey's Sex Research

John Bancroft, director of the Kinsey Institute for Research in Bloomington, Indiana, defends Kinsey from his contemporary critics.

K insey's research is discredited, we are told by opponents of the Kinsey institute, because, having interviewed sexual criminals, he then did not report them to the police.

At the time of Kinsey's research, virtually all forms of sexual activity outside marriage and several forms of sexual activity within marriage (not including raping one's wife) were illegal. He attached great importance to the confidentiality he guaranteed his subjects, and this was crucial to the success of his whole research endeavor.

Kinsey's mission, his detractors claim, was to undermine

fined to lectures in the hygiene-type courses that had been established on many campuses in the second decade of the twentieth century, largely through the efforts of the American Social Hygiene Association. The approach to sex of these hygiene classes was quite different from that of the marriage and family courses, as they generally emphasized the dangers of sexually transmitted diseases and masturbation. In a sense, these hygiene-type courses were conceived to preserve sexual purity, whereas the sexual portions of marriage and family courses provided information, following the outlines of the better sex manuals of the time.

Kinsey went even further in his discussion of sexuality than the sex-positive marriage manuals, and soon clashed with Thurman Rice, a bacteriology professor who had written extensively on sex, primarily from the point of view of eugenics. For many years, Rice had delivered the sex lectures in the required hygiene course, where the males were separated from the females when he gave his lectures. Kinsey deliberately had

sexual morality as we know it. In his last book, the volume on the female, he was principally concerned about the lack of sexual understanding between men and women and how this undermined the stability of marriage. Ironically, considering how Kinsey so often has been accused to the contrary, the book underscores that he saw heterosexual marital sex as the norm. True, Kinsey is not beyond criticism. He made mistakes; with the benefit of 50 years of hindsight, one can say that he was naive in several respects. But he was a pioneer who broke through the social taboos to carry out the first substantial survey of sexual behavior, which remains the largest and richest collection of data on sexual behavior ever collected and is used by researchers today.

John Bancroft, *Insight*, March 30, 1998.

not included Rice in his recruited faculty, which probably furthered Rice's antagonism. Rice was typical of an earlier generation of sex educators in that he considered moral education an essential part of sex education. He believed and taught that masturbation was harmful, condemned premarital intercourse, and was fearful that Kinsey's course on marriage was a perversion of academic standards. For example, he charged Kinsey with asking some of the women students about the length of their clitorises. To show that his accusations were based on more than gossip, Rice demanded the names of students in Kinsey's class so that he could verify such classroom voyeurism. Rice opposed Kinsey's questioning of students because he believed that sexual behavior could not and should not be analyzed by scientific methods because it was a moral topic, not a scientific one. Rice's perspective thus was perhaps typical of the hygiene approach to sex.

Kinsey had probably been doing at least some of the things that Rice mentioned because he had approached sex as a taxonomist—as one interested in classifying and describing—as a dispassionate scientist and not as a reformer or politician. In a sense, he was a political innocent. He believed that science could speak for itself, and he criticized his faculty colleagues who took any kind of political stand. He refused to join organizations that he felt had any kind of political agenda, including the Society for the Scientific Study of Sexuality (SSSS) in its early years.

AN UNEXPLORED NEW FIELD

There is, however, much more to Kinsey's interest in sex than the dispassionate scientist. In his personal life, he was not inhibited about body functions. Even before starting his course on marriage, he had sought information about the sex life of his students. His openness about sex was what Rice objected to.

It might well be that when Kinsey began teaching the sex course, he was undergoing a kind of midlife crisis, feeling that he had come to know all he wanted to know about gall wasps and needing to explore new fields. Sex to him represented an unexplored new field where comparatively little was known, and where there was much information to be gleaned. He began his study as he had that of gall wasps: finding out what was known and, in the process, building up a personal library of serious books on sex (hardly any of these had found their way into university libraries) and reading extensively. He also sought first-hand information by questioning his students about topics such as their age at first premarital intercourse, frequency of sexual activity, and number of partners.

All this gave fodder to Rice and his allies, including a number of parents who, perhaps at Rice's urging, complained about the specific sexual data given in the course and particularly about questions that Kinsey asked of his students. The president of the university, Herman Wells, a personal friend of Kinsey who had appointed him coordinator of the course, counseled him and gave him two options: to continue to teach the course and give up some of his probing of student lives, or to devote more time to his sex research and not teach the course.

Because Kinsey had already begun to extend his interviews off campus, the answer was perhaps inevitable. Although Kinsey continued to teach courses in biology, his load was reduced, and much of his life came to be devoted to sex research.

KINSEY'S RESEARCH

Because Kinsey was already well connected to the scientific establishment, his initial efforts to study sex received encouragement from the CRPS. He received an exploratory grant from them in 1941, during which time he would be evaluated as to suitability for a larger grant. George W. Comer, a physician member and later the chair of the CRPS, visited Kinsey as one of the grant investigators to determine whether Kinsey deserved further funding. He was tremendously impressed and reported that Kinsey was the most intense scientist he had ever met. He added that Kinsey could talk about little besides his research. According to Comer, Kinsey was an ideal person for a grant to study sex:

> He was a full professor, married with adolescent children. While carrying on his teaching duties in the zoology department he worked every available hour, day and night, traveling anywhere that people would give him interviews. He was training a couple of young men in his method of interviewing. Dr. Yerkes and I submitted separately to his technique. I was astonished at his skill in eliciting the most intimate details of the subject's sexual history. Introducing his queries gradually, he managed to convey an assurance of complete confidentiality by recording the answers on special sheets printed with a grid on which he set down the information gained, by unintelligible signs, explaining that the code had never been written down and only his two colleagues could read it. His questions included subtle tricks to detect deliberate misinformation.

Important to the continuation of the grant was the support of the university administration and its president, which Kinsey received despite sniping by some fellow faculty members such as Rice and others who regarded Kinsey's interest in sex with suspicion. As Comer's reference to Kinsey's family indicates, the committee wanted to make certain that the researcher had no special agenda except, perhaps, to establish some guides to better marriages. Kinsey satisfied them on this account and was well aware that any indication otherwise might endanger his grant. Thus, his own sex life remained a closed book, only to be opened by later generations of scholars. The CRPS came to be so committed to Kinsey that by the 1946–1947 academic year, he was receiving half of the committee's total budget.

Before the interviews stopped with Kinsey's death, about 18,600 individuals had been interviewed, 8,000 by Kinsey himself. Kinsey strongly believed that people would not always tell the truth when questioned about their sexual activities and that the only way to deal with this was through personal interviews in which the contradictions could be explored. He did not believe that self-administered questionnaires produced accurate responses: He regarded them as encouraging dishonest answers. He also recognized that respondents might lie even in a personal interview, but he provided a variety of checks to detect this and believed his checks were successful. Subjects were usually told that there were some contradictions in their answers and were asked to explain them. If they refused to do so, the interview was terminated and the information not used. Kinsey was also aware of potential bias of the interviewer. He sought to overcome this bias by occasionally having two people conduct the interviews at different times and by relying mainly on four interviewers, including himself, to conduct the study. If there was a bias, it came to be a shared one. The questions, however, were so wide-ranging that this too would limit much of the potential for slanting the data in any one direction. Following taxonomic principles, he wanted to gather data from as many subjects as possible, and he hoped initially to conduct 20,000 interviews and later to conduct 80,000 more. He did not live to achieve this. Before he died, the funding sources had dried up for such research, and other methods based on statistical sampling grew more popular.

CHALLENGING THE ASSUMPTIONS ABOUT SEXUALITY

Kinsey's major accomplishment was to challenge most of the assumptions about sexual activity in the United States. In so doing, he aroused great antagonism among many who opposed making sexual issues a matter of public discussion and debate. One reason for the antagonism is that he brought to public notice many sexual practices that previously had not been publicly discussed. Although Kinsey prided himself as an objective scientist, it was his very attempt to establish a taxonomy of sexual behaviors—treating all activities as more or less within the range of human behavior—that got him into trouble. Karl Menninger, for example, said that "Kinsey's compulsion to force human sexual behavior into a zoological frame of reference leads him to repudiate or neglect human psychology, and to see normality as that which is natural in the sense that it is what is practiced by animals."

Most sex researchers today accept the fact that total objectivity in our field is probably impossible. Some of Kinsey's difficulty resulted from his belief that he could be totally objective. He did not realize that the way he organized his data sometimes could challenge his objectivity, even though the organization seemed logical. For example, Kinsey developed a seven-point bipolar scale, which was one of the standard methods of organizing data in social science research at that time. He did not trust people's self-classification as homosexual or heterosexual. Therefore, he decided that regardless of how they might have classified themselves, the only objective indicator that he could use was to define sex in terms of outlet—namely, what activity resulted in orgasms.

In most seven-point scales, the extremes are represented by 0 and 6 (or by 1 and 7, depending upon the number with which the scale starts). Most people tend to respond using the middle of the scale. When one rates heterosexual orgasm as 0 and homosexual orgasm 6, a logical decision in terms of taxonomy, he in effect weights the scale by seeming to imply that exclusive heterosexuality is one extreme and exclusive homosexuality the other. Although his data demonstrated that far more people were identified as exclusively heterosexual than as any other category, his scale also implied that homosexuality was just another form of sexual activity, something that I think Kinsey believed was true. For his time and place this was revolutionary. His discussion of homosexuality and its prevalence resulted in the most serious attacks upon him and his data.

CRITICISM AND CONTROVERSY

Kinsey was a trailblazer, openly and willingly challenging many basic societal beliefs. It was not only his dispassionate discussion of homosexuality that roused controversy, but also his tendency to raise questions that society at that time preferred to ignore. In his book on males, for example, he questioned the assumption that extramarital intercourse always undermined the stability of marriage and held that the full story was more complex than the most highly publicized cases led one to assume. He seemed to feel that the most appropriate extramarital affair, from the standpoint of preserving a marriage, was an alliance in which neither party became overly involved emotionally. Concerned over the reaction to this, however, he became somewhat more cautious in the book on females. He conceded that extramarital affairs probably contributed to divorces in more ways and to a "greater extent than the subjects themselves realized."

Kinsey was interested in many different sexual behaviors, including that between generations (i.e., adults with children or minors). One of his more criticized sections in recent years is the table based on data he gathered from pedophiles. He is accused of not turning these people over to authorities, although one of the major informants was already serving time in jail for his sexual activities when interviewed. Kinsey gathered his data wherever he could find it, but he also reported on the source of his data. His own retrospective data tended to show that many individuals who experienced intergenerational sex as children were not seriously harmed by it, another statement that got him into trouble.

Kinsey is also criticized for his statistical sampling. Although his critics (even before his studies were published) attempted to get him to validate his data with a random sample of individuals, he refused on the grounds that not all of those included in the random sample would answer the questions put to them and that, therefore, the random sample would be biased. It is quite clear that Kinsey's sample is not random and that it overrepresents some segments of the population, including students and residents of Indiana. Part of the criticism, however, is also due to the use and misuse of the Kinsey data without his qualifications. This is particularly true of his data on same-sex relationships, which are broken down by age and other variables and therefore allowed others to choose the number or percentage of the sample they wanted to use in their own reports.

Another assumption of American society that Kinsey also challenged was the asexuality of women. This proved the issue of greatest controversy in his book on females. A total of 40% of the females he studied had experienced orgasm within the first months of marriage, 67% by the first six months, and 75% by the end of the first year. Twenty-five percent of his sample had experienced orgasm by age of 15, more than 50% by the age of 20, and 64% before marriage. On the other hand, he also reported cases in which women failed to reach orgasm after 20 years of marriage. In spite of the controversies over his data on orgasms, it helped move the issue of female sexuality on to the agenda of the growing women's movement of the late 1960s and the 1970s, and to encourage further studies of female sexuality.

In light of the challenges against him, Kinsey ignored in his writings what might be called sexual adventurers, paying almost no attention to swinging, group sex, and alternate lifestyles such as sadism, masochism, transvestism, voyeurism, and exhibitionism. He justified this neglect by arguing that such practices were statistically insignificant. It is more likely that Kinsey was either not interested in them or not interested in exploring them. He was also not particularly interested in pregnancy or sexually transmitted diseases. However, he de-mystified discussion of sex insofar as that was possible. Sex, to him, was just another aspect of human behavior, albeit an important part. He made Americans and the world at large aware of just how big a part human sexuality played in the life cycle of the individual and how widespread many kinds of sexual activities were. . . .

Changing Attitudes

In sum, Kinsey was the major factor in changing attitudes about sex in the twentieth century. His limitations and his personal foibles are appropriately overshadowed by his courage to go where others had not gone before. In spite of the vicious attacks upon him during his last few years of life, and the continuing attacks today, his data continue to be cited and used (and misused). He changed the nature of sexual studies, forced a reexamination of public attitudes toward sex, challenged the medical and psychiatric establishment to reassess its own views, influenced both the feminist movement and the gay and lesbian movement, and built a library and an institution devoted to sex research. His reputation continues to grow, and he has become one of the legends of the twentieth century. As one of those recognized by the SSSS to receive the Alfred Kinsey award, I thank him for his pioneering efforts.

How the Birth Control Pill Changed Women's Lives

ANN MARIE CUNNINGHAM

In the following selection, originally written for *Ladies' Home Journal* in 1990, freelance writer Ann Marie Cunningham discusses how the birth control pill profoundly changed the lives of American women. First introduced in 1960, the pill contributed to the sexual revolution by enabling women to have intercourse more frequently without fear of unwanted pregnancy. Access to the pill also encouraged women to challenge traditional teachings on ethical matters—such as religious prohibitions on abortion and contraception—and gave women more freedom to pursue careers and to abandon unsuccessful marriages. The pill did have its drawbacks, Cunningham states: An increasing number of men expected women to engage in casual sex, but many women who had "no-strings" affairs found it difficult to separate their emotions from their sexual feelings. All in all, however, the pill fostered a new and healthy assertiveness among women.

In June 1960, the oral contraceptive was approved for sale—and transformed our lives like nothing before or since. The Pill, we called it, and everyone from teenage boys to country singers to eminent theologians knew just what we meant. In this age of AIDS, when the very idea of sexual revolution seems both archaic and dangerous, it's easy to forget how truly liberating the Pill seemed to be in 1960. Nothing else in the twentieth century—perhaps not even winning the right to vote—made such an immediate difference in women's lives. Overnight, the Pill gave women control of their reproductive

Excerpted from "The Pill: How it Changed Our Lives," by Ann Marie Cunningham, Fran Snyder, and Nelly Edmondson Gupta, *Ladies' Home Journal*, June 1990. Copyright © 1990 by *Ladies' Home Journal*. Reprinted with permission.

systems; no longer was biology our absolute destiny.

Used properly, this contraceptive was virtually 100 percent effective, and it provoked profound social change. The Pill helped lower the birth rate and end America's baby boom in 1964. It spurred sexual frankness and experimentation. It allowed women to think seriously about careers because they could postpone childbirth. And it sparked the feminist and pro-choice movements; once women felt they were in charge of their own bodies, they began to question the authority of their husbands, their bosses, their doctors and their churches. As Founding Feminist Betty Friedan says today [in 1990]: "In the mysterious way of history, there was this convergence of technology that occurred just as women were ready to explode into personhood." Yet for many women, the Pill turned out to have a decidedly bitter aftertaste. The early versions were at best inconvenient and at worst dangerous, with alleged side effects ranging from dampened libido, depression and weight gain to blood clots, strokes and cancer.

Today's Pill is far safer, and 10.7 million American women now use it. It continues to be the nation's number-one method of birth control. But the profile of the Pill user has altered: Those now most likely to take it are aged fifteen to twenty-four.

Many of these young women, like their sixties' moms before them, regard taking the Pill as a rite of passage. "Most of my friends start the Pill when they begin going steady; it's part of a commitment you make," says Elizabeth, a twenty-two-year-old book editor from New York.

Some of the women who once shared that feeling now express a deep ambivalence, however. The Pill allowed Boomers to postpone childbearing for a long time—in some cases until they were too old to conceive. "I think maybe the Pill made us think we could turn our fertility on and off," says Jan, thirty-five, a college administrator from New Orleans who started taking the Pill as a teenager and decades later found herself unable to have a baby.

There are many other second thoughts about the Pill. Some

women wonder if it didn't really do more for men, who availed themselves of the increased sexual opportunities while expecting women to automatically assume the responsibility for contraception. Says University of Washington sociologist Pepper Schwartz, "Since the Pill, men tend to assume that women will take care of protection."

THE DEVELOPMENT OF THE PILL

The Pill was developed by a team of Massachusetts-based researchers, including a Catholic physician, John Rock. Its biggest proponent was Margaret Sanger, the founder of the Planned Parenthood Federation of America. "No woman can call herself free who does not own and control her own body," she declared. Produced by the G.D. Searle pharmaceutical company and called Enovid, the original Pill combined synthetic forms of the hormones estrogen and progestin to suppress ovulation.

By 1965, six other companies were marketing their own brands of oral contraceptives. And by the end of the decade, nearly ten million women were taking the Pill, making it America's contraceptive of choice. But almost with its introduction, reports of serious problems began to surface, including blood clotting, heart disease, depression and strokes. After Congress held a hearing on the Pill's health effects, the Food and Drug Administration (FDA) forced manufacturers to include a package insert warning users of all possible side effects. Women heeded the caveats, and during the seventies usage dropped by 20 percent. Consumption recovered to present levels in the eighties, with the development of formulas containing as little as one fifth the estrogen and one twenty-fifth the progestin.

SEXUAL DEALINGS

The Pill's greatest effect may have been that it not only kept women from getting pregnant, it helped them change their sex lives. Finally, they could enjoy lovemaking wholeheartedly, without dreading the consequences. Says author Erica

Jong, whose 1974 novel *Fear of Flying* was a textbook of sexual liberation, "Because women could control their fertility, they could start thinking of sexual pleasure instead of just pregnancy."

Most experts agree that the Pill contributed mightily to the sexual revolution. Effective forms of birth control—notably condoms—were already available, and sexual mores had begun to change in the postwar era. But the Pill made it easier for women to engage in sex more frequently. One 1965 study of married women who used oral contraceptives found that they had sex up to 39 percent more often than women using other methods of contraception.

And it encouraged public discussion of sex as well. For the first time, women's magazines could talk to their readers about sexual fulfillment, even headlining the word "orgasm" on their covers. Recalls Malcolm Potts, M.D., president of Family Health International, a nonprofit contraceptive-research organization, "You wouldn't mention condoms at cocktail parties, but you could talk about the Pill." And wisecracks about single women who were "on the Pill" were a shorthand for women who had stopped worrying about their reputations and started enjoying sex, just like men.

Here, too, however, the Pill brought mixed blessings. No longer were women looked on as fragile beings to be protected because they were vulnerable to pregnancy; instead they came to be regarded as independent equals who could—and should—take care of themselves. Gone were differentiations between "good girls" whom men would marry, and "bad girls" with whom they'd play around. "Before the Pill," says William Simon, Ph. D., professor of sociology at the University of Houston, "a woman who came prepared for contraception was making a statement about being prepared for sex which moved her to the slut end of the spectrum. The invisibility of the Pill muted that considerably." By the time the sexual revolution was at its height, many men expected women to have casual affairs and even one-night stands. "The key was that this was done without any expectation that it would end in marriage," says

132 • THE SEXUAL REVOLUTION

John Money, Ph.D., professor emeritus of medical psychology at Johns Hopkins University and Hospital, in Baltimore.

But while some female sexual behavior changed, attitudes did not always keep pace: Many women still wanted emotional as well as physical fulfillment. "One of the characteristics of women that remained true throughout all this was their inability to become sexually aroused without becoming emotionally attracted," says William Simon. "Men can go to bed with someone they don't necessarily like. That was never true of women." For the multitudes of women who did engage in no-strings sex, it soon became an empty exercise.

Nowadays, while we may take a certain degree of sexual frankness and freedom for granted, the excesses of the sixties seem emotionally empty and downright dangerous: We're haunted by AIDS, not to mention more than thirty other sexually transmitted diseases—against which the Pill is useless. In 1990, the social and sexual winds have shifted. Says Helen Singer Kaplan, Ph.D., a specialist in sexual disorders, "The Pill freed young men and women to have sex, but in 1990 the new fears are forcing them to learn to communicate, to put more energy into making their relationships work instead of seeking out more partners."

DIFFICULT QUESTIONS

One change wrought by the Pill is still with us today: It raised women's expectations of their lives, and they soon were unwilling to bear a child if the pregnancy was accidental. "Having a baby when you didn't want a baby became unthinkable," says Rosalind Pollack Petchesky, professor of women's studies at Hunter College, in New York City. This attitude, Petchesky says, "undoubtedly contributed to the rise in abortions for women who did not use the Pill and sometimes for those who did."

For some women, the Pill's ramifications went beyond pregnancy and sex. Its reliability encouraged Catholic women to ignore the church's centuries-old prohibition against artificial birth control. Today, between 80 and 85 percent of Catholic women in the U.S. approve of the use of some form of contraception. For most U.S. Catholic women, using the Pill was their first significant rebellion against the church, and it meant that their attitude toward its teachings on other matters would never be quite the same. Says Rev. Andrew Greeley, the sociologist and author, "It has prompted them to question the church. They now make their own decisions on ethical and religious matters when they think the official church is wrong."

In some ways, the Pill has had as great an effect in the office as in the bedroom. In the early sixties, increasingly, numbers of women had already begun trickling into the job market. Their opportunities expanded just as the cost of living exploded, making it both more possible and essential for women to work. The Pill abetted these forces by allowing women for the first time to plan how they would mesh their new opportunities with their reproductive lives. As they did so, the birth rate fell until 1976, when Baby Boomers decided to conceive, creating the baby boomlet. Between 1970 and 1987, the rate of first births among women in their thirties more than doubled, according to the National Center for Health Statistics. For those aged forty to forty-four, it increased 75 percent.

If the Pill helped keep women in the office longer, it also may have made it easier for them to walk out of unsuccessful marriages. "The major influence on a woman's decision to leave her husband is probably whether she can find a job and support her family," says Pepper Schwartz. "But she is more likely to be able to leave if she has two children, not four.". . .

THE TEENAGE SCENE

Some parents and religious commentators worry that the Pill has encouraged adolescent promiscuity and teenage pregnancies. It's true that the rate of adolescent pregnancies in the United States, currently stable, remains the highest in the Western world. But a more likely culprit is lack of the Pill and of information about contraceptives. In 1988, the Alan Guttmacher Institute, the reproductive-health research organization in New York, found that U.S. women, especially teenagers, take the Pill less frequently than do women of other nationalities. One major reason: In the 1980s, state and federal cuts in social services severely limited teens' access to birth control and sex education. "We suffer from incredible ignorance about sexual matters in this country," says Louise Tyrer, M.D., vice-president of medical affairs for the Planned Parenthood Federation of America.

THE MALE FACTOR

In some ways, the Pill's very effectiveness has been unfortunate; American medical researchers have made little subsequent effort to develop a male contraceptive. But researchers have lagged on finding better birth-control methods for women as well. Today, this contraceptive gap is crucial, because the Pill cannot defend women against AIDS and sexually transmitted diseases that were no particular threat when it was invented. Says Susan C.M. Scrimshaw, Ph.D., professor of anthropology and public health at the University of California at Los Angeles, "In some cultures where AIDS is raging, women find it next to impossible to enlist their partners in using barrier methods." She calls on the drug industry to develop an entiviral spermicide that women could use without their partners' permission. "In a way," she adds, "it's appalling that after thirty years, the Pill is the best we have."

For all its shortcomings, however, the Pill brought the average American woman a degree of freedom that had previously been unimaginable. Given that freedom, women began to look more thoughtfully at sex, work, marriage, motherhood—and themselves. Even the Pill's considerable drawbacks prompted a new assertiveness: Women are now more willing to question their doctors and their drug companies. As a method of contraception, the Pill may be antiquated before the twenty-first century, but the power it conferred on women remains considerable, and its legacy enduring.

The Problem That Has No Name

BETTY FRIEDAN

In the early 1960s, many American women began admitting that they were painfully dissatisfied with their lives as housewives and mothers, writes Betty Friedan in the following selection. She attributes this discontent to a discrepancy between a certain cultural ideal of womanhood and women's actual lives. The feminine ideal or "mystique" assumes that women find ultimate fulfillment in passivity, male dominance, and motherhood. Friedan maintains that this mystique, which pervades popular culture in the 1960s, forces women to deny their intelligence, autonomy, and full humanity. However, women's need to develop their own potential beyond their stereotyped gender roles has begun to assert itself. Friedan, a writer and founding member of the National Organization for Women (NOW), is the author of *The Feminine Mystique*—a 1963 book often cited as a major influence on the feminist movement.

W hy have so many American wives suffered this nameless aching dissatisfaction for so many years, each one thinking she was alone? "I've got tears in my eyes with sheer relief that my own inner turmoil is shared with other women," a young Connecticut mother wrote me when I first began to put this problem into words. A woman from a town in Ohio wrote: "The times when I felt that the only answer was to consult a psychiatrist, times of anger, bitterness and general frustration too numerous to even mention, I had no idea that hundreds of other women were feeling the same way. I felt so completely alone." A Houston, Texas, housewife wrote: "It has been the feeling of being almost alone with my problem that has made it so hard. I thank God for my family, home and the chance to care for them, but my life couldn't stop there. It is an awakening to know that I'm not an oddity and can stop being ashamed of wanting something more."

That painful guilty silence, and that tremendous relief when a feeling is finally out in the open, are familiar psychological signs. What need, what part of themselves, could so many women today be repressing? In this age after Freud, sex is immediately suspect. But this new stirring in women does not seem to be sex; it is, in fact, much harder for women to talk about than sex. Could there be another need, a part of themselves they have buried as deeply as the Victorian women buried sex?

If there is, a woman might not know what it was, any more than the Victorian woman knew she had sexual needs. The image of a good woman by which Victorian ladies lived simply left out sex. Does the image by which modern American women live also leave something out, the proud and public image of the high-school girl going steady, the college girl in love, the suburban housewife with an up-and-coming husband and a station wagon full of children? This image—created by the women's magazines, by advertisements, television, movies, novels, columns and books by experts on marriage and the family, child psychology, sexual adjustment and by the popularizers of sociology and psychoanalysis—shapes women's lives today and mirrors their dreams. It may give a clue to the problem that has no name, as a dream gives a clue to a wish unnamed by the dreamer. In the mind's ear, a geiger counter clicks when the image shows too sharp a discrepancy from reality. A geiger counter clicked in my own inner ear when I could not fit the quiet desperation of so many women into the picture of the modern American housewife that I myself was helping to create, writing for the women's magazines. What is missing from the image which shapes the American woman's pursuit of fulfillment as a wife and mother? What is missing from the image that mirrors and creates the identity of women in America today?...

THE IMAGE OF AMERICAN WOMEN

The image of woman that emerges from a 1960 *McCall's* is young and frivolous, almost childlike; fluffy and feminine; passive; gaily content in a world of bedroom and kitchen, sex, babies, and home. The magazine surely does not leave out sex; the only passion, the only pursuit, the only goal a woman is permitted is the pursuit of a man. It is crammed full of food, clothing, cosmetics, furniture, and the physical bodies of young women, but where is the world of thought and ideas, the life of the mind and spirit? In the magazine image, women do no work except housework and work to keep their bodies beautiful and to get and keep a man.

This was the image of the American woman in the year Castro led a revolution in Cuba and men were trained to travel into outer space; the year that the African continent brought forth new nations, and a plane whose speed is greater than the speed of sound broke up a Summit Conference; the year artists picketed a great museum in protest against the hegemony of abstract art; physicists explored the concept of anti-matter; astronomers, because of new radio telescopes, had to alter their concepts of the expanding universe; biologists made a breakthrough in the fundamental chemistry of life; and Negro youth in Southern schools forced the United States, for the first time since the Civil War, to face a moment of democratic truth. But this magazine, published for over 5,000,000 American women, almost all of whom have been through high school and nearly half to college, contained almost no mention of the world beyond the home. In the second half of the twentieth century in America, woman's world was confined to her own body and beauty, the charming of man, the bearing of babies, and the physical care and serving of husband, children, and home. And this was no anomaly of a single issue of a single women's magazine.

I sat one night at a meeting of magazine writers, mostly men, who work for all kinds of magazines, including women's magazines. The main speaker was a leader of the desegregation battle. Before he spoke, another man outlined the needs of the large women's magazine he edited:

> Our readers are housewives, full time. They're not interested in the broad public issues of the day. They are not interested in national or international affairs. They are only interested in the family and the home. They aren't interested in politics, unless it's related to an immediate need in the home, like the price of coffee. Humor? Has to be gentle, they don't get satire. Travel? We have almost completely dropped it. Education? That's a problem. Their own education level is going up. They've generally all had a high-school education and many, college. They're tremendously interested in education for their children—fourth-grade arithmetic. You just can't write about ideas or broad issues of the day for women. That's why we're publishing 90 per cent service now and 10 per cent general interest.

Another editor agreed, adding plaintively: "Can't you give us something else besides 'there's death in your medicine cabinet'? Can't any of you dream up a new crisis for women? We're always interested in sex, of course."

At this point, the writers and editors spent an hour listening to Thurgood Marshall on the inside story of the desegregation battle, and its possible effect on the presidential election. "Too bad I can't run that story," one editor said. "But you just can't link it to woman's world."

As I listened to them, a German phrase echoed in my mind—*"Kinder, Kuche, Kirche,"* the slogan by which the Nazis decreed that women must once again be confined to their biological role. But this was not Nazi Germany. This was America. The whole world lies open to American women. Why, then, does the image deny the world? Why does it limit women to "one passion, one role, one occupation?" Not long ago, women dreamed and fought for equality, their own place in the world. What happened to their dreams; when did women decide to give up the world and go back home?

A geologist brings up a core of mud from the bottom of the ocean and sees layers of sediment as sharp as a razor blade deposited over the years—clues to changes in the geological evolution of the earth so vast that they would go unnoticed during the lifespan of a single man. I sat for many days in the New York Public Library, going back through bound volumes of American women's magazines for the last twenty years. I found a change in the image of the American woman, and in the boundaries of the woman's world, as sharp and puzzling as the changes revealed in cores of ocean sediment.

In 1939, the heroines of women's magazine stories were not always young, but in a certain sense they were younger than their fictional counterparts today. They were young in the same way that the American hero has always been young: they were New Women, creating with a gay determined spirit a new identity for women—a life of their own. There was an aura about them of becoming, of moving into a future that was going to be different from the past. The majority of heroines in the four major women's magazines (then *Ladies' Home Journal, McCall's, Good Housekeeping, Woman's Home Companion*) were career women—happily, proudly, adventurously, attractively career women—who loved and were loved by men. And the spirit, courage, independence, determination—the strength of character they showed in their work as nurses, teachers, artists, actresses, copywriters, saleswomen—were part of their charm. There was a definite aura that their individuality was something to be admired, not unattractive to men, that men were drawn to them as much for their spirit and character as for their looks.

These were the mass women's magazines—in their heyday. The stories were conventional: girl-meets-boy or girl-gets-boy. But very often this was not the major theme of the story. These heroines were usually marching toward some goal or vision of their own, struggling with some problem of work or the world, when they found their man. And this New Woman, less fluffily feminine, so independent and determined to find a new life of her own, was the heroine of a different kind of love story. She was less aggressive in pursuit of a man. Her passionate involvement with the world, her own sense of herself as an individual, her self-reliance, gave a different flavor to her relationship with the man. The heroine and hero of one of these stories meet and fall in love at an ad agency where they both work. "I don't want to put you in a garden behind a wall," the hero says. "I want you to walk with me hand in hand, and together we could accomplish whatever we wanted to" ("A Dream to Share," *Redbook,* January, 1939). . . .

One heroine runs away from home when her mother insists she must make her debut instead of going on an expedition as a geologist. Her passionate determination to live her own life does not keep this New Woman from loving a man, but it makes her rebel from her parents; just as the young hero often must leave home to grow up. "You've got more courage than any girl I ever saw. You have what it takes," says the boy who helps her get away ("Have a Good Time, Dear," *Ladies' Home Journal,* May, 1939). . . .

These stories may not have been great literature. But the identity of their heroines seemed to say something about the housewives who, then as now, read the women's magazines. These magazines were not written for career women. The New Woman heroines were the ideal of yesterday's housewives; they reflected the dreams, mirrored the yearning for identity and the sense of possibility that existed for women then. And if women could not have these dreams for themselves, they wanted their daughters to have them. They wanted their daughters to be more than housewives, to go out in the world that had been denied them.

It is like remembering a long-forgotten dream, to recapture the memory of what a career meant to women before "career woman" became a dirty word in America. Jobs meant money, of course, at the end of the depression. But the readers of these magazines were not the women who got the jobs; career meant more than job. It seemed to mean doing something, being somebody yourself, not just existing in and through others.

I found the last clear note of the passionate search for individual identity that a career seems to have symbolized in the pre-1950 decades in a story called "Sarah and the Seaplane"

(*Ladies' Home Journal*, February, 1949). Sarah, who for nineteen years has played the part of docile daughter, is secretly learning to fly. She misses her flying lesson to accompany her mother on a round of social calls. An elderly doctor houseguest says: "My dear Sarah, every day, all the time, you are committing suicide. It's a greater crime than not pleasing others, not doing justice to yourself." Sensing some secret, he asks if she is in love. "She found it difficult to answer. In love? In love with the good-natured, the beautiful Henry [the flying teacher]? In love with the flashing water and the lift of wings at the instant of freedom, and the vision of the smiling, limitless world? 'Yes,' she answered, 'I think I am.'"

The next morning, Sarah solos. Henry "stepped away, slamming the cabin door shut, and swung the ship about for her. She was alone. There was a heady moment when everything she had learned left her, when she had to adjust herself to be alone, entirely alone in the familiar cabin. Then she drew a deep breath and suddenly a wonderful sense of competence made her sit erect and smiling. She was alone! She was answerable to herself alone, and she was sufficient.

"'I can do it!' she told herself aloud. . . . The wind flew back from the floats in glittering streaks, and then effortlessly the ship lifted itself free and soared." Even her mother can't stop her now from getting her flying license. She is not "afraid of discovering my own way of life." In bed that night she smiles sleepily, remembering how Henry had said, "You're my girl."

"Henry's girl! She smiled. No, she was not Henry's girl. She was Sarah. And that was sufficient. And with such a late start it would be some time before she got to know herself. Half in a dream now, she wondered if at the end of that time she would need someone else and who it would be."

"OCCUPATION: HOUSEWIFE"

And then suddenly the image blurs. The New Woman, soaring free, hesitates in midflight, shivers in all that blue sunlight and rushes back to the cozy walls of home. In the same year that Sarah soloed, the *Ladies' Home Journal* printed the prototype of the innumerable paeans to "Occupation: Housewife" that started to appear in the women's magazines, paeans that resounded throughout the fifties. They usually begin with a woman complaining that when she has to write "housewife" on the census blank, she gets an inferiority complex. ("When I write it I realize that here I am, a middle-aged woman, with a university education, and I've never made anything out of my life. I'm just a housewife.") Then the author of the paean, who somehow never is a housewife (in this case, Dorothy Thompson, newspaper woman, foreign correspondent, famous columnist, in *Ladies' Home Journal,* March, 1949), roars with laughter. The trouble with you, she scolds, is you don't realize you are expert in a dozen careers, simultaneously. "You might write: business manager, cook, nurse, chauffeur, dressmaker, interior decorator, accountant, caterer, teacher, private secretary—or just put down philanthropist. . . . All your life you have been giving away your energies, your skills, your talents, your services, for love." But still, the housewife complains, I'm nearly fifty and I've never done what I hoped to do in my youth—music— I've wasted my college education.

Ho-ho, laughs Miss Thompson, aren't your children musical because of you, and all those struggling years while your husband was finishing his great work, didn't you keep a charming home on $3,000 a year, and make all your children's clothes and your own, and paper the living room yourself, and watch the markets like a hawk for bargains? And in time off, didn't you type and proofread your husband's manuscripts, plan festivals to make up the church deficit, play piano duets with the children to make practicing more fun, read their books in high school to follow their study? "But all this vicarious living—through others," the housewife sighs. "As vicarious as Napoleon Bonaparte," Miss Thompson scoffs, "or a Queen. I simply refuse to share your self-pity. You are one of the most successful women I know.". . .

And the American housewife is reminded that Catholic countries in the Middle Ages "elevated the gentle and inconspicuous Mary into the Queen of Heaven, and built their loveliest cathedrals to 'Notre Dame—Our Lady.' . . . The home-maker, the nurturer, the creator of children's environment is the constant recreator of culture, civilization, and virtue. Assuming that she is doing well that great managerial task and creative activity, let her write her occupation proudly: 'housewife.'"

In 1949, the *Ladies' Home Journal* also ran Margaret Mead's *Male and Female.* All the magazines were echoing Farnham and Lundberg's *Modern Woman: The Lost Sex,* which came out in 1942, with its warning that careers and higher education were leading to the "masculinization of women with enormously dangerous consequences to the home, the children dependent on it and to the ability of the woman, as well as her husband, to obtain sexual gratification."

THE FEMININE MYSTIQUE

And so the feminine mystique began to spread through the land. . . .

The feminine mystique says that the highest value and the only commitment for women is the fulfillment of their own femininity. It says that the great mistake of Western culture, through most of its history, has been the undervaluation of this femininity. It says this femininity is so mysterious and intuitive and close to the creation and origin of life that man-made science may never be able to understand it. But however special and different, it is in no way inferior to the nature of man; it may even in certain respects be superior. The mistake, says the mystique, the root of women's troubles in the past is that women envied men, women tried to be like men, instead of accepting their own nature, which can find fulfillment only in sexual passivity, male domination, and nurturing maternal love.

But the new image this mystique gives to American women is the old image: "Occupation: housewife." The new mystique makes the housewife-mothers, who never had a chance to be anything else, the model for all women; it presupposes that history has reached a final and glorious end in the here and now, as far as women are concerned. Beneath the sophisticated trappings, it simply makes certain concrete, finite, domestic aspects of feminine existence—as it was lived by women whose lives were confined, by necessity, to cooking, cleaning, washing, bearing children—into a religion, a pattern by which all women must now live or deny their femininity.

Fulfillment as a woman had only one definition for American women after 1949—the housewife-mother. As swiftly as in a dream, the image of the American woman as a changing, growing individual in a changing world was shattered. Her solo flight to find her own identity was forgotten in the rush for the security of togetherness. Her limitless world shrunk to the cozy walls of home.

The transformation, reflected in the pages of the women's magazines, was sharply visible in 1949 and progressive through the fifties. "Femininity Begins at Home," "It's a Man's World Maybe," "Have Babies While You're Young," "How to Snare a Male," "Should I Stop Work When We Marry?" "Are You Training Your Daughter to Be a Wife?" "Careers at Home," "Do Women Have to Talk So Much?" "Why GI's Prefer Those German Girls," "What Women Can Learn from Mother Eve," "Really a Man's World, Politics," "How to Hold On to a Happy Marriage," "Don't Be Afraid to Marry Young," "The Doctor Talks about Breast-Feeding," "Our Baby Was Born at Home," "Cooking to Me Is Poetry," "The Business of Running a Home."

By the end of 1949, only one out of three heroines in the women's magazines was a career woman—and she was shown in the act of renouncing her career and discovering that what she really wanted to be was a housewife. In 1958, and again in 1959, I went through issue after issue of the three major women's magazines (the fourth, *Woman's Home Companion,* had died) without finding a single heroine who had a career, a commitment to any work, art, profession, or mission in the world, other than "Occupation: housewife." Only one in a hundred heroines had a job; even the young unmarried heroines no longer worked except at snaring a husband. . . .

With the career woman out of the way, the housewife with interests in the community becomes the devil to be exorcised.

Even PTA takes on a suspect connotation, not to mention interest in some international cause (see "Almost a Love Affair," *McCall's*, November, 1955). The housewife who simply has a mind of her own is the next to go. The heroine of "I Didn't Want to Tell You" (*McCall's*, January, 1958) is shown balancing the checkbook by herself and arguing with her husband about a small domestic detail. It develops that she is losing her husband to a "helpless little widow" whose main appeal is that she can't "think straight" about an insurance policy or mortgage. The betrayed wife says: "She must have sex appeal and what weapon has a wife against that?" But her best friend tells her: "You're making this too simple. You're forgetting how helpless Tania can be, and how grateful to the man who helps her . . .".

"I couldn't be a clinging vine if I tried," the wife says. "I had a better than average job after I left college and I was always a pretty independent person. I'm not a helpless little woman and I can't pretend to be." But she learns, that night. She hears a noise that might be a burglar; even though she knows it's only a mouse, she calls helplessly to her husband, and wins him back. As he comforts her pretended panic, she murmurs that, of course, he was right in their argument that morning. "She lay still in the soft bed, smiling in sweet, secret satisfaction, scarcely touched with guilt."

The end of the road, in an almost literal sense, is the disappearance of the heroine altogether, as a separate self and the subject of her own story. The end of the road is togetherness, where the woman has no independent self to hide even in guilt; she exists only for and through her husband and children. . . .

REDEFINING THE "WOMAN'S PROBLEM"

Woman's political job [according to Adlai Stevenson] is to "inspire in her home a vision of the meaning of life and freedom . . . to help her husband find values that will give purpose to his specialized daily chores . . . to teach her children the uniqueness of each individual human being."

This assignment for you, as wives and mothers, you can do in the living room with a baby in your lap or in the kitchen with a can opener in your hand. If you're clever, maybe you can even practice your saving arts on that unsuspecting man while he's watching television. I think there is much you can do about our crisis in the humble role of housewife. I could wish you no better vocation than that.

Thus the logic of the feminine mystique redefined the very nature of woman's problem. When woman was seen as a human being of limitless human potential, equal to man, anything that kept her from realizing her full potential was a problem to be solved: barriers to higher education and political participation, discrimination or prejudice in law or morality. But now that woman is seen only in terms of her sexual role, the barriers to the realization of her full potential, the prejudices which deny her full participation in the world, are no longer problems. The only problems now are those that might disturb her adjustment as a housewife. So career is a problem, education is a problem, political interest, even the very admission of women's intelligence and individuality is a problem. And finally there is the problem that has no name, a vague undefined wish for "something more" than washing dishes, ironing, punishing and praising the children. In the women's magazines, it is solved either by dyeing one's hair blonde or by having another baby. "Remember, when we were all children, how we all planned to 'be something?'" says a young housewife in the *Ladies' Home Journal* (February, 1960). Boasting that she has worn out six copies of Dr. Spock's baby-care book in seven years, she cries, "I'm lucky! Lucky! I'M SO GLAD TO BE A WOMAN!". . .

The ultimate, in housewife happiness, is finally achieved by the Texas housewife, described in "How America Lives" *(Ladies' Home Journal,* October, 1960), who "sits on a pale aqua satin sofa gazing out her picture window at the street. Even at this hour of the morning (it is barely nine-o'clock), she is wearing rouge, powder and lipstick, and her cotton dress is immaculately fresh." She says proudly: "By 8: 30 A.M., when my youngest goes to school, my whole house is clean and neat and I am dressed for the day. I am free to play bridge, attend club meetings, or stay home and read, listen to Beethoven, and just plain loaf."

"Sometimes, she washes and dries her hair before sitting down at a bridge table at 1:30. Mornings she is having bridge at her house are the busiest, for then she must get out the tables, cards, tallies, prepare fresh coffee and organize lunch. . . . During the winter months, she may play as often as four days a week from 9:30 to 3 P.M. . . . Janice is careful to be home, before her sons return from school at 4 P.M."

She is not frustrated, this new young housewife. An honor student at high school, married at eighteen, remarried and pregnant at twenty, she has the house she spent seven years dreaming and planning in detail. She is proud of her efficiency as a housewife, getting it all done by 8:30. She does the major housecleaning on Saturday, when her husband fishes and her sons are busy with Boy Scouts. ("There's nothing else to do. No bridge games. It's a long day for me.")

"'I love my home,' she says. . . . The pale gray paint in her L-shaped living and dining room is five years old, but still in perfect condition. . . . The pale peach and yellow and aqua damask upholstery looks spotless after eight years' wear. 'Sometimes, I feel I'm too passive, too content,' remarks Janice, fondly, regarding the wristband of large family diamonds she wears even when the watch itself is being repaired. . . . Her favorite possession is her four-poster spool bed with a pink taffeta canopy. 'I feel just like Queen Elizabeth sleeping in that bed,' she says happily. (Her husband sleeps in another room, since he snores.)

"'I'm so grateful for my blessings,' she says. 'Wonderful husband, handsome sons with dispositions to match, big comfortable house. . . . I'm thankful for my good health and faith in God and such material possessions as two cars, two TV's and two fireplaces.'"

IMAGE VERSUS REALITY

Staring uneasily at this image, I wonder if a few problems are not somehow better than this smiling empty passivity. If they are happy, these young women who live the feminine mystique, then is this the end of the road? Or are the seeds of something worse than frustration inherent in this image? Is there a growing divergence between this image of woman and human reality?

Consider, as a symptom, the increasing emphasis on glamour in the women's magazines: the housewife wearing eye makeup as she vacuums the floor—"The Honor of Being a Woman." Why does "Occupation: housewife" require such insistent glamorizing year after year? The strained glamour is in itself a question mark: the lady doth protest too much.

The image of woman in another era required increasing prudishness to keep denying sex. This new image seems to require increasing mindlessness, increasing emphasis on things: two cars, two TV's, two fireplaces. Whole pages of women's magazines are filled with gargantuan vegetables: beets, cucumbers, green peppers, potatoes, described like a love affair. The very size of their print is raised until it looks like a first-grade primer. The new *McCall's* frankly assumes women are brainless, fluffy kittens; the *Ladies' Home Journal,* feverishly competing, procures rock-and-roller Pat Boone as a counselor to teenagers; *Redbook* and the others enlarge their own type size. Does the size of the print mean that the new young women, whom all the magazines are courting, have only first-grade minds? . . .

I helped create this image. I have watched American women for fifteen years try to conform to it. But I can no longer deny my own knowledge of its terrible implications. It is not a harmless image. There may be no psychological terms for the harm it is doing. But what happens when women try to live according to an image that makes them deny their minds? What happens when women grow up in an image that makes them deny the reality of the changing world?

The material details of life, the daily burden of cooking and cleaning, of taking care of the physical needs of husband and children—these did indeed define a woman's world a century ago when Americans were pioneers, and the American frontier lay in conquering the land. But the women who went west with the wagon trains also shared the pioneering purpose. Now the American frontiers are of the mind, and of the spirit. Love and children and home are good, but they are not the whole world, even if most of the words now written for women pretend they are. Why should women accept this picture of a half-life, instead of a share in the whole of human destiny? Why should women try to make housework "something more," instead of moving on the frontiers of their own time, as American women moved beside their husbands on the old frontiers?

A baked potato is not as big as the world, and vacuuming the living room floor—with or without makeup—is not work that takes enough thought or energy to challenge any woman's full capacity. Women are human beings, not stuffed dolls, not animals. Down through the ages man has known that he was set apart from other animals by his mind's power to have an idea, a vision, and shape the future to it. He shares a need for food and sex with other animals, but when he loves, he loves as a man, and when he discovers and creates and shapes a future different from his past, he is a man, a human being.

WHAT HAPPENED TO THE NEW WOMAN?

This is the real mystery: why did so many American women, with the ability and education to discover and create, go back home again, to look for "something more" in housework and rearing children? For, paradoxically, in the same fifteen years in which the spirited New Woman was replaced by the Happy Housewife, the boundaries of the human world have widened, the pace of world change has quickened, and the very nature of human reality has become increasingly free from biological and material necessity. Does the mystique keep American woman from growing with the world? Does it force her to deny reality? . . .

Why, with the removal of all the legal, political, economic, and educational barriers that once kept woman from being man's equal, a person in her own right, an individual free to develop her own potential, should she accept this new image which insists she is not a person but a "woman," by definition barred from the freedom of human existence and a voice in human destiny?

The Changing Sexual Morality of the 1970s

VICTOR BONDI AND PETER C. HOLLORAN

In the following selection, historians Victor Bondi and Peter C. Holloran discuss some of the social changes that accompanied the sexual revolution of the 1970s. Spurred on by the availability of the birth control pill and other forms of contraception, many Americans became more adventurous and open to sexual experimentation, premarital sex, promiscuity, homosexuality, and graphic pornography. Critics charged that the new sexual freedom was destroying genuine intimacy and causing an increase in teen pregnancy, divorce, and sexually transmitted diseases. Despite the permissiveness of the decade, the authors conclude, the majority of Americans eventually "settled down" to a lifestyle of monogamous heterosexuality.

The so-called sexual revolution was considered by many to be the most shocking social trend in the 1970s. The sexual revolution, an outgrowth of the counterculture, cast aside traditional sexual restraints and began a decade of alternative eroticism, experimentation, and promiscuity. In part facilitated by the development of the birth-control pill and other contraceptives, Americans in the 1970s broke many sexual taboos. Interracial dating, open homosexuality, communal living, casual nudity, and dirty language all seemed to indicate a profound change in sexual behavior. Sexual activity among the young especially increased. Surveys during the 1970s reported that by age nineteen, four-fifths of all males and two-thirds of all females had had sex. Fashion designers promoted a new sensuality, producing miniskirts, hot pants, halter tops, and formfitting clothes designed to accentuate women's sexuality. Abandoning the censorious production code, Hollywood used nudity and eroticism to attract audiences (and, all too often, to cover shortcomings in screenplays). Hard-core pornography annually earned $4 billion. Graphic suggestion and profanity became a staple of rock music and popular novels. Public schools offered sexual education courses for adolescents. Most of these developments took place without the hand-wringing and guilt that had formerly characterized American attitudes toward sex.

PORNOGRAPHY

The growing visibility of pornography in the 1970s was one sign that sexual attitudes were changing. Nudity and sex had been used by countercultural artists in the late 1960s to challenge social convention. Artists in the 1970s continued to use such techniques, often tying graphic sex to larger statements about the human condition. Films such as Bernardo Bertolucci's *Last Tango in Paris* (1973) tied explicit sex to themes of human loneliness and madness. Erica Jong's 1973 novel *Fear of Flying* described uninhibited sexuality as a feminist act. Most pornography, however, was not nearly so high-minded, being for the most part voyeuristic displays of acrobatic intercourse with little or no plot. Much film pornography was shown in adult-movie theaters and peep shows in seedy urban districts such as New York's Times Square, Boston's Combat Zone, or San Francisco's North Beach. Often closely associated with prostitution and organized crime, the pornography business nonetheless became increasingly acceptable. In the 1970s pornographic films such as *Deep Throat* and *Behind the Green Door* were genuine hits, and their stars, Linda Lovelace, Harry Reems, and Marilyn Chambers, achieved celebrity status. Established men's magazines such as Hugh Hefner's *Playboy* were forced by the popularity of more-explicit competitors such as *Penthouse* and *Hustler* to become more graphic. Even women became consumers of pornography. Eroticized romance novels with titles such as *Royal Bondage* and *Sweet Savage Love* sold twenty million copies a year, primarily to women. A female-oriented magazine filled with pictures of naked men, *Playgirl*, began publishing in 1973. Sexual liberation, which in the 1960s was supposed to lead to greater self-expression and transcendence, became, in the 1970s, a coarse consumer business.

SEX MANUALS

The growth of pornography was connected to increased middle-class sexual exploration and adventurism. Sexual manuals such as *The Joy of Sex, Everything You Always Wanted to Know about Sex But Were Afraid to Ask* and *The Sensuous Man* provided frank and explicit advice concerning a host of sexual activities, in a tone that presented sex as a healthy human pleasure. These best-sellers were popular with millions of American couples, especially those living together before or in place of marriage. A small minority of American couples also experimented with traditional, heterosexual marriage, sometimes introducing extra partners into their relationships, sometimes experimenting with same-sex partners. Open marriage and wife swapping were practiced occasionally in 1970s suburbia, often after consulting the popular sex manuals. Given the decade's mania for self-help, seeking instruction on sex in these users' manuals often seemed a trendy solution to sexual problems.

CRITICS OF THE SEXUAL REVOLUTION

Critics of the sexual revolution ranged from conservatives to clergymen to public-health officials to feminists. Although the National Commission on Obscenity and Pornography reported in 1970 that there was no connection between pornography and crime, delinquency, or sexual deviation, President Richard Nixon rejected their findings, condemning the report as "morally bankrupt." Like Nixon, conservatives argued that sexual promiscuity was part of a larger decline in society. Sexual promiscuity, they argued, was immoral and dangerous, ultimately compromising social discipline. Some linked the new sexual freedom to rising divorce rates, to an epidemic of sexually transmitted diseases, and even to the failure of the United States to win the war in Vietnam. Clergymen often echoed the concerns of conservatives, condemning the new sexual toleration and guiltless attitudes toward premarital sex and single motherhood. Public-health officials sometimes shared these concerns, pointing to increased incidence of teenage pregnancy. Despite the wider availability of birth control and abortion, teenage pregnancies reached one million per year; about 87 percent of these teenagers kept their children. While many of these critics blamed feminism for such problems, some feminists were themselves deeply troubled by the new sexual adventurism and the growth of pornography. Feminist writers such as Judith Rossner, in her novel *Looking for Mr. Goodbar* (1975), objected that one-night stands and the singles scene were predatory, consumerist, and meaningless. Lesbian feminists such as Andrea Dworkin protested that pornography objectified women and acted as a catalyst for male dehumanization of women, wife battering, and rape. As Susan Brownmiller argued in her 1975 study *Against Our Will: Men, Women and Rape*, "Pornography, like rape, is a male invention, designed to dehumanize women, to reduce the female to an object of sexual access, not to free sensuality from moralistic or parental inhibition." All the critics of the liberalization of sex in the 1970s saw the phenomenon as emptying sexuality of its mystery, joy, and intimacy.

CONSEQUENCES OF THE REVOLUTION

Aside from the growth of sex as a consumer item and the increase in premarital sex and teenage pregnancies, the long-term consequences of the sexual revolution remained unclear. Most Americans continued to practice monogamous heterosexuality, usually within marriage. Sexual explorers of the 1970s generally settled down to monogamous relationships in the 1980s. Even Tony Manero, the barhopping sexual buccaneer portrayed by John Travolta in *Saturday Night Fever* (1977), ended the film disgusted with the meaninglessness of the New York singles scene. Kinsey Institute researchers revealed in a

1989 report that the sexual revolution had not been as common as the media and its critics believed. The researchers could find no revolution in American attitudes toward sexuality, and they noted that many groups remained hostile to sexual permissiveness, especially Fundamentalists and pious Christians, those with less education and less sexual experience before marriage, rural people, and those from restrictive backgrounds. Relegated to the background during the sexual consumerism of the 1970s, such groups became outspoken in the 1980s, continuing the debate over the limits of legitimate sexual activity begun in the 1960s.

The Gay and Lesbian Liberation Movement

MARGARET CRUIKSHANK

The liberal sexual values that found increased acceptance in the 1960s helped to invigorate a late–twentieth century gay and lesbian rights movement. This activism, as Margaret Cruikshank explains in the following selection, first appeared in the small 1950s "homophile movement" that sought the integration of homosexuals into mainstream society. The gay liberation movement grew dramatically after the Stonewall riot of 1969—an incident in which gays and lesbians battled against a police raid on a Greenwich Village bar. Gay and lesbian organizations proliferated in big cities throughout the 1970s and 1980s despite the onslaught of AIDS and resistance from powerful political opponents. Cruikshank, editor of *The Lesbian Path*, *Lesbian Studies*, and *New Lesbian Writing*, teaches at the City College of San Francisco, California.

World War II was important for American homosexuals because it brought large numbers of them in contact with each other for the first time. After the war, many chose to live in big cities, knowing their relative anonymity there would make a homosexual life easier. War work was empowering for many lesbians who struck out on their own in the late 1940s, and the war gave many men time to consider alternatives to the husband and breadwinner role they might automatically have assumed in peacetime. Unjust and irrational treatment of homosexuals by the military during World War II, documented in Allan Berube's *Coming out under Fire,* did not lead to an organized resistance movement but it did allow many lesbians and gay men to see themselves as belonging to a group. A postwar novel by John Horne Burns, *The Gallery*, described homosexuals as "a minority that should be left alone."

This view . . . took root finally in 1950, when a small band of southern California men founded the Mattachine Society, taking the name from medieval masked singers, to indicate that homosexuals were an unknown people. As Marxists, Harry Hay and other founders of Mattachine believed that prejudice against them was not a problem individuals could solve because it was deeply ingrained in American institutions. Gradually they came to view homosexuals as an oppressed minority, made up of people who for the most part did not place this interpretation on their private lives. Their goal therefore was to popularize the idea of a homosexual minority, to develop group consciousness. Their discussions allowed participants to feel their self-worth for the first time. Hay resigned from the Communist Party so that it would not be associated with homosexuals at a time when Senator Joseph McCarthy was attacking both groups. A split developed in Mattachine between the founders, who envisioned a separate homosexual culture, and members who thought this strategy would only increase hostility to them and who preferred to integrate into mainstream society because they felt no different from heterosexuals except in their sexual lives. This latter view prevailed, with the result that a philosophy of individualism replaced that of collective, militant action. The founders thought they could validate homosexuality through their own positive experience of it, while the integrationists deferred to experts on sexuality.

Another way of describing these divergent viewpoints is to say that, for the leftists, homosexuality was not a problem; the problem lay in institutions. The integrationists saw social rejection as their problem, one which they wanted mainstream professionals to treat sympathetically rather than by condemning them. In the McCarthy era, one of the most repressive periods in American history, being different was dangerous. Even socializing with other homosexuals took great courage. In every state, homosexual acts were illegal, and even the American Civil Liberties Union (ACLU) supported these repressive laws. The integrationists' safe position had strong appeal, therefore, to people who were keenly aware of the punishment they could face if their homosexuality became known. At that time, purges of homosexuals were supported by the newspapers, and "medical researchers tinkered with lobotomies, castration, and electric shock" to "rehabilitate" them.

Members of Mattachine and the pioneer lesbian group Daughters of Bilitis (DOB), named for a woman who was thought to be Sappho's contemporary, described themselves as "the homophile movement," literally "love of same." This was a more positive, broader term than "homosexual," suggesting a philosophy or attitude as much as a sexual practice. De-emphasizing sex was strategic because it was sex acts that called down opprobrium on homosexuals.

A SLOW-GROWING MOVEMENT

In the 1960s the movement grew slowly. By then, gay subcultures were thriving in the United States, and heterosexuals began to be aware of their existence. A few books, mostly negative, were published on the subject of homosexuality. Lawyers began to argue for repeal of sodomy laws. As the topic of homosexuality began to lose some of its shock value, homophiles could be more assertive; but the change had a negative consequence as well because the medical view that homosexuality is a mental illness could be more widely disseminated. In 1965, for the first time, small numbers of militant homophiles picketed and paraded for their rights. [Historian John] D'Emilio notes that on the same day in May that 20,000 anti-war protesters gathered at the Washington Monument, seven men and three women marched for homosexual rights in front of the White House. Targets of other demonstrations were the Pentagon, the State Department, and Independence Hall in Philadelphia July Fourth. Del Martin and Phyllis Lyon, two founders of DOB, recall that on New Year's Day 1965, a costume ball was held in San Francisco to benefit the newly formed Council on Religion and the Homosexual. Police obstructed the entrance with a paddy wagon, flooded the entrance with lights, and took photos of everyone who entered the hall. Five hundred lesbians and gay men, accompanied by many ministers and their wives, defied police by entering. Several people, including lawyers, were arrested. The next day, seven ministers held a press conference to denounce the police, and the ACLU persuaded the judge to dismiss charges. The importance of this incident is that homosexuals were no longer isolated and cowed into submission. A coalition of homosexuals and progressive heterosexuals vigorously protested gross injustices that would previously have been known only to the victims.

In August 1966, movement groups created the North American Conference of Homophile Organizations, which established a legal fund, sponsored protests against discrimination by the federal government, and encouraged new groups to form. In New York Mattachine passed out literature in Greenwich Village and sent many members to appear on radio and television shows and to speak to hundreds of non-gay groups. In 1967, the ACLU reversed its earlier position by saying that consensual sex acts between adults were protected by the constitutional right to privacy. Despite many other signs of progress, a daunting problem remained: most homosexuals had not taken the step of joining the homophile movement. From 1950 to 1969, the membership of all the groups totalled only about 5,000.

AFTER STONEWALL

Stonewall was the shot heard round the homosexual world. On that day, patrons of the Stonewall Inn, a Greenwich Village bar popular with Puerto Rican drag queens and lesbians, responded to a police raid by throwing beer cans and bottles because they were angry at police surveillance of their private gathering places. In the ensuing riot, which lasted two nights, a crowd of 2,000 battled 400 policemen. Before, the stigma attached to homosexuality and the resulting fear of exposure had kept homosexuals in line. Stonewall was a symbolic end to victim status. Homosexuals had acquiesced to police brutality; gay people fought back. It was fitting that a new phase of the old struggle for acceptance of homosexuals had its start in a bar, for bars held a central place in gay culture: often they were the only places where people could be open. The first visit to a gay bar was often an initiation rite for a person coming to terms with his or her sexuality or for those who accepted their orientation but had never met another homosexual. Also, bars drew people from different races and classes.

After Stonewall, "gay power" graffiti began to appear in Greenwich Village. The Gay Liberation Front (GLF), a New Left group, and the Gay Activist Alliance (GAA) were formed, and similar groups quickly sprang up in other parts of the country. GLF stood for coalitions with other progressive groups, while the GAA, which took a single-issue stance, became more influential in the movement. Gay liberation could not be subsumed by the left, in the view of long-time activist Barbara Gittings, because of its "sheer chaotic nature." In addition, gay liberation tends to promote a high degree of individualism because sexual identity politics rises directly from private experiences that lead to feelings of being different from others. Nevertheless, Marxism exerted a strong influence on the movement: inspired by revolutionary rhetoric, activists no longer feared being known as homosexuals. Through the lens of Marxism the homophile goal of tolerance for homosexuals could be seen as inadequate; sexual freedom required structural change, not just changes in laws. In the 1970s, academic Marxists began to challenge the assumption that homosexuality is fixed and unchanging by examining the social forces that shape its definitions.

"The Personal Is the Political"

Some homosexuals have been drawn to Marxism out of a sense of disenfranchisement and alienation, but class privilege and the freedom to express homosexuality have also been closely linked historically. When Marx urged workers to unite, he knew who and where they were; in industrialized nations they were highly visible and their numbers could be estimated. But the Victorian homosexuals who believed their lives were as healthy and as productive as the lives of heterosexuals had no idea how many people this radical notion might directly apply to. Neither did the "silent pioneers," the name given to homophile activists of the 1950s. Only in the 1970s did conditions allow isolated individuals who had been invisible to each other to name their sexual difference, come together, and forge a common bond. Now a cliché, the phrase "the personal is the political" made a great impact on homosexuals who heard it for the first time in the 1970s. Declaring their most private feelings was a radical political act. It called on everyone, not just the sexual minority, to rethink their most basic assumptions about love, sex, marriage, the family, and the legitimate role of the state in controlling private life. It rejected centuries of religious teaching and decades of medical hypothesizing. It said that sexual self-determination was a fundamental human right. Homosexuals could not be driven back into the closet because they had left in large numbers. Coming out made gay liberation possible.

Though it had political meaning, the act of coming out was highly personal as well. Some people achieved self-respect as lesbians and gay men and were accepted by friends and families relatively easily; others needed years to become completely comfortable with their sexual orientation. Some were "out" to only a handful of people; others went on television to promote gay rights. Coming out was a different experience for those who risked being fired than it was for lesbians and gay men in secure jobs. It was riskier for married homosexuals than for singles. Coming out was not the same for women and men. People of color found it an especially complex process because they needed to keep the allegiance of their families for protection in a white-ruled society. Often they remained in their communities of origin. In general, greater economic privilege gave white gays more options when families, friends, or employers rejected them. Activist Billy Jones, a founder of

Goals of the Homosexual Revolution

Sociologist Ira L. Reiss contends that an important goal of the gay and lesbian liberation movement was to increase Americans' tolerance for sexual diversity.

The increased formation of gay and lesbian identities and the attempts to liberate heterosexuals from biases about gay and lesbian homosexuality were essential parts of the homosexual revolution in this country. As British social scientist Jeffrey Weeks sees it, the homosexual revolution of the 1970s had the objective of encouraging the realization by heterosexuals of the sexual diversity that exists in all societies, and helping to build possible ways that heterosexuals and homosexuals could coexist.

It seems that just as straight women sought equality in the heterosexual revolution, the goal of the homosexual revolution was for homosexuality to be recognized as a legitimate option and for homosexuals to be treated as equals rather than as inferiors. In this sense, for both homosexuals and heterosexuals, the last sexual revolution was a movement toward greater social equality with sexuality serving as one of the lead vehicles in that pursuit.

Ira L. Reiss, "An End to Shame: Shaping Our Next Sexual Revolution," 1990.

the National Coalition of Black Gay Men and Lesbians, recalls feeling torn between primary allegiance to the gay movement and to Black issues, a dilemma that remains current for many people of color who join gay and lesbian liberation.

The experience of discovering an identity or reassessing a familiar one, shared by thousands of people all over America, quickly united strangers. Like people accustomed to blurred vision who suddenly see sharp images, the lesbians and gay men who came out in the 1970s found pieces of their lives forming a coherent pattern for the first time. The childhood and adolescent feelings for which there was no name, fantasies, marriage resistance or discomfort in marriage, attractions to certain movie stars, all bore meaning. Anyone who cannot remember a time when homosexuality was absolutely unmentionable may not fully understand the high spirits of the gay rights movement in its first decade.

The euphoria of coming out and of joining a new movement was channeled into much hard work, organizing, fund raising, and consciousness raising in the 1970s. Gay and lesbian groups were formed all over the country, especially in big cities. A major focus of the movement was the passage of laws protecting those who had come out from housing and job discrimination. Aside from addressing real problems, these laws had a strong symbolic significance for lesbians and gay men because they equated gays with established, respected minorities. Initial victories sparked a right-wing backlash epitomized by Anita Bryant and her "Save Our Children" campaign, which led to repeal of a gay rights ordinance in Dade County, Florida, and in several cities.

In the 1970s, the movement drew many people who didn't have the option of being closeted, according to veteran activist Eric Rofes. They felt queer, and they tended to have a leftist perspective. The mobilization of gays in response to Anita Bryant's homophobic crusade brought into the movement many who wanted assimilation into American society. They were established in careers and had different values from people radicalized in the 1960s. Echoing Rofes, long-time Los Angeles activist and gerontologist Sharon Raphael says that the movement changed in the late 1970s. Until then, volunteers ran everything; gay liberation was a grassroots movement. Another characteristic of the movement in the 1970s is that it took Stonewall as the beginning of liberation. Naturally lesbians and gay men wanted a total break with the past because the past had been so oppressive. But many in the 1970s knew nothing of the homosexual emancipation movement or the homophile movement that began in 1950; that story had to be recovered by lesbian and gay historians.

SAN FRANCISCO IN 1978

The gay community in San Francisco, in California, and across the country experienced a traumatic year in 1978. A huge campaign was needed to defeat the Briggs initiative, Proposition 6, which would have required schools to fire homosexuals or any teacher who mentioned homosexuality positively in a classroom. This was one of the most serious threats gay Americans ever faced, not only because it jeopardized the livelihood of some but also because it declared in the most emphatic way that lesbians and gay men were morally unfit; they could not be trusted with children. Like other homophobic demagogues, Briggs encouraged previously silent bigots to voice their hatred for gay people. In the fall of 1978, lesbians and gay men in San Francisco feared their meeting places and their clubs would be bombed.

There were no bombs that fall in San Francisco but everyone who worked in a downtown office housing the Gay National Educational Switchboard sensed danger. They tried to avoid paranoia but jumped when cars backfired. The outpouring of hatred inspired by Briggs awakened white lesbians and gay men to the ugliness of a society in which difference is condemned. It taught them, too, that the struggle for gay rights would be harder than they had imagined earlier in the decade. A state-wide defense against Briggs led to his overwhelming defeat at the polls in November, a victory not only for gay Californians but for those in other states who knew that similar attacks on teachers would be attempted elsewhere if Proposition 6 passed. But the campaign was exhausting because it often seemed that the struggle for equality was really a struggle for survival.

A far greater trauma, however, was the November 27 assassination of San Francisco supervisor Harvey Milk, the first gay person elected to office in a major city, and liberal mayor George Moscone. The candlelight procession that night from the Castro district to City Hall united the San Francisco gay community more deeply than the political victory a few weeks earlier. Thousands of San Franciscans who were not gay joined marchers from the Castro in a spontaneous ritual of grief. On the steps of City Hall friends and colleagues of Moscone and Milk paid tribute to them and played a tape Milk had made in anticipation of his murder. In campaigning against Briggs, he realized that his high profile made him an inviting target for a violent right-wing extremist. It was an eerie experience hearing Milk say, "Let the bullet that rips my brain open every closet door in America."

City supervisor Dan White, a conservative ex-policeman and ex-fireman who represented a blue-collar district of San Francisco, entered City Hall through a basement on the morning of November 27, 1978, so that he could evade the metal detectors at the main entrance. After shooting the mayor several times in the mayor's office, he reloaded his gun, walked to Milk's office, and shot him repeatedly. Ostensibly, he was angry at the mayor for refusing to reinstate him after he resigned from the board and angry at Milk for supporting the mayor. The real reason the two men were killed is that San Francisco had become too gay. Thousands of new gay and lesbian residents had arrived from all over the country in the 1970s. They were flexing their political muscle, as Milk's election in 1977 demonstrated. Though he alone fired the shots, Dan White represented a collective right-wing attempt to drive gay people back underground. No evidence of a conspiracy was found, but the identity of the man who murdered Milk and Moscone was less significant than the gathering storm of anti-gay hatred waiting to burst. After the police arrested Dan White, they treated him like a hero.

By eradicating a perceived threat to the well-being of many San Franciscans, Dan White escaped identification as a cold-blooded murderer. Gay people and their supporters saw him in that light, of course, but gay people were not powerful enough to be avenged. Before the trial, they were excluded from the jury. Neither the prosecution nor the defense wanted the political trial that would have exposed both White's underlying motive for the killings and the entrenched bigotry of the police department. It was safer for both prosecution and defense to portray the murders as the aberrations of an individual rather than as manifestations of a sick social system. Homophobia could not yet be named a social fact. Psychiatrists said White had overdosed on sugar and thus suffered "diminished capacity." The gay press and the liberal *Bay Guardian* scorned the "Twinkies defense."

Five months later, the verdict was manslaughter, the sentence seven years (of which White served five). California law allowed the death penalty for the murder of public officials. Outraged by this exoneration, 5,000 gay people took to the streets. They marched on City Hall and smashed its front doors. They overturned police cars and set them on fire. Hoards of police who were furious because their chief would not let them fight the City Hall demonstrators invaded the Castro district and attacked pedestrians. At the Elephant Walk, a gay bar, they went on a rampage, destroying the bar and beating many men, some of them severely. The night's casualty toll was 100 gay people hospitalized and 61 policemen. Gay San Franciscans, mindful of the bar raids of the past and inured to occasional police brutality, were nevertheless shocked by the violence of the retaliatory attack on the Elephant Walk. Like the assassinations, it was a political act, intended to intimidate and silence them.

The "White Night Riots" left the gay community divided over the question of the violence of their own members. Some leaders deplored it; others said, "consider the provocation." The barbarity of the verdict took time to absorb: the jury had said that premeditated murders were not serious crimes if the victims were a gay man and a mayor sympathetic to the gay community.

An astute grassroots politician, Harvey Milk embodied both the radical and reform strands of gay liberation. As a former

Marine and former stockbroker, he had mainstream credentials. As a much-televised debater against Briggs, he wore a suit and spoke about the American tradition of civil liberty. Nearly everywhere else, Milk wore jeans and a T-shirt. He reached out to every minority in San Francisco. He spoke of a time when ordinary people would be empowered. Like Edward Carpenter, he had a vision extending beyond the gay community. [English socialist Edward Carpenter believed that homosexuals would one day lead a mass movement against various social oppressions.] Witty, irreverent, charismatic, and theatrical, Milk was very different from mainstream politicians. He celebrated his gay identity so exuberantly that he became a folk hero to lesbians and gay men.

GAYS AS A POWERFUL MINORITY

By 1980, gay people seemed to have securely established themselves as a powerful minority. Even though the goal of changing the minds of an entire society about homosexuality seemed utopian, given the relative newness of the idea that "gay is good," thousands of organizations were created and, even more important, a new pride in being gay was expressed. The popular button "We Are Everywhere" signified this radical change.

Before the gains of the 1970s could be completely consolidated, however, a mysterious virus began killing gay men and, as years passed with a mounting death toll and no cure, the movement was deeply affected in ways that only future historians will be able to assess. Much political work was carried on, but not in the seventies' spirit that gay liberation was unstoppable. The right-wing backlash of the late 1970s intensified in the Reagan years. Anti-gay violence increased. Because of AIDS, homosexuality was linked to disease. Gay men and lesbians once again were forced to defend their right to exist.

Although AIDS took an inestimable toll on the gay community, the movement continued, partly because the AIDS crisis resulted in new political organizations and because other gay and lesbian groups kept springing up. Many people who were not ready to come out in the 1970s were ready in the

1980s, and many young people came out then as well. Gay groups in the 1980s tended to be more specialized than earlier ones: youth groups and senior groups, for example, recovery groups, a political action committee to lobby in Washington, groups for gay men and lesbians of color, the Gay Olympics, and campus gay groups.

In the 1970s gay identity was so novel and compelling that it tended to overshadow one's other identities. The more people saw their lesbian or gay identity as the center of their lives, the more likely they were to become politicized. But in the 1980s many people wanted to be gay *and*—gay and Black, for example, gay and working class, gay and disabled, gay and Democratic, gay and old. Although this proliferation of groups tended to diffuse the energy of gay liberation, the movement became stronger both because it became more institutionalized (paid work and permanent organizations assuming more importance) and because it was too large and diverse to be contained by formal organizations. The gay lobbyists who visited Congressional offices were representing an important tendency in gay liberation, the tendency to carve out a secure niche in American society, but they could hardly speak for gay Native Americans, lesbian separatists, working-class lesbian mothers, drag queens, gay teenagers, or all the homosexuals who still remained in the closet.

The old radical impulse in gay liberation, which appeared at the beginning of Mattachine in the early 1950s and again in the Gay Liberation Front after Stonewall, sparked the creation of AIDS Coalition to Unleash Power (ACT UP). In three years it had branches in sixty cities. ACT UP came to life because going through official channels was not saving the lives of gay men. Confrontation and civil disobedience seemed the only alternative. ACT UP members unfurled safe sex banners at baseball games, disrupted many meetings, sat in at the Food and Drug Administration, chained themselves to a balcony in the New York Stock Exchange, covered buildings with red tape to symbolize government delays in helping those with AIDS, and spray-painted outlines of bodies on Castro

Street in San Francisco to represent those who had died. These attention-getting tactics were reminiscent of the feminist and gay liberation zaps of the early 1970s when both concepts were still shocking (zaps were disruptions of meetings or events by protestors, often using satirical humor to publicize their cause). The direct action tactics of ACT UP are forcing drug companies and the medical bureaucracy to consider radical changes in drug research and regulation.

A low point for gay liberation in the 1980s was the 1986 Supreme Court decision upholding the constitutionality of sodomy laws. Another setback was the May 1988 passage of Clause 28 by the British government, saying that a local authority shall not "intentionally promote homosexuality or publish material with the intention of promoting homosexuality" or "promote the teaching in any maintained school of the acceptability of homosexuality as a pretended family relationship." This repressive measure does not distinguish between mentioning homosexuality in a neutral spirit—acknowledging, for example, the existence of a gay and lesbian rights movement—and "promoting." The bias of the phrase "pretended family relationships" is obvious, for they are not pretended to those who enter into them. In the year following the passage of Clause 28, many lesbian mothers lost custody of their children, attacks on lesbians and gay men rose by 11 percent, and the suicide rate among gay youth went up 20 percent.

The high point for the movement was the October 1987 March on Washington, which drew 600,000 people. Assuming that each marcher had five friends or acquaintances at home, the gay and lesbian movement is 3 million strong. It may be much larger, however, because the US gay population is estimated to be 22 million.

CHAPTER 4

THE LEGACY OF AMERICA'S SEXUAL REVOLUTION

AMERICAN
SOCIAL
MOVEMENTS

The Sexual Counterrevolution

SCOTT STOSSEL

Liberals and conservatives strongly disagree about the results of the sexual revolution, explains Scott Stossel in the following selection. While liberals applaud America's growing acceptance of birth control, sex education, premarital cohabitation, and equal rights for gays and women, conservatives maintain that the loosening of sexual mores in the twentieth century has led to increased promiscuity, infidelity, and an explosion of sexually transmitted diseases. Many observers claim that the United States is undergoing a backlash against the sexual revolution as cultural critics decry nonmarital sex and advocate a return to more traditional sexual values. Stossel concludes that although the sexual revolution had its flaws, its liberal political gains should not be abandoned for a stifling new puritanism. Stossel is a freelance journalist.

During the 1984 primary season, Ronald Reagan worried publicly that Americans were having too much sex. Promiscuity, he lamented, had become "acceptable, even stylish." The very word "promiscuity," with its reproachful moral overtones, had been replaced by the more accepting term "sexually active." What had once been "a sacred expression of love," had become "casual and cheap." The country's moral fabric was fraying dangerously. Who had set us on this road to Sodom? Liberals.

Accusations like Reagan's do not necessarily presume that liberals are friskier than other people—believe it or not, one study actually found that the very conservative are 10 percent more likely than the very liberal to be conducting extramarital affairs and three times more likely than the very liberal and the moderate to find sadomasochism an acceptable practice. Rather, Reagan's comments represent a typical version of the traditional conservative's interpretation of the "sexual revolution": It was part of the sinful sixties-seventies counterculture; it was a weakening of morals caused by trends and policies, such as wider availability of contraceptives and broader acceptance of premarital sex, that liberals advocated; and it was bad.

The sexual revolution is clearly one of those ideological battlegrounds—like the conflicts over college curricula, abortion, and "the sixties"—where liberals and conservatives clash over culture, politics, and religion simultaneously. Many liberals would insist—rightly—that the sexual revolution helped bring about changes for the better: broader rights for gays and women, wider use of contraceptives, acceptance of premarital cohabitation. Many conservatives would insist—also rightly— that the sexual revolution undermined traditional social and religious bonds and that this loosening of mores caused an explosion of sexually transmitted diseases (STDs). Conservatives have used the epidemics of AIDS and other STDs to reenergize their traditional moral arguments against sex outside marriage. Liberals, on the other hand, still champion what they consider to be the revolution's moral gains; they advocate improving contraceptive availability and sex education to preserve these gains while fighting disease and raising awareness.

Today we live with what many people believe—despite some studies showing sexual activity today to be as promiscuous as, if not more promiscuous than, at the height of the revolution—is a counterrevolution ushered in by AIDS. But is this backlash against the revolution a reality? What is the connection between public morality and public health? And who has more authority to speak on these issues: liberals advocating sex education and public health, or conservatives advocating abstinence and self-discipline?

On May 10, 1960, the Food and Drug Administration (FDA) announced the approval of a new drug produced by G.D. Searle & Company, called Enovid. Some 21 years later, on

June 5, 1981, *Morbidity and Mortality Weekly* reported the appearance of a strange new pneumonia in five otherwise healthy gay men. On neither day were the consequences of these events imaginable to most people. But "the pill" and AIDS serve in the popular imagination as the watershed developments that catalyzed and then killed the sexual revolution.

It is not entirely clear, however, that a discrete "sexual revolution" is anything more than a cultural artifact. Although there is clearly a countervailing trend toward more puritanical attitudes in some segments of society, the preponderance of evidence shows that sexual behavior has remained "loose"— and may even be continuing on a loosening trend—in the time of AIDS. Nor, contrary to popular mythology, did the revolution really begin with the birth control pill: The same trends can be traced back to the end of World War I.

By 1918 sex had begun to escape its institutional confinement in marriage and was starting to become an accepted— or at least acknowledged—part of the culture. During the 1920s, for example, the number of young women engaging in premarital sex jumped sharply, to about 50 percent of the cohort. Economic prosperity after World War II shifted values away from puritanical self-denial and toward a demand for consumer goods; by the 1960s, having lots of sex had become almost a commercial moral imperative. Business began catering to nonmarital sex: A new kind of establishment, the "singles bar," became a standard feature of the urban land scape; convenience stores sold "one-night-stand kits" that came with a toothbrush, condoms, razors, and, for women, an extra pair of underwear; and the concept that "sex sells" became ever more apparent in the proliferation of sexual scenes and innuendoes in entertainment and advertising.

In the 1950s, less than 25 percent of Americans thought premarital sex was acceptable; by the 1970s, more than 75 percent found it acceptable. Between 1960 and 1980, the marriage rate dropped by about 25 percent; the average age of marriage for both men and women rose steadily; and the number of divorced men and women jumped by 200 percent. All told, according to a study by *Adweek* magazine, single people as a percentage of the total American adult population rose from 28 percent in 1970 to 41 percent in 1993. The sexual revolution was in full swing.

It is significant that most people attribute the rise and decline of the revolution—now consolidated by popular understanding into a finite event—to developments that are not strictly speaking "moral" or "political." The birth control pill was a technological advancement; AIDS was a medical threat. Thus the vaunted loosening and then tightening of sexual mores that bracket the revolution are in some sense more reducible to biology and technology than to changes in religion or politics or morality per se.

This blending of science and morality is not a new phenomenon. In nineteenth-century America, physicians began to take the place of both church and state as the authoritative source of sexual norms. Victorian-era doctors and much of the public understood sex by analogy to the second law of thermodynamics, believing that profligate sex led to mental and physical degeneration. With this in mind, entrepreneurial inventors developed such devices as a genital cage that would ring an alarm when a boy wearing it had an erection, to prevent masturbation. STDs lent scientific urgency to calls for stricter sexual morality: In the 1890s, conservatives were quick to label a burgeoning syphilis epidemic divine retribution for an era in which the rules governing sexual behavior were losing their force.

A century later, AIDS was—literally, for some on the religious right—a Godsend. "AIDS is God's judgment on a society that does not live by its rules," declaimed Reverend Jerry Falwell. For the biblically inclined, this argument had a certain logic to it. After all, we had been warned: The herpes virus, afflicting as many as 30 million people by the early 1980s, had been deemed "the new scarlet letter" in a 1982 *Time* magazine cover story explicitly linking the disease to promiscuity. AIDS led to invigorated calls for monogamy and abstinence by religious leaders and public health officials. Both religious and secular authorities now had a powerful weapon, in the form of a medical threat, with which to bring the sexual revolution to a crashing halt.

Today, science has become so woven into moral discourse about sexuality that it is hidden in plain sight. Ironically, this conflation of scientific and moral rhetoric in discourse about sexual activity owes much to the work of an obscure midwestern entomologist who in the 1940s set out to separate religious and moral shibboleths about sex from actual sexual practices.

NATURAL, NORMAL, AND MORAL

In 1938, Alfred Kinsey, a professor in the zoology department at Indiana University, was known only for being the world's foremost expert on a small, stinging insect called the North American gall wasp. But that year, when the university inaugurated a new course on marriage and asked Kinsey to give lectures for it, the sexual world shifted on its axis. Kinsey, frustrated at not having enough statistical material for his lectures, began collecting his own data by surveying students in the marriage class. Finding that data insufficient, he distributed questionnaires to students and the faculty at large. Finally, relying on the help of a legion of colleagues, research assistants, and graduate students, Kinsey began surveying anyone who would consent to be interviewed, ultimately collecting data on 18,000 people. With funds from the National Research Council's Committee for Research in the Problems of Sex (underwritten by the Rockefeller Foundation), Kinsey stopped teaching and devoted himself full-time to his survey, founding the Institute for Sex Research in 1947.

Sexual Behavior in the Human Male, which became known as the Kinsey report, dropped like an 800-page bomb into American culture in 1948. No one—certainly not Kinsey or his publisher, who brought out a first printing of only 5,000 copies—expected the reaction it elicited. Rocketing to the top of the bestseller list, where it stayed for 27 weeks, the report introduced facts and statistics into America's dinner table conversations that dramatically altered perception of sexual behavior in America. The statistics shocked and scandalized: 86 percent of men said they had engaged in premarital sex; 50 percent said they had committed adultery before turning 40; 37 percent of men reported at least one episode of homosexual sex; and 17 percent of men who had grown up on farms claimed to have had sex with animals. The Kinsey report blew the lid off the container in which sexual experience had been sealed. Sexual activity previously labeled "deviant" or "immoral" seemed rampant among the very people who outwardly condemned it.

One of Kinsey's explicit goals in publishing the report was to export discussion of sexual practices from the realm of morality to that of science. In a scientific context, whatever the surveys found was "natural" and whatever was "natural" was "normal" and whatever was "normal" was morally okay. In other words, he sought to demolish "normal" as a meaningful category of sexual behavior.

> Whatever the moral interpretation . . . there is no scientific reason for considering particular types of sexual activity as intrinsically, in their biological origins, normal or abnormal. . . . Present-day legal determination of sexual acts which are acceptable, or "natural," and those which are "contrary to nature" are not based on data obtained from biologists, nor from nature herself.

Because previous study of sexual behavior had been little more than "a rationalization of the mores masquerading under the guise of objective science," the report aimed, in the words of its authors, to accumulate "scientific fact divorced from questions of moral value and social custom."

But despite its claims to separate sex from morality by inoculating it with science, what the Kinsey group managed to do was pretty much the opposite—to reify science as morality. Sex, one of the areas of life most laden with taboos, myths, and rules in every society, had historically been governed by traditional cultural authorities—religion, folklore, literature, law. The Kinsey report solidified science's role as the new, preeminent cultural authority. And Kinsey's version of the Word of Science was that, sexually speaking, anything goes. Whatever he found in his survey—and he found great quantities of adultery, homosexual sex, oral sex, prostitution, bondage, and bestiality—was by definition acceptable. Our moral values needed to be brought more scientifically in line with our sexual practices—and the sexual goal of society, the Kinsey report implied, was to maximize the number of orgasms per week. The sexual revolution, though it owed much to interpretations (and misinterpretations) of Sigmund Freud and Wilhelm Reich, found its intellectual underpinnings here.

Kinsey's methodology was badly flawed. Many of his respondents were simply the most eager volunteers; his statistical sample, while large, was hardly representative of the larger population. Thus the numbers he published in his reports were very likely grossly inflated. But this hardly mattered. Conservative critics attacked him on their terms, not his. It was not the specific quantities of "immoral" sexual activity reported by Kinsey that riled them; rather it was the report's attempt to use an implicitly moralizing social science to justify an anything-goes sexual ethos. "It is impossible to estimate the damage this book will do to the already deteriorating morals of America," declared the evangelist Billy Graham when the Kinsey report's companion volume, *Sexual Behavior in the American Female*, came out in 1953. Tennessee Congressman Carroll Reece formed a committee to investigate foundation support of "un-American activities," targeting in particular the Rockefeller Foundation's funding of the Kinsey Institute.

From the Kinsey reports onward, this constant tension between permissiveness and restraint, between old cultural authorities and new ones, led to a growing moral bewilderment. What was right? Nobody knew anymore. The sexual revolution and its aftermath caused this tension to intensify. A 1977 *Time* poll found that 61 percent of Americans believed it was harder and harder to tell sexual right from wrong than in the past. And the most striking feature of the 1993 *Janus Report on Sexual Behavior* was the increase in uncertainty between its two polling periods. "For most items . . . the no opinion responses in Phase Two [1988–1992] were two to three times what they had been in Phase One [1983–1985]. We observed significantly less firm opinion and more irresolution in the second phase sample than in the first." Perhaps the most confusing thing was that "science," deployed by Kinsey to establish what Lionel Trilling called a "democratic pluralism of sexuality," was now, in the age of herpes and AIDS, fused to moral arguments for monogamy and restraint. The Age of Aquarius turned into the Age of Confusion. . . .

THE GIRLS STRIKE BACK

In 1995, Warner Books published one of those advice-for-the-lovelorn pop-psychology books that line the self-help shelves of bookstores. Sales of *The Rules: Time-tested Secrets for Capturing the Heart of Mr. Right,* by Ellen Fein and Sherrie Schneider, chugged along modestly for a few months. Then the authors went on Oprah. All of a sudden, the Rules were everywhere. In 1996, the book reached the top spot on the *New York Times* bestseller list. Articles about the Rules started appearing everywhere from *Cosmopolitan* and *Glamour* to the *New Republic* and the *New Yorker.* The authors started offering phone consulting—at $250 an hour. My copy of the paperback even comes with an application form for a Rules seminar.

The Rules consists of 35 simple precepts such as "Don't Talk to a Man First," "Don't Accept a Saturday Night Date After Wednesday," "Let Him Take the Lead," and "No More than Casual Kissing on the First Date," arranged in rule-per-chapter sequence. "The purpose of the Rules is to make Mr. Right obsessed with you. . . . What we're promising you is 'happily-ever-after.'" The Rules amount, in aggregate, to a recommendation of playing "hard to get"—and to a rolling back of women's liberation by maybe 40 years. A "Rules Girl," according to Fein and Schneider, doesn't put out. She also never tells a man what to do, always lets him be in control, and doesn't let her children (from a previous marriage) become an intrusive presence in the relationship. "In a relationship, the man must take charge. . . . We are not making this up—biologically, he's the aggressor.". . .

The Rules no doubt taps eternal fears about spinsterhood, but its commercial success can be largely attributed to a neat intersection with the zeitgeist. The Rules may be inane (they recommend studying the mawkish film *Love Story* like the Bible), but they appeal smartly to an American society that won the sexual revolution—and then realized the spoils of victory were not all they were cracked up to be.

> Modern women aren't to talk loudly about wanting to get married. We had grown up dreaming about being the president of the company, not the wife of the president. . . . Still, we had to face it: as much as we loved being powerful in business, for most of us, that just wasn't enough. . . . We didn't want to give up our liberation, but neither did we want to come home to empty apartments. Who said we couldn't have it all?

This weirdly inverts the yearnings of 1950s housewives, for whom family and laundry were not enough. The question is a good, forward-looking one—why can't women have it all?—but the solution Fein and Schneider provide is retrograde.

Kinsey and the sexual revolution that followed him erased all the rules of romantic relations; the Rules, which the authors describe as "a simple working set of behaviors and reactions," put them back. The authors use a typical combination of pop science, fear mongering, practicality, and moral cajoling to urge sexual restraint. "Never get in a car with a man you meet at a party," they tell us, because "you might end up in his trunk." "Forget all the 'free love' theories from the swinging sixties," they tell us, summarily discarding the sexual revolution. It's not "cool to have an unwanted pregnancy or a disease."

SEXUAL ECOLOGY

The sexual counterrevolution is not limited to pabulum like the Rules. The most vitriolic backlash is reserved for gay men, who were in many ways both the primary catalysts and short-

The Sexual Backlash

A proliferation of sexually transmitted diseases provoked a backlash against the sexual revolution, explains feminist writer Lillian B. Rubin.

By the 1980s, first herpes, then AIDS became household words, while a host of other sexually transmitted diseases, many of them so rare they were generally unknown until then, became epidemic, part of the reality of everyday life. As these diseases increasingly brought illness, infertility and death, newspapers, magazines and television began to feature stories proclaiming the death of the sexual revolution and the return of the sexual conservatism of the past.

Lillian B. Rubin, *Erotic Wars: What Happened to the Sexual Revolution?* 1990.

term beneficiaries of the sexual revolution—and who have also suffered far more than anyone else its costs. Gabriel Rotello's *Sexual Ecology: AIDS and the Destiny of Gay Men* argues that it was radical changes in the sexual behavior of homosexual American men that led to a large, sudden increase in the prevalence of STDs among the gay and bisexual population. AIDS, it should be made clear, is not a "gay" disease—outside of the United States, 90 percent of its victims are heterosexual. But the new intensity and variety of sexual activity among homosexual males during the sexual revolution generated an environment in which diseases previously "held in check" could thrive. The gay New York bathhouses of the 1970s made possible licentiousness on a positively Roman scale. According to the Centers for Disease Control, the first few hundred gay men with AIDS had an average of 1,100 (!) lifetime sexual partners. Rotello, who is gay, makes the argument that, contrary to what many in the gay political community like to believe, the AIDS epidemic wasn't something that "just happened." The sexual revolution caused it.

Given the facts, this seems an obvious point, and an important one to acknowledge. But whether by ignorance or design, many people—gays and liberals in particular—don't accept it. To do so, they believe, would be playing into the moralist rhetoric of fundamentalist conservatives like Falwell and Pat Buchanan, for whom AIDS is a punishment visited by God upon the sexually deviant. "The poor homosexuals," Buchanan sneers. "They have declared war on Nature, and now Nature is exacting an awful retribution." AIDS confers such a moral stigma because conservatives have—incorrectly—managed to connect AIDS to homosexuality, which they consider intrinsically immoral, rather than to the specific behavior patterns in the sixties and seventies that in the United States made gays the focal point of the epidemic.

Rotello, like Kinsey, tries explicitly to distance himself from any moral claims ("So let me say simply at the outset that what I describe below are biological, not moral, events") in making his epidemiological arguments advocating sexual restraint and safe sex. But Rotello's book effectively—if unintentionally—illustrates that science, pragmatism, and morality are clearly interwoven in ways that resist untangling. Morality and public health are both concerned to protect and enhance the commonweal. But both can also be used to ostracize and deny rights—and they do so most effectively when they are mixed together.

IT'S OVER! NO, IT'S NOT!

The sexual revolution is such a contentious topic that even ostensibly objective social science gets tinged with the ideological predispositions of researchers. Though the data are now 50 years old, and though most experts believe its findings of sexual activity to be grossly inflated, the Kinsey reports remained the standard source for information about sexual activity until at least 1994. Various academic studies contradicted aspects of Kinsey's findings, but these studies were of much narrower scope. And broad studies of society that captured some data about sex, such as the General Social Survey (GSS), found quantities and varieties of sexual activity much lower than what Kinsey found. Would-be exegetes of the sexual revolution and its aftermath were left with a morass of conflicting and outdated information.

In 1993, Cynthia and Samuel Janus tried to rectify this situation, publishing *The Janus Report on Sexual Behavior*, for which they collected data between 1983 and 1992. Their findings only made things more confusing: They were unable to determine whether they were witnessing a backlash against the sexual revolution or a continuation of it. On the one hand the AIDS epidemic had made people claim to be more cautious about sex. On the other hand, they were having more sex with more people—especially among the most at-risk groups. Sixty-two percent of young men and 66 percent of young women reported that their sexual activity increased compared to three years earlier. Serious decline in sexual activity was shown by only 5 percent of the men and 9 percent of the women in the youngest group. Moreover, 24 percent of men and 20 percent of women reported "much more" sexual activity than three years earlier, and 44 percent of men and 41 percent of women reported "more" sexual activity. All told, 73 percent of men and 68 percent of women reported having the same or more sex in 1988–1992 than in 1985–1988.

Confronted with the conflicting data, the Januses weakly hedged their bets. This increase in sexual activity was, they said, the "Second Sexual Revolution." "The enormous tensions and backlash generated by these devastating sexually transmitted diseases made the practice of casual sex pause; from this hesitation, and the reaction to it, came the beginning of the Second Sexual Revolution." In other words, there was the revolution. Then there was the backlash against the revolution. Then there was the backlash against the backlash against the revolution. No wonder everyone is so confused.

The Janus report was based on a statistical sample of only 2,795, and many of the older respondents were found at sex-therapy clinics—so there is good reason to believe that many of their estimations of activity, like Kinsey's, are greatly overstated. But the following year another study appeared. Billed as the most comprehensive survey since Kinsey's, the National Health and Social Life Survey (NHSLS), popularly published as *Sex in America: A Definitive Survey*, dropped into American culture in 1994 like the original Kinsey report had nearly a half century earlier. Only while the Kinsey report had titillated and horrified with its previously unimaginable picture of sexual variety in the United States, *Sex in America* did quite the opposite.

What happened to the sexual revolution? *Sex in America* seemed to provide clear evidence that it was dead and gone, swept away by AIDS and a revival of sturdy family values. Some findings from its random sampling of 3,432 subjects: 94 percent of Americans were faithful to their spouses (up from around 60 percent in the Kinsey, Janus, and other surveys); only 33 percent of Americans had sex twice or more per week; the median number of lifetime sex partners for women was two, for men six. One of its more telling findings was that married people had the most sex, single people the next most, and divorced people the least. "The more partners you have," the report's authors wrote, "the more time you are going to spend finding and wooing them—time that a married couple could be having sex." In other words, if you like sex it doesn't pay to be a swinging single. Instead, get married and stay married. "Our findings," the authors wrote, "often directly contradict what has become the conventional wisdom about sex. They are counterrevolutionary findings, showing a country ... that, on the whole, is much less sexually active than we have come to believe."

Some found the study's conclusions dubious and its methodology biased, arguing that the opposition of politicians like Senator Jesse Helms—who in 1987 had blocked congressional funding for the study (and all sex surveys), forcing the researchers to apply for foundation money—had conservatized its results. John Heidenry, for example, writes in *What Wild Ec-*

stasy: The Rise and Fall of the Sexual Revolution that the *Sex in America* survey was "the logical culmination of the new and improved puritanism of the United States, dressed out in the guise of objective science." This is precisely the opposite of what critics of the Kinsey report had said: that its "objective science" gave moral license to sexually deviant practices. And while Kinsey had set out to abolish the whole concept of "normal"—or moral—sexuality, the NHSLS authors strove explicitly to preserve moral norms by warning that, "Of course, a survey cannot tell us what is normal, only what is frequent."

While the NHSLS's conclusions about sexual activity were generally much more conservative than the Janus report's, there were places where Janus's findings supported theirs. Though the NHSLS found that most young people did not have large numbers of sexual partners (more than 50 percent of 18- to 24-year-olds had just one partner in 1992), it also found that "the very sexually active people in the population, who are most at risk of being infected with HIV, did not seem to have been slowed by fears of AIDS." For example, 8.7 percent of people ages 25 to 29 claimed to have had 21 or more partners since age 18; 11.5 percent of 30- to 39-year-olds claimed to have had that many. The authors point out that if fear of AIDS had affected sexual activity, the highly promiscuous proportion of the younger group, who came of age after the explosion of AIDS, ought to have been much lower than it was relative to the older group.

But the most recent sex studies tell a more heartening story. On May 1, 1997, the National Survey of Family Growth, a government survey conducted every five years, released its most recent data, collected during 1995: The data showed that, for the first time since 1970, the percentage of teenagers having sex had declined. The percentage of girls aged 15 to 19 having sex declined from 55 to 50 between 1990 and 1995 (the number of married teenagers is so small these days, that even if marital sex is excluded, the percentage of girls having sex in 1995 falls by only 2 percent); and 55 percent of teenage boys had sex in 1995, down from 60 percent in 1988. Conservatives, no doubt, will take this as evidence that the sexual counterrevolution is, albeit slowly, taking hold. (And many adults think it should be taking hold faster; a March 1997 survey found that 95 percent of people surveyed believe teens should be completely abstinent.) But while something of a conservative sexual counterrevolution may finally be trickling down to younger Americans, the most encouraging data vindicate liberal sex-education policies: Condom use among young women has risen sharply, from 18 percent in the 1970s to 36 percent in the 1980s to 54 percent in 1995; in 1995, 91 percent of women said they had been taught safe-sex methods of preventing AIDS transmission. If condom use is up while sexual activity is down, then the conservative argument that sex education and contraception availability increase "immoral" and dangerous promiscuity looks less credible.

WHO WON THE SEXUAL REVOLUTION?

"Uninhibited sex," writes the conservative political scientist Harvey Mansfield in *Reassessing the Sixties*, "received a rude shock from the emergence of AIDS. Perhaps you should listen more carefully to the vague menaces of your mother . . . about what happens to people who do funny things for sex." Well, perhaps that's true—to a point. But then Mansfield continues. "Since the sixties, feminine modesty has reasserted itself, though partly in the guise of feminism. There are now plenty of nice girls . . . but they are confused, apologetic, and unsupported by social norms. What they get for advice is 'safe sex.'"

Mansfield's tone—with his derisive "under the guise of feminism" and his patronizing "nice girls"—gives away the conservative game here. What conservatives like Mansfield want is less a curb on sexual excess than a rolling back of the political gains that women (and gays) have won under the auspices of the sexual revolution. It is difficult, of course, to tie victories in the political and social realms directly to victories in the sexual realm—maybe a right to sexual assertiveness is directly linked to a right to political assertiveness and maybe it isn't. But at the very least the sexual revolution for women was bound up in the larger revolutionary changes of the period that led to an improvement in their social status. You can't have the one without the other. Conservatives like Mansfield and Falwell would like to erase both.

Mansfield's strategy for achieving this erasure is typical. In fact, it's roughly what *The Rules* does. First, point out that sexual liberation had a tangible, "science"-based cost: AIDS and other STDs. Next, cast the net more widely so that if sexual liberation was associated with women's liberation, for example, and sexual liberation caused AIDS, then women's liberation caused AIDS. All forms of liberation and political change connected to the sixties and seventies get implicated in this way. Women's rights, gay rights, woman's right to choose, and the freedom to do what you like in the privacy of your own bedroom all get thrown out the window with the bathwater.

In 1885, the prestigious British scientific journal the *Lancet* published an article arguing that the best method for protecting the young against STDs was the "cultivation of purity"— was "purity" a scientific concept or a moral one? The ambiguous rhetoric of "purity," neither clearly scientific nor clearly moral, is what for so many years has enabled traditional conservatives to extract from biology and epidemiology moral messages that are broader than the science merits.

The sexual revolution eliminated some hypocrisy. Those who trace the ruination of society to the breakdown of sexual morality forget that the old sexual morality was honored in the breach as often as not. Sure, in 1960 colleges had curfews and sexually segregated dorms. But remember that even then—no matter if Kinsey significantly overstated things— when the curfew bell rang, the campus shrubbery would quiver as young men and women emerged frantically pulling up their pants and smoothing down their dresses ready to run back to their single-sex dorms. Failing to acknowledge this, the anti-fornication crusaders are either dishonest (Jimmy Swaggart, Jim Bakker) or totally lacking in self-awareness (Robert Bork). In *Slouching Towards Gomorrah: Modern Liberalism and American Decline,* Bork writes:

One evening at a hotel in New York I flipped around the television channels. Suddenly there on the public access channel was a voluptuous young woman, naked, her body oiled, writhing on the floor while fondling herself intimately. . . . I watched for some time—riveted by the sociological significance of it all.

The sociological significance? Right. If Bork had been confirmed as a Supreme Court justice, we can guess the Court might have taken a lot more pornography cases for careful review.

The sexual revolution may not, in an important sense, have been worth its costs. Most gay men, the group most galvanized by the sexual revolution, would not say that the considerable political gains and social acceptance they've won over the last few years was worth human losses now numbering in the hundreds of thousands. But they would not want to give up those political gains and social acceptance. The Terror did not nullify all that the French Revolution achieved. Similarly, the ravages of AIDS do not mean that we should now abandon the liberal advances won by the sexual revolution. Less sexually wanton, yes; safer sex, yes; but we should not give in to rhetorical appeals for an oppressive new puritanism.

How Women Turned the Sexual Revolution to Their Advantage

PAULA KAMEN

Women helped to lay the foundation of the sexual revolution as more of them entered the paid workforce in the 1960s, explains Paula Kamen in the following selection. Women's increasing economic independence gave them more control over their sex lives, which in turn enabled them to expand their views on relationships, marriage, and family. Initially, however, women often had to contend with men who did not perceive them as equals but who wanted to enjoy women's increased sexual availability. Feminists responded to this sexism by organizing to redefine sexual freedom, securing reproductive rights, and garnering work and educational opportunities for women and minorities. Kamen, a Chicago-based journalist, lecturer, and playwright, has written several articles and books on contemporary feminism and gender roles.

If there is going to be a breakthrough in human sexuality—and I think that such a breakthrough might be in the wind—it is going to occur because women will start taking charge of their own sex lives. It is going to occur because women will stop believing that sex is for men and that men (their fathers, their doctors, their lovers and husbands, their popes and kings and scientists) should call the shots.

—Barbara Seaman, *Free and Female,* 1972

Excerpted from *Her Way: Young Women Remake the Sexual Revolution*, by Paula Kamen (New York: New York University Press, 2000). Copyright © 2000 by New York University Press. Reprinted with permission.

Until relatively recently, women in the mainstream society did not always conduct sex or family lives on their own terms. Rather, because they lacked power, they were dependent on male authorities such as husbands, clergy, psychologists, and doctors, who prescribed and proscribed their proper places, often within a submissive and self-sacrificing female framework. These men, previously as women's only sources of official knowledge, enforced their own sexual agendas, telling women only what they thought they needed to know. But for the past four decades, various interconnected social forces have converged to give more women more authority over their own lives and to create and propel the sexual evolution. This effect has followed a greater pattern that sociologists have documented: *the people possessing the most power in society also enjoy the greatest sexual permissiveness.*

First, social movements emerging in the 1960s and 1970s provided a foundation. Women gained economic power and greater social status by entering the labor force and becoming better educated in greater numbers. The ensuing sexual revolution helped weaken the double standard, which had confined sex for women purely to procreation, not recreation. On a more organized and political level, the women's movement reframed sex from a woman's point of view, giving women more power and control, and securing equal rights in the home, in relationships, and in the family.

Second, boosted by these social movements, young women have overcome the most restrictive sexual authority of women: organized religion. American culture has traditionally allowed men to define religion and morality on their own terms, and women have always been expected to take the role of follower. Now, however, taking the lead of the spiritually seeking boomer generation, young women are redefining religion and are becoming their own moral authority.

Third, the information age, accelerating in the 1990s, has had a profound effect on women making their own sexual choices. With better and more accessible information and safer-sex campaigns, women are now less isolated and know more about sex, thus making them less reliant on and more critical of male "experts."

WOMEN'S FINANCIAL INDEPENDENCE

The basic source of women's control over their sex lives is their financial independence. As some of the most prominent feminist writers of the twentieth century predicted, financial power, assisted by education, raises women's expectations and abilities to do things their own way, as well as shaping their views of men, marriage, family, sexual satisfaction, and romance. As Simone de Beauvoir wrote in *The Second Sex* in 1952:

> It is through gainful employment that woman has traversed most of the distance that separated her from the male; and nothing else can guarantee her liberty in practice. Once she ceases to be a parasite, the system based on her dependence crumbles; between her and the universe there is no longer any need for a masculine mediator.

When my interview subjects talked about sex, they frequently brought up their work and education goals. This was especially true for Stacie S., 27, who kept returning our conversation to the topic of money.

She isn't rich. But her job as a social worker, her small sales business, and her graduate degree give her a sense of independence that governs even the most personal aspects of her life. She has surpassed the economic and educational reach of her mother, a postal worker with a high school education. She just bought a small condo in a modest low-rise in a middle-class Chicago suburb and hopes some day to have a summer home, as her older coworkers do. "[Money] gives you power," she said. "It gives you freedom. You know, if I want to go somewhere, I go. If I want to go to Jamaica in November, I'll go. If I want to go to Cancún in January, I'm going to go. I'm not going to ask anyone. As long as my bills are paid, you know, I can do what I want to do."

Stacie repeatedly insisted that she is looking for a man who can be her companion, not her meal ticket. She makes more money than do most of the men she dates and doesn't need them to take care of her. Her financial independence also enables her to leave a relationship. "I don't need them to pay my mortgage, or I don't need them to pay my car note, or I don't need them to give me money to get my hair done, a manicure, my pedicure. That's why I go to work every day. . . . In the past, [women and men] kind of traded off. 'We'll give you sex if you give us the money to go to the beauty salon on Saturday.' What's up with that?"

Although poor women have always had to work, more middle-class and upper-class women are now in the workforce than ever before. In fact, working outside the home is more the rule than the exception for young women of all backgrounds. Three out of four women aged 25 to 54 were in the workforce in 1994, twice the proportion for this group shortly after World War II. In 1994, women accounted for 46 percent of the labor force, up from 24 percent in 1940. What has changed most in the past fifty years is women's steady long-term work patterns, which now resemble those of men. In the years immediately after the war, the majority of women workers were under 25, and most quit when they had children. Today, the greatest workforce participation is by women in their late thirties and forties (eight in ten are in the workforce). Their financial goals have also become more ambitious. Just a few generations ago, almost all women, even those with a college education, were relegated almost exclusively to the lowest-paying "female" jobs, almost never on a serious "career" track. When married middle-class women worked, it was often part time, and they were thought to merely be seeking "pin money" or extra change. Women's most dramatic employment gains have been in managerial and professional jobs, the occupational groups in which men and women are most equally represented, with women accounting for three in ten of these jobs.

Women began entering the job market in large numbers in the early 1940s, spurred by the war, which created labor shortages because of the loss of male workers and the need for increased production. As a result, 5.2 million more women were in the labor force in 1944 than in 1940, reaching a proportion of 36 percent. After the war, the percentage dropped slightly to 31 percent, which was still above prewar levels. In the 1950s, married women continued to work to support their families. In the 1980s, women's labor force participation continued to grow, but at slower levels. In the early 1990s, it reached a plateau of 57.2 percent, but in 1994, it started to climb, reaching an all-time high in 2000 of 60 percent of women participating in the labor market.

In general, today women also earn more than ever before. In 1963 women earned 59 cents for every dollar earned by men; today women earn 73 cents for every dollar earned by men. (This is widely understood to be the result of discrimination, which still keeps disproportionate numbers of women routed to and stuck in low-wage jobs with little opportunity for advancement.) However, this progress has not been shared by all. Gender differences are still apparent in the less elite occupations, with the majority of women working in low-paying clerical, sales, and service jobs. White women have gained more than black women, who are much more likely than white women to be stuck in low-wage service jobs. Women's overall career growth is also overshadowed by the general state of poverty for a substantial subset of women, mainly single female heads of families, who account for 14 percent of all households in 1993, compared with 9.4 percent in 1970. Half of these households are poor, compared with 10 percent of the general population.

Just a short time ago, college was a male pursuit and women were called *coeds,* reflecting their novelty and secondary status, but today the number of women has surpassed that of men on all educational levels (except the number earning doctorates). In 1998, the U.S. Census Bureau reported that for the first time, young women are completing both high school and college at a higher rate than are their male peers. According to 1999 statistics, in the past decade the annual number of women receiving Ph.D.s increased by more than 50 percent, now accounting for about 40.6 percent of the total. As their entry into the professions indicates, women have made particularly great gains in securing degrees in traditionally male fields. In the thirty years between 1961/62 and 1991/92, women's share of all business degrees sextupled, and their share of biology degrees almost doubled. By 1991/92, the number of women who received dentistry degrees had nearly tripled from 1976/77. The number of women receiving degrees in medicine and law more than doubled over that same time. In computer and information sciences, engineering, and the physical sciences, however, women remain significantly underrepresented.

This greater amount of education is a powerful force in shaping women's sexual attitudes and behavior. The authors of the University of Chicago's 1994 National Health and Social Life survey point out that education is an especially significant variable for young women, determining their level of recreational sexual exploration. They discuss this issue most directly in a section about same-sex partners. Although educational level is not a variable for males for homosexuality, it does correlate strongly with lesbian behavior. The women college graduates surveyed were eight times more likely than high school graduates to claim a homosexual or bisexual identity and were more than twice as likely to have had same-gender sex since puberty. The Chicago survey noted other nontraditional behaviors that are more common among highly educated women. Sixty percent of women who had attended graduate school reported having masturbated in the past year, compared with 25 percent who had not finished high school. Women with at least some college were 40 percent more likely to have received oral sex than were women with less than a high school degree, and women with graduate degrees were 40 percent more likely to have had anal sex than were women with high school degrees.

The 1993 *Janus Report on Sexual Behavior* also found that educated women had greater sexual options:

They report much greater gratification in their sexuality, are aware of the sexual double standard, demand parity in initiating sex rather than playing the traditional passive female, have had the most premarital sexual experience, and report being the most sensual. Women in the more highly educated groups were more easily able to assert their sexual opinions and preferences and to maintain a greater level of control over their sex lives.

In addition, the *Janus Report* found a related variable, career, to be such a strong influence on women that it divided women into two categories: homemakers (those not employed outside the home at all) and career women employed outside the home. (Data on part-time workers were not specifically tabulated.) These two groups were "two distinctly different populations" regarding sex life and lifestyle in general. In fact, the *Janus Report* found that "one of the most striking indications of our data" is the similarity of agreement between men and the career women (55 to 56 percent). Educated women also have sex later and are more careful. The 1994 National Health and Social Life survey discovered a positive correlation between education and delaying sex and using birth control as a teenager. In addition, the odds of becoming an unmarried mother fall sharply as education rises and opportunity broadens. Almost 50 percent of births to high school dropouts occur out-of-wedlock, whereas among college graduates, the proportion is just 6 percent, according to U.S. Census Bureau statistics. In contrast, by the time they reach thirty, about 10 percent of the less-educated women, compared with 30 percent of those with a college education, still did not have a child, according to the Chicago survey.

Young women today are more aware of this connection between jobs and gaining power in their relationships. The social critic Florynce Kennedy, 77, an African American attorney and activist, described the main difference she had observed over the years: "I think they don't believe so much in men. They used to be so round eyed about men and relationships. I think now they're not. I think women are much more skeptical that their romances are going to be all right. . . .

The fact was that they were fixed on romance because that was the way you hooked a guy, so that you can get him to pay the rent and everything. But now that women are better educated and can pay their own bills, they don't have the same need for romance. What they thought was romance was really the need for economic arrangement."

THE SEXUAL REVOLUTION: A MIXED LEGACY

As women left home and joined the workforce in the early 1960s, they began laying the foundation of the sexual revolution. The expansion of pink-collar service and clerical jobs drew more women to the cities and helped contribute to a new urban singles culture. More women also were going away to college, ready to experiment with sex. Birth control pills first became available in 1960, giving women more confidence in avoiding pregnancy than with the less effective and obtrusive diaphragm (often restricted by doctors to married women). Hugh Hefner, founder of *Playboy* in 1953, helped glamorize the swinging single life for men, who were waiting in the wings from their martinis- and modern art-stocked bachelor pads for their female counterparts to emerge. But men knew that for the sexual revolution really to begin, women still needed cultural permission, as premarital sex was still frowned on.

The tide started changing in 1963 with Betty Friedan's book *The Feminine Mystique,* which exposed many married women's feelings of suffocation. Helen Gurley Brown's *Sex and the Single Girl* in 1962 had already put a new spin on the single life. (Of all the writers of that period, Friedan and Brown, both radicals, particularly influenced exactly how future generations of women would shape their married and single identities and expectations.) Challenging traditional images of the single woman as a pathetic spinster or a neurotic leftover, Brown portrayed her as complete, fulfilled, and not necessarily in hot pursuit of a husband. She also put a large dent in the double standard, reducing women's shame for having sex outside marriage. "Perhaps you will reconsider the idea that sex without marriage is dirty. . . . You inherited a proclivity for it. It isn't some random piece of mischief you dreamed up because you're a bad, wicked girl," she wrote. She then widely promoted these beliefs for the next thirty years as editor in chief of *Cosmopolitan* magazine, which has both enhanced other women's magazines' sexual content and carried her beliefs to future generations of women.

In another influential and emblematic best-seller, *The Sensuous Woman,* published in 1969, the anonymous author, "J," continued this discussion. As Brown did, "J" begins her book discussing the actual benefits of sex for women outside marriage, namely, to obtain pleasure and to snare a man. In fact, she devotes an entire chapter to assuring readers they have nothing to feel guilty about:

> Now I know a few people are going to try to beat you down and force you into a corner marked "shame," if you don't play the virgin role. But you don't have to abide by their rules. . . . Our world has changed. It's no longer a question of "Does she or doesn't she?" We all know she wants to, is about to or does. Now it's only a question of how tastefully she goes about it.

The mass media first discovered this sexual revolution or "new morality" in the mid-1960s, culminating with a *Time* cover story on January 24, 1964. In 1963, *Time, Mademoiselle,* and *America* also referred specifically to this "sexual revolution." This term won out over other popular labels such as the "morals revolution" (*Newsweek,* April 6, 1964) the "moral revolution" (*New York Times,* May 7, 1965), and the "sexplosion" (*Christian Century,* January 29, 1964). Today, despite reports that the sexual revolution is dead, it continues to influence women's lives and choices. But its legacy is mixed. On the one hand, we now have a "sexualized marketplace," the result of society's greater openness about sex. Sexualized pictures of women are everywhere, used to sell every product possible, but in a market still dominated by male tastes and defining female sexuality as what is attractive to men. On the other hand, women now have more control over their sex lives because of their better access to sex education, erotica, and information about their bodies.

For many traditionally oriented women, however, the sexual revolution has meant a loss of power because sex is no longer a bargaining tool for a long-term commitment. In the past, not having sex until marriage merited a big reward: being supported for life by a man. But after the sexual revolution, when sex was given freely, it became a less precious commodity. Just as many men lost their financial bargaining power with women as women started to earn their own money, many women lost their sexual bargaining power with men. But the most sweeping criticism of the sexual revolution was that it was conducted entirely according to men's rules. Women still knew little about their own bodies and how they could have an orgasm, as sex was still being defined in men's terms. Women continued to have little protection against pregnancy because abortion was illegal. Moreover, women no longer could say no without being labeled as repressed or frigid. They also had no defense against forced sex; date rape, sexual harassment, and sexual abuse. In other words, even though women's behavior had changed, society had not. Now many women felt trapped in another role, that of sex object.

ORGANIZING FOR SEXUAL CONTROL

When the women's movement began in the late 1960s (in what has been called "the second wave" of feminism), these problems were at the top of the agenda. Some of these early feminist activists were inspired by their work in the civil rights and antiwar movements, in the process of which they were made aware that they were second-class citizens themselves. Despite the rhetoric about the importance of equality and of ending oppression, their supposedly enlightened fellow male activists often didn't take them seriously as peers and relegated them to a strictly sexual role.

"I think the 1960s sexual revolution was really a way where

more women were supposed to be available to more men," said longtime leader Gloria Steinem in an interview, describing women's experiences in the New Left. "It wasn't about autonomy. It was about you ran the mimeograph machine and you were sexually available."

Steinem remarked that the first issue of *Ms.*, which she co-founded in 1972, featured an article entitled "The Sexual Revolution Isn't Our War." The author, Anselma Dell'Olio, while affirming women's right to sexual pleasure and rejecting the double standard of the past, talked about the "sexual revolution" as a male invention, a "more free sex for us revolution." She wrote that the revolution neglected, however, to address women's sexual pleasure and orgasms, along with women's infinitely greater risks, such as pregnancy and unreliable contraception.

Women's activism for change began with the powerful process of consciousness raising, talking to one another about their own experiences. The slogan that emerged from such discussions was "the personal is political," referring to no longer seeing individual problems exclusively as personal, random, or idiosyncratic but as related to the greater systemic oppression of women. The more conservative feminists concentrated on gaining more work and education opportunities, whereas many radical feminists explored the intimate sphere of life to which women were restricted and in which so many of women's oppressions were rooted. They recognized that questions of sexuality and reproduction were not just private matters but concerns that determined women's freedom and status. Issues like abortion, rape, welfare for single mothers, child care, marriage, heterosexuality, motherhood, and women's sexual pleasure didn't take place in a vacuum but were shaped and influenced by the greater male-dominated culture.

These insights into "sexual politics" provided the spark for women organizing as a group to take control and start to change attitudes. As a result, feminists of the 1960s and 1970s had a powerful impact on future generations of women's being able to conduct their sex lives "her way." They redefined sex and sexual freedom from a woman's point of view, broadened women's knowledge of their own bodies, secured reproductive rights, and began to expand freedoms for lesbians and minorities. With new rights in education and the workplace, women were able to become independent, by either remaining single or divorcing, and to better control every aspect of their sex lives. Much of this work continued in the 1980s and beyond, as the women's movement became more firmly established in American culture. Even though the media repeatedly report that we are in a postfeminist age and that activism is dead, feminists are continuing to push for change, which often comes gradually and behind the scenes. . . .

HIGH EXPECTATIONS AND MORE CHOICES

Young women as a whole and those in my sample have been profoundly influenced by the past forty years of feminist organizing. Ideas that used to seem radical are commonplace today, and young women have higher expectations than ever about their sexual rights. In the 1960s, it was radical for an unmarried woman to use birth control; thirty years later young women on college campuses are passing out condoms to one another. In the 1970s, it was radical to not blame a woman for rape, even if the perpetrator was a stranger. Now, young feminists are moving the debate to the next level, labeling it rape even if the assailant is an acquaintance or family member. Women used to have trouble being accepted in the workplace at all; now they are addressing issues affecting the quality of their work lives, such as sexual harassment. In the 1970s, considering lesbianism was radical; in the 1990s, lesbians are fighting for their rights in marriage, the family, and the workplace.

The older women I interviewed also recognized the younger generation's greater sense of entitlement, from how they are treated personally to how they define their career paths. "What encourages me is that my students and the young people I meet on college campuses have a much better self-concept," said Sarah Weddington, 50, who teaches law at the University of Texas. "They feel more self-confident than I ever was at that age. And I think part of that was I was raised in West Texas, in a little town with people . . . in the community often saying, 'Women don't, women can't, women shouldn't.'. . . So if they're starting far ahead of where I was, I think they can make a longer, a better race than I did." In an interview, syndicated sex columnist Isadora Allman described the greater variety of life choices: "When I was growing up, a woman was married with children, or not yet. Those were the only choices. If you weren't married, clearly you were a leftover. If you didn't have children, it must have been God's will, not a choice. And if you didn't marry or have children, then you were something weird, like Marion the Librarian. If you were a career gal, sexless, peculiar. Nowadays a person can be a nurse or an astronaut, male or female, can be monogamous or not, be with a person of the same sex or not, marry several times, not marry at all, have children whether you're married or not. There are more choices for making a life that's personally more rewarding."

Mary Ann Hanlon, 54, who raised five children while her husband worked, said the lesson of the women's movement was that "women had a value. We had a right to a job, equal pay with men. We didn't have to sit home and wash dishes." She added that young women also demand better treatment from men, willing to get divorced if they are not satisfied. "Women feel we're not to tolerate certain forms of behavior. Whereas in the past, in my generation, or my mother's generation, it just went with the turf." Hanlon now appreciates these effects, although she was not a supporter of the women's movement in the 1960s when she was at home raising four children. In fact, after she read Betty Friedan's *The Feminine Mystique* in the 1960s, she hurled it across the room in disgust because she viewed the book, a critique of women's compulsory housewife role, as a "put-down of what I did."

As Hanlon suggested, another challenge for the new generation is to raise the value of women's various choices. As the women's movement matures, it is becoming more sensitive to differences in race, class, and sexuality. If their goal is to be inclusive and to attract broader support, young feminists must avoid making and enforcing a list of requirements of what it means to be a feminist. Accordingly, they have largely abandoned the heated feminist arguments of the 1970s and 1980s about what a true feminist is. This defiance of strict rhetoric is the legacy of young activists, known as the "third wave" feminists. They are freer to explore gray areas and apparent contradictions such as bisexuality as opposed to lesbianism or heterosexuality, making and using pornography but also being critical of it, and looking at the dark side of abortion as well as its necessity. . . .

THE INNER STRUGGLE

To attain sexual self-determination, all women must also face another overall struggle, an inner one. Planning one's life requires active attention to one's needs and desires and a willingness to create new roles instead of passively following old ones. After the influx of women into the labor force, the sexual revolution, and the women's movement, we are living in a more democratic society than our mothers and grandmothers did, and even though we should not complain, life can still be tough. "It is easier to live through someone else than to become complete yourself," wrote Betty Friedan in the 1963 *The Feminine Mystique*. "No woman in America today who starts her search for identity can be sure where it will take her. No woman starts that search without struggle, conflict, and taking her courage in her hands."

The Evidence Against Sexual Liberation

FREDERICA MATHEWES-GREEN

The so-called sexual revolution that was lauded in the 1960s and 1970s has led to "divorce, disease, abortion, illegitimacy, and multiplying heartbreak," writes Frederica Mathewes-Green in the following selection. She contends that these negative social trends are causing young people to question the ideals of feminism and sexual liberalism. As a result, an increasing number of teens and young adults are becoming sexually conservative, rejecting premarital sex, promiscuity, and abortion. The growing influence of religious values may be having an effect on young people's views on sexual morality, she concludes. Mathewes-Green is a syndicated columnist and a commentator for National Public Radio.

Ideas don't only have consequences, they have companions. For thirty years a ragtag trio has been running across the cultural landscape, linked like escapees from a chain gang and causing similar havoc: "sexual liberation," "economic independence," and "reproductive choice." Even as the bad news is that these notions rose and flourished together, the good news is that hints of their common fall are becoming discernible.

Take sexual liberation (i.e., promiscuity). As recently as 1989 the Centers for Disease Control found that 59 percent of high schoolers had had sex. In subsequent years, similar CDC studies showed the numbers dropping: 54 percent in 1990, and 43 percent in 1992. In 1994, the Roper Organization released a study done in conjunction with SIECUS (the Sex Informa-

Excerpted from "Now For Some Good News," by Frederica Mathewes-Green, *First Things*, August/September 1997. Copyright © 1997 *First Things*. Reprinted with permission.

tion and Education Council of the U.S.), which found that only 36 percent of high schoolers had had sex.

A 23 percent drop in five years is notable, if not amazing. What's happening?

THE FALLOUT FROM SEXUAL LIBERATION

"Sexual liberation" sounded like an excellent idea in the seventies, when contraception was abundant and venereal disease rare. Why should men have all the fun? Why should there be an unfair double standard? Women's sexual desires were as strong as men's, and if they weren't they ought to be. In fact, anything men wanted ought to be what women wanted too; in the fretful and self-contradictory thinking of nascent feminism, men were scum, but their values were objects of envy.

Although hammering men for exploiting women and treating them as sex objects, feminists tacitly adopted the "*Playboy* Philosophy" of sex without commitment as the new standard for female sexuality. But gradually women began to realize it was a bad bargain. If girls give sex in order to get love, while boys give love in order to get sex, dumping free sex on the market inevitably drove the cost of love through the roof. Female bargaining power was demolished. Girls had to fling enormous quantities of sex at boys in desperate attempts to buy the smallest units of love. One teen told a friend of mine: "I slept with Rick last night. Do you think he likes me?"

Though "sexual liberation" is still viewed confusedly as something that helps women own and enjoy their sexual feelings, the negative fallout has been hard to ignore: divorce, disease, abortion, illegitimacy, and multiplying heartbreak. Free sex made women feel free in the sense that you feel free falling from a twelve-story building: exposed, vulnerable, and headed for disaster. Thus the phenomenon of "date rape," which is largely the result of uncertainty over what the current rules are for behaving "like a gentleman."

Not only are church-sponsored abstinence clubs booming, but anti-promiscuity messages are popping up in unexpected places as well, perhaps indicating the mainstreaming of the movement. A popular dating handbook, *The Rules*, advises women to refuse sex, reminding them how painful it is when last night's lover doesn't phone, and what power there is in recovering the word "No." And teens in the "straight edge" movement refuse sex, drugs, and alcohol—while dressing like punks, screaming in hardcore bands, belligerently espousing vegetarianism and animal rights, and having no discernible ties to religion.

While rising numbers of teens are saying no to sex, the most telling evidence against "liberation" comes from the kids who said yes. A survey published in the *American Journal of Preventive Medicine* in 1991 asked sexually experienced inner-city junior and senior high students what they thought was the ideal age to begin having sex: 83 percent suggested ages older than they had been. Twenty-five percent of these sexually experienced kids also said that they believe sex before marriage is wrong. (This point of view has continued to grow in popularity. The UCLA Higher Education Research Institute surveys 250,000 new college freshmen every year. In 1987, 52 percent of the students said that casual sex was acceptable; only 42 percent of the 1996 class agrees.)

In the 1994 Roper survey cited above, 62 percent of sexually experienced girls, and 54 percent of all experienced high schoolers, said they "should have waited." And, most poignant, a study published in a 1990 issue of *Family Planning Perspectives* described a questionaire distributed to one thousand sexually active girls, asking them to check off which item they wanted more information about. Eighty-four percent checked "how to say no without hurting the other person's feelings."

WOMEN'S ATTEMPTS FOR ECONOMIC INDEPENDENCE

Of all the problems that can be caused by sexual promiscuity, the hardest to ignore is pregnancy. Unexpected pregnancy can be disruptive in many ways, but the bottom line is money: a new mouth to feed historically required the care of two, a full-time caretaker and a full-time breadwinner. Thus, if sexual promiscuity was to be practically feasible, it required that women be economically self-supporting, just in case children came along. Otherwise, a one-night stand might turn into a lifetime commitment. A lifetime commitment might be what women would prefer, but that would undermine the noble goal of "sexual liberation."

Rather than the interdependence of family life, women were exhorted to grasp the mirage of empowerment through "economic independence." As a result, having a high-paying career became the locus of meaning in life. This marked an ironic reversal at the time. The sixties were characterized by rejection of the "corporate rat race" and the material success and status that implied. Instead, we were going to get back to the land, live simply, wear tie-dyes and munch granola.

The feminism that grew out of the sixties did an about-face on this. By the early seventies, the struggle was to get women into that corporate rat race, which now looked all the more appealing for having been off-limits. If men wanted to spend their lives at ulcer-churning work, never seeing their kids, and dying early of stress-related disease, it must be what women wanted too. Particularly in those early days of feminism, child-rearing was disparaged as mindless work for drudges; in this, supposedly progressive women adopted the condescending and contemptuous male chauvinist attitude toward housewives, and toward the work women have done nobly for millennia. It was a wholesale rejection of women's heritage and an adoption of masculine values—values that were, in fact, not very healthy for men either.

"The two-paycheck family is on the decline," reported the financial weekly *Barron's* in 1994; "the traditional one-paycheck family is now the fastest-growing household unit." Those leading the charge are the youngest moms, between the ages of twenty and twenty-four. One says, "My mother worked; my husband's mother worked; we want our child to have more parental guidance at home." According to William Mattox of the Family Research Council, these young parents feel they were cheated by parental absence growing up, and 62

Reproductive Freedom?

Author and researcher Barbara Dafoe Whitehead contends that the "contraceptive revolution" increased pressures on unmarried women to have sex without commitment.

Something happened on the road to reproductive freedom. Men were liberated from the old bargain that held them responsible for an unwanted pregnancy. Before the contraceptive revolution, a young man who got a girlfriend pregnant came under family and social pressures to marry her and support the family. But shortly after the advent of legal abortion and contraception for unmarried women, the shotgun wedding began to disappear. According to [Brookings Institute economist George] Akerlof, a woman's right to choose enlarged male choice as well. If women had the option to choose to have a baby, men had the option to marry and support the mother and child—or not. Akerlof quotes an Internet contributor to a dad's-rights newsgroup: "Since the decision to have a child is solely up to the mother (see *Roe v. Wade*), I don't see how both parents have responsibility to that child."

At the same time that the new bargain gave men greater freedom to pursue their own interests, it also increased pressures on women to have sex without the promise or expectation of marriage. Akerlof argues that this deal created winners and losers. The losers were the women who had sex and then babies with the old-fashioned expectation that their sex partners would be faithfully committed to them and their offspring.

Barbara Dafoe Whitehead, *City Journal*, Summer 1999.

percent say they intend to spend more time with their kids than their parents did with them.

While feminists continue to wring their hands over the gender wage gap, the fact is that the gap has shrunk to 2 percent—that is, when corrected for variation in lifestyle choices. Childless men and women between the ages of twenty-seven and thirty-three earn nearly the same amount. But a great many women earn less than men because, putting child rearing and family life first, they choose to work at less stressful and demanding jobs.

Changing Opinions on Abortion

In a world where women are expected to be sexually available, but also expected to be financially self-supporting, the prevention of childbirth—"reproductive choice"—becomes a necessity. Contraception is a partial solution to this problem, but contraception fails, or participants fail to use it for one reason or another. Thus abortion becomes the necessary third link in the chain of companions.

The first year abortion was available, about three-quarters of a million were done; by 1981, the number had doubled to one and a half million. Invention was the mother of necessity: something that people had always managed without (often by turning to adoption plans or marriage) turned into such a handy solution it became nearly indispensable. At the same time, the availability of abortion took away one of women's classic reasons to turn down casual sex, and even made less urgent her insistence on contraception. ("I'll take a chance this one time; I can always have an abortion.") Thus the availability of abortion contributed to an increased rate of unwed sex, "unplanned" pregnancy, and (coming full circle) subsequent abortion. It also made it easier for career to be moved to the top of a woman's agenda, since the distraction of children could so easily be eliminated; indeed, it seemed that abortion was the course a responsible career woman was expected to take, while bearing an unexpected child was unprofessionally whimsical and selfish.

In recent years, the number of abortions has dropped slightly, and public acceptance of the procedure has dimmed. An August 1996 Harris poll found that public support for *Roe v. Wade* had slipped to 52 percent, the lowest point in a decade. The pro-choice movement had dropped nine approval points since 1992, while the pro-life movement had risen five. Polls by CBS News/*New York Times* can be compared as well: in 1989, 40 percent of respondents agreed that "abortion is the same thing as murdering a child." In 1995, that figure had risen to 46 percent.

But that's not the most startling element to the story. In the later CBS poll, one particular age group emerged as the most likely to call abortion murder; they raised the average ten points, to 56 percent. The age group wasn't pious behind-the-times grannies. It was young adults, ages eighteen to twenty-nine.

MANY YOUTHS FEEL ABORTION IS WRONG

[At the time of this writing,] *Roe v. Wade* is twenty-four years old, which means that every person in America under the age of twenty-four could have been aborted. Of course, a great many were; the ratio has hovered around two or three births to each abortion, and over those years some thirty-five million children were lost. High school and college students can imagine every third or fourth classroom chair reserved for the ghost of an aborted would-be friend or sibling. They know themselves to exist only due to their parents' choice, not due to any inherent value or dignity of their own. Thoughts like these can radicalize.

A study in the April 1992 *Family Planning Perspectives* stumbled over a tendency of teens to oppose abortion. Authors Rebecca Stone and Cynthia Waszak were dismayed to find that the "vast majority" of adolescents in focus-group studies were united in believing abortion to be medically dangerous, emotionally traumatic, and wrong. This finding transcended ethnicity, income level, and gender. Indeed, the young women were even more "judgmental of other women's motives" than the young men, with some opposing abortion even in the case of rape, or alleging that a rape exception would induce some women to lie.

Contraceptive failure was not seen as justification for abortion, since the possibility of conception came with the choice of having sex. Abortion was called "selfish" and "a cop-out," and associated consistently with words like "murder," "blood," and "death." The authors attribute this to successful propagandizing by an "intensive antiabortion campaign" (implausibly implying that these kids haven't had sufficient exposure to the arguments for "choice"). Participants believed that life begins at conception, and the right solution to an unexpected pregnancy was having the baby: "Anything's better than killing it," one said.

While reading this study one can almost hear the authors wringing their hands. Though they certainly intended to listen, not lead, in the focus groups, glimpses of ideology struggling against professional restraint slip through. One young woman reminds the group of something the author/facilitator had said earlier: "Religion is legal; we have our choice. Abortion is legal; they have their choice." Perhaps under the influence of such encouragement, most of the adolescents do affirm legal access to abortion (while presuming erroneously that it is presently illegal nearly everywhere, and under nearly all circumstances). In this they reflect the prevalent American compromise: abortion is wrong, but it should be legal. What distresses the authors is the fervency and obstinacy with which the teens think it is wrong; this may "guide their votes later." (Indeed, the UCLA study of college freshmen found that in 1990 65 percent believed abortion should remain legal, but by 1996 only 56 percent agreed.)

A RETURN TO BALANCE

For all three of these links in a chain of consequential ideas—promiscuity, careerism, and abortion—an inevitable return to balance and health is beginning to occur. In all three cases, the way is being led by teens and young adults, the most encouraging sign of all. What is eliciting such a change is a matter of speculation; perhaps it's the undeniable evidence of past failure, the dawning of reality, a deeper understanding of what really satisfies in life, or a renewed respect for the guidelines offered by biology.

Or maybe it's something else. The authors of the study cited above blamed "antiabortion views, conservative morality, and religion" for forming the teens' attitudes, and throughout the discussions religion did keep rearing its threatening head. The authors report, in a mix of headscratching bewilderment and dread: "Many of the participants described having personal relationships with God, and some quoted Scripture and said God was the only source of the right advice." The following conversation is quoted:

"A male participant said, 'At the end, legal or illegal, at the end you are gonna pay consequences. Not to man but to God. 'Cause the Bible warns you of what's gonna happen.'

"A young woman added, 'Judgment Day.'

"The young man replied, 'Exactly.'"

The Sexual Revolution Among Today's Youth

Parents and educators are witnessing a troubling increase in sexual activity and an openness about sex among children and teenagers today, reports *Time* magazine journalist Ron Stodghill II. One benefit of this increased sexual candor among youths is that more of them are taking measures to protect themselves from pregnancy and sexually transmitted diseases. However, teens often lack the maturity to deal with the complexities of sexual relationships, and many observers fear that too much sexual permissiveness is adversely affecting young people's attitudes about love and commitment. Another downside to the youthful sexual revolution is an increase in sexual harassment and sexual violence in schools. Such difficulties are aggravated by the mixed messages youths receive from the entertainment industry, parents, and sex education curricula, writes Stodghill.

The cute little couple looked as if they should be sauntering through Great Adventure or waiting in line for tokens at the local arcade. Instead, the 14-year-olds walked purposefully into the Teen Center in suburban Salt Lake City, Utah. They didn't mince words about their reason for stopping in. For quite some time, usually after school and on weekends, the boy and girl had tried to heighten their arousal during sex. Flustered yet determined, the pair wanted advice on the necessary steps that might lead them to a more fulfilling orgasm. His face showing all the desperation of a lost tourist, the boy spoke for both of them when he asked frankly, "How do we get to the G-spot?"

Whoa. Teen Center nurse Patti Towle admits she was taken aback by the inquiry. She couldn't exactly provide a road map. Even more, the destination was a bit scandalous for a couple of ninth-graders in the heart of Mormon country. But these kids had clearly already gone further sexually than many adults, so Towle didn't waste time preaching the gospel of abstinence. She gave her young adventurers some reading material on the subject, including the classic women's health book *Our Bodies, Ourselves*, to help bring them closer in bed. She also brought up the question of whether a G-spot even exists. As her visitors were leaving, Towle offered them more freebies: "I sent them out the door with a billion condoms."

G-spots. Orgasms. Condoms. We all know kids say and do the darndest things, but how they have changed! One teacher recalls a 10-year-old raising his hand to ask her to define oral sex. He was quickly followed by an 8-year-old girl behind him who asked, "Oh, yeah, and what's anal sex?" These are the easy questions. Rhonda Sheared, who teaches sex education in Pinellas County, Fla., was asked by middle school students about the sound *kweif*, which the kids say is the noise a vagina makes during or after sex. "And how do you keep it from making this noise?"

There is more troubling behavior in Denver. School officials were forced to institute a sexual-harassment policy owing to a sharp rise in lewd language, groping, pinching and bra-snapping incidents among sixth-, seventh- and eighth-graders. Sex among kids in Pensacola, Fla., became so pervasive that students of a private Christian junior high school are now asked to sign cards vowing not to have sex until they marry. But the cards don't mean anything, says a 14-year-old boy at the school. "It's broken promises."

It's easy enough to blame everything on television and entertainment, even the news. At a Denver middle school, boys rationalize their actions this way: "If the President can do it, why can't we?" White House sex scandals are one thing, but how can anyone avoid Viagra and virility? Or public discussions of sexually transmitted diseases like AIDS and herpes? Young girls have lip-synched often enough to Alanis Morissette's big hit of a couple of years ago, "You Oughta Know," to have found the sex nestled in the lyric. But it's more than just movies and television and news. Adolescent curiosity about sex is fed by a pandemic openness about it—in the schoolyard, on the bus, at home when no adult is watching. Just eavesdrop at the mall one afternoon, and you'll hear enough pubescent sexcapades to pen the next few episodes of *Dawson's Creek*, the most explicit show on teen sexuality, on the WB network. Parents, always the last to keep up, are now almost totally pre-empted. Chris (not his real name), 13, says his parents talked to him about sex when he was 12 but he had been indoctrinated earlier by a 17-year-old cousin. In any case, he gets his full share of information from the tube. "You name the show, and I've heard about it. Jerry Springer, MTV, *Dawson's Creek*, HBO After Midnight . . ." Stephanie (not her real name), 16, of North Lauderdale, Fla., who first had sex when she was 14, claims to have slept with five boyfriends and is considered a sex expert by her friends. She says, "You can learn a lot about sex from cable. It's all mad-sex stuff." She sees nothing to condemn. "If you're feeling steamy and hot, there's only one thing you want to do. As long as you're using a condom, what's wrong with it? Kids have hormones too."

In these steamy times, it is becoming largely irrelevant whether adults approve of kids' sowing their oats—or knowing so much about the technicalities of the dissemination. American adolescents are in the midst of their own kind of sexual revolution—one that has left many parents feeling confused, frightened and almost powerless. Parents can search all they want for common ground with today's kids, trying to draw parallels between contemporary carnal knowledge and an earlier generation's free-love crusades, but the two movements are quite different. A desire to break out of the old-fashioned strictures fueled the '60s movement, and its participants made sexual freedom a kind of new religion. That sort of reverence has been replaced by a more consumerist attitude. In a 1972 cover story, *Time* declared, "Teenagers generally are woefully ignorant about sex." Ignorance is no longer the rule. As a weary junior high counselor in Salt Lake City puts it, "Teens today are almost nonchalant about sex. It's like we've been to the moon too many times."

The good news about their precocious knowledge of the mechanics of sex is that a growing number of teens know how to protect themselves, at least physically. But what about their emotional health and social behavior? That's a more troublesome picture. Many parents and teachers—as well as some thoughtful teenagers—worry about the desecration of love and the subversion of mature relationships. Says Debra Haffner, president of the Sexuality Information and Education Council of the United States: "We should not confuse kids' pseudo-sophistication about sexuality and their ability to use the language with their understanding of who they are as sexual young people or their ability to make good decisions."

One ugly side effect is a presumption among many adolescent boys that sex is an entitlement—an attitude that fosters a breakdown of respect for oneself and others. Says a seventh-grade girl: "The guy will ask you up front. If you turn him down, you're a bitch. But if you do it, you're a ho. The guys are after us all the time, in the halls, everywhere. You scream, 'Don't touch me!' but it doesn't do any good." A Rhode Island Rape Center study of 1,700 sixth- and ninth-graders found 65% of boys and 57% of girls believing it acceptable for a male to force a female to have sex if they've been dating for six months.

Parents who are aware of this cultural revolution seem mostly torn between two approaches: preaching abstinence or suggesting prophylactics—and thus condoning sex. Says Cory Hollis, 37, a father of three in the Salt Lake City area: "I don't want to see my teenage son ruin his life. But if he's going to do it, I told him that I'd go out and get him the condoms myself." Most parents seem too squeamish to get into the subtleties of instilling sexual ethics. Nor are schools up to the job of moralizing. Kids say they accept their teachers' admonitions to have safe sex but tune out other stuff. "The personal-development classes are a joke," says Sarah, 16, of Pensacola. "Even the teacher looks uncomfortable. There is no way anybody is going to ask a serious question." Says Shana, a 13-year-old from Denver: "A lot of it is old and boring. They'll talk about not having sex before marriage, but no one listens. I use that class for study hall."

Shana says she is glad "sex isn't so taboo now, I mean with all the teenage pregnancies." But she also says that "it's creepy and kind of scary that it seems to be happening so early, and all this talk about it." She adds, "Girls are jumping too quickly. They figure if they can fall in love in a month, then they can have sex in a month too." When she tried discouraging a classmate from having sex for the first time, the friend turned to her and said, "My God, Shana. It's just sex."

Three powerful forces have shaped today's child prodigies: a prosperous information age that increasingly promotes products and entertains audiences by titillation; aggressive public-policy initiatives that loudly preach sexual responsibility, further desensitizing kids to the subject; and the decline of two-parent households, which leaves adolescents with little supervision. Thus kids are not only bombarded with messages about sex—many of them contradictory—but also have more private time to engage in it than did previous generations. Today more than half of the females and three-quarters of the males ages 15 to 19 have experienced sexual intercourse, according to the Commission on Adolescent Sexual Health. And while the average age at first intercourse has come down only a year since 1970 (currently it's 17 for girls and 16 for boys), speed is of the essence for the new generation. Says Haffner: "If kids today are going to do more than kiss, they tend to move very quickly toward sexual intercourse."

The remarkable—and in ways lamentable—product of youthful promiscuity and higher sexual IQ is the degree to which kids learn to navigate the complex hyper-sexual world that reaches out seductively to them at every turn. One of the most positive results: the incidence of sexually transmitted diseases and of teenage pregnancy is declining. Over the past few years, kids have managed to chip away at the teenage birthrate, which in 1991 peaked at 62.1 births per 1,000 females. Since then the birthrate has dropped 12%, to 54.7. Surveys suggest that as many as two-thirds of teenagers now use condoms, a proportion that is three times as high as reported in the 1970s. "We're clearly starting to make progress," says Dr. John Santelli, a physician with the Centers for Disease Control and Prevention's division of adolescent and school health. "And the key statistics bear that out." Even if they've had sex, many kids are learning to put off having more till later; they are also making condom use during intercourse nonnegotiable; and, remarkably, the fleeting pleasures of lust may even be wising up some of them to a greater appreciation of love.

For better or worse, sex-filled television helps shape young opinion. In Chicago, Ryan, an 11-year-old girl, intently watches a scene from one of her favorite TV dramas, *Dawson's Creek*. She listens as the character Jen, who lost her virginity at 12 while drunk, confesses to her new love, Dawson, "Sex doesn't equal happiness. I can't apologize for my past." Ryan is quick to defend Jen. "I think she was young, but if I were Dawson, I would believe she had changed. She acts totally different now." But Ryan is shocked by an episode of her other favorite show, *Buffy the Vampire Slayer*, in which Angel, a male vampire, "turned bad" after having sex with the 17-year-old Buffy. "That kinda annoyed me," says Ryan. "What would have happened if she had had a baby? Her whole life would have been thrown out the window." As for the fallen Angel: "I am so mad! I'm going to take all my pictures of him down now."

Pressed by critics and lobbies, television has begun to include more realistic story lines about sex and its possible consequences. TV writers and producers are turning to groups like the Kaiser Family Foundation, an independent health-policy think tank, for help in adding more depth and accuracy to stories involving sex. Kaiser has consulted on daytime soaps *General Hospital* and *One Life to Live* as well as the prime-time drama *ER* on subjects ranging from teen pregnancy to coming to terms with a gay high school athlete. Says Matt James, a Kaiser senior vice president: "We're trying to work with them to improve the public-health content of their shows."

And then there's real-life television. MTV's *Loveline*, an hourlong Q.-and-A. show featuring sex guru Drew Pinsky, is drawing raves among teens for its informative sexual content. Pinsky seems to be almost idolized by some youths. "Dr. Drew has some excellent advice," says Keri, an eighth-grader in Denver. "It's not just sex, it's real life. Society makes you say you've got to look at shows like *Baywatch*, but I'm sick of blond bimbos. They're so fake. Screenwriters ought to get a life."

With so much talk of sex in the air, the extinction of the hapless, sexually naive kid seems an inevitability. Indeed, kids today as young as seven to 10 are picking up the first details of sex even in Saturday-morning cartoons. Brett, a 14-year-old in Denver, says it doesn't matter to him whether his parents chat with him about sex or not because he gets so much from TV. Whenever he's curious about something sexual, he channel-surfs his way to certainty. "If you watch TV, they've got everything you want to know," he says. "That's how I learned to kiss, when I was eight. And the girl told me, 'Oh, you sure know how to do it.'"

Even if kids don't watch certain television shows, they know the programs exist and are bedazzled by the forbidden. From schoolyard word of mouth, eight-year-old Jeff in Chicago has heard all about the foul-mouthed kids in the raunchily plotted *South Park*, and even though he has never seen the show, he can describe certain episodes in detail. (He is also familiar with the AIDS theme of the musical *Rent* because he's heard the CD over and over.) Argentina, 16, in Detroit, says, "TV makes sex look like this big game." Her friend Michael, 17, adds, "They make sex look like Monopoly or something. You have to do it in order to get to the next level."

Child experts say that by the time many kids hit adolescence, they have reached a point where they aren't particularly obsessed with sex but have grown to accept the notion that solid courtships—or at least strong physical attractions—

potentially lead to sexual intercourse. Instead of denying it, they get an early start preparing for it—and playing and perceiving the roles prescribed for them. In Nashville, 10-year-old Brantley whispers about a classmate, "There's this girl I know, she's nine years old, and she already shaves her legs and plucks her eyebrows, and I've heard she's had sex. She even has bigger boobs than my mom!"

The playacting can eventually lead to discipline problems at school. Alan Skriloff, assistant superintendent of personnel and curriculum for New Jersey's North Brunswick school system, notes that there has been an increase in mock-sexual behavior in buses carrying students to school. He insists there have been no incidents of sexual assault but, he says, "we've dealt with kids simulating sexual intercourse and simulating masturbation. It's very disturbing to the other children and to the parents, obviously." Though Skriloff says that girls are often the initiators of such conduct, in most school districts the aggressors are usually boys.

Nan Stein, a senior researcher at the Wesley College Center for Research on Women, believes sexual violence and harassment is on the rise in schools, and she says, "It's happening between kids who are dating or want to be dating or used to date." Linda Osmundson, executive director of the Center Against Spouse Abuse in St. Petersburg, Fla., notes that "it seems to be coming down to younger and younger girls who feel that if they don't pair up with these guys, they'll have no position in their lives. They are pressured into lots of sexual activity." In this process of socialization, "no" is becoming less and less an option.

In such a world, schools focus on teaching scientific realism rather than virginity. Sex-ed teachers tread lightly on the moral questions of sexual intimacy while going heavy on the risk of pregnancy or a sexually transmitted disease. Indeed, health educators in some school districts complain that teaching abstinence to kids today is getting to be a futile exercise. Using less final terms like "postpone" or "delay" helps draw some kids in, but semantics often isn't the problem. In a Florida survey, the state found that 75% of kids had experienced sexual intercourse by the time they reached 12th grade, with some 20% of the kids having had six or more sexual partners. Rick Colonno, father of a 16-year-old son and 14-year-old daughter in Arvada, Colo., views sex ed in schools as a necessary evil to fill the void that exists in many homes. Still, he's bothered by what he sees as a subliminal endorsement of sex by authorities. "What they're doing," he says, "is preparing you for sex and then saying, 'But don't have it.'"

With breathtaking pragmatism, kids look for ways to pursue their sex life while avoiding pregnancy or disease. Rhonda Sheared, the Florida sex-ed teacher, says a growing number of kids are asking questions about oral and anal sex because they've discovered that it allows them to be sexually active without risking pregnancy. As part of the Pinellas County program, students in middle and high school write questions anonymously, and, as Sheared says, "they're always looking for the loophole."

A verbatim sampling of some questions:
- "Can you get aids from fingering a girl if you have no cuts? Through your fingernails?"
- "Can you gets aids from '69'?"
- "If you shave your vagina or penis, can that get rid of crabs?"
- "If yellowish stuff comes out of a girl, does it mean you have herpes, or can it just happen if your period is due, along with abdominal pains?"
- "When sperm hits the air, does it die or stay alive for 10 days?"

Ideally, most kids say, they would prefer their parents do the tutoring, but they realize that's unlikely. For years psychologists and sociologists have warned about a new generation gap, one created not so much by different morals and social outlooks as by career-driven parents, the economic necessity of two incomes leaving parents little time for talks with their children. Recent studies indicate that many teens think parents are the most accurate source of information and would like to talk to them more about sex and sexual ethics but can't get their attention long enough. Shana sees the conundrum this way: "Parents haven't set boundaries, but they are expecting them."

Yet some parents are working harder to counsel their kids on sex. Cathy Wolf, 29, of North Wales, Pa., says she grew up learning about sex largely from her friends and from reading controversial books. Open-minded and proactive, she says she has returned to a book she once sought out for advice, Judy Blume's novel *Are You There God? It's Me, Margaret*, and is reading it to her two boys, 8 and 11. The novel discusses the awkwardness of adolescence, including sexual stirrings. "That book was forbidden to me as a kid," Wolf says. "I'm hoping to give them a different perspective about sex, to expose them to this kind of subject matter before they find out about it themselves." Movies and television are a prod and a challenge to Wolf. In *Grease*, which is rated PG and was recently re-released, the character Rizzo "says something about 'sloppy seconds,' you know, the fact that a guy wouldn't want to do it with a girl who had just done it with another guy. There's also another point where they talk about condoms. Both Jacob and Joel wanted an explanation, so I provided it for them."

Most kids, though, lament that their parents aren't much help at all on sexual matters. They either avoid the subject, miss the mark by starting the discussion too long before or after the sexual encounter, or just plain stonewall them. "I was nine when I asked my mother the Big Question," says Michael, in Detroit. "I'll never forget. She took out her driver's license and pointed to the line about male or female. 'That is sex,' she said." Laurel, a 17-year-old in Murfreesboro, Tenn., wishes her parents had taken more time with her to shed light on the subject. When she was six and her sister was nine, "my mom sat us down, and we had the sex talk," Laurel says. "But when I was 10, we moved in with my dad, and he never talked about it. He would leave the room if a commercial for a feminine product came on TV." And when her sister finally had sex, at 16, even her mother's vaunted openness crumbled. "She talked to my mom about it and ended up feeling like a whore because even though my mom always said we could talk to her about anything, she didn't want to hear that her daughter had slept with a boy."

Part of the problem for many adults is that they aren't quite sure how they feel about teenage sex. A third of adults think adolescent sexual activity is wrong, while a majority of adults think it's O.K. and, under certain conditions, normal, healthy behavior, according to the Alan Guttmacher Institute, a non-profit, reproductive-health research group. In one breath, parents say they perceive it as a public-health issue and want more information about sexual behavior and its consequences, easier access to contraceptives and more material in the media about responsible human and sexual interaction. And in the next breath, they claim it's a moral issue to be resolved through preaching abstinence and the virtues of virginity and getting the trash off TV. "You start out talking about condoms in this country, and you end up fighting about the future of the American family," says Sarah Brown, director of the Campaign Against Teen Pregnancy. "Teens just end up frozen like a deer in headlights."

Not all kids are happy with television's usurping the role of village griot. Many say they've become bored by—and even resent—sexual themes that seem pointless and even a distraction from the information or entertainment they're seeking. "It's like everywhere," says Ryan, a 13-year-old seventh-grader in Denver, "even in *Skateboarding* [magazine]. It's become so normal it doesn't even affect you. On TV, out of nowhere, they'll begin talking about masturbation." Another Ryan, 13, in the eighth grade at the same school, agrees: "There's sex in the cartoons and messed-up people on the talk shows—'My lover sleeping with my best friend.' I can remember the jumping-condom ads. There's just too much of it all."

Many kids are torn between living up to a moral code espoused by their church and parents and trying to stay true to the swirling laissez-faire. Experience is making many sadder but wiser. The shame, anger or even indifference stirred by early sex can lead to prolonged abstinence. Chandra, a 17-year-old in Detroit, says she had sex with a boyfriend of two years for the first time at 15 despite her mother's constant pleas against it. She says she wishes she had heeded her mother's advice. "One day I just decided to do it," she says. "Afterward, I was kind of mad that I let it happen. And I was sad because I knew my mother wouldn't have approved." Chandra stopped dating the boy more than a year ago and hasn't had sex since. "It would have to be someone I really cared about," she says. "I've had sex before, but I'm not a slut."

With little guidance from grownups, teens have had to discover for themselves that the ubiquitous sexual messages must be tempered with caution and responsibility. It is quite clear, even to the most sexually experienced youngsters, just how dangerous a little information can be. Stephanie in North Lauderdale, who lost her virginity two years ago, watches with concern as her seven-year-old sister moves beyond fuzzy thoughts of romance inspired by Cinderella or Aladdin into sexual curiosity. "She's always talking about pee-pees, and she sees somebody on TV kissing and hugging or something, and she says, 'Oh, they had sex.' I think she's going to find out about this stuff before I did." She pauses. "We don't tell my sister anything," she says, "but she's not a naive child."

Mothers, Daughters, and the Pill

PAULA J. ADAMS HILLARD

Paula J. Adams Hillard is a professor in the department of obstetrics and gynecology at the University of Cincinnati College of Medicine. In the following essay Hillard maintains that the contraceptive pill has helped to transform relationships between mothers and daughters. In the 1960s, when the pill first became available, young women did not feel they could tell their mothers they were sexually active or that they were taking oral contraceptives. Today, those women are the mothers of teenagers, and many of them want to have better communication with their children about sex than their parents did with them. Mothers often accompany their teenage daughters to consult clinicians about sexual health concerns and contraception. Hillard concludes that this signifies progress in health education and family relationships.

In the 1960s and 1970s, oral contraceptives were new. Some observers argued that the pill ushered in the sexual revolution by freeing women from the worry that sexual intercourse would inevitably lead to pregnancy. Indeed, trends in rates of sexual activity among adolescents over the years suggest that there really have been changes in sexual behavior: In 1970, fewer than 50% of 19-year-olds had experienced intercourse, while by 1985, more than 50% of 17-year-olds were sexually experienced.

In the 1960s and 1970s, most young women did not tell their mothers that they were sexually active or that they were taking oral contraceptives. They were introduced to responsibility about reproductive issues through visits to family planning clinics, and most of those visits were made alone or with a girlfriend, not with their mother. Many of the clinicians who provided contraceptive services for adolescents in that era were aware that assurances of confidentiality were of paramount importance to many teenagers.

THE PILL AND FAMILY COMMUNICATION

The teenagers of the 1960s and 1970s have now reached middle age; many have adolescent children. Has the pill made a difference in how we relate to our daughters (and sons)? Has the pill made a difference in our beliefs about family communication? I believe that it has. About 80% of women born since 1945 have taken oral contraceptives. They grew up with the pill. They took it for granted. They assumed that their sexual lives could be separated from their decisions about parenting and conception. And so do their daughters. But their own mothers did not have the same confidence that they could control their reproductive lives as successfully. This change, occurring over two generations, is attributable to oral contraceptives.

Today's mothers know that their daughters can receive oral contraceptives without parental involvement, much as they themselves did. But because they know this, many of them have made decisions about how they want to parent, based on their own experiences as adolescents. They have decided that they want to do a better job of communicating with their children about healthy sexuality than their parents did with them. They talk about many things that their parents left undiscussed—contraception, STDs, HIV, homosexuality and oral sex. Not that these conversations are easy. They talk about these things with their children in part because they feel that they are too important to ignore, but also because the times in which they live have made it dangerous not to. They talk about these things because they can't ignore the availability of oral contraceptives, nor would they want to. As parents, they know that they need to talk about oral contraceptives as an option for their daughters. For some of today's mothers, the pill changed life for the better (fewer menstrual cramps, predictable periods and reliable contraception), while for others it caused uncomfortable or even frightening side effects.

As a consequence of this knowledge, many mothers of adolescents help their daughters obtain medical and gynecologic care; they often make the appointments and accompany their daughters to see a clinician who will provide appropriate health education and preventive guidance. The clinicians who provide care for today's adolescents recognize the importance of confidentiality, but also understand that adolescents grow up within the context of a family.

In my practice, I see many adolescents; I see most of them with their mothers. As I have grown as a clinician, I have come to recognize the importance of fostering healthy communication between mothers and daughters. When I see a new patient, I allow time to talk with the mother and daughter together, to speak with each privately, and then to meet again together. This process allows an adolescent to keep whatever information she chooses confidential, but allows the sharing of information and health concerns.

When I talk about oral contraceptives, I feel that it is most helpful if both mother and daughter can hear about the risks, benefits and potential side effects. Of course, many daughters today still choose not to tell their mothers of their need for contraception. They may instead request that oral contraceptives be described to their mothers as therapy for cramps, irregular periods or heavy bleeding. In addition, many older adolescents come for gynecologic visits alone. But I encourage them to try to talk with their mothers. I do believe that this is easier today than in years past, in part because so many of today's mothers have themselves taken the pill, and because the pill has evolved from a revolutionary new pharmacologic development into an assumption of modern life and health.

KNOWLEDGE IS POWER

Most mothers of adolescents know or will soon come to know the essential fact of parenting—that they are preparing their children to make decisions for themselves. While they would like to protect them from making foolish, dangerous or inappropriate choices, they can only provide them with the information, support and encouragement to make smart and healthy choices.

But most mothers of adolescents today recognize that knowledge is power. They want to provide knowledge about contraceptive options to their daughters. They want them to know that they can effectively protect themselves from unintended pregnancies, but that sexually transmissible infections are a potentially problematic, morbid or even life-threatening possibility. They want them to be safe—from pregnancy, from infections and from emotional hurt; they want to protect them from an intimate relationship that is premature, exploitive, unequal or ill-advised. They would like for them to postpone having intercourse until they are cognitively, socially, emotionally and developmentally mature enough to make responsible choices. And mothers and daughters today do talk about these issues—and I believe that is so because oral contraceptives helped to set the stage, shaped the mothers' own behaviors and helped them think about how they would like to have been parented.

The pill becomes the focus of many mother-daughter discussions relating to adolescent growth and development, achievement of independence, individuation and responsible choices. That is a good thing; these issues need to be addressed.

In general, the interactions that I observe between today's mothers and adolescents seem healthier than those of a generation ago. The fact that women can successfully postpone childbearing until they actively choose to parent is an assumption of modern life. I believe that this assumption has and is shaping today's families, and that the pill played and is playing a major role in the transformation of relationships between mothers and daughters.

CHRONOLOGY

1834
A group of New York Protestant women found the Female Moral Reform Society, an organization that works to reform prostitutes and challenge the double standard that tolerates male sexual licentiousness.

1847
The American Medical Association (AMA) is founded. Many physicians discourage higher education for women, claiming that it interferes with women's reproductive and child-rearing functions.

1848
The first women's rights convention is held at Seneca Falls, New York.

1850s
Several short-lived utopian communities, including Long Island's Modern Times and Cleveland's Berlin Heights, form. These communities promote "free love"—the idea that sexual unions should be based on love and attraction rather than marriage.

1868–1870
In New York, Chicago, and other locales, state legislatures consider bills that would legalize and regulate prostitution. The AMA supports such regulation as a means to curb the spread of venereal disease.

1870s
A social purity movement, composed of women's rights activists, clergy, and temperance advocates, forms to abolish prostitution. They also begin a campaign to establish a "single standard" of sexual morality for men and women.

1873

Congress passes the Comstock Act, which prohibits the mailing of "obscene and indecent" materials, including literature about contraception and abortion.

1874

Activist Victoria Woodhull's speech, *Tried as by Fire*, is printed. Woodhull denounces marriage and contends that couples should be free to establish relationships based purely on mutual love, desire, and benefit.

1876

Ezra Hervey Heywood, founder of the New England Free Love League, publishes the free-love tract *Cupid's Yokes*. He is convicted and imprisoned for printing obscenity.

1909

Psychoanalyst Sigmund Freud lectures at Clark University in Worcester, Massachusetts. He introduces the American public to his idea that sexuality is a central part of life and identity.

1912

The National Education Association endorses sex education.

1914

Margaret Sanger founds the National Birth Control League, which later becomes Planned Parenthood.

1917

The United States enters World War I. American soldiers overseas encounter the more relaxed sexual mores of Europe.

1920

The Nineteenth Amendment, granting women the right to vote, is ratified; the United States enters a decade of sexual adventurousness, prompted by the advent of economic affluence, the automobile, jazz music, and sexually charged literature, ads, and movies.

1936

Sanger forms the National Committee on Federal Legislation for Birth Control, arguing that the economic crisis is intensifying the need for family planning. A federal appeals court overturns the anticontraception provisions of the Comstock Law.

1945

Pharmaceutical companies produce large amounts of penicillin, an effective treatment for the venereal diseases that had become rampant in the armed forces.

1950

Margaret Sanger first meets with biological researcher Gregory Pincus, a collaboration that leads to the development of an oral contraceptive for women.

1953

Alfred Kinsey publishes *Sexual Behavior in the Human Female*. This study, along with his 1948 landmark book, *Sexual Behavior in the Human Male*, become known as the Kinsey Report. Hugh Hefner publishes the first issue of *Playboy*, a glossy monthly magazine featuring photos of nude women. The magazine suggests that men should "enjoy the pleasures a female has to offer without becoming emotionally involved."

1960

The birth control pill is approved for use in the United States.

1961

The National Council of Churches, an organization of Protestant, Anglican, and Orthodox denominations, issues a proclamation supporting married couples' use of birth control.

1962

Helen Gurley Brown publishes *Sex and the Single Girl*, encouraging single women to have multiple sexual affairs.

1963

Betty Friedan publishes *The Feminine Mystique*, which attacks the then-popular notion that women's true vocation is in the home.

1966

Friedan founds the National Organization for Women (NOW), an organization that pushes for "full equality for women in America in a truly equal partnership with men." William Masters and Virginia Johnson publish *Human Sexual Response*, which contends that women's sexual desires and responses are equal to those of men.

1966–1968

A counterculture grows in which young adults experiment with freer sexual behavior, hallucinatory drugs, rock music, and communal living. In 1967, thousands of hippies congregate in San Francisco's Haight-Ashbury district for the "summer of love."

1968

In *Ginsberg v. New York*, the Supreme Court rules that some sexually explicit materials are obscene for minors but constitutionally protected for adults. Feminists protest the objectification of women at the Miss America pageant in Atlantic City.

1969

On June 28, gays and lesbians battle against a police raid on the Stonewall Inn, a gay bar in New York City; the riot marks the beginning of a movement in which gays and lesbians demand civil rights and greater societal acceptance of homosexuality.

1973

The Supreme Court's *Roe v. Wade* decision legalizes abortion during the first two trimesters of pregnancy.

1974

The American Psychiatric Association removes homosexuality from its list of mental illnesses.

1981

The federal Centers for Disease Control issues a report on Acquired Immunity Deficiency Syndrome (AIDS), caused by the human immunodeficiency virus (HIV). AIDS-related illnesses are initially observed in gay men, Haitians, and IV drug users.

1986

In *Bowers v. Hardwick*, the Supreme Court upholds laws declaring sodomy illegal.

1992

In *Planned Parenthood v. Casey*, the Supreme Court rules that states can regulate access to abortions, as long as no "undue burden" is placed on women seeking abortions. Some states begin requiring counseling sessions and twenty-four-hour waiting periods for abortion seekers.

1996

President Bill Clinton signs the Defense of Marriage Act, which forbids federal recognition of same-sex marriages and gives states the right to refuse to recognize gay marriages performed in other states.

2000

RU-486 is approved for inducing nonsurgical abortions during the early weeks of pregnancy. Vermont legalizes civil unions for homosexual couples.

FOR FURTHER RESEARCH

Barry D. Adam, *The Rise of a Gay and Lesbian Movement*. New York: Twayne, 1995.

David Allyn, *Make Love, Not War: The Sexual Revolution, an Unfettered History*. Boston: Little, Brown, 2000.

Terry H. Anderson, *The Movement and the Sixties*. Oxford, NY: Oxford University Press, 1995.

Linda J. Beckman and S. Marie Harvey, eds., *The New Civil War: The Psychology, Culture, and Politics of Abortion*. Washington, DC: American Psychological Association, 1998.

Helen Gurley Brown, *Sex and the Single Girl*. New York: Random House, 1962.

Anthony Comstock, *Frauds Exposed: Or, How the People Are Deceived and Robbed, and Youth Corrupted*. Montclair, NJ: Patterson Smith, 1969.

Danielle Crittendon, *What Our Mothers Didn't Tell Us: Why Happiness Eludes the Modern Woman*. New York: Simon and Schuster, 1999.

Flora Davis, *Moving the Mountain: The Women's Movement in America Since 1960*. New York: Simon and Schuster, 1992.

Maggie Gallagher, *The Abolition of Marriage: How We Destroy Lasting Love*. Washington, DC: Regnery, 1996.

Cynthia Gorney, *Articles of Faith: A Frontline History of the Abortion Wars*. New York: Simon and Schuster, 1998.

John Heidenry, *What Wild Ecstasy: The Rise and Fall of the Sexual Revolution*. New York: Simon and Schuster, 1997.

Ezra H. Heywood, *Uncivil Liberty: An Essay to Show the Injustice and Impolicy of Ruling Woman Without Her Consent*. Princeton, MA: Cooperative Publishing, 1870.

James Howard Jones, *Alfred C. Kinsey: A Public/Private Life*. New York: W.W. Norton, 1997.

Wendy Kaminer, *True Love Waits: Essays and Criticism*. New York: Perseus, 1997.

Lawrence Lader, *The Margaret Sanger Story and the Fight for Birth Control*. Garden City, NY: Doubleday, 1955.

Ronald David Lawler et al., *Catholic Sexual Ethics: A Summary, Explanation, and Defense*. Huntington, IN: Our Sunday Visitor, 1998.

William Martin, *With God on Our Side: The Rise of the Religious Right in America*. New York: Broadway Books, 1996.

James R. Peterson, *The Century of Sex: Playboy's History of the Sexual Revolution, 1900–1999*. New York: Garden Grove, 1999.

Judith A. Reisman, *Kinsey: Crimes & Consequences the Red Queen & the Grand Scheme*. Crestwood, KY: Institute for Media Education, 1998.

Ira L. Reiss, *Solving America's Sexual Crises*. Amherst, NY: Prometheus Books, 1997.

Paul Robinson, *The Modernization of Sex: Havelock Ellis, Alfred Kinsey, William Masters, and Virginia Johnson*. New York: Harper & Row, 1976.

John Charles Rock, *The Time Has Come: A Catholic Doctor's Proposals to End the Battle over Birth Control*. New York: Knopf, 1963.

Katie Roiphe, *Last Night in Paradise: Sex and Morals at the Century's End*. Boston: Little, Brown, 1997.

Lillian B. Rubin, *Erotic Wars: What Happened to the Sexual Revolution?* New York: Farrar, Straus & Giroux, 1990.

Wendy Shalit, *A Return to Modesty: Discovering the Lost Virtue*. New York: Free Press, 1999.

Diane Silver, *The New Civil War: The Lesbian and Gay Struggle for Civil Rights*. Danbury, CT: Franklin Watts, 1997.

Rickie Solinger, ed., *Abortion Wars: A Half Century of Struggle, 1950–2000*. Berkeley: University of California Press, 1998.

Madeleine B. Stern, ed., *The Victoria Woodhull Reader*. Weston, MA: M & S Press, 1974.

INDEX

Santelli, John, 216
"Save Our Children" campaign, 163
Schneider, Sherrie, 178
Schopenhauer, Arthur, 111
Schwartz, Pepper, 131, 134
Seaman, Barbara, 188
Second Sex, The (Beauvoir), 190
Sensuous Woman, The ("J"), 196
Sex and the Single Girl (Helen Gurley
 Brown), 21, 195
sex education
 by parents vs. schools, 218–21
 vindication of liberal polices in, 185
Sex in America: A Definitive Survey, 183
Sex in Education (Clarke), 28
Sex Information Council of the U.S.
 (SIECUS), 202–203
Sex in Our Changing World
 (McPartland), 95
sexual activity
 academic studies on, 181–85
 among adolescents, 215, 218–19
 decline in, 184–85, 202–203
 among women, influences of
 education on, 193–94
Sexual Behavior in the Human Female
 (Kinsey), 19, 177
 see also Kinsey report
Sexual Behavior in the Human Male
 (Kinsey), 19, 175
 see also Kinsey report
sexual counterrevolution, 171–87
 gay backlash and, 179–81
 religious component of, 174–75
*Sexual Ecology: AIDS and the Destiny of
 Gay Men* (Rostello), 180
sexuality
 debate within free love movement
 about, 44–45
 early research on, 117–19
 Victorian attitudes toward, 10–12
 20th century challenges to, 14–15
 in 1920s, 16–17, 98–107
 in 1940s–1950s, 18–19
 in 1960s, 19–24
sexual liberation
 fallout from, 203–204
sexually transmitted diseases (STDs)
 awareness of, among teens, 215

sexual counterrevolution and, 172,
 174
 treatment of, 18
sexual revolution, 20–24
 backlash against, 153–54, 171–87
 harbingers of
 in early 20th century, 14–19
 in 19th century, 10–14
 legacy of, 25, 154–55
Sheared, Rhonda, 212, 220
Simon, William, 132, 133
Sims, J. Marion, 28
Skriloff, Alan, 218
Slenker, Elmina Drake, 45
*Slouching Towards Gomorrah: Modern
 Liberalism and American Decline*
 (Bork), 186–87
social purity movement, 11, 27
 preservation of maternal authority
 and, 33–35
 voluntary motherhood and, 32–33
sodomy laws
 moves to repeal, 158
Stanton, Elizabeth Cady, 45
 marriage/prostitution parallel and,
 31
Stein, Nan, 218
Steinem, Gloria, 198
Stevenson, Adlai, 147
stockbrokers
 first women as, 40
Stockham, Alice, 32
Stodghill, Ron, II, 211
Stone, Rebecca, 208
Stonewall riot (1969), 24, 159–60
Storer, Horatio, 28, 29
Stossel, Scott, 171
suffrage movement
 prostitution and, 30
Sumner, John S., 73
Sunday, Billy, 68
Supreme Court
 rulings of
 on abortion, 24
 on sodomy laws, 169
surveys
 on abortion, 208
 on sexual activity, 182, 183
 among adolescents, 184, 204

on sexual morality, 177
see also Janus Report on Sexual Behavior; Kinsey report
Susan Lenox (Phillips), 73
Swaggart, Jimmy, 186

television
effects on adolescent sexuality, 213, 216–17
theater
New York, sexual realism in, 104–105
Thompson, Dorothy, 143
Tilton, Elizabeth, 42
Time (magazine), 174
Tolstoy, Leo, 38
Towle, Patti, 212
Traps for the Young (Comstock), 37, 60
Tried as by Fire: Or, the True and the False Socially (Woodhull), 46
Trilling, Lionel, 178

Vanderbuilt, Cornelius, 40
van Gelder, Sarah, 26
venereal disease, 18
see also sexually transmitted diseases
Victoria, 11
Vietnam War protests, 21

wages
gender gap in, 192, 207
Waisbrooker, Lois, 43
Walker, Edwin, 43
Ward, Lester, 45
Waszak, Cynthia, 208
Weddington, Sarah, 199
Weeks, Jeffrey, 162
Wells, Herman, 122
West, Mae, 105
What Wild Ecstasy: The Rise and Fall of the Sexual Revolution (Heindenry), 183–84
White, Ann, 108
White, Dan, 165–66
White, William Allen, 74
Whitehead, Barbara Dafoe, 206
"White Night Riots" (San Francisco, 1979), 166
white slave panic, 71–72

Wilde, Oscar, 45
Wolf, Cathy, 221
Woman Rebel, The (newsletter), 15
women
Catholic, use of birth control among, 133–34
economic gains of, 189–92
educational gains of, 192–93
influences on sexual attitudes/behavior, 193–94
effects of birth control pill on lives of, 129–35
erotic claims of, 82–83
as housewives, dissatisfaction with, 136–50
ideal of, in 1950s, 138
in labor force, 191–92
issues affecting, 199
in 1920s, 100–101
love-rights of, 75–83
sexual fulfillment
should not be highest aim in life, 108–14
sexuality of
Kinsey's findings on, 127
19th century view, 10–11, 28
women's magazines
messages from
in 1920s, 109
in 1930s, 140–42
in 1950s, 138, 145–46, 145–49
women's movement, 22–23
gains of, 189
in financial independence, 190–192
in higher education, 192–93
in sexual options, 193–95
legacy of, 195–201
second wave, 197
third wave, 201
women's rights
threats to, from sexual counterrevolution, 185–86
Woodhull, Victoria, 13, 38, 46
and free love movement, 40–42
Word, The (journal), 42, 44
World War I
changes in sexual attitudes following, 16, 95–96